Arming Freedom

The Freedom Saga, Book Four

Also by the author

The Freedom Saga
Book 1: *Cloning Freedom*
Book 2: *Freedom's Law*
Book 3: *Freedom's Myth*
Book 4: *Arming Freedom*
Book 5: *Freedom's Plan* (forthcoming)

Tinker's World
Book 1: *Tinker's Plague*
Book 2: *Tinker's Sea*
"Tinker's Toxin"
(in *The Light Between Stars*)

The Chronicles of Ray McAndrues
Book 1: *Nukekubi* (Dark Dragon)
Book 2: *Revenant* (Dark Dragon)

Worlds Apart (Dark Dragon)

The Bastard Prince Saga (Pendelhaven Press)
Book 1: *Horn of the Kraken*
Book 2: *The Mistletoe Spear*

Cats (Ankh Shen Publishing)

Havens in the Storm (Ankh Shen Publishing)

War of the Worlds 2030 (Damnation Press)

ARMING FREEDOM

STEPHEN B. PEARL

Milton, Ontario

First edition, December 2024
Published by Brain Lag
Milton, Ontario
https://www.brain-lag.com/

ISBN: 978-1-998795-11-6 (softcover)
ISBN: 978-1-998795-12-3 (ebook)
ISBN: 978-1-998795-19-2 (dyslexia-formatted edition)

Cover artwork by Catherine Fitzsimmons

"The Cremation of Sam McGee" by Robert W. Service, 1907; "In Flanders Fields" by John McCrae, 1915; "The Charge of the Light Brigade" by Alfred, Lord Tennyson, 1854; "She Walks in Beauty" by Lord Byron (George Gordon), 1832; quotes provided courtesy of Poetry Foundation, https://www.poetryfoundation.org/

Library and Archives Canada Cataloguing in Publication

Title: Arming freedom / Stephen B. Pearl.
Names: Pearl, Stephen B., 1961- author
Description: Series statement: The freedom saga ; book four
Identifiers: Canadiana (print) 20240420896 | Canadiana (ebook) 20240420950 | ISBN 9781998795116
   (softcover) | ISBN 9781998795123 (EPUB)
Subjects: LCGFT: Space operas (Fiction) | LCGFT: Science fiction.
Classification: LCC PS8631.E255 A89 2024 | DDC C813/.6—dc23

Content warnings: Death, gore, medical procedures, sexual assault (mentioned)

Dedication

I dedicate this book to my late father, Vernon Wilmont Pearl. Speak his name for when a man's name is spoken he lives.

My dad taught me to look at what others called garbage and see a resource. The house I grew up in was largely made from construction waste repurposed from the city dump. It may have been because my father was raised poor during the depression of the nineteen thirties that he acquired a mindset that made the best of things. In a world where everything is running short, this mindset is again essential for our survival. It also forms a major element of my Tinker's World series but more apropos, much of *Arming Freedom* is a far future scrounging expedition. In space suits surrounded by radiation, facing death at every turn, but it's still scrounging.

I also want to mention my wife who puts up with my wood pile and reluctance to throw anything out. :) And of course Catherine Fitzsimmons, the proprietor of Brain Lag Publishing, who accepts the fact that sometimes I will use the wrong here/hear in a rough draft and corrects this dyslexic author in a calm and gentle manner. If I'd had school teachers like you, Catherine, I might actually be able to spell today. Probably not, but the issue wouldn't be as bad. There is nothing quite like being called a stupid, stupid boy to shut down the learning facility.

Note to all, Catherine doesn't see anything I write professionally before it is run through at least two grammar checkers and multiple edits. One thing I want people to take away from my issues with a literacy handicap is that in a professional setting one must do one's best to not let their handicap(s) burden others. Others, in their turn, should recognize the difference between a social setting (social media) and a professional setting. But really, even professionally, a little consideration. "Cow, spelt just as well with a small k as a large." (Mark Twain).

On that issue, I also dedicate this book and series to those who have literacy handicaps who struggle every day to be given the respect their intellect deserves.

Try to be kind to one another and look at the world from the other guy's perspective, please. Let's strive to express empathy, understanding, tolerance and inclusion.

Let's not be afraid to use proper dictionary English, or acknowledge the reality of biology, but on the other hand, let's give people the space they need to be who they perceive themselves to be.

Arming Freedom

OUT OF THE ION STORM, INTO THE NOVA

Rowan massaged her temples, hoping to ease the throbbing in her head that using her telekinesis had caused, then looked at her instruments as they scanned the Murack side of the stargate. "Oh, stardust!"

Ryan shifted forward in the pilot's seat beside Rowan, his fit, medium-built body reflecting tension. "What?"

Rowan's pale-skinned hands flew over the navigator's console, putting a graphic interpretation of the data she was receiving on screen. The result looked like a dome made of a web of blue lines. Each line ended in a dark speck. Dim stars glowed through the gaps. "Those are ionized gas trails. Twenty-five... correction, thirty-five ships in a rough dome formation on the sunward side of the stargate's exclusionary sphere." Rowan's blue eyes traced over her readouts. "They're just floating there."

Ryan ran a copper-skinned hand through his brown hair. "Stay on course. The sycamorezoids and dichrostigmazoids can stick their tongues out at each other as much as they want. It has nothing to do with us. Our job is to get the relief supplies to Murack Five, and we're travelling under a Republic Writ of Passage." Only Rowan and Henry heard the tremor in their captain's voice.

"Sorry, hotty boss, but these Hiss-ass-toos—" Henry shook his android head where he was wired into the *Star Hawk*'s computer control station. The unmutilated side of his face looked worried, the scorched side macabre.

Kitoy made a squeaking sound and lashed her tail as her cat-like body stiffened and her cougar tan fur stood on end. She sat at the communications console beside Henry on the horseshoe-shaped bridge. "Watch your mouth!" The translator nanobots allowed all to understand her. The nostrils on her cheetah-like face trembled, then flared. "Besides, you need to hold the middle consonant longer. It sounded like you were asking for a cocktail."

"Sorry, sexy kitty. No *Homo sapiens* word does those sycamorezoid terrorists justice. They tried to blow up a stargate and decimate a planetary population. Now we've got to fly through a blockade of the buggers." Henry drummed the fingers of his remaining arm on the computer console.

"On this side of the stargate, all the sycamorezoids know is that their scheme didn't work. I'm betting the dichrostigmazoids had no idea what was going on. They aren't going to try and eradicate their own planet. If the sycamorezoids try anything, it will be sneaky. They can't risk Republic reprisals for attacking a ship under a Writ of Passage." Ryan focused his green eyes on the blue lines on the main screen.

"Incoming message. Audio only." Kitoy's pointed ears twitched nervously as her tail lashed with anxiety.

"Play it," ordered Ryan.

"Alien vessel, this is sycamorezoid traffic control. You are ordered to stall your momentum and leave this system," growled a deep voice through the speakers.

"Sycamorezoid control. This is *Homo sapiens* H L T C-two-nine-seven - D - R C named *Star Hawk*. I am travelling under a Republic Writ of Passage carrying supplies to the relief efforts on Murack Five. You have no authority to block my transit. Please advise on safe exit trajectory from the Republic zone around the Murack stargate. There seems to be a lot of traffic at the perimeter. Henry, take over piloting." Ryan moved to the command chair in the middle of the bridge, brushing smooth the blue UES space services coverall uniform he wore as he did so. The retiree's braids, over-the-shoulder patches and civilian captain's pin in the collar were all that marked him as separate from the government forces. "Rowan, focus the screen on one of those ships, maximum magnification."

Rowan pressed the controls, changing the image on the big screen at the front of the bridge, then reached to nervously toy with her long, dark hair only to find it was cut short. The main screen filled with an oblong craft with rounded sections on both ends. Spikes poked from its surface in rings along its length.

"That's a dichrostigmazoid heavy cruiser," observed Ryan. "Rowan, bring up another vessel."

The screen shifted to a ship that looked like a furry egg with fins projecting along its length from front to back.

"It looks sycamorezoid, but I don't recognize the class." Ryan stroked his clean-shaven chin.

"It's their new type of destroyer." Henry swivelled the computer control station chair where the upper part of his mutilated android body was strapped in. A mass of wires and fibre optic cables came from where his hips would have been, connecting him to the ship.

Ryan looked at the android, who was to his right at the back of the control stations that ringed the front and sides of the horseshoe-shaped bridge. "You've been keeping up with them?"

"I got bored, so I updated the friend and foe recognition files." Henry shrugged his remaining shoulder.

"Good work. Send the rec-files to my private system. I'll need to update when there's time."

"Message coming in from the transfer and monitoring ship," said Kitoy from the station one forward of Henry's.

"Play it," ordered Ryan.

"*Star Hawk*, welcome to the Murack system. This is Dichrostigmazoid Space Traffic Control. On your current heading and speed, you will be leaving Republic territory in two point five *Homo sapiens*' minutes. Be advised this vessel is not equipped to intervene on your behalf after that." The voice was high-pitched and had a friendly cadence.

"You cannot do that! It is the sycamorezoids' time to have primacy over emerging ships." The deeper voice blasted from the speakers.

"You are in dereliction of your duty, sycamorezoid. As such, I step in to fulfill it as is permitted under Republic regulations. You are not allowed to hamper the entrance of ships into the Murack system." The dichrostigmazoid's voice was annoyed.

"Nova blast! They're at it again. Boss, turn us around," pleaded Henry.

Ryan smiled, then spoke to his crew but mainly for the benefit of Tim and Rowan. "Murack Six and Seven have been spitting in each other's eyes for over a century. The sycamorezoids of Murack Six are galactic separatists and hate other species. I should have worn my brown trousers."

Nervous laughter coursed around the bridge, breaking the paralysis that had seemed to grip the organic crew members.

Ryan straightened his uniform.

Rowan turned her athletic form in her chair at the navigator's station at the front left of the bridge to glance at her lover. He was no longer the tender, compassionate man that shared her bed. Not the determined warrior who would fight through all obstacles to achieve his end. This Ryan was colder, harder, and frightening. Every line of face and form was as solid as a sabre's edge, and his voice was a breath from the graves of dead and forgotten men from ages past.

"Kitoy, broadband transmission, uncoded. On my mark. Mark.

"Murack gate monitor ships. Thank you for your greetings. The *Star Hawk* is a Hawk Class Heavy Lander reclassified to carry light to moderate civilian cargo. As a point of fact, it is the same vessel that broke the blockade on Murack Seven during your last conflict. We are travelling under a Republic Writ carrying relief supplies to Murack Five. As such, we are outside any interspecies conflicts. I am transmitting my course on an open subfrequency and would ask that all ships cooperate with the delivery of Republic aid supplies.

"Kitoy, download all ship's status updates to a communications probe. Navigator, do a running update on the probe's course to see it enters the stargate.

"Republic Gate Monitor ships. I will also mention that I am Captain Ryan Chandler. The *Star Hawk* is the ship I commanded during your last declared war. If anyone should consider violating the Republic Writ of Passage, keep in mind that I only have to survive long enough for my communications probe to reach Republic space. Also, be warned. I will be most annoyed if actions are taken against me! End transmission!"

"Stardust, we're vapour! Could somebody let me cop a feel before the end," said Henry.

"Dad, you are bluffing, right?" Tim stared at his father from the environmental control station one down on the left from the navigator's console. Since Ryan's cloning, no one with eyes could be faulted for thinking that Tim was Ryan's older brother.

Ryan shrugged.

"I… They… I'll key in the transmission." Kitoy put her audio on speaker.

"Captain Shuka, do not be stupid! That is the one the felinezoids called Space Mink. The *Homo sapiens* are mad to let that one have a Bird of Death as his own," spoke a deep voice.

"Admiral, our orders," objected an equally deep voice.

"You were not bridge crew during the blockade on Murack Seven. He is within his rights to take relief supplies to Murack Five. If we act against him and the Republic learns of it, the cost would be enormous. We will do nothing to stop him. I will relay his flight plan to Murack

Six. The reigning monarchs can decide what to do. I order you to move your vessel."

A higher-pitched voice came over the speaker. "Admiral Bukk, this is Commodore Vrignet of the dichrostigmazoid. We have heard your inter-ship communications and concur. It is not our place to violate Republic law. Captain Chandler, I am sure you are monitoring this. I promise you, the dichrostigmazoid will take no action against you."

Rowan checked her instruments. "The ships are clearing a path along our flight path. Wait a moment. One ship is—"

"Captain, we have a message coming in from a dichrostigmazoid freighter," blurted Kitoy.

"Put it up, audio only," ordered Ryan as he moved to the pilot's station.

"*Star Hawk*, this is the *Swift Flyer*. We are a civilian ship trying to exit the Murack system. We humbly ask permission to share your flight corridor. Our home is Lazadd, and we have no intention of returning to this uncouth place."

Ryan nodded. "Kitoy, transmit.

"*Swift Flyer*, maintain five thousand kilometers distance at apogee and fair voyage. End message.

"Rowan, plot the pull points for the gravity laser drive to keep us clear of the other ship. Ziggy, be ready to use the particle beams as an anti-missile system."

"Aye, sir." The podgy middle-aged man in a U.E.S. ground forces uniform with retiree braids over the shoulder patches sat at the weapons station at the back left of the captain's chair.

Ryan drew the gravity laser drive's pull points from the file and steered the *Star Hawk* down the left side of the passage the other ships had opened. The *Swift Flyer*, which looked like a tube with rings around it and bulbous ends, plotted a course parallel but opposite to the *Star Hawk*. A small wedge-shaped ship followed five thousand kilometers behind the *Star Hawk*.

"We are out of Republic territory." Rowan toyed nervously with the sleeve of the floral print blouse she wore.

"Keep steady," said Ryan.

"The *Mary* is following us." Rowan looked to her side. To anyone else, Ryan would have appeared calm. Only she noticed the cording of his neck muscles.

"We'll focus on not getting blown up for now. The assassins we'll deal with later." Ryan's eyes stayed glued to the exterior display.

"We have an incoming message," said Kitoy. "It's from the dichrostigmazoid's gate monitor ship."

"Put it on." Ryan gestured to the big screen.

"Captain Ryan Chandler, I wish you good voyage and caution that the Murack system has experienced an increase in illegal activity. Pirates may not be inclined to respect the Republic Writ of Passage as the government forces have law-abidingly done."

"Thank you for the warning," said Ryan before the screen blanked. "I hate this system. Henry, take over piloting." Ryan returned to the captain's chair.

"Do you want stealth?" asked Henry.

Ryan considered. "No. We haven't been shown an overt threat, and stealth can be considered a hostile act. I'd rather not get back to the Switchboard Station to face a charge of provoking a space conflict."

"So, we wait until someone shoots at us?" asked Kitoy.

"Stupid rule, isn't it?" agreed Ryan. "Everyone, stay at station. I want some distance between us and those ships back there. Rowan, Ziggy, keep scanning for other ships. I want to see what's coming."

"Aye," chorused the crew. It brought back memories for Ryan. Memories he'd tried hard to leave behind. His hand traced over the name plaques on the side of his chair. One for each captain who had died in the line of duty on the *Star Hawk*. His eyes skipped to the backs of the chairs around the bridge. Not one had less than two plaques attached to its back. He sighed and focused on keeping his current crew alive.

THROUGH THE LOOKING GLASS

"It was so romantic. Like something out of the stories of Camelot. The heroic knight saving his lady fair." The slender, red-haired, middle-aged woman with perfect pale skin and classical features paused to sip from a champagne flute.

Kendra leaned against a tree on the studio producer's palatial mansion's grounds. She'd spent the evening eavesdropping on the guests of the *Freedom's Run* series launch. Overhead, the sky had gone from dark blue to silver-flecked black. A crow roosted in the tree.

"I know. And to think it plays out in the real world. I logged into my home system and had it pull the public records of the pursuit. It's going to be as much fun reviewing it as experiencing it. And Ryan. He isn't what you'd call classic, but I like that in a man. He looks real, and he cares so much." An attractive Asian woman, who, with the state of cosmetic surgery, could be any age, stood opposite the redhead. Both wore evening gowns.

"I did a check on Ryan with my watch." The redhead held up her wrist, displaying a large black bead on a silver band. She tapped the top of the bead, which folded out into a paper-thin screen the size of a softcover book.

Kendra suppressed a gasp at the technical display.

"I've seen those advertised. Do they work as well as a handheld?"

"They're delicate. The screen can rip, and they're light on

RAM. I only wear mine when I don't want to carry a purse. Now look." The redhead held her arm so her friend could stare into the screen.

"Saviour of the kangazoid species. Prevented the forced revision of five Republic member species to a neolithic level. Jupiter commendation with a platinum cluster. I thought I recognized Ryan. Judging from this, he'll give the authorities a run for it." The Asian woman took a sip from her glass. "I hope he stays ahead of them long enough for he and Rowan to, well, you know."

"You and me both, but don't tell Ken. He gets jealous when I use the e-rig to experience intimate encounters. What did you think of the third-party emotional perspective for Mildred and Arlene's viewpoint?"

"Interesting and a bold experiment. As they weren't configured for emotional download, what else could they do? Still, though..."

The two women wandered off. Kendra pushed away from the tree. Scanning the grounds, she noticed that most of the guests had left. A small group clustered around the buffet tables that had been consolidated into a quarter of their original number. Red-jacketed waiters were collapsing and removing the unused tables. Other figures were using tubular devices to levitate the e-interface units, which looked like loungers with a hood that could descend to cover the head, onto a sledge-like platform. The sledge filled up, then levitated a meter off the ground and sped away.

Obert held Carol's hand. They seemed to be conversing with a handsome middle-aged couple. They were all elegantly dressed, though Obert looked a little mussed. Medwin appeared from the tent that held the e-interfaces and made a beeline for what remained of the buffet. Kendra started toward Medwin, then she heard a voice in her head. *'Wait up.'*

Kendra paused as a fit-looking, twentyish woman with light brown hair that fell past her shoulders and an oval face, clad in a little black dress, rushed up to her. Kendra formed the words carefully in her mind. *'Hi, Jessica.'*

Jessica laughed, then spoke softly. "You don't have to try so hard. It doesn't make a difference. I didn't want to yell."

"What have you found out?" Kendra resumed her stroll towards the food tent with Jessica at her side.

"Only those involved with the production know anything about Mike's hopes for *Freedom's Run*. About two-thirds of the people have never given the status of clones a second thought. We're just part of life and blend into the background. Of the other third, half think we should remain property and/or second-class citizens. The other half would welcome changes that saw us treated better, but there isn't enough emotional outrage to drive them to action, and they lack focus."

"We'll need to brief Medwin and—" Kendra began.

"And you should give him time," finished Jessica.

"What, I... I never. I..." Kendra stopped walking as a blush filled her features, which blended the best of the Asian and Caucasian genotypes.

Jessica took the arm of the beautiful late teen girl and squeezed it. "Telepath, remember?"

"Does everybody know?" Kendra stared at the ground.

"Everybody but Medwin. I wouldn't have to be a telepath to see it. I'm telling you this as a friend. Armina's suicide hit Medwin hard. He loved her, though to hear Obert, you can only guess why. Medwin blames himself both as the leader of our group and as her man. Personally, I think finding out she was a clone designed to make an entertainment that didn't even make it past its first season was too much for her. No one's fault. We all have things that will break us.

"If you want Medwin, stand back. Be his friend. That's what he needs now. Let him grieve, don't be a rebound. You may think you'd be helping, but it would be like using a bandage to stop an arterial bleed. When the time is right, when he is with you, Kendra, and not the ghost of Armina, you'll know it."

Kendra nodded. "Thanks. We still need to re-group and get out of here with the handhelds. Those little computers are the best way to arm ourselves." She resumed her walk to the food tent.

They reached Medwin as he stepped away from the food table with a platter heaped with chicken wings, pizza, and sushi rolls.

"There's still good pickings, but they're out of suicide chicken wings," he greeted them.

"I'm still full from earlier. Did you experience the show?" asked Kendra.

"The first episode." Medwin's voice dropped to a near whisper. "Being forced to feel what someone else felt..." He shuddered. "It isn't me."

Kendra smiled. "Ditto, though I went through both episodes. It's obvious the controllers are using us to fill in the blanks when the story shifts to people not set up for empathic feeds."

"I'm getting some food. It's a long way home." Jessica sauntered off. Medwin couldn't keep his eyes from focusing on her backside.

"Keep your mind on the job and off our girlfriend's butt." Obert walked up arm in arm with Carol, a classically beautiful redhead in her early twenties.

"Our?" Kendra blushed. "I see. I... Oh."

Obert chuckled. Jessica returned with a tray heaped with food. "I snagged the last of the Hawaiian pizza."

Medwin nodded. "We eat, go to the room Michael supplied us with, change into our travelling clothes and head back for Sun Valley. We have a lot to report to Gunther and the gang."

"Shouldn't we sleep first?" asked Obert.

Medwin shook his head. "We are in the dragon's lair. Maybe Michael is what he wants us to think. Maybe he isn't. In any case, I want distance between him and us before we make ourselves that vulnerable. Besides, I don't know about you, but there is no way I'm sleeping with all this going through my head."

Everyone considered, then nodded. "It beats camping rations." Kendra moved to the nearly empty buffet.

Gunther lay on the couch. Two loungers and an entertainment console with a television and stereo made up the rest of the furnishings for what appeared to be an upscale middle-class living room from the early twenty-first century. He closed his eyes and enjoyed the silence in his thoughts. The background drone of Jessica's mind had stilled when Medwin's team left Sun Valley. He cringed as his manhood shifted in his pants. The side effects of the telepathic merging with Jessica had been disturbing. He heard Willa enter the living room from the kitchen. Opening his eyes, he appreciated his wife's slender, athletic build with her silver-streaked red hair and Celtic features. His heart warmed to see her. He knew this was where he belonged. She had been the recipient of the frenetic eroticism that had resulted from his telepathic bonding with Jessica, and strangely it had drawn the married couple closer together.

"Here." Willa passed him a cold pack.

Gunther reached out a well-muscled arm and took the pack, resting it over the groin of his track pants. His handsome middle-aged features relaxed as the cold eased his pain.

Willa chuckled and ran her fingers through her husband's short, salt-and-pepper hair. "Not as young as you used to be." She smiled.

Gunther chuckled. "Not as old as I'm going to be." He pulled Willa close and kissed her.

Willa knelt beside him, resting her head on his chest. "It's a good thing that Carl is bringing the pirate healer. I think we both need time to recover."

Gunther looked to the window by the entry door. It was night outside. "I hope he gets here soon. I have patients in the morning."

As if on cue, the doorbell rang.

Willa rushed to open the door, which let onto a short hallway separated from the living room by a half wall.

Carl, his Hispanic features reflecting discomfort and his muscular, early-twenties body clad in jeans and a T-shirt, pushed a shopping cart into the room. A blanket covered something in the cart.

Carl closed the door as Gunther shifted to a sitting position.

Willa stepped closer to the shopping cart. Carl backed away but couldn't stop his eyes from tracing over the form of his ex-lover. Despite her age, she drew him like a moth to a flame.

Gunther scowled and came to his feet, moving to the shopping cart's side.

What looked like a huge, mahogany-furred otter with an elongated head pushed out from under the blanket and eyed Willa. "You are the cyborg."

"I prefer Willa." Willa stood ready to choke the life from the otterzoid pirate.

"Willa. I am sorry. I did not expect to have dealings with you before Carl approached me. I am called Chelaa." Chelaa sneezed violently into the blanket covering him.

Gunther stared at the otterzoid, noting a greying of the small black nose and how he moved as if trying not to aggravate sore ribs. "I take it you are infected."

"Stage one. I do not know if it is transmissible to *Homo sapiens*. My investigations have found nothing. Not even a transmission vector, but I would suggest..." Chelaa began.

Gunther held up his hand. "We have all been exposed treating Valaseau. For the moment, *Homo sapiens* appear to be immune. My own investigations haven't uncovered a transmission vector either. I doubt they will. Let's go to my clinic. I can examine you while we talk. Are you here with your leader's sanction?"

"The acting captain is a fool. She doesn't take the sickness seriously. I told her collaborating with you might be our only hope. She still forbade me making contact."

"There is cause for distrust on both sides," observed Willa.

"I must agree. Much blood clouds the stream."

"Willa, if you could help our guest to the treatment room, we can get started. We have a drug comparison file matching human medications with the database on the enforcer's ship that crash-landed and gave us our abilities. We'll share it with you before you leave as a show of good faith," explained Gunther.

Willa picked up the otterzoid, which was nearly as large as herself, and with the strength of her cybernetic form, easily carried him from the living room and down a flight of stairs into the basement.

One side of the basement was an infirmary with an ambulance gurney at its centre. The other side was full of electronics and tools. The jammer that could create a place safe from the studio's motoring stood against one of the walls.

Willa placed Chelaa on the gurney and stepped back as Gunther moved to the otterzoid's side.

"Have you noted any similarities in disease progression between the felinezoid and otterzoid?" asked Gunther.

"They are nearly identical. Though my fever seems to be worse." Chelaa rested his chin on the gurney. "I... The truth is, you are a primitive, but I am not qualified to deal with this. I am hoping that by combining our efforts, something can be done. So far, the disease is one hundred per cent lethal. All our felinezoid population is infected, and it is creeping into the otterzoid population. The other species seem immune, but I do not know how long that will last. Each infection is a laboratory for creating new variants. When I joined the pirates, it seemed like it would be exciting and get me away from my legal troubles. Now, I will probably die on an alien world that hates me."

"Maybe if you hadn't tried to invade and enslave us, we'd have a little more sympathy," snipped Willa.

Chelaa glared at Willa and made a chittering sound with his teeth.

"I think a little mutual insight might help here. I'm going to boot up the telepathy enhancer." Gunther moved to his jammer unit and turned it on.

Willa's cybernetics twitched as the field expanded over her.

"You built a telepathy enhancer? How is that possible with the state of *Homo sapiens* technology? I don't feel anything. Are you sure it works?" Chelaa looked at the mass of equipment that was the jammer.

Gunther moved to the otterzoid's side. "You're a telepath. I won't try to make you see the truth without your consent. All we know is a lie. We are clones being used to make VR5 plus emotion entertainments. Humans have been part of the Galactic Republic for hundreds of years. We live in the Set Region. Our show is called *Angel Black*. It involves a group of pirates attempting to invade a pre-contact Earth and the efforts of genetically altered humans to stop them without panicking the population."

"This is a good story, but why should anyone believe it?" Chelaa shifted his gaze to Carl, who stood by the stairs. "His surface thoughts are in agreement with you."

"I offer this as proof." Gunther held a handheld towards Chelaa. "Handheld, record current settings, then reset Chelaa surrogate to norms."

Chelaa gasped, coughed up a mass of phlegm that fell to the floor, then took an almost fearful deep breath. "The symptoms are gone. What have you done?" he demanded.

"The plague is a plot in the program. It is the result of bio-manipulation by the controllers. Will you accept a telepathic information transfer? I swear I will show you only the truth." Gunther stared at the otterzoid.

"I will open my thoughts. This delusion intrigues me." Chelaa stared at Gunther.

Gunther focused his mind and sent his knowledge about the reality of those in Sun Valley into the otterzoid.

Chelaa blinked. "Thank the Divine! All this time, I thought the fish droppings that make up my life were my own 'Divine avatar performing an unnatural act with a snail-like sea creature's fault. The plague being bio-manipulation makes sense. These controllers are orca-like predators!"

"You're taking it well," observed Carl.

"If you had made the mistakes I made, you'd be happy to find out it was all a lie, *Homo sapiens*... Carl. This means I never stole drugs from the hospital, never killed a patient because she had murdered my uncle. Never joined the pirates. Those were all stories your controllers implanted. This news washes clean my soul. If we can escape this 'set region,' I can start in clean water. What can I do to help you?"

Greg split his attention between recording Gunther's recruitment of Chelaa and monitoring Medwin and his group as they left Michael's estate. The wall screens of the two-meter-wide rectangular box that was the *Freedom's Run* control room showed the sensory inputs of the surrogates. All the emotional monitors were reading within acceptable norms for the final cut of the e-entertainment.

"Look, cars." Obert's vision tracked over a line of identical small orange vehicles that waited beside the gate to Michael's estate. Each had a shaft sticking out of its front that plugged into a port at the top of a small pole. A canopy of black panels covered the parking area, and tulip blade wind turbines turned lazily at the peak of the canopy.

"It's a charging station." Carol shrugged. She, like all her colleagues, wore durable camping clothes.

Greg took a moment to appreciate the view of her from

Medwin's eyes. "Divine, ssshe isss a beautiful woman." Greg's forked reptilian tongue flicked from his mouth, and his green, scaly skin deepened in shade. "*Freedom'sss Run* hass a great-looking casst."

"It's a long walk back to where we left the water gear," observed Medwin.

Obert opened the trunk of the closest car and deposited his pack inside. "Not as bad if we drive part of it." He left the trunk open and moved to the car's back door.

"We can't steal a car!" Kendra sounded exasperated.

"We wouldn't be. These are public transport. I scanned the mind of a guest who was leaving. He was thinking about them." Jessica moved to the car where Obert had shuffled to the middle of the back seat, put her backpack in the trunk, then slipped in beside him.

"Dibs on the back." Carol followed Jessica's example and slipped in on Obert's open side.

"Do you know how to drive?" Medwin focused on Kendra.

"If it isn't stick." Kendra's perspective scanned the vehicle's dash. "No controls anyway."

Medwin and Kendra stowed their packs, then took the front seats.

"Please register your travel account." A pleasant woman's voice came from the dash.

"I..." began Medwin.

"Use the handheld Ulva gave you. You told us she said it had money on it," prompted Kendra.

Medwin took out the handheld and held it up to the dash. "Transfer funds for the trip from this account."

"Searching handheld. Have you considered the convenience and savings of maintaining a dedicated travel account? The planetary transport system can configure an account to your personal specifications. Planetary transport systems—" rambled the machine's voice.

"Computer, will you take us where we want to go?" demanded Kendra.

"State destination."

Medwin and Kendra shared a confused look.

"Take us as close to the Sun Valley set region as the roads allow. Most direct route," Obert's voice ordered from the back seat.

"That would be the western terminus of Alda Boulevard. Transport cost will be seven point seven two standard trade credits."

"Do it," ordered Medwin.

There was the click of locking doors. The vehicle backed away from the recharge station and sped into the night.

Greg adjusted the biologies of Medwin's group, inducing sleep despite their excitement. "Resst now, my friendss. You've had a bussy night."

Greg shifted the board's focus to Gunther as he returned Chelaa's medical condition to what it had been before he activated his jammer.

"I will give you any information I find on the disease," said Chelaa.

Willa carried the otterzoid up the stairs and put him into the shopping cart. Carl pushed him out the door. Gunther and Willa retired to sleep. Greg manipulated their biologies, ensuring it would be restful.

He then pressed a button, and Medwin jerked awake.

"We have reached your destination. We have reached your destination. We have—" The computer spoke in increasing volume.

"Computer, we hear you." Medwin opened his door and

stepped out onto a deserted two-lane road. The others joined him. They retrieved their packs from the trunk before the car drove off by itself.

Kendra checked the diver's compass strapped to her wrist as Medwin brought up a map on the handheld's screen. Kendra looked at the map, then turned the screen so north matched north by her compass. "This way." She pointed into the darkness.

"Are we there yet?" Obert said in a whiny voice. Everyone released a snort and started walking.

Greg turned to a console labelled 'telemetry unit'. He typed *Owl One* on a keyboard. The console lit up. Greg directed the owl-shaped drone to circle Medwin's group. The press of a button set the drone to relay the signals from the surrogates' built-in monitors.

PAST GLORIES

Hours had passed since the *Star Hawk* pierced the blockade at the Murack stargate.

Rowan sat at the navigator's station, scanning space for ships. "Henry."

"Yes, oh hot and desirable captain's mate."

Rowan rolled her eyes. "Why didn't we get killed when we left the stargate?"

Henry sighed. "It is a long story. Short version, sycamorezoids lose wood when someone mentions the space mink."

"Do they even have trees? I..." Rowan swivelled her chair to look at Henry. The smirk on his face spoke volumes.

"Oh... Why are they so afraid of Ryan?"

"You heard about the blockade on Murack Seven?"

"Emergency rations and recycled water for three months," replied Rowan.

"It was worse than that. No spare parts or armaments. We spent half our time hiding, the other half running. We were outgunned, outmanned, and out of luck."

"How'd you escape?" Rowan focused on Henry.

"Watch your board, sweetness. You don't need to see me to hear me."

"Sorry." Rowan turned back to the navigator's instruments.

"You're learning. Give it time, and you'll be as jaded, uptight and paranoid as Ryan and me."

"Ryan's not... uptight." Rowan checked her instruments.

"Ryan carried the Murack Seven defensive. It may be

suicidal, but hotty boss always has a plan. We needed to break the sycamorezoids and felinezoids' line ships' hold on the system to get out, and we were rogered for firepower. We also needed to preserve the dichrostigmazoid industry if we were going to take the war at large.

"At the start of the siege, the sycamorezoids were bombing Murack Seven at will. Ryan screwed that but good."

"How?" Rowan adjusted her scanners and did another sweep.

"Ryan figured we had three hundred ground pounders laying around eating supplies and shagging like bunnies. I didn't mind the second part, but troops get nasty when they eat even worse than they're used to. So Ryan put them to work.

"The dichrostigmazoid had a strong orbital defence array, so the sycamorezoid and felinezoid heavy ships were held at bay. The smaller, more manoeuvrable landers, their equivalent of the Hawk class, we called them gnats because they looked like bugs, could penetrate gaps in the defence, dip into the atmosphere, dump a payload and blast out before the big guns could get a target acquisition. The Hawk class ships were manoeuvrable enough to cut across the gaps in the defence grid so we could tag the gnats, but we didn't have the firepower to stop them before they blasted through the atmosphere and out to where the big ships could supply cover fire."

"You were forced to play defence." Rowan brought an image up on the big screen. "That's Murack Seven, isn't it?"

A gas giant with swirling clouds of atmosphere in yellow and orange hung against an ocean of black. Moons sped around the main planet, and a ring system girded its middle.

"That's the gas ball. Nasty piece of real estate."

"How did Ryan stop the bombers?" Rowan shifted the high-resolution image, vectoring over sectors of space that might house a ship on an intercept course.

"He deployed ground forces in suits into the airlocks, then moved in fast and close, grabbing the sycamorezoid ships with our gravity lasers while they were still in vacuum. We took some hits, but Hawks are tough, and the gnats weren't built for inter-ship combat. They couldn't do much if we stayed clear of their bomb bay. We deployed troops onto the bombers' surface, and they used explosive grapplers to secure polycarbonate cables into the gnats' 'upper' hull. The cables were attached to the *Star Hawk*. After that, it was a tug of war, and we had more mass. We'd pull up, forcing the gnat to drop momentum and show their bellies as we hit atmosphere. We made them a heat shield. They burnt, and we held them to the flames. When we cut out of the upper atmosphere, the gnat we'd latched onto was half-cooked. Our people hunkered down behind the gnat's hull under our belly. When we were in clean space, they scrambled up the cables and were back in the ship. Most of them at least." Henry's voice became haunted for the last. "*Star Hawk*, we will never forget," he whispered. "The names are on the old barracks' walls."

Rowan reached back and traced the memorial plaques on the back of her duty chair. "Ryan must have known he'd lose people."

"He knew, hotty. Same way he knew that each bomb that got through was costing dichrostigmazoid lives. They may look like something you'd crush for eating your turnip leaves, but they have their version of families. Each bomb we stopped saved civilians. Our people who died saved little dichrostigmazoid from the pain of never seeing their caregivers again. Preserved the integrity of the hive. That's what Ryan tells himself to stay sane."

"I suppose I don't know him as well as I should," remarked Rowan.

"Hotty, no one knows the shaggable one as well as they should. There's too much to know. You know the him he wants you to know. You might not like some of the other bits.

"The sycamorezoids could not defend against our attack. The Hawks were just better in atmosphere.

"We took the first bomber as proof of concept. The other Hawks followed our example. When we were done, the dichrostigmazoid evaced what was left of the sycamorezoid crews to POW camps they set up beside their major industrial complexes. The ships were left floating in orbit.

"Each interception cost personnel, but it made the sycamorezoids bleed. Ryan received the Jupiter commendation for that one."

"And that broke the siege?"

"Not hardly, hot stuff. But it stopped the bombing and left a load of ordnance floating around Murack Seven. What broke the siege was Murack Seven C."

"The third-largest moon," reflected Rowan.

"Give the girl a prize. You can collect when I get my hips back." Henry leered at Rowan.

Rowan kept her attention on a silver spot about the size of the head of a pen that was barely visible in the screen's centre. She started running some calculations. "What did break the siege?"

"We were still shagged. The sycamorezoids couldn't get in, but we couldn't get out, and hydrogen breathers don't have much that you rocky planet types can eat. We needed a resupply bad. For the war on a broader scale, we needed a respite. The sycamorezoids came into the war with more ships than the dichrostigmazoid. Part of what the dichrostigmazoids were doing was making ship components. If they could have a week to launch and assemble, they could have a fleet to secure their own space. Ryan figured that if he could give the sycamorezoids a black eye, he might buy the dichrostigmazoid time and get his crew out of the pooch-pleasuring the UES government landed us in."

Rowan stopped herself from a futile attempt to correct

Henry's speech. "The dichrostigmazoid did offer better tech as payment."

"And they'd never won a war without help. I could have told you how that would pan out before we started. I did tell them, but I'm just an AI line unit who's seen actual battle, not some armchair strategist who got his rank playing war games." Henry snorted derisively.

"It's done now," soothed Rowan.

"For too many." Henry sighed. "Ryan started docking with the sycamorezoid bombers we'd left crippled in orbit. We looted them. Fun fact, things that go boom are things that go boom, no matter who makes them. We had bombs stacked on empty racks in the ground pounder quarters. The galley shelves were stacked with detonators. If we'd taken a hit, you would have thought a nova went off. We took all that ordnance to the C moon. The moon wasn't much but stardust. The dichrostigmazoids had mined it out. Only reason they didn't crush it to pulp was the minerals were in seams. It was cheaper to tunnel. This left useless rock riddled with mine shafts.

"Ryan brought us into one of the old mines. We barely fit. It was as tight as a virgin's—"

"Henry!" Rowan glanced back at the android, then returned to her calculations.

Henry grinned mischievously. "Long, hard, story short, the ground troops carried all that ordnance and the contents of our bomb bay into those tunnels and wired it up. We set the timer for an hour and a half, then Ryan ordered us out of our cave.

"We made orbit around the moon looking like we were going to use a slingshot and gravity bounce to maximize velocity."

"Exactly what you'd do if you were running the blockade," remarked Rowan.

"Very good, hot stuff. The sycamorezoids were on us like the new girl at the swinger's club. Their admiral was still smarting from how we stopped his bombers. They knew hotty boss by name. Six sycamorezoid cruisers closed on the C moon despite the fire from the defence array. The felinezoids had the sense to stay back. The sycamorezoids weren't going to let us do a run-up. Ryan kept building momentum, holding to moon C with the grav lasers. The cruisers started firing, but we were zigging and zagging across our orbital plain. At det minus one minute, we cut the tethers. The sycamorezoids were close enough to smell us, and we were taking hits. We blasted past them and would have been fried in a crossfire as a second wave of five ships was closing in. But before the ships on the moon side of us could get their first volley off, the whole nova-blasted moon exploded. Rocks were flying in all directions. Four of the cruisers near the moon were scrapped. The other two were in space dock for an Earth year.

"Ryan ordered all grav lasers locked on Murack Seven. That had two effects. One, it made our course curve, so we passed below the incoming ships. Two, it pulled a mass of atmosphere up into orbit behind us. When the sycamorezoids from the second wave tried to follow us, they were in dirty space. They were deep void craft, not landers. Their scanners were occluded, and the random gas particles were sucked into their gravity laser ports, jamming them up.

"The guns from the orbital array blasted them.

"We were rounding the planet when Tansy Denardo in the *Hurn* with a half dozen light cruisers at her back hit from outside the blockade on the out-system side of the planet. The sycamorezoids' formation was disrupted. Between the *Hurn*, its fleet and the orbital defence array, the blockade fell apart like a homophobe in a gay bar."

"What's a homophobe?" Rowan continued to run numbers.

"A thing humans outgrew, sweetness. A thing you outgrew. Anyway, the sycamorezoid fleet was in disarray.

"We came screeching around the planet and killed our

grav lasers. We hurtled out of orbit like a particle beam, laying down missiles as we did. Between our out-orbit velocity, the enemy's incoming velocity, and our missiles' acceleration, our missiles topped a quarter light speed relative velocity when they impacted the sycamorezoid cruisers on our flight path. Kinetic force scrapped anything we hit. The *Star Hawk* is the only Hawk class ever to take out a line ship in direct combat." Henry paused as if allowing the statement to sink in.

"The blockading force was in tatters. This bought the dichrostigmazoid the time they needed to get the prefabricated ships into orbit and assemble them, balancing the numbers for the war in space. We used the momentum we'd built up to steer for the stargate so we could resupply at the Switchboard Station. Four weeks later, we were re-manned, re-supplied and on Murack Five.

"They gave Ryan a platinum cluster on his Jupiter commendation for breaking the siege. Not that he wanted it. The body count was too high for hotty boss."

"He blew up a moon. Is there anything left of Murack Seven C?" asked Rowan.

"Bits have joined the ring system. The dichrostigmazoid put up an orbital satellite with a message to mark the location."

"What's the message?" Rowan finished checking her numbers.

"A rough translation. 'Here once was Murack Seven C. Let it stand as a reminder that dichrostigmazoids choose their allies wisely. The *Star Hawk*, a small *Homo sapiens* ship under the command of Captain Ryan Chandler, known as the Space Mink, defended Murack Seven's sentients. We recall our valiant champions who, outnumbered and outgunned, did take the planetary rotation. We here list the *Homo sapiens* heroes and those who fell in battle against them. We pray to the Divine in its myriad forms that no such thing will happen again.' It then lists the *Star Hawk*'s crew, after which it lists the dead of the sycamorezoids' forces. The message is an hour and a half long. Then it repeats."

"That is some memorial." Rowan fiddled with her station's controls.

"Ryan hates it. Too many dead. It's as much a threat as anything. I think the dichrostigmazoids want to remind the sycamorezoids that they and *Homo sapiens* are friends and that the crazy mammals might come back. The memorial also serves as a navigational warning. There's rubble around where the moon was," observed Henry.

Rowan shook her head. "Henry, can you confirm my calculations? It's only a reflection a little more intense than the ambient light around it, even at maximum magnification, but I think a ship is coming around the sun on a course for Murack Five."

"Your math is right, sweetness. Course, they could shift pull points and go anywhere." Henry drummed the fingers of his one arm against the side of the computer station chair. "Moving slow."

"I've back run the numbers. The most likely launch point is Murack Six, the planet's sun-blocked. Should I wake Ryan?" Rowan made to stand.

"Only if you want to shag him back to pleasant dreams, sweetness. It will be days before we can tell what kind of ship they are. Could be a freighter that will divert to the stargate. For now, we'll track it. And Rowan."

Rowan turned at the mention of her name.

"Good catch." Henry smiled in a way free of innuendo.

Hilda stood before the *Homo sapiens* court bench in a tube skirt, blouse, and jacket. Physically, she looked like a middle-aged, blonde-haired version of Rowan. But the beginnings of lines on her face indicated that she was more accustomed to scowling than smiling. Her gaze tracked up to the grey-haired, Chinese-looking man in judge's robes that sat at the simulated wood court's bench and podium.

She turned to the large screen on the courtroom's wall. The screen displayed a magnified line of text. "Justice Haynes, I cannot say where Parry Johansson's residence is, but it most definitely is not the residence of my client, Parry Johanssan. As such, the search and seizure of items in my client's residence was illegal, and all evidence gained must be excluded, as must all evidence gained in investigations reliant on, or inspired by, said illegally found items. It is all fruit of the poisonous tree, Your Honour." She gestured to the greatly enlarged letter in question.

"Your Honour, I object. When viewed at the magnification level used in a standard handheld or police readout, the letter can be interpreted either way. The defence is trying to cloud the issue with an inconsequentiality," spoke the twenty-something, dark-haired Caucasian lawyer in a cheap, grey suit that sat at the prosecutor's desk.

The judge took a breath and let it out slowly. "A technicality, Mr. Pertwee. The law is built on technicalities. We must always err on the side of the individual's rights."

"Yes, Your Honour, but given the offences aligned with the Johansson name, my office finds this highly suspicious. We are conducting an in-house review looking for outside interference with our computer system that may have resulted in this oversight."

Justice Haynes leaned forward in his seat. "And do you have evidence that the prosecutor's office computers have been hacked to this effect?"

"Your Honour, the people ask for the time to conduct such an investigation." Pertwee gazed up pleadingly.

"Your office may conduct an internal review, but I cannot let unfounded suspicions weigh upon the circumstances of this case. I find the warrant invalid and am recusing the drugs found in the defendant's parents' residence and all evidence found due to the illegal search of said residence."

The gavel came down as Mr. Pertwee slumped into his chair.

"Your Honour, given that the prosecution's case is based wholly on excluded evidence, I request that the charges against my client be dismissed." Hilda smiled at the judge.

Mr. Pertwee stood up, but Justice Haynes held up his hand, forestalling any objections.

"This court, with reluctance, dismisses the drug trafficking charges against Parry Johanssan. Mr. Pertwee, we do not hold the son guilty of the father's sins. If your internal investigations find evidence of malfeasance regarding the disallowed warrant, you may refile the charges and challenge the warrant's dismissal."

"Yes, Your Honour." Pertwee sounded defeated.

"Thank you, Your Honour." Hilda turned her gaze to her client. He was a man in his late teens dressed in a suit that cost more than most people earned in a year. His green skin and slit-pupil eyes had the shallow quality that usually came when the genetic splices hadn't fully integrated. "I'll expect the rest of the money transfer from your father," she whispered.

Justice Haynes cleared his throat, attracting everyone's attention. "However, the defendant is old enough to know right from wrong. The charges for possessing an illegal weapon stemming from the search of the stolen and demolished grav-vehicle he was operating without certification and the charges for operating a grav-vehicle without a licence are still outstanding. Mr. Johanssan, you are fortunate that the owners of the vehicle you stole agreed not to press charges, or I would be adding grand theft to this list. The recused evidence has no weight regarding those charges."

"But Your Honour, his place of residence being searched is why my client felt compelled to steal the grav-vehicle and flee." Hilda kept her tone even.

"The motivation for his crime may be considered in sentencing, but it does not invalidate the crime. Given your client's juvenile record and his family's off-planet residences, I am remanding him without bail and setting a short court date. I suggest the prosecutor's office use this time wisely." Justice Haynes brought down his gavel.

The defendant leapt to his feet. "Thiss iss becaussse I have been genetically altered. It iss biasss againsst the reptile ssocssiety."

"Mr. Johanssan, you took a grav-vehicle from your neighbour's property without permission and crashed it into a mature tree, damaging the vehicle and killing the tree. That has nothing to do with the fact that you have reptilian DNA spliced into your genome and everything to do with your actions as an individual." Justice Haynes shook his head. "Bailiff, please return Mr. Johanssan to his cell, then bring in the next case."

Hilda spoke softly to her client before a large, dark-skinned man dressed in a bailiff's uniform escorted him from the room.

"Tell me you aren't going to play the altered genetic card?" Mr. Pertwee walked to Hilda's side.

"Whatever works, Jim." She smiled at her young colleague.

"He's following in his parent's footsteps. Don't you care about the suffering his drug dealing causes?"

"Everyone is entitled to a defence. It's not as if he ties people down and forces them to become junkies. If they weren't frying their brains with the restricted stuff, they'd use one of the legal rec-chems or e-entertainments. Same difference."

Jim shook his head and walked away. Hilda followed him from the court into a utilitarian hallway, then paused, staring at a fat, Caucasian man with thinning brown hair dressed in a trendy style decades too young for him. "John, what are you doing here?"

John turned to face her. "You haven't been taking my calls."

"I gave you an update yesterday. I do have other cases."

"Half our case has been dismissed. You said you could get Michael." John's pudgy features reddened with anger.

"A public hallway is not the place to discuss this! Come." Hilda led the way to a door. "Computer, attorney for the defence, Hilda Strongbow, requests access to client interview room three."

The door slid into the wall, revealing a small room with a central table flanked by two chairs. "In here."

"I think—" began John.

"No, you don't! That's your problem." Hilda pushed John back until he half fell into one of the chairs.

"I'll... I'll... I'll have you disbarred," snapped John.

Hilda rolled her eyes and settled in the remaining seat. "Don't threaten me, John. Half of my clients, if they say they will kill you, you update your will. You don't scare me! Nor do you impress me. You ripped off ideas from some old entertainment archives, combined them and came out with one hit. Good for you, don't go acting like it's an achievement."

I—I—I—" John sputtered. "They've dismissed all the criminal charges. It was in the information dispatch."

Hilda shrugged. "Of course they have. That was taken care of before we met. It was a training exercise, as such a blanket immunity for anything short of a capital offence was issued."

"If it was just going to be dismissed...?"

Hilda reached across the desk and patted John's cheek. "Silly man. Millions of people will have read that dispatch. A good two-thirds of them will have never heard of a Pygmalion delusion. Now they have."

"And they know Michael doesn't have one," blurted John.

"Do they? Or do they know his name was mentioned in the same article as a Pygmalion delusion? Will they look at pictures of that little wife of his and wonder? Long after the details of the article are forgotten, people will remember Pygmalion delusion and that Marcy Strongbow looks like a character from Mike's first big hit and *Angel Black*." Hilda pulled her hand back.

"But the legal charges…" John sat back, looking confused.

"Forget them. We won't win in court. In fact, I'm counting on us losing the first round of suits. All we need to do is get enough into the public eye that the S.E.T.E. shareholders unify against Michael. That will remove his power base. Then we launch a second civil suit for the damages he has done to your professional reputation with his manipulations of the storyline to *Angel Black*."

"But it will be the middle of the next season before the changes he ordered come out."

"Exactly, but all people will see is the mess you made at the start of season eight. He'll get blamed for your incompetence. We can exploit that."

"My—"

"John, I don't even like e-entertainments, and I can see that the relationship disruptions you forced into the show won't fly with the audience. People like the illusion that love triumphs. Cheap sex only goes so far. Killing off Rowan, your most popular character, was stupid. It doesn't matter who made the mess. What matters is Mike will be seen as the one in charge and take the blame for it. With a little luck, Mike and that fakey he married will be playing for food vouchers on a street corner by the time we're done."

John was red-faced but managed to choke out, "How long?"

"A year, maybe a year and a half. This isn't some e-entertainment where you edit out all the boring bits and solve the world's problems in a half hour. This is reality, and we are at war."

"What am I supposed to do for a year?" demanded John.

Hilda rolled her eyes. "Get back into the studio and do your shifts on the *Angel Black* control board like a good boy."

"I hate working the board, especially with Michael's restrictions." John pouted like a child.

"Tough. I need you to watch what's going on at S.E.T.E. And sober up. I can smell the rum from here. Now, I have other cases I need to attend to. Unless something urgent comes up, don't call me. I'll call you."

"I'm starting to regret this." John looked sour.

"Tough. Is there anything you haven't told me that could make us vulnerable?" Hilda stood.

John looked at the wall and began to sweat. "Of course not!"

"Right. We'll deal with it when it comes to bite us in the ass. I have to depose a witness. Get to the studio and sign up for whatever work keeps you there. We need to know what Michael's side is up to. Computer, open door."

The door slid into the wall. Hilda strode into the hallway, followed by a subdued John.

IT'S GOOD TO HAVE FRIENDS

Ryan stood in the *Star Hawk*'s workshop, gesturing towards what looked like a pair of huge bat wings sitting on a work counter that dominated the side of the room opposite the entry. A similar counter with a series of robotic arms on trackways above it filled the wall to his right. The wall to his left contained a nanobot manufacturing unit, a three-dimensional printing system, and a schematic display system with a computerized drafting board.

A table filled with tools dominated the middle of the room. Drawers and cabinets occupied the spaces under the cabinets and table.

"They are lovely." Asalue stretched the burnt and broken wings of his bat-like form and nervously tapped the foreclaws of the six-fingered hands on his front pair of legs. "You shouldn't have gone to the trouble."

Ryan looked at the mutilated batzoid archaeologist he was transporting for the Murack Five relief effort and was surprised by the banality of the reaction.

Asalue let out a sigh. "I do not mean to be ungrateful, but looking whole only reminds me of what has been taken from me."

Ryan smiled. "Asalue, they're functional."

The batzoid swivelled his snake-like neck as his forked tongue flicked from his mouth. "Functional? You mean..." The beady black eyes in the python-like face darted from Ryan to the wings.

"It may take you a while to get used to them, but with practice, you should be able to fly again. And they don't break any of the batzoid theocracy's tech restrictions."

Asalue's tongue flicked from his mouth so far and so fast it was like he was trying to spit it out, and he did what could only be described as a dance in place. "I... You are giving me back the skies?"

"Tim and Yipya helped. The cybernetics would be better if we could have used a direct neural interface, but these should work. Yipya suggested that you could begin the acclimation process on board, so you'd be ready to try flight when we reach Murack Five."

Ryan moved to the wings. "Would you like to try them on?"

Asalue flicked his tongue in joy. "What do I need to do?"

Medwin lay on his sleeping bag and stared at the sky. They had started walking before dawn, and now it was late afternoon. They'd reached the spot where they'd hidden their water gear. The wetsuits, masks, fins, and mini-diving tanks were as they had left them. Exhaustion pulled at him. Aside from the brief nap in the car, they were all going on forty-eight hours since they'd slept. His tired mind strayed to Armina. He missed her, though he had to admit he didn't miss having to jump up every few minutes to do something she could easily do for herself. The camping side of the current trip was the simplest it had been since they'd gotten together. He also didn't miss the constant stream of complaints.

He needed to burn off nervous energy so that he could sleep. Medwin came to his feet and started working the hand pump to recharge the mini diving tanks. Kendra already lay stretched out on the top of her sleeping bag. He stared at her. She had been lovely in the fancy dress. He wondered why he never noticed. Gone was the geeky, grade-nine girl of the science fiction club. She'd grown into a dynamic, beautiful woman. A flash of guilt tore through him as if he was being unfaithful to Armina. She had been his first, his love. Her memory lingered.

"Why did you leave me?" Medwin whispered. He longed to have her as a rock in the insanity that his life had become. Anger fought up against his fatigue. He fell back onto the sleeping bag and plummeted into unconsciousness.

It seemed like minutes later, someone shook his shoulder. "Medwin, it's sunset."

Medwin kissed the hand before he realized it was Kendra's. Her hand felt warm. It brought a vague comfort followed by a bolt of guilt. Armina had wakened him that way many times.

"I've made dinner. Camping rations, but it's hot," observed Obert.

Medwin opened his eyes to see the first stars. He sat up and scanned the rocky barren with occasional clumps of vegetation that made up much of Gaia's surface. "No one spotted us?"

"If they did, they thought we were a bunch of campers. From what Gunther says, the satellites don't scan much past the river." Carol stood up and stretched.

Medwin wanted to look away but couldn't. "Right, we eat, then suit up and hit the river."

"Remember to swim across the current. We have kilometers before the current carries us past the set region. The tanks will give us about ten minutes bottom time, and the wetsuits should be enough to prevent hypothermia. Make sure the plastic wrap around your clothes is sealed. You'll want them dry on the other side." Kendra repeated her lecture while scraping the last of the camp stew in her travel bowl together.

"Why are we making this so hard on ourselves?" asked Jessica.

"We can't let the controllers see us moving in and out of Sun Valley. The less time we're visible going in and out, the better. Being underwater will hide us," explained Kendra.

"Mike would cover for us. I saw that in his mind." Jessica shrugged and started packing her bag.

"The less he has to do, the more he can do. We shouldn't lean too heavily on him." Medwin accepted a bowl of stew from Carol and started wolfing it down. "Once we get to the other side, I'll set up the camping lantern on a rise of land. We'll meet there. Depending on where we land, we may have to walk around the tree-planting sector. All the workers will be off shift, so it shouldn't be too bad. Once we reach forest, we can set up camp and wait for morning."

"Right, then eat up and let's go." Obert began stowing their gear.

Minutes later, they raced to the bank of the Wolf River. Sweat collected in their wetsuits, and their packs felt heavy on their backs. Reaching a sloping section that led into the fast-flowing water, they pulled on their fins and masks. An otter watched them from the shore.

Ulva sat in the *Freedom's Run* control room. She ran through her mental checklist.

"All satellite surveillance diverted.

"All feeds secured.

"Otter bot in place.

"Hawk bot waiting on the other side of the river."

The screens were mostly dedicated to Medwin's team. The emotional monitors for Kendra, Medwin and Obert showed stress. Jessica's and Carol's monitors indicated that they were more excited than worried.

Ulva adjusted the primary track of the preliminary edit to focus on Jessica and Carol.

Medwin pushed into the river, followed by Kendra, then the others. The screens showing their sense of sight went black as the combination of night and water blocked all light. The sensation of cold water on the bits of exposed skin. The water filling the wetsuits almost made muscles cramp before their body heat could warm it.

Ulva hugged herself in reflex as she watched the sensory monitors. She refocused the primary feed to Kendra, who swam with the confidence of her training as a lifeguard. She pushed across the bottom using fins and feeling with her gloved hands. The air entering her lungs was chilly. She kept her side to the current and made steady progress through the blackness. The bottom sloped up. She scrambled out of the water onto a pebbly shore.

Ulva shifted the board's focus to Medwin.

Medwin fought to stay sideways to the current. He felt himself drifting up and kicked hard to stay against the bottom. His head crested the water, then he hauled himself ashore. Tufts of grass dotted the rocky barren. Shivering despite his wetsuit, he stood and looked around. Spotting a hill, he started towards it.

Ulva scanned the feeds from Carol, Obert and Jessica. Carol made shore on a long shallow bank where the river channel looped. Obert and Jessica soon followed. They were less than thirty meters apart. They all stumbled inland and clumped together.

Ulva scanned Jessica's readouts. Her stress levels were mounting.

Obert's visual feed showed a light on a nearby hill. They started towards it.

Jessica's screen kept looking across the river. Her emotions were conflicted. "Stardust! Stardust, stardust, stardust!" she muttered.

Ulva watched as the party assembled on the hill around the electric lantern, dressed in their camping clothes, and started towards the town proper.

Ulva watched Kendra's screen as the surrogate stole glances of Medwin.

"Can't blame her." Ulva sighed. "Being single sucks!"

"No sign of the Wolf River serpent," quipped Obert.

"After the last few weeks, I'm not going to say impossible to anything," remarked Carol.

"What do you think, Jess?" Obert turned to his other

girlfriend.

"What... Oh. What?" Jessica looked distracted.

"Do you believe in the Wolf River serpent?" asked Kendra.

"I... I don't know. Guys, Gunther is dreaming. The connection's back."

"Stardust!" remarked Medwin and Ulva at the same moment.

"Piles of it," agreed Jessica as Obert and Carol moved to embrace her.

"Gene, *Freedom's Run* action log. Priority note to all controllers and administrative functions. The telepathic link between Gunther and Jessica was re-established after the inbound Wolf River crossing. Gene, run the math. Would terrain and planetary curvature result in Gunther and Jessica having a direct line of transmission between them at present?"

"Yes."

Ulva scanned the readouts from Jessica. They showed stress, confusion, underlying arousal and strange blips of happiness and contentment. Ulva brought up Gunther's readings on an auxiliary panel and compared them. Whatever Gunther was dreaming was echoing into Jessica's mental landscape.

"Not good. Gene, amend the last message. Surrogates' relative positions imply a line-of-sight limitation for telepathic transmissions.

"Gene, end message. We have got to keep those two apart. Super telepath evil genius set on galactic domination is not on the production roster." Ulva paused for a moment. "Gene."

"Yes, Ulva," replied the studio computer.

"Open my personal idea file and record."

"File open." The computer's voice was soothing.

"Super telepath evil genius set on galactic domination. That should be enough to spark the idea. Close file."

Tim sat at the navigator's console on the bridge, poring over the sensor inputs.

"I need the pull points now!" Kitoy sat beside him at the pilot's station.

"Coming up." Tim pressed the button that loaded the gravity sources he'd located into the pilot's system.

Kitoy executed the manoeuvre, propelling the ship away from a potential collision with an oncoming craft, then stalled their outbound momentum.

The image on the front screen began to tumble. The words 'Unstable Diversion, FAIL' flashed in red letters.

"Stardust," swore Tim.

Kitoy growled low in her throat.

"Congratulations, oh shaggable organics. If it had been a real course correction, we'd be in a spin." Henry sounded disgusted.

"It's not as easy as you'd think." Tim scowled at the navigator's board. "You can take it out of training mode, Henry. I'm done. Dad wanted me to check on that incoming ship Rowan spotted."

"Unlocking navigation board, oh cute and cuddly captain's son. What about you, sexy kitty? You want to have another go?" Henry's voice dripped innuendo.

Kitoy stood up, stretching her tail from where the human-style flight seat had crushed it. "No, but you could tell us what we did wrong."

Henry regarded his crewmates through his android eyes. "Mostly, you both overreached, sweetheart. You're working for a General Operational Procedures rating, not to be a pilot and navigator. You went for the Kama Sutra when you're only up to heavy petting."

"What?" Kitoy lashed her tail, and her ears turned forward.

"Kama Sutra, an ancient *Homo sapiens* text on spirituality and eroticism. Henry, do you have to sexualize everything?" Tim glowered at the decrepit android.

"Makes you nervous?" Henry smirked at Kitoy. "All a GOP needs to do in the scenario is add a few kilometers per hour sideways momentum to avoid the collision and call the bridge crew proper to course-correct afterwards. The point of the GOP is to deal with an immediate threat without making too much of a mess."

Tim hesitantly pressed a button on the navigator's console. The big screen filled with a small sector of space. Murack Seven appeared to be a brown-blue sphere about the size of a ping-pong ball at one side of the screen. Two of its moons were visible and about the size of eraser ends on a pencil. The background was yellow. A dark speck tracked a course across the yellow towards the planet.

"Is it still heading towards Murack Five?" Kitoy moved behind Tim and placed her hand on his shoulder. Tim took a moment to brush his cheek against the soft fur on the back of her hand. Her tail swished happily.

"Still on track, sweetness. What you gonna do?" asked Henry.

"Log it, Captain's orange notification, so Dad sees it when he wakes up," answered Tim.

"Good call. Still too far off to bother waking hotty boss. I'll let him know when he gets out of bed. Rowan is on her night. I wouldn't want to rush them." Henry leered.

"Henry, there are things about my father I don't need to be reminded about." Tim shook his head.

Kitoy rolled her eyes. "One can only hope that stamina runs in the family." She lashed her tail playfully. "I should get in some exercise before my watch."

Tim stood and turned to face her. Tentatively he reached out and took her hand in his, then gently ran his thumb in a circular motion over its back.

Kitoy's tail swished as she brushed the back of her free hand against Tim's cheek, then stepped away and gently stroked the red sash she wore over one shoulder. Her nostrils twitched, and a bit of clear liquid leaked from them, but her voice stayed steady. "Have a good watch." She left the bridge.

"She misses Kadar," observed Henry.

"She's worth waiting for. I just want her to remember I'm interested." Tim moved to the environmental console and began the systems checks.

"Kid, you are your father's son."

Tim was startled to hear what he knew was Henry's highest praise.

"Gene, put the call on speaker, voice only," ordered a diminutive woman with short cut hair, dressed in a business suit and sitting at a large, utilitarian desk in a four meter by four meter office. Her back was to a side wall, which held an oil painting of her and a lean man with short-cropped black hair. He was a head and a half taller than she was. They were both in formal wear. He was embracing her from behind, and they were smiling. Small oil paintings of two young men that strongly resembled the man in the first painting flanked the central image. The wall to her left was transparent and had a sliding door to a rooftop garden. The wall facing her was a view screen displaying a map of the set region covered with annotations in little boxes. The remaining wall had a central sliding door flanked by smaller display screens. A sofa against the bottom of the opposite wall and two rolling chairs completed the furnishings. "This is Mildred Tallman, head of S.E.T.E. studio security. I'm told you wish to speak to me."

"Hello, Major. I mean, Ms. Tallman," spoke a male voice.

"Chow." Mildred stopped adjusting annotation boxes on her wall screen and smiled. With a press of a button, the map was replaced by the image of a muscular Malaysian man in his early twenties with squarish features. He sat in a comfortably furnished but basic living room about the same size as her office and wore a dress shirt and slacks.

An e-interface occupied the space to his left.

"If you're calling about my offer, it's still good, but I need a couple more weeks. This thing with Chandler and Rowan just won't go to bed. It shouldn't be long now that Mike has let the cat out of the bag," opened Mildred.

"I'm still interested in the job, but that's not why I'm calling. I thought you'd like to know. A lawyer has been trying to get me to answer questions about the retrieval mission. I've ducked her so far, but she is persistent."

Mildred leaned back in her chair and steepled her fingers. "Who is she?"

"Hilda Strongbow. At first, I thought she might be related to the studio head, but that's not the vibe she's giving off."

"Hilda Strongbow." Mildred shook her head and tapped some keys. A bio appeared on the small screen on her desk. "That's a surprise. It seems that Mike has an ex-wife. He never mentioned her, but we're more work friends. What kind of questions was she asking?"

"She seemed keen to know if I thought any outside influence was brought to bear to obstruct our pursuit. She also kept asking about you and if I thought you did your best during the pursuit. She seemed to imply that you let Ryan and Rowan get away."

"Did she now?" Mildred's voice was ice.

"I haven't told her anything," remarked Chow.

"Nothing to tell. We did our best. Chandler was better. I broke my own rule about chasing things I can't do anything about and reviewed his record." Mildred drummed her fingers on her desk.

"And?" prompted Chow.

"Let's say, we're lucky he didn't feel lethal force was called for. What they have declassified from his service file, which isn't much, scares me, and I do not scare easily."

"What should I tell this lawyer?" Chow paled a little.

"Tell her the truth. We were put up against a captain who earned the Jupiter commendation with a platinum cluster, and he beat us."

"What's going on?" Chow leaned forward and spoke softly.

"All I have is rumours. I'll call you back this evening. That will give me time to arrange everything, and Chow. We'll have a chat about hours and wages then. And call me Mildred. Michael likes to run an informal shop."

"Thank you, Ma... Mildred."

Mildred closed the line. "Gene, where is Michael Strongbow, S.E.T.E. studio chief executive?"

"Mr. Strongbow is working from home. He has office availability logged starting in two hours and thirty-three minutes."

"Book me in for his first appointment." Mildred pressed several keys. The wall filled with an image of the interior of the Garlic Palace from the set region. A fat man with brown hair stood in the corner of the room. Rowan took her regular table.

"That appointment slot is filled by Rana Khatri, producer of *Detective Dave*."

Mildred rolled her eyes. "Bump her. How that show stays in production..."

"Do you wish an analysis of audience trends and psychology? The latest paper referencing *De–*"

"It was a rhetorical question. Book me the appointment slot and tell Rana to rebook. Probably wants to complain about her budget again."

⚬

Chow returned his wall screen to the image of a moving seascape.

"What did she say?" asked a dark-haired, early-twenties woman with lovely, classic Italian features and a body that most women would envy. She wore a form-fitting floral print dress that showed off her legs.

Chow smiled and marvelled at his luck. "It looks like I'll be giving my notice to the customs authority tomorrow."

Tracy smiled, displaying dazzling white teeth, and rushed to sit beside Chow. Throwing her arms around him, she kissed him firmly on the lips. "I am so happy for you."

"I'm happy for me too. This means I won't get shipped off-planet. I'll keep my reserve commission, but with the renewal, I can accept the option that they will only activate me for off-Gaia work if somebody directly attacks the UES. I'll stay on the convict retrieval rotation and won't be farmed out as a mercenary." Chow leaned back as tension flowed out of his body.

"You were worried about that, weren't you?" Tracy snuggled into his side.

"Maybe I'm a coward, but I don't like the idea of fighting for the highest bidder. I'll defend my species, but getting the next upgrade to grav-nullifiers isn't a good enough reason to kill." He drew Tracy closer in.

"No coward, a man of conscience. My mother regrets a lot of the things she did in the service. Not protecting her people, but running here and there to fight somebody else's war so the UES could get a new planet or some shiny piece of tech. She always says…"

Chow listened attentively, but Tracy went quiet and pulled back emotionally and physically. "Chow. Tell me the truth. I know you felt chemistry with my mom when you were with her on the *Saber*."

"Tracy," began Chow, but she held up her hand.

"It's okay. My mother has that effect on men. I don't know how my dad copes with it."

Chow shook his head. "Your mother is extraordinary, and yes, I fell under her spell. Beautiful, intelligent, accomplished, determined and classy without being stuck up. She is also very married to your father and old enough to be my mother. You, you are everything she is and more. You're real. She was a fantasy. I don't think I could take your mother to a Cat's Paw concert."

"Divine, no. She hates felinezoid music. Says it sounds like ball bearings dropping on a tin roof." Tracy smiled.

"It's you I like, Tracy. You. It's you that I want to see where things go with. You're real." Chow leaned in and kissed Tracy.

"I... I need to tell you something before this goes any further." Tracy took a deep breath.

"If it's that you're a clone, it makes no difference. I like you. How original your DNA is doesn't matter."

Tracy sat on the couch with her mouth hanging open. "How?"

"You and your mother look like twins, just a few years apart. It made me think, and I have an aunt that caught aboral-736. The family doesn't talk about it, but my cousin, Fumi, is a clone of her mother. She was carried in her mom's womb but is genetically identical. S.E.T.E. donated their lab facilities to the victims of aboral-736 to create the zygotes. It was one of the options doctors gave to couples that couldn't have families, but you'll know all about that. The timeline fits with when you would have been born. I put two and two together."

"I... You don't mind?" Tracy closed her mouth and stared into Chow's face.

"What difference does it make? You don't beat a drum and shout about it, so we won't become a target for idiots. I told you, I think medical clones should have equal rights."

Tracy kissed Chow, then pulled away without removing her hand from his shoulder. "There's more. I... This body is a clone of my mother, mostly. I was born with Nutters Syndrome."

"But there's no cure."

Tracy smiled sadly. "A human physician working in the common area of the Switchboard Station spliced parts of my DNA onto the template of my mother. He used alien techniques banned in the UES. I lived for fifteen years in a broken shell, expecting to die each morning until the transfer could happen. I'm sorry I didn't tell you before. It's just..."

Chow pulled Tracy to himself and held her close before

backing up enough to look her in the face. "What were you supposed to do? Shake my hand and say, 'hi, I'm Tracy, and I'm an illegal genetic experiment gone right, so what's your name?'" Chow smiled.

"I…" Tears brimmed in Tracy's eyes. "This is the part in the script where you throw me out of your apartment and never want to see me again or sleep with me once and never call."

"If that is how it's been, I can only thank the Divine that those other guys were idiots. Tracy, if it comes to it, we'll have to be careful when we have kids in case the gene-splicing carries over like the children in the reptile society. Other than that, you are the most beautiful, intelligent, funny, warm, and fun woman I have ever known. Why would I throw that away?"

"When we have kids, pretty sure of yourself there." Tracy smiled and batted his nose.

"One can dream." He kissed Tracy. This time it progressed to necking on the couch.

"Chow." Tracy came up for air.

"Yes."

"One last thing. About what you said regarding beating a drum. I'm involved with a group, Humans Inclusive. It's a clones' rights movement on campus and…"

Chow kissed her. "They may not like it at the studio or in the squad, but what I do with my own time is my business. I'm in."

Tracy buried his lips with her own and pushed him down on the couch, lying on top of him. "Let's eat in. I'm sure we can find something better than ball bearings on a tin roof to fill our time."

"You don't like them either," observed Chow.

"I like the fact that they drive my mother nuts. I love my mom, but it's tough being the admiral's daughter."

"Then, by all means, let us find something better to do, my beautiful, original girl." Chow went back to kissing her.

GUILT AND PROJECTION

Michael sat at his desk, staring at his computer screen. His eyes flicked up at the sound of his door. "Mildred? I thought I was seeing Rana in this time slot. Between you and me, you're an improvement. If she doesn't stop nagging, I'm thinking of cancelling *Detective Dave* out of spite."

"You've got to be kidding. I don't think much of the show, but isn't it consistently mid-list in the ratings?" Mildred moved in front of Michael's desk.

"For nine years. People like the 'policeman is your friend' theme." Michael stood and indicated his informal meeting area with a subtle hand gesture. "Beverage?"

"Chamomile tea, please." Mildred led the way to the lounge and took a seat. Her feet dangled off the floor. "The Dave character is likeable."

"He plays well to the early teen girl demographic. Never tops five, but always in the top twenty crushes. Rana wants to push things without considering the character's appeal or the show's nature. Her latest idea is that Dave should take the lead investigator spot on a *Homicide: Life on the Street* sequence. It's too dark for the character." Mike took a breath. "Gene, please ask Teresa to bring in a coffee, black, light roast, and a chamomile tea." He then took a seat facing Mildred.

"A lawyer named Hilda Strongbow has been asking if Chow thinks someone interfered with the pursuit of Ryan and Rowan." Mildred watched her boss like a hawk.

Michael sighed. "How much do you already know about

what's going on?"

"Hilda Strongbow is your ex-wife. Why didn't you ever mention her?"

The door opened. An attractive, smartly dressed, blonde woman entered carrying a tray with two cups. She deposited the cups on the coffee table.

"Thank you, Teresa. Have you finished compiling the requisitions for the new set region?" asked Mike.

"They'll be in your system before the end of business today." The woman smiled in a friendly way.

"Once you get them done, go home. I can cope for an hour or two without you." Mike sipped his coffee.

"Sir, I..."

"Go. You should be with Christine. She must be due any day now."

"She is. Two bouts of false labour. I know it's worse for her, but the stress is killing me. I want it over with." Teresa unconsciously hugged herself.

"Then the fun really begins. I remember when Marcy and I had Richard. I was a wreck, but it all came out fine. The half-and-half baby pool has nearly ten thousand credits in it. That will give your little one a nice start. Now, get those requisitions done so you can go look after your wife."

"Thanks, Mike." Teresa left the room.

"Teresa and her wife are expecting their first." Mike sipped his coffee.

"I know. I bought three tickets in the pool. If Christine pops tomorrow at two, three or five, I'm five thousand richer. Christine dated my oldest boy back in high school. Nice girl. Now back on topic."

"I was hoping my diversion would allow me some privacy." Mike shook his head.

"You know me better than that." Mildred picked up her tea.

"Hilda belongs to my time in the Ground Forces. We divorced while *Kids in the Band* was in its second year of production." Mike put his mug on the table, stood up and started pacing.

"Why is she back now?" Mildred regarded her boss. For him to show signs of anxiety in front of her was a testament to two things. One, he trusted her. Two, there was a vast sea of stress he was holding back by force of will.

"I think the situation with John afforded her an opportunity. I'm not concerned about myself. I have enough set aside to live quietly on Silvanus for the rest of my days. I don't like the harm she could do to Marcy."

"Jealous ex-wife." Mildred nodded.

"No… Not the Hilda I knew. Machiavellian, conniving, amoral, and ruthless, yes. Petty, no. If she is doing this, she sees a chance to forward her agenda. She's in it for the money."

"John?"

"He's in it to be petty and take vengeance. He wants people to think I suffer from a Pygmalion delusion. He somehow thinks that will get him back control of *Angel Black*."

Mildred steepled her fingers and made a humming sound.

"What is it?" queried Michael.

"It's classic psychology. Project what is true of yourself onto those you decide to hate. Would you like some help dealing with John?" Mildred smirked.

"What is the help, and what will it cost?" Michael watched his security chief suspiciously.

"Gene, my voice print authority. Open the file 'John Wilson', open sub file 'sculptor' and play its contents on Michael's wall, please."

The wall filled with an image of the Garlic Palace. Rowan sat at a table looking forlorn. John moved towards her.

"I thought those files had been blanked," observed Michael.

"You aren't the only one who needs leverage once in a while." Mildred donned a cat that ate the cream expression.

"You look unhappy, my dear." John's voice came from the speaker amongst a garble of bar sounds.

There was the sound of an alarm coming through a walkie-talkie. The perspective surrogate brought the device to his ear. "Automotive pedestrian accident, Main Street and Oak Boulevard, respond code four." The surrogate dashed from the restaurant. The view shifted to an overhead shot of a man and woman sitting at a table. Rowan and John were in the background. The man pulled a ring from his pocket and presented it to the woman.

In the background, Rowan pushed John away. Her face was red, and she looked ready to spit.

"I've seen this before. So, what you're saying is when they try to paint me with a Pygmalion delusion, I turn it back on John. One recording won't be enough. We'd have to establish a pattern. The fact that Marcy looks like an AH-F has been a great source of fun for me, but now it can be used against me."

"Skip to the next segment, Gene," ordered Mildred.

John was in a set region shopping centre. He approached Willa, who was inspecting melons. "Skip," ordered Mildred. John was dressed as a traffic cop, giving Angel a ticket and offering to let her off for a 'favour'. Several scenes followed with various e-entertainers, ending with a considerably younger John approaching a woman that looked like a middle-aged Fran. All the images were incidental to the focus of the recording.

"This last is from when he was a technician on one of Veda's shows," observed Mildred.

"Why didn't you tell me it was a pattern? This is unacceptable! He should be in counselling," blurted Michael.

"He should be fired! Relax. He never got anywhere with any of the fa… surrogates, and I didn't know until I caught him in the Rowan incident. After that, I had Gene scan the archive with facial recognition when it had free ram, and the rest turned up. John always approached the surrogates when they were on low priority time."

"So, the catches are all incidental. It will be hard to convince people that don't know him."

"The backup they performed during the last maintenance on his Luba bot could corroborate the pattern." Mildred gently drummed her fingers on the arm of her chair.

"I could call..." Mike looked at Mildred. "You already have the files."

"I can neither confirm nor deny that I possess such files."

"How?" Mike focused his attention on Mildred.

"John was rude to me. Since returning from the Rowan pursuit, I've made him a project. You came clean with me, and the payoff—"

"Bonus in appreciation for you accepting your expanded role in the entertainment creation side of studio operations," corrected Mike.

"Really?" Mildred rolled her eyes. "I feel that we're even. John did nothing to apologize. I did not appreciate that, not at all. A few years ago, Hedonism Incorporated wanted a scan of the Toronk clone for their Taste for Fur line. The interspecies legalities were killing them."

"I understand that. Getting the DNA and permissions to use it for the *Angel Black* antagonists almost killed the series before it started."

"Hedonism wanted to use their contract with us granting the use of the images of e-entertainers as the basis for their alien models. The problem was that the contracts' wording didn't expressly include non-*Homo sapiens*. Legal was out to make points by bringing in money for a change. My husband plays golf with the vice president of marketing from Hedonism Inc. They asked me to ease the way to get the contracts amended. I didn't see the harm in having a quiet word with legal. In the end, S.E.T.E. got a reasonable funds transfer, and I banked a favour which I called in to get a copy of John's backup data."

"Nicely done." Mike took a large swallow of coffee. "What do the files show?"

"That John is utterly obsessed with the characters from his show and their variant forms."

"We've got him." Mike slapped the fist of one hand into the palm of the other.

Mildred cleared her throat. "We have him?"

Mike regarded her. "What do you want?"

"Nothing you can't afford." Mildred leaned back in her chair, projecting an air of confidence.

"What?"

"Two things. First, I want the studio to help my husband get elected. The race for the U.E.S. Parliament seat is tight. A minor shift in public perception could tip the first-round elimination in anybody's favour."

"What makes you think I can help with that?" asked Mike.

"I've been at this studio long enough to hear things. Portray characters who look like a politician positively. People carry the association to the polls. Portray characters that resemble the politician as a villain, and people respond accordingly. The studio has done it before."

"People still have free will," objected Mike.

"But most don't use it." Mildred's smile was predatory.

"I know the trend. The studies show it only really works for the elimination elections. Once the field is thinned down to two or three contenders, the issues and candidate history became overriding concerns."

"Salvador can win on his character and platform. He just needs the chance." Mildred bit her lip.

Michael smiled. "Done."

"That easy?" Mildred looked suspicious.

Mike ticked points off on his fingers.

"One. Salvador supports the biological equality movement.

"Two. You've both served in the forces. We have to stick together.

"Three. I support my friends.

"Four. I've already told you that having you off to the side while Sun Valley is decommissioned will make my life easier. You take your job seriously and are good at it. That is useful in the long term. For the next few years, it will likely put us in opposition."

"You planned this." Mildred went red in the face.

"No. Not really. I just see advantages. Haven't you noticed an uptick in positive background characters that are medium-brown skinned, of average height with brown eyes, on the shows I'm involved with? Or that the bumbling scoundrel of a mayor on *Our City Hall* resembles the incumbent minister in Salvador's riding?"

"You were already doing it," blurted Mildred.

"I don't like Minister Lisng's politics. Too much in the back pocket of Humans Ascendant." Mike sighed. "Terra noster sors. Too many of our brothers and sisters in arms have been treated like dirt after sacrificing their first bodies for the good of *Homo sapiens*. I do what I can. Now, what was your second request?"

"It's about Chow. The reservist that joined me on the initial Rowan pursuit. I want to bring him in as my aide immediately. Helen has transferred over to *A Cat's Life* as an assistant controller. Thank you for that. Being rid of that fool is most welcome."

"She seems to have a knack for working with Fluffy. The cat is only slightly more intelligent than her. Chow is more competent than I would like for your successor, but if Salvador wins, you'll be gone before he's half-trained. I can work with that."

"This only stands if you keep him on. He's too good to waste by throwing him in the deep end without support, then canning him for it."

"Mildred, have you ever known me to be like that? He'll have considerable slack to make honest mistakes. I'll see he receives the guidance he needs."

"Then we have a deal." Mildred stood and held out her hand.

Mike took the proffered hand and shook it. "Bump his pay ten thousand annually from what we were giving Helen. It only seems fair since he is qualified for the position."

Jessica walked down a tree-lined suburban street with Obert on one side and Carol on the other, guiding her by her hands. Her feet moved mechanically, and she wasn't looking where she was going.

Gunther sat in his work office. Its only furnishings were a therapist couch, desk, and a rolling office chair. Late afternoon light streamed through the window. The walls were soothing pastel shades. His eyes were closed, and Jessica's voice filled his thoughts.

'It seems like this Michael is more or less on our side. The telepathic meshing is because we're... What are we? Brother and sister? Twins?' Jessica's voice spoke in Gunther's mind.

'A science experiment gone wrong.' The Gunther/Jessica gestalt felt worry flowing in from both sides.

'I want to...'

'We want to...' The gestalt swirled with erotic thoughts.

Gunther forced the thoughts away. *'I now know everything you learned. We should break contact.'*

'Yes.' The Jessica side felt regret. *'Brother. I think it will help Jessica if she thinks like that.'*

Gunther's mind accepted the logic. *'Sister. Daughter would be better for the Gunther side.'*

'Daddy.' Jessica tried the thought on for size and found the attraction swimming against a current of ingrained social conditioning. *'That works better, Dad.'*

'Go home, daughter. They'll be expecting you back on

your show soon.'

'You and Willa…'

'Nearly recovered. Obert and Carol…'

Jessica blushed as she walked through the real world.

'Have fun, but I do not need the memories, daughter.'

Jessica pulled away from the gestalt but couldn't close the connection. She opened her eyes and squeezed her lovers' hands. "I briefed Gunther, a.k.a. Dad. It helps keep me from marching over there and giving Willa something to worry about. I should start being careful. Mike can only keep the *Defenders of the Crystal* board offline for so long. I'll be actively monitored soon. No voice communications about the liberation movement after that."

"Did Gunther have any orders?" Medwin walked with Kendra to one side of the triplet.

"Do nothing obvious. He wants your help in recruiting more augments. Something about the four of you serving as lures for a vampire. He'll tell you at the meeting."

"Who said my life wasn't working out," remarked Obert.

⟨━━◇➤

Angel dozed on the chair in the shed in Gunther's backyard. Valaseau lay on a cot beside her. The felinezoid's breathing was laboured, and her temperature high, but she seemed stable.

The door opened, admitting Willa.

"What?" Angel started awake. Her large bat-like wings spread until they touched the shed's walls.

"It's me. Gunther doesn't think *Homo sapiens* are at risk from the sickness, so I thought I should take over here and let you get some real sleep."

Angel stood and stretched her petite, dark-skinned form. The sports bra and shorts she wore were black. All told, she was nearly invisible in the dark shed. "I don't want to risk going back to my apartment until we're sure. Toronk is stuck there with his leg. I won't risk him."

Willa smiled. "I thought you might say that. I've made up the bed in Rowan's room." Sadness devoured Willa's smile. "I know she wouldn't mind. I..." A sob shook Willa's slender form.

Angel hugged her best friend's mother. "I miss her too. She's in a better place." Angel chose her words so the controllers wouldn't guess she knew the truth.

Willa nodded and returned the hug. "Sleep in Rowan's room. She'd want you to. I'll watch Valaseau. Funny, with all she's done, we end up looking after her."

"I keep asking myself why?"

"Because we are better than the pirates. And because what we learn here may help us save Toronk." Willa moved to the side of the felinezoid and, taking the hose of a portable suction unit, began sucking the mucus from the alien's airway.

"Gunther met with the otterzoid healer. Turns out pseudoephedrine sulphate is safe for felinezoids at half the human dose. Gunther prepared a shot to add to the IV solution." Willa produced a syringe from her pocket and injected it into the IV flowing into Valaseau.

"What the stardust is pseudoephedrine sulphate?" Angel blinked as she tried to stay awake.

"Antihistamine, you can get it in any drug store. Go to bed."

Angel nodded. "Is the plague as bad as Gunther feared?"

"Worse, it's infecting the otterzoids. For now, all we can do is keep Toronk isolated."

Angel shuffled from the shed, closing the door behind her. The afternoon sun felt good on her face as she crossed to Gunther and Willa's back door. Soon, she was in Rowan's old room. Memories of sleepovers and all-night sessions talking about boys assailed her, then she plummeted into unconsciousness. The 'alien plague' the controllers made up to supply a conflict for the season could wait for morning.

Michael sat in the lounge area of his office. An image of a twenty-something man struggling across an institutional room with a walker filled a wall. Michael cradled a crystal goblet of amber liquid in one hand. A crystal decanter sat on his desk, surrounded by tumblers.

"Richard, what else could I do? I swore I'd always put you before the job. One year away, because I love my son, and everything turned to stardust. Damn you, John!" Glancing up, Mike noted the local time, ten thirty-five p.m.

A chime sounded, and the door to his office retracted into the wall.

"All right, I'm here. What was so nova blasted urgent it couldn't wait until morning?" Mildred stomped into the room.

"Gene, blank wall, please." Michael stood, then lurched a little to one side. "Thank you for coming, Mildred. Drink?"

"This better be good." Mildred half threw herself into an easy chair. She was dressed in a t-shirt with the caption 'Small But Perfect' across it and a pair of jeans.

"I need you in your capacity as the studio military liaison officer. There's been a problem with the Gunther McPherson and Jessica Safehaven clones."

"Jessica, the telepath from *Defenders of the Crystal*?" Mildred's brow wrinkled as she mentally pulled up information.

"Yes. Their telepathies have gotten locked together. I'd hoped separating them would undo the effect, but it resumed when they moved closer together. Sun Valley isn't large enough to keep them apart. I need to know what our military partners found out about it. My sources have hit a brick wall."

Mildred sighed and closed her eyes. "I'll make the calls, but you know what the forces are like about information sharing. When is the fallout of that damn bomb going to settle? And yes, pun intended. I was getting ready for bed when you called. May I use your terminal?"

"Please. The open code is…" Mike gestured towards his desk.

"Marcy plays the flute. You need to change that." Mildred walked to the desk, hopped up and knelt in Mike's chair.

"My internal passwords are more secure."

Several minutes passed as Mildred sent e-mails to a variety of military personnel. When she looked up, Mike had brought a map of the set region up on his wall. It showed six dots surrounding the Sun Valley core. One by one, the dots turned from orange to green, except for one that turned red. A red streak arched over the northeast corner of the town and burst.

"RPGs with a dispersal charge packed with whatever radioactive garbage those idiots could find." Mildred shook her head. "It's frightening how vulnerable we are."

"Dirty bombs have been a threat for thousands of years," added Mike.

"I should have been faster." Mildred sighed.

"You stopped five out of six of their teams. Sun Valley would have been a write-off if it wasn't for you. It would have cost us billions, not to mention setting back the terraforming operation. You did a damn fine job, Milly."

Mildred looked up at the use of the hated abbreviation. Seeing Mike's expression of support and worry, she took it as the gesture of friendship it was meant to be.

"You made lemonade out of it," she observed.

Mike closed his eyes and sipped his drink. "The military jumped at the chance to run their science experiment. Ten per cent of the surrogates in northeast Sun Valley died within a month, even with the military-funded treatments. Nova blasted shareholders caring more about profits than lives."

"They were only fa… surrogates."

"Are they, Mildred? Are they really? Four thousand two hundred irradiated. Two hundred and seven dead before we could start the advanced treatments or flush the worst of the radioactive dust off the city. Another hundred died despite the treatments. Then the experiment, seventy-five per cent expelled the alien-abilities retroviruses and went on with their shows, their lives unchanged, except for the ticking time bomb of even more impending cancer and having a 'kill me first' sign hung over their consoles. Half of those left developed cancers induced by the retroviruses that we couldn't treat. *Vampire Tales* came into being to cull the terminal cases so they wouldn't suffer." Mike scowled and pitched his voice in guttural tones. "Them's good eating."

Mike paused to take another swallow of his drink, emptying the glass. He reached for the bottle and poured himself another. "The body count for those first two years was three times what it was in the preceding year, and we still couldn't keep ahead of the terminal cases. An average of ten survived in each of the five augmentation groups that displayed alien abilities. Half of them became deformed and/or psychotic. We used those we could keep on track. The rest became disposable antagonists. Of the few that worked, the military took half. Get right down to it, creating one Jessica that could read minds cost five hundred lives. That's not counting the first run that formed the base for the technology by creating Gunther. And now it seems that some of the seventy-five per cent have dormant abilities that can activate at random."

Mike sipped his drink.

"Maybe you should put the drink down," suggested Mildred.

Mike nodded. "I probably should." He then drained the glass and set it on the table. "Marcy will be here soon to take me home. She had a concert. My musical maiden."

"Mike." Mildred sounded concerned.

"Oh yes, speaking of dormant. *My Psychic Sister* is a cute idea for a show, and Zilla is a sweet kid. I always liked her on *School Friends*. If you ever feel like something light and fluffy, check it out."

Mike looked at his hand. "Funny how you don't see it."

"What?" asked Mildred.

"The blood. Twenty years a ground pounder on the front lines. The things I saw, the things I did. All the stardust we do here. You'd think I'd be swimming in it. But I can't see a speck." Mike's eyes sharpened. "I didn't want to do experiments on the clones, but it was the only way I could get the money to treat them. The shareholders wouldn't pony up. Extra years of life for thousands at the cost of hundreds, all of them dying. What could I do?"

Mildred looked at her boss as something inside her bled. She'd known enough combat vets to know that this was a pit that any of them could fall into, and she couldn't pull them out. Behind her, the door retracted into the wall as Marcy entered the office.

"Hi Mildred, Mike." Her eyes took in the decanter. "Is the work done?"

"Yes," replied the shorter woman. "At least until tomorrow."

"Leave him to me. Thanks for being here. He doesn't like to bother me at work. Silly, but you don't command a man like Mike. You steer him." Marcy moved beside her husband and embraced him.

"Dead. So many dead." Mike pushed his cheek into Marcy's side. "Warm. Alive. I did that much."

Mildred left the room.

GETTING THROUGH THE DAYS

"All crew to bridge stations. All crew to bridge stations." Ryan stood by the communications console and made the announcement. He could hear the system echoing the call throughout the ship. He turned to gaze at the main screen. The centre displayed a tennis ball-sized sphere against a backdrop of flaming yellow. Minuscule black specks flashed into and out of visibility as they seemed to round the planet's edge before entering its shadow.

"Are you sure they're going to attack us?" Ziggy's voice held sad resolve.

"They are orbiting Murack Five. Why would a sycamorezoid or dichrostigmazoid ship go there when they can't survive in the environment? According to the records, there aren't any other species ships in system except us."

"Supply delivery?" Ziggy's voice held forced hope.

Ryan shook his head. "I prefer to think the worst of beings who tried to blow me up and fry an inhabited planet. We'll know more when we can see the class of ship." Ryan settled in the captain's chair.

"Why aren't they running cloaked?" Ziggy fidgeted with the gunnery controls.

"Most ships can't cloak. What would be the point? Hawks can because we were built to sneak past blockades and make landings. For most classes, it's a waste of resources. Henry, can you make out any details?" Ryan stroked his chin.

"You got the same scanners as I do, hotty boss." Henry

blinked. "Not enough definition to get a match. The *Star Hawk* has sharp eyes, or we wouldn't be able to see them at all. We need to get closer."

The bridge door opened. Rowan rushed in, taking the navigator's station. She reviewed her instruments. Before she finished, Kitoy was at the communications station. Tim entered next and settled at environmental control.

"That ship I was following is in orbit around Murack Five, and I think they have company," observed Rowan.

"Told you you'd be as paranoid as Ryan and me eventually, sweetness," quipped Henry.

"Kitoy, transmission delay?" Ryan leaned forward in his seat.

"Around four and a half hours out and four hours twenty minutes back, given relative velocities and assuming consistent courses." Kitoy's tail flicked back and forth through the slot cut for it in the communications chair.

Ryan leaned back and pondered. "Rowan, how long will the period of effective weapons range be if we decelerate with a full twenty-five G pull to planetfall and forgo orbit?"

Rowan's fingers danced across her console.

"We could cut the intercept down to ten minutes." Rowan focused on her instruments.

"If they don't mine the approach," added Henry.

"One disaster at a time. I wish I knew what class those things are. Rowan, find me pull points for a twenty-five G deceleration entry for Murack Five atmospheric incursion. If they have standard deep-space weapons, a layer of air will be a good shield. I want as many pull points to change our approach vector as possible. Update it as we get closer."

"It will be a day or more before we're close enough for the scanners to pick up any details," interjected Rowan.

Ryan leaned back in the captain's chair, gazing at the big screen. "Rowan, replot our flight plan for a thirty per cent light speed coast and find the pull points to make that happen. I'd rather show up early for the party. Henry, talk

Ziggy through activating stealth. With no other ships about, they can hardly claim we are inciting hostilities. When the new course is ready, activate stealth, then initiate course correction."

"Should I inform Dichrostigmazoid Space Traffic Control of the revised flight plan?" asked Kitoy.

"We're in open space, and there are no other ships aside from the *Mary* behind us for light minutes. Let's surprise everyone. Once we make the course correction, I want checks on all stations, then non-watch personnel are dismissed. Expect to be called back out of schedule."

"All crew to bridge stations. All crew to bridge stations," blasted from the *Star Hawk*'s speakers.

A tremor ran through Wispy's blue, wasp-like body, and he furled and unfurled his translucent wings.

"I would not be overly concerned." Krakkeen stretched the ten legs of his wolfhound-sized, spider-like form. "Captain Ryan Chandler is more likely to avoid a problem than engage in one. He undoubtedly is doing that now."

Wispy clicked his mandibles and waved the feelers beside his mouth. "I have reviewed Captain Chandler's declassified file. He seems to be a magnet for trouble. This ship was built for battle. He has done little to change that. Not that our captain is not a polite sentient as far as *Homo sapiens* go, but they are a violent species. Have you heard that they have social taboos about eating their dead? I mean, as long as the cause of death wasn't a contagious vector, it is the last gift you can give your family. On Hive, after the young have finished with their father, we would harvest the legs. They are considered a delicacy and a way of being close to the father, who is now sister. It is such an alien thing to not eat the dead. And the fact that the males of the species can survive the mating process and never become female. How can it not make them value life less and view the opposite gender as other because they know they will never experience their perspective? When I am done on Murack Five, I think I will examine it. My sister/father…"

Krakkeen stared at the walls of the *Star Hawk*'s mess. A rectangular table dominated the centre of the room, and the walls displayed a three-dimensional rendering of a forest scene from Gallab, his homeworld. Yet another example of what he found to be the overwhelming courtesy of Ryan and Rowan, who ruled the *Star Hawk* like a family tree of the highest quality. It was all he could do to keep from tapping his pincer-clawed feet in frustration as the waspzoid babbled cruel words against sentients who had shown their passengers nothing but courtesy and kindness.

Wispy stopped to take a breath.

Krakkeen rushed to speak. "We should get our rations. I do not want to be here when the mammals eat. It is what their biology demands, but I do not want to watch it. All that cutting and chewing before intaking it." He clicked his mandibles together.

"Oh, I know. They could liquefy their food, so they'd be less disgusting."

Krakkeen snapped his mandibles closed. "I did not say anything like that. Wizziminipzzy, Captain Chandler has accommodated our sensibilities by setting separate eating times. Our dining form is as uncomfortable for the mammals as theirs is for us. My words held no harsh judgment."

The spiderzoid scuttled to the food dispenser after releasing what, for his species, was an extremely aggressive attack.

Wispy stood silent for a full thirty seconds. "I am sorry. I did not know you felt so strongly. I haven't had much interaction with *Homo sapiens*. We know very little about them in the bio-zone my species can occupy because they carry lethal pathogens. I am the only waspzoid that has had the enhancements to my immune systems so that I can share an environment with *Homo sapiens*, felinezoids and otterzoids. You spiderzoids are lucky to be able to share environments with so many species."

Krakkeen expanded his cephalothorax and then let the air out in a sigh as his fellow passenger babbled on. Looking at the tray, he noticed an old fruit husk with a circular hole in it plugged with wax. "Pardon me," he interrupted Wispy. "Henry, if I may ask? What is this shell full of?"

A series of squeals, some in the ultrasonic range, issued from the ship's speaker. "That, my ten-legged friend, is from hotty boss. He thought you might like to try some human food, so he searched the database for something safe for you and used one of your empty fruit husks to make a container. It's the pulped meat of a fruit called," the speaker sang in a high soprano, 'apples.' "*Homo sapiens* call it applesauce."

Krakkeen tried to repeat the odd word. "Ales. Ales." He gave up. "It is most kind of Ryan to do such a thing." Extending his proboscis, Krakkeen injected his digestive juices into the fruit husk. "How long should I digest?"

"A minute should do it. It is already a semi-liquid," explained Henry in spiderzoid.

"What are you and the artificial intelligence saying?" asked Wispy.

"Ryan has prepared a *Homo sapiens* food for me. I mentioned to him that the Republic's rations, though adequate for health, leave much to be desired."

"I know exactly what you mean. My rations are remote survival packs. I don't know what the Republic was thinking. I..."

Krakkeen let Wispy ramble through another disjointed liturgy as the spiderzoid pushed his proboscis into the husk, sucking up its contents. Setting the husk aside, he rubbed his forelegs together as he savoured the taste. "Henry, please convey my thanks to Ryan. This is delicious."

Minutes later, Krakkeen managed to slip away from Wispy as the waspzoid tore layers off a ball of what may have been processed meat with the small pincers by his mouth, stuffing the partially digested meat into his orifice. The waspzoid then exuded a clear liquid over the ball and repeated the process.

A spasm of pain tore up from the spiderzoid's silk gland. Thinking about how he had helped his tree family in the stars made Krakkeen feel warm. That and how appreciative they all were towards him. Unlike his aunt's tree. His life as an aid worker may have come because of the shame of debt, but it was starting well.

Entering the *Star Hawk*'s main space crew passage, Krakkeen supported his weight on his back legs and scuttled along the wall of the meter-wide, two-meter-high corridor. Coming to the end away from the bridge, he pressed the lift's call button. The doors opened, and he collapsed into the three meter by three meter elevator.

"Where to?" asked Henry in spiderzoid.

"Medical. Is Doctor Pikeman there?"

"He's on sleep right now, but I can call him. Yipya is on a wake shift." Henry started the lift moving.

"If you could ask Yipya to meet me in medical. Doctor Pikeman is quite brilliant, but he is lacking in compassion. Also, a healer of many species is more accustomed to working outside the parameters of their own species."

"Vets make the best interspecies medics," agreed Henry.

The elevator stopped. Krakkeen began a sideways shuffle down a meter-wide *Homo sapiens* corridor. Henry opened the door to medical. Krakkeen clambered into the large room with its three *Homo sapiens*-style examination cots and walls lined with monitors and equipment. With ease, the spiderzoid hopped onto the central examination cot. The monitors started screaming and blipping as they read vital signs outside the *Homo sapiens*' norms.

"Henry, could you please..." began Krakkeen. The

warning went silent.

"There you go, my splendidly-legged friend. Yipya's on his way."

"It is probably nothing, but that was a lot of silk to produce in such a short time." Krakkeen tried to settle comfortably on the narrow cot.

"You saved our collective asses. That net wrapped around the missile like it was a fly."

"A fly?" echoed Krakkeen.

"An insect that Earth spiders catch in their webs, then encase in webbing before injecting digestive juices."

Krakkeen shuddered. "I will stay with fruit. Earth sounds like a savage world. It is no wonder *Homo sapiens* rate so highly on the Species Aggressiveness Assessment Table."

The door opened, admitting the k-no-in veterinarian. "Henry said you were having a problem."

"I am sore from extruding so much silk," explained Krakkeen.

Yipya moved to the bottom of Krakkeen's cephalothorax and examined the area. He made a quiet growling sound as he probed the silk expulsion gland.

Krakkeen's mandibles clicked together in pain.

"Yes, of course. To be expected."

"Please, friend veterinarian, I am vocal," observed Krakkeen.

"My apologies. I am not used to dealing with creatures that can talk back. It is good you called. This is a small thing that could become serious if left untreated. Henry, please list antibiotic and/or tissue constrictive medications, cross-reference for what is safe for use on spiderzoids and give their k-no-in names."

"What is wrong with me?" Krakkeen sounded concerned.

"You have distended blood vesicles around your expulsion gland resulting in swelling and pain. It opens a path for infection as well. With treatment, the pain will stop in a day or two, then a few days of no silk production will result in total recovery." Yipya examined the boxy script that Henry displayed on the wall. "Do we have a supply of this one?" He tapped a word.

"In the cupboard by the door," replied Henry.

Yipya opened the cupboard, revealing rows of containers labelled in *Homo sapiens* script.

"Which one?" asked Yipya.

The image on the wall shifted to a bottle bearing the *Homo sapiens* script for 'Witch Hazel' and a chemical formula below it.

"It is a pretty language, though it is confusing. I have learned to read it a little." Yipya paused, the toes of his four hind legs flexing as he concentrated. "Metaphysical practitioner Brown."

"That is a strange name for a medicine," observed Krakkeen.

"It is a plant extract that *Homo sapiens* have used since before they were technological. The name probably comes from then," observed Henry.

"Fascinating the things that are preserved. *Homo sapiens* are quite interesting when one takes the time to study them. Not much history and a great preoccupation with violence, but very involved. I've been reading *A Space Traveller's Guide to Homo Sapiens*," observed Krakkeen.

"You as well. They could do much better for themselves with a well-thought-out eugenics program." Yipya moved behind Krakkeen and started dabbing witch hazel onto the spiderzoid's silk gland, followed by a topical antibiotic.

"Eugenics got a rotted reputation with the political progenitors of their second global conflict. As a species, they threw the pulp out with the husk." Krakkeen clicked his leg pincers happily as the witch hazel drew out the inflammation.

"I could do more with dedicated pharmaceuticals, but this should work. I'll want to check on you tomorrow. If there is more pain, call me immediately. I admit I am failing the breeding exam for lack of study. This is the point in a treatment I normally give my patient a treat, then let them go with their owner." Yipya released the low growling sound that served his kind as a laugh.

Krakkeen clicked his mandibles. "Thank you. It no longer hurts. Now I need to find a way to fill the day."

"Jacques and I were playing Thwart the Dictator. You are welcome to join us." Yipya moved to a cleansing tray and pressed his forehands into it. Flea-sized robots swarmed over his skin, removing dirt and bacteria.

"I do not know. I am disinclined from confrontational activities." Krakkeen waved his legs.

"There are political and diplomatic avenues to success." Yipya stepped away from the cleanser.

"I will try it." Krakkeen clicked his pincers. "Anything, so I need not listen to Wispy."

Yipya clicked his claws on the deck in sympathy.

Medwin slid from the back of the flatbed truck onto the pavement in front of the three-storey building that housed his mother's apartment. The tree planter's coverall he wore was grubby with rock dust, and his nose was stuffed and irritated from his time on the drill. Everything ached. All he wanted to do was lie down. He found the mindless repetition of his job exhausting, but it demanded just enough attention that he had to stay focused on what he was doing or risk losing a finger or worse. Somehow Armina had made it bearable. Though he didn't know how because, with her demands and complaints, she had been a different type of exhausting.

He barely noticed the trees growing along the street as he plodded past them, then turned up the lane to the apartment building's entrance.

The familiar halls faded into the background as his mind swam with all he'd learned, and his body struggled against exhaustion. Waiting at the elevator, he saw Mrs. Henderson come out of her apartment. The middle-aged woman wore tight clothing that did nothing to flatter her less-than-fit body.

Medwin closed his eyes and thought, *I wonder what kind of show they made you for. Is it still active? Are you classed as non-vital, do not assist?*

The elevator arrived. Medwin stumbled into it and went to the second floor. In minutes he stepped into his mother's living room.

"Medwin, you're home. Good. I need to talk to you." Nancy smiled at him. Her brown eyes were full of warmth. Her red hair was cut short, and her wiry body reflected the hard work of nursing. She was still in her blue scrubs.

Her smile warmed him. He knew intellectually that they were nothing to each other biologically, but all his 'memories' and his experience since he was 'activated' for the show they made him for said she was his mum. He loved her. A smile came to his face as he thought, *So what? I'm adopted, like everyone else in Sun Valley.* "Let me grab a shower. I know you hate it when I get rock dust on the couch."

Nancy smiled. "I'll put dinner on. I've made spaghetti."

Medwin plodded to the bathroom. Minutes later, he sat at the small kitchen table in his tattered housecoat. A plate of noodles steamed in front of him, covered in a sauce with just enough meat added to flavour it.

"You wanted to talk?" Medwin twirled his noodles around his fork and let his gaze take in the kitchen. It was small, and the enamel on the appliances was chipped, but the room was clean.

Nancy sat at the round two-seater table with her own dinner. The pots were stacked in the sink to her right, and the scuffed counter was clean.

"It's maybe a good thing. I'm not sure. I know you've been through a lot with Armina, but I need your help to make this decision." She toyed her fork through her noodles.

"You're scaring me." Medwin took a mouth full of pasta.

"Do you remember when I worked a couple of weeks at the Shady Rest Care Home last year?"

"The disgusting dump that should be shut down, where management abused the staff and the staff passed it on to the residents? You hated that place."

"I know. Something's happened. The city inspector that covered that zone was in a traffic accident. Ken, the inspector from the northeast quadrant, took on the southwest quadrant duties to cover. He is an honest man. The Shady Rest administrator tried to bribe him. It spun out into a major investigation. Long story short, the city has taken over management of Shady Rest and canned half the staff and all the management."

"From what you told me, that is a good thing." Medwin tried to think what show those events could be playing out in.

"Ken has asked me to become the head nurse at the facility. I'd have the authority to clean it up and make it a safe, pleasant place for the residents. It also pays twice what my job at the hospital pays."

Medwin closed his eyes, remembering Ulva's words about a new job coming up for his mother. "Take it, Mom."

"It would mean working every second weekend and some nights until I get things settled. I worry about you." Nancy stared at her son.

"Mom, I'm eighteen. Take the job. You've wanted to get away from the hospital ever since..." Medwin trailed off and busied himself with his food.

"There are a lot of memories there. It is easy to forget that you're growing up. With the extra money, I should be able to help with tuition. Pay back some of what you gave me since your father died."

"I live here too. It's only right I help with the rent." Medwin smiled at his mother.

"Not at sixteen. Not in this day and age. I know it cut into your college fund. I'll call Ken and tell him I'll take the job."

"I have focus group tonight. I need to get dressed."

Medwin finished his spaghetti and stood.

"I'll get the dishes. Are you taking the car?" Nancy cleared the table.

"Kendra is giving me a lift." Medwin didn't see the smile spread across his mother's face. Moving into his room, he closed the door and whispered. "Michael kept his word. Points to you, controller."

"Points to you, controller." The whisper was clear in the *Freedom's Run* control room. Arlene smiled as she blanked the words from the record.

"You're welcome, Medwin. I always thought Nancy deserved better than what the studio gave her." Sighing, she reached beside herself and picked up a small plastic box. Pressing a button on the box's side, she waited several seconds, then opened the lid. A rich aroma of mutton stew filled the room. "Mom could always cook." She smiled at the care package and what it said about mended bridges. "I guess what I do can make a difference. Thanks, Armina. You got us talking even though you didn't mean to."

The focus group sat in loungers, watching a large-screen television as an audio-video cut of *Freedom's Run* played. Medwin and his friends knew they were supplying emotions to be dubbed into the e-version and that the events they witnessed were of intense interest to Gunther, Willa, and the rest of Rowan's friends, who longed for news of her.

On the screen, Rowan fidgeted as she sat in the *Star Hawk*'s captain's chair. "So, now what?"

The image cut to Ryan at the pilot's station. "Now, we wait. I don't want to violate space traffic control regulations."

Rowan shook her head. The image panned around the six consoles that filled the horseshoe-shaped bridge's walls, then came to rest on Ryan's back.

"Why? I mean, you already committed grand theft, trespassing, stealing power and all that other stuff. I'd have thought that air traffic control regulations wouldn't be much," asked Rowan's voice.

Henry's mutilated form filled the screen. "Really is a fakey, ain't she?"

The shot cut to Ryan, who swivelled in his chair to glare at the android. "I've told you. I don't like that word, *robot!*"

The image cut to Arlene in the *Freedom's Run* studio control room. She watched a monitor leap into the red. "Boy-o, I didn't think they made 'em like you anymore. Take anything about yourself. Let the mech dis your lady fair, and you're a tiger."

She glanced at Henry's meters that bounced up and down at astounding speed and then levelled out.

Arlene pressed a button on the console. "General note: slow and adapt Henry's emotional process before market. The AI processing speed is too fast to make good human entertainment." She paused. "Keep a version in original format with a view to breaking into the AI market."

The screen cut to the bridge of the *Star Hawk*. Henry spoke. "I'm sorry, hotty. Ryan, point taken."

Ryan nodded, then turned to Rowan. "So far, I've only committed crimes of a planetary nature, aside from a weapons violation they don't know about. Once we're away from Gaia, the theft charge doesn't apply because of ambiguity about your status in the United Earth Systems and Republic spheres. The trespassing charges are petty, and they'd have to deport me to prosecute. The power theft might apply in the United Earth Systems, but it's iffy, it wouldn't apply to the Republic."

"Interstellar law is nova blasted," added Henry.

"So away from this planet, am I legally a person?" Rowan sounded hopeful.

Henry let out a bark of laughter.

Ryan hung his head. "Only on Silvanus and Frigga. On Earth, you'd be killed the minute you left the ship. Even on Silvanus and Frigga, you'd be deported unless you managed to evade detection for five standard years."

Medwin let his thoughts rove over the implications of what he heard. Knowing it was real and how intimately it affected him and everyone he knew gave his emotional response an intensity not in keeping with a TV show, but he couldn't help himself.

EQUIPPING THE TROOPS

Troy stood on a barren rock field strewn with a jumble of equipment. A large, two-storey building built out of the native stone rose, sporting a peaked roof covered in solar panels, about two hundred meters in front of him. He knew the smaller and more delicate set props were housed within it. What looked like three early twenty-first century RVs and a powerboat on a trailer rested under tarps to his right. A battered cube of polycarbonate, three meters in all dimensions, was to his left. An internal pressure door from a spacecraft provided access to the cube's interior. Inside was a jumble of broken machines.

Troy ran his long-fingered hand through his straw-coloured hair and smoothed the t-shirt and slacks on his gawky twenty-one-year-old body. The day was fading, and he needed to be ready for the transfer into the set region in the wee hours. Only a couple of months on the job, and he was responsible for a prop dump. He was overwhelmed, proud and more than a little scared. When the duty had appeared on the board, he'd felt sure John would be given it because of his experience, but the disgraced producer hadn't even been considered.

Troy folded out the screen of his handheld and spoke. "Handheld, connect me to studio control. Gene, voice print access to studio props inventory. Requisition and transport to…" Troy glanced up at a sign on a nearby post. "G9. Inventory, four octozoid military-grade land scuttling suits, thirty octozoid hunting rations, five octozoid data tubes, seven replacement air filter kits for a type two civilian octozoid land scuttling suit, two octozoid subsurface aquatic rifle systems. Three power clips for octozoid subsurface aquatic rifles, seventy per cent degeneration. Six dead crayfish, two dead trout, fifty kilograms of lake silt, and one standard distressing kit."

"Authorization required," stated the handheld.

"Authorize Troy Mac, controller, *Angel Black* Employee Number TM–512. Clearance for action Michael Strongbow, head studio producer."

"Authorization accepted. Preparing inventory."

Troy stuck his head into the polycarbonate box. He knew it was part of a spacecraft the studio had pulled off a scrap heap to mimic a crashed alien ship. Depowered clamp systems stuck out from the wall, and a jumble of smashed tech littered the floor. Holding up his handheld, he projected a beam of light. Something that may have been a battle robot was smashed in half against the far wall. A human-looking cybernetic arm stuck out of a pile of mouldy rags.

"That's a tip-off." Troy walked over the garbage and pulled out the arm. He set it by the path that gave access to the storage sector before returning to the cube. By the time a flat-surfaced robotic platform stacked with his order had arrived, he had a pile of battered clothing, a *Homo sapiens* doll, the arm, a human skull, and an antique keyboard bearing human lettering.

Taking a pair of meter-and-a-half-long, pole-like grav-lifts from a rack at the front of the platform, he began arranging the items in the container. On the first scuttle suit, he took a piece of pipe and slammed it onto one of the leg seals, dislodging it before arranging the suit inside the cube. Three of the suits he loaded with no damage but jumbled them together. The rest he caused impact effects that could be readily fixed. He considered the ration packs.

"Stardust, not their fault the studio made them pirates. Let them have a decent meal." Troy placed the storage crate on the heaped detritus.

When he was finished, he looked in through the door. "Not bad if I do say so myself," he muttered. "Looks like it could have gone through a crash, then spent eight years at the bottom of a lake." He popped open a panel beside the door and grabbed the auxiliary operation lever. Turning a knob to close, he pumped the lever. With a grating sound, the hatch slid shut. He then replaced the panel.

Opening his handheld, Troy checked the time. "24:30. Almost tomorrow. I need to hurry."

Opening a red toolbox, as long as his forearm in all dimensions, that sat on the corner of the robotic platform, he pulled out a block of a Plasticine-like material and some small tubes. Clambering over the cube, he placed the charges and detonators. Returning to the distressing kit, he put on a set of earphones and pressed a button on a boxy device. Hot air flowed over him as scorch marks and battered indentations appeared on the cube. Retrieving a sledgehammer from the kit, Troy pounded at the braces where the cube would have ripped free of the crashing ship until the couplings were bent and crumpled. He returned the sledgehammer to the distressing kit, then folded out his handheld. "Handheld, connect me to the studio control computer. Gene, props inventory. Return sledge three to the staging area, restock and file found items."

The sledge rolled away, carrying the arm, skull and other items.

Troy looked at the sky. Clouds had closed in, making for a dark night. A large, flat platform appeared above him, a darker shadow against the dark sky. His handheld chirped. Troy jumped, then folded open the device.

"Could give a guy a little warning, Hope. You scared the stardust out of me." Troy looked into the screen, which displayed the face of a middle-aged woman with bright blue eyes and short brown hair.

"What would be the fun in that? Besides, it's a good test of the stealth. This old bird has been mothballed for a couple of years. I really wish they'd upgrade it. I mean, how much would it cost? There's enough newer military surplus floating around. You ready?" The pilot smiled mischievously.

"Ready. Let's load her up. Confirming drop location, hydroelectric lake silt zone."

"Location confirmed. The file work matches. What are they sending the pirates this time? With the loss of Rowan, you'd think they'd want to disempower the antagonists, not build them up," remarked Hope as cables descended from hidden ports in her craft.

"Need to know, and Mike would have my head. It will bring out a new twist with the octozoids. I'll say that much."

"I'll look forward to experiencing it. I always felt the octozoids were underutilized. Cables down and locked."

Troy pushed the cables against the sides of the cube, allowing the rows of mini grapplers along their length to find hold points. Minutes later, he stood back as the cube lifted into the air. The delivery ship was invisible with its stealth technology. The cube's naturally dark colour made it blend with the night. Troy checked the time on his handheld. "2:35 hours. Right on schedule." Turning, he walked down the prop storage avenue.

Hope drifted over the set region, watching her screen as the rocky barren gave way to the forestation project, then the lake behind the hydroelectric dam. She checked the latest current chart against the supposed location of the spaceship crash and selected her site. It was the dead of night on a Wednesday. The clones were all in their beds, and any in her sector that weren't would have inexplicably, from their perspective, fallen asleep.

She drifted silently over the water and brought the old military grav-hauler to a halt. She scanned the cockpit instruments, which wouldn't have been out of place in a

20th-century aircraft, then pressed the button that lowered her cargo.

The polycarbonate box dropped into the water with a plop.

The press of another button signalled the cables to release and rewind.

Hope watched on the monitor as the payload sank, sending bubbles to the surface. "I hope Mike knows what he's doing. Farley has enough trouble dealing with the aquatics as it is."

She watched until the box went under, then flew silently out of the set region.

Grell's voice issued from the answering machine. "Rydro-electric lake. Somering big. Now!"

Carl didn't reach his phone before his k-no-in informant broke the connection. Carl stood beside the battered couch in his living room, staring at the phone on his end table and blinking stupidly. Sighing, he shuffled back to the bedroom, emerging in a blue housecoat and slippers shaped to resemble dragon heads. Picking up the phone, he hit a speed dial button.

"What?" Farley's voice came over the line.

"There's something up at the hydroelectric lake. We'll need you and Quinta. I'll call the others." Carl's mind cleared as he threw off sleep.

"Time for coffee?" asked Farley.

Carl glanced at the clock on the wall. 5:55 AM. "Going to have to be. Angel is useless before her first cup, and we'll need aerial surveillance. Rally at Gunther's."

"See you there."

Hanging up, Carl hit another speed dial key.

"Carl, this had better be important," answered Gunther's grumpy voice.

"Something is going down at the hydroelectric lake."

"I'll tell Angel and Willa. There will be coffee waiting. Pick up some danishes on your way over."

The line went dead.

"Trouble?" asked the beautiful Navajo woman who padded naked from the bedroom. Fran moved to Carl and kissed him.

"Something at the hydroelectric lake. The pirates have probably found another part of their ship. The less tech they recover, the better for us. We're meeting at Gunther's. He wants me to pick up danishes."

"We must be why Bill the Baker's opens early." Fran leaned against Carl and kissed him. "And here I had plans for the morning."

With matching sighs of regret, they moved to the bedroom to dress.

⊂══◇►

Gunther opened the door to his house. Quinta, wearing a collar and leash held by Farley, scuttled into the living room.

"A leash and collar?" Willa sounded disgusted from her seat in one of the loungers. She was dressed in durable camping clothes with a coffee in one hand and a danish in the other.

"In shadows, people think I'm walking a dog. It's easier than the shopping cart," explained Farley.

Quinta flared her nostrils. "When I am undercover, it is the only time *I* wear it."

Farley blushed crimson.

"Sometimes being a telepath has disadvantages. I did not need that mental image." Gunther shook his head.

Quinta made a splashing motion with her paws. "My apologies."

Willa shook her head and rolled her eyes.

"You are one twisted puppy!" Angel glared at Farley, then turned to the rest. "I'll fly ahead and see what I can see.

Gunther, keep in touch."

'Of course,' Gunther's voice echoed in everyone's mind without him moving his lips.

"Any idea of what we're facing?" Gunther turned to Carl.

"None. Just a call from Grell saying something was happening." Carl gulped his coffee.

"Everyone, listen. If you have to go in the water, the currents are dangerous. If they open the gates on the dam, it can go from still to ten kph in a flash. If that happens, there will be a lot of silt stirred up. In places, the sides of the lake are undercut. If you go up, you may find a roof before reaching air. Stay out of the water. If you have to go in, keep track of where you are and remember there are back eddies. You can't trust the current to give you a sense of direction." As he spoke about aquatic matters, confidence entered Farley's voice.

"We'll take the SUV. The back roads give better access. Carl, you hang back and take care of Valaseau. Suction her airway and refresh the IV if needed." Gunther finished his tea, then led the way from his house. Angel glanced around to be sure they weren't being watched, then leapt into the air, caught a thermal and sped towards the lake.

By seven-thirty, Gunther was driving along a tree-lined dirt road that ended at the lake's edge. He took a pair of binoculars from his glove compartment and scanned the water.

'Two o'clock from your position.' Angel's voice sounded in his mind.

'What, who's that?' Jessica's sleepy mental voice intruded.

Gunther pushed down the desire to merge with the young telepath. *'Not now, daughter. We're on mission for the masters.'*

'Enjoy the charade and keep our cover.' Jessica's intrusion faded.

Gunther shifted the binoculars. A mid-sized powerboat floated on the water. Several figures moved on the deck.

"Two k-no-in and three humans. I recognize two of the humans as vilicsa addicts." Willa gazed along Gunther's line of sight, the magnification of her cybernetic eye far outstripping his binoculars. "They're pulling things out of the water, and... I saw a tentacle crest the surface."

"Farley, Quinta, you're up. We'll back you up as soon as we can." Gunther moved to open the back hatch of the SUV.

"Gunther. No!" Farley's voice was adamant. "It's too dangerous. Maybe Willa is strong enough to deal with the currents in this lake. Maybe. The rest of you..." Farley shook his head.

"He is correct in this. I am evolved to the water, and I would not enter so close to a hydroelectric plant except for dire need. It is better we spend our efforts dealing with the pirates than rescuing you." Quinta rose on her hind legs, throwing her tail out behind her for balance, the show of strength emphasizing her point.

"We'll wait. Angel can at least drop some surprises on the boat." Gunther reached into the SUV and pulled out a box of glass jars filled with a yellow-coloured liquid.

Farley strapped a diver's knife to his leg and took a bang stick and a belt of replacement shells out of the weapons store in the SUV. He and Quinta leapt into the water and vanished from view. Angel landed by the SUV.

"You called?" She smiled at Gunther.

"We'll give them ten minutes, then start dropping bombs." Gunther indicated the box of jars.

"I don't like operating in daylight. People might see." Angel picked up two of the bottles.

"Can't be helped. It's the only real backup we can give. I'm going to see what I can do from a distance. The rest of you, keep your eyes peeled. We don't want to be ambushed." Gunther settled with his back against a tree and focused his mind on the boat's occupants.

Farley and Quinta raced through the water. The gills on the sides of Farley's neck extracted oxygen from the water, and the extra membrane on his eyes kept his vision clear for the three meters the silt allowed. The water sped over his skin like silk, and the exhilaration of movement was enough to make him forgive the controllers for forcing his freak show of a body on him. He glanced at Quinta. Here she was everything he knew her to be. Lean, sleek, beautiful and, to him, sexy. In free water, she was nearly his match. She broke from his side and sped to the surface, catching a breath and then returning to him. So far, the lake water was clear. Weeds grew on the bottom amidst stretches of rock and silt. Fish sped away at their approach.

He pinged his sonar, even though it always gave him a sinus headache. Soft things moved around a large, hard box in the distance.

'Gunther, we found them,' Farley thought.

'Quinta is getting a breath. She says not to attack without her,' Gunther relayed the message.

Quinta sped to the surface, then returned. Farley readied his bang stick.

They burst into the range of vision around the boxy construct. Six octozoids removed objects from the box, which was half-buried in silt. The octozoids' bulbous bodies pulsed as they drew water in and out of themselves. The four tentacles that projected off the base of each of their bodies were lined with suckers. Beak-like mouths opened in the centre of the tentacles, and a ring of beady eyes surrounded the mouths. There was a mound of trash to one side of a hatch in the box, while at the other stood several of what looked like fishbowls mounted on four corrugated legs. There were nondescript crates around the legs attached to the fishbowls. One of the fishbowls on legs was being hoisted up from the bottom.

Farley sped to the closest octozoid, thrusting with his bang stick. The octozoid swept to the side and tried to circle the human. Two others stopped securing items from the box and picked up kinetic rifles. Quinta, with her telekinesis, pushed a rifle to one side as a tentacle squeezed its trigger mechanism. The blast of water hammered into an octozoid, slamming it into the side of the box. One of the octozoids vanished into the silty waters.

Farley thrust at another octozoid, driving his bang stick home. It detonated, tearing a chuck the size of a man's fist out of his foe.

The octozoids threw off their surprise and formed a rank before charging the human and the otterzoid. There was the sound of a splash from above. A human in scuba gear plummeted to the bottom.

A muffled whoop sounded as light blazed above.

'There are too many, and they all have hydrokinetic rifles.' Farley projected the thought even as he pulled his dive knife and fell on an octozoid trying to entangle Quinta from behind. A short wrestling match later, two octozoid tentacles drifted towards the surface while the alien propelled itself away with the other two. Three octozoids swam to the fishbowls with legs and slipped into them while the others menaced Farley and Quinta. Lights blinked at the base of the fishbowl-like section on the devices. Each grabbed a crate with the pincer at the end of one of its limbs and ran across the lake bed on the other three legs.

An octozoid entwined Quinta in its tentacles and squeezed. The otterzoid released a stream of bubbles from her nose, then closed her eyes and seemed to go limp. An invisible force pried the waste sphincter at the top of the octozoid's bulb open. Cold water rushed into the alien. Its tentacles spasmed as its bowels cramped. It released Quinta, who sped to the surface.

Farley tried to hide behind a rock.

Two more octozoids entered the suits and, hoisting other crates, ran away from the box.

With a force like hitting a wall, the current shifted. Farley was swept back as visibility dropped to zero. Silt clogged his gills like thick smoke. He drove down through the maelstrom, barely avoiding hitting something, be it octozoid or junk from the chamber he couldn't guess. He swept past another rock outcrop and pulled down for all he was worth, finding a small area of still water in the lee of an underwater cliff. Here the silt was thin enough that he could breathe. *'Gunther, is Quinta all right?'*

'Angel has her. It's taking them both to lift her. What's your status?'

'They got away with several… I don't know what to call them.'

'Land scuttling suits. I skimmed Tony's mind. Running off with the suits was his idea. He thought a retreat would save lives on both sides.'

'Good squid.'

'Are you safe?' demanded Gunther's thoughts.

'I can hole up here until the current changes. What do you think the octozoids got?'

'Less than they would have. When the current changes, check the status of that cube, then get back here.'

Minutes passed as the water sped over Farley's crude shelter like a howling wind. Then it slowed and back surged. Using his sonar, Farley swam to where the box had been. Silt had piled up on one side of it and flowed into it through the open door. Inside, it was too dark to see, and outside, he could barely make out his hand at the end of his arm. He knew from experience that the shifting silt would re-bury the box in a few hours.

Quinta appeared at his side with a flashlight in her mouth. Farley took the light and shined it into the box, spotting a tube made of bone or coral. Taking the device, he followed Quinta to shore.

CHANGING HEARTS AND MINDS

Gunther sat in his basement, trying not to yawn. The jammer ticked down towards failure. Medwin and his team sat amongst the cast from *Angel Black* and Willow from *The Station House*. The beautiful, dark-haired, twenty-something firewoman sat hand in hand with a muscular thirty-something man with dark brown hair and rough features. The man was shaking his head in disbelief.

"The show is now being shown. Michael claims he wants to reform society's attitude towards clones. The rebellion is the show's B story. Rowan made it to Ryan's ship, but the episodes didn't go that far," summarized Medwin.

"Rowan always dreamed of being an astronaut." Willa watched the floor.

Carl yawned where he sat on the stairs leaning on Fran.

"James, is there anything you want to ask before the jammer overheats?" Gunther visually scanned the team. The only ones that didn't look exhausted were the fire officers.

James looked at Willow. "You say all the stuff in my head is true."

"All of it. Every word... Well, thought." Willow cupped her companion's cheek.

James took a deep breath. "I'm in. Though I don't know how much use I can be."

"I thought the same thing." Kendra smiled. "I've surprised myself. Even my lifeguarding has come in handy."

"Emergency skills always do. I view lifeguards as part of the fraternity. Cops, firemen, ambulance, and lifeguards. All us crazies who run, or swim, towards when sane people head in the other direction." James smiled at the young woman.

"For now, we organize. We have to be careful about whom we recruit," began Gunther.

Medwin interrupted him. "Not everyone can handle having their world turned upside down. Some people..." He trailed off.

"Medwin's girlfriend killed herself," explained Obert.

James strode over and embraced Medwin. "You are not alone. We should arrange to meet in a way these controllers will not suspect. It helps to talk to others who have been left behind."

"You?" Medwin sounded surprised.

James released the younger man. "When my wife found out that we couldn't have children, it was too much for her." James shook his head. "Now I learn that no one in Sun Valley can have children. Silly, how many of the things that mattered before I entered this basement now count as nothing. Medwin, was it?"

"Yes."

"It wasn't your fault, and I am sure you did whatever you could. Make some excuse to drop by the station. We'll play-act a meeting so we can talk about what really matters."

The jammer started beeping. Everyone scrambled to return to their hiding places. Gunther threw the switch that shut it down.

"Given what we know, I think Angel, Farley and Quinta should check out the Link River connecting the hydro-electric lake to Lake Edgley. The scuttle suits may still be walking that way. Willa, I'll need you to examine the data storage device Farley retrieved. And..." Gunther yawned.

"We all need to get some sleep," stated Carl. "I say we patrol the river once, then hit the hay."

Gunther nodded. "One quick check, then bed."

The cast of *Angel Black* dispersed to provide the distraction for the controllers that would allow their allies to sneak from Gunther's house and disperse.

Greg sat in the *Freedom's Run* control room and sighed. When he'd seen the suicide element in James's back story, he'd hoped things would go exactly as they had.

"Now you have sssomeone to talk to, my friend." Greg let his green-skinned hand rest in his lap and flicked his slender forked tongue. He kept the board focused on James and Willow as they snuck out of the basement.

James took Willow's hand. Willow let him walk in silence, giving him time to sort out having his world turned upside down.

"I've always believed in guardian angels, spirits, ancestors. Whatever you want to call them." James spoke softly.

"I..." Willow smiled as she caught the game of semantics. "There are nasty ones too."

"Undoubtedly. My Granny was into spiritualism. She used to say, 'Just because someone is a spirit, it doesn't mean they are a nice person.' Still, it's comforting to think someone is looking out for you."

"Especially in our line of work. Though I don't think the spirits are watching all the time. There are a lot of people in Sun... the world. The spirits would each have to watch over several people."

James smiled. "You can only wonder how they'd do things. Maybe leading people to other people who could make a difference."

The conversation continued as they made their way to

James's house.

Ryan adjusted the pilot station, stilling the gravity lasers' pull.

"I read zero acceleration, drift speed thirty point zero one per cent light speed. Course is on target," stated Rowan from the navigator's station.

"Stealth is engaged," added Ziggy from the weapons station.

"Only remnant chatter. Mostly space traffic control. Our system entry made the news for both the sycamorezoids and the dichrostigmazoids. Ryan, did you know you are either a war criminal and thief or a great champion of sentient rights and hero, depending on which side you listen to?" Kitoy flicked her tail in amusement, where she sat at the communications console.

"I did. The sycamorezoids tried to place charges against me for the destruction of Murack Seven C. It was a dead moon, and the dichrostigmazoids didn't mind, so the case had no traction. Tim?"

"Environmental station is green. I need to adjust the temperature in Krakkeen's quarters again. The system keeps trying to slip back to *Homo sapiens* norms." Tim rubbed the back of his neck.

"Do it when you're done here. Henry, computer status?"

"I'm doing fine, thank you. For someone with no hips and no one to play with. Hotty, you sure sharing our sexy captain is out of the question?"

"Henry!" Ryan and Rowan shouted in unison, then smiled at each other.

Rowan focused on her console. The image on the big screen zoomed in. Murack Five was now a slightly blurry image that crowded the screen with the sun's yellow filling in the background. Two dots about the size of pinheads appeared against the sun on the planet's horizon. Red arrows pointed to them to aid vision. The moons were out of frame.

"Henry, have you compiled the images?" Ryan moved to the engineering station and ran the safety checks while locking down the gravity laser drive.

"They're still blurry as a voyeur cam in a muddy swim hole." Henry blinked. The image on the big screen changed to a black field with what looked like a fuzzy egg about half a centimeter long in the centre.

"There are three ships now," observed Rowan.

"They all look alike from this distance, hotty." Henry's voice reflected frustration. "This image is built up over hours of compilation."

"We'll get closer all too soon. At least we know they're sycamorezoid. That's more than we had yesterday. Rowan, restore real-time image. What are their orbits like?"

The big screen changed in time for them to watch the fly speck move behind the planet.

Rowan took several minutes to correlate her data. Everyone else busied themselves with station checks.

"They keep looping up and down on the orbital planes." Rowan's voice was concerned.

"Seeding mines." Ryan smoothed his clothing but showed no other signs of agitation. "Henry, how many kinetic missiles do we have in the feeder system?" Ryan settled in the captain's chair.

"Point two-five per cent of a load, and with the way we're jammed up with cargo, no way to set more up even if we had them." Henry drummed the fingers of his remaining hand on the edge of his console.

"What we have is time and the fact they can't know exactly when we're reaching planetfall. Unless they have exceptional sensors and know how to use them, they won't see us until we drop stealth at the edge of the Republic safe zone."

"Dad, maybe we should return to the Switchboard Station and report that..."

Ryan turned to look at Tim. "Report what? That three ships are in orbit around a planet? Add to that, the last two supply runs didn't get through. If the aid workers on Murack Five are still alive, they will be desperate. Likely starving. If the aid workers die, the kangazoids die. If the kangazoids die, there are good odds the Republic will re-open the case to reduce the species responsible to a neolithic level. Failure is not on our list of options."

"Stardust," whispered Tim.

"We'll shut her down for now. Everyone, I want suggestions for getting past those ships and mines. Don't worry if it sounds crazy."

"Or suicidal," interjected Henry.

"Henry," admonished Ryan.

"Hotty boss, I've served with you longer than anyone. I know your pattern." Henry twisted his chair to stare at Ryan with his android eyes.

"Crazy and/or suicidal. We're on it. I haven't been aboard as long as Henry, but I know the score." Rowan turned in her chair to smile at Ryan. "And I worried that life would be boring once I got away from the U.E.S."

Ryan chuckled. "Dismissed, except for the watch. Standing orders."

Chow held Tracy's hand as if it were a lifeline. The mostly late teens and early twenties of the university chapter of Humans Inclusive filled the seminar room. The soothing forest scene on the walls did nothing to cut the sense that these people were convinced they would change the galaxy and closed off to any thought that didn't fit their group's notion of what was right. Even though they currently shared Chow's goals, their nature sent a chill down his spine.

The room was familiar. Lines of VR5 interface recliners, each with an attached tray table, keyboard, and voice interface, were separated by narrow walkways. The front of the room was open to allow lecturers a place to stand.

He scanned the mostly students in the crowd. Even as an undergrad, he had never been part of this group. His free time had been spent pulling reservist hours to cover expenses. These students' trendy clothing and what he'd come to recognize as a false self-assurance masking doubt and confusion spoke of pampered lives. Most of them were young in years and experience. For them, the slums of the Earth cities were a thing of sensory news broadcast and fiction.

Chow remembered Medan. The crowding, the crime, the ever-present threat of violence. He'd been fifteen when his father got a job on Gaia. They'd left the homeworld and his mother behind. His mother had pulled herself away from her John of the day to say goodbye at the spaceport. She'd told him not to cry, not realizing that he had no tears left for her. He would never again come home to find her stealing what little he and his father had saved so she could buy a fix of the latest rec-chem. Or find her passed out on his bed, covered in vomit.

Poor as they had been upon reaching Gaia, they had been able to build towards something with her light years away.

Chow shook off the mood and looked at Tracy. She outshone all present like a sun outshining its planets. The dress she wore was flattering but modest. Classy. Her Italian features were drawn into a professional smile.

"Tracy. I'm so glad you could make it." A muscular man with rainbow-dyed hair and bright blue teeth strode up. His clothing shifted colour in an ever-changing mosaic that hurt the eyes.

Chow felt Tracy's hand clasp his tighter.

"Hello, Amberford. I'd like you to meet my boyfriend, Lieutenant Chen Chow."

"Pleasure. I go by Chow." Chow held out his hand, but he didn't like the predatory way Amberford's eyes tracked over

Tracy.

"Lieutenant." Amberford ignored the proffered hand. "I've read about you. You headed the squad that tried to recapture Rowan. What are you doing here? Spying for Captain Denardo? Get out. We don't tolerate bio-bigots here."

"Amberford, don't be an ass!" Tracy's eyes seemed to blaze.

Chow brought her hand to his lips, kissed it, then released it and stepped to one side, his arms loose, ready to move, as he'd been trained. "I did pursue Rowan. Those were my orders. I don't have to agree with the politics behind an order to know I have a duty to follow it. Once you put on the uniform, you give up the luxury of a measure of your free will to preserve that luxury for others. It doesn't mean you can't stand against the underlying injustice when you take the uniform off."

"Very convenient, bio-bigot. Get out of here. I won't have you reporting back to that bitch of a captain."

"My mother is not a bitch! Just because she made you look like a fool that time, and you deserved it, spouting misinformation and conspiracy theories like you were."

"She denied the truth. She is a lying tool of the state, and you are no better! How can you be with the man that tried to capture Rowan, a clone? How can you take his side? Your whole family are hypocrites." Amberford glowered at Tracy.

"Have a care, little man. I know and like the captain. She and Tracy are not hypocrites, much the opposite. Keep a civil tongue in your head. It will be better for your health!" menaced Chow.

"Are you threatening me? You'll beat me up, is that it? You parasite. The military is a drain on resources and a home for bio-bigots."

"Do you like your shirt?" Chow asked nonchalantly.

"What? I... Yes. It is an Emanual Sani." Amberford seemed taken aback.

"The refractive filament technology that lets it shift colour came out of the payment for the Batzoid Pirate Suppression. Where it is estimated that closing the pirate cells prevented the deaths of over twenty thousand civilians. Millions of people are alive today who wouldn't be if our troops hadn't traded their lives for tech and planets. Many of them live because of the advances we gained as a species. Many others as a direct result of ending criminal conglomerates and stopping conflicts sooner and more effectively. Politicians make wars, not the personnel that fight them. Put the blame where it belongs or be labelled a fool."

"You're an attack dog. You should never have hunted Rowan." Amberford glowered at Chow.

"I don't get to pick and choose my orders. Two missions before the one with Rowan, I had an escaped convict retrieval of one of the terrorists that dirty bombed the set region. Suppose I was anti-clone. Would it have been right for me to ignore that order and let her go so she could kill again?"

"That's not the same thing!" Amberford was red in the face, and his fists clenched.

"Isn't it?" A short, swarthy youth who appeared to be in his early teens, dressed in a t-shirt and blue jeans, walked up.

"Frances, this is none of your business!" sputtered Amberford.

Frances shook Chow's hand. "Major Frances Lopez, retired. Terra noster sors."

"Lieutenant Chen Chow. Terra noster sors." Chow smiled.

Frances looked at Amberford with an assurance that made a lie to his youthful appearance. "If it isn't the business of an actual clone who served in the U.E.S. ground forces, then whose business is it?"

"Frances, is that you?" Tracy eyed the newcomer up and down.

"As I was, I am again. Older and perhaps a little wiser. Bernadette feels like a cradle robber. I always liked older women." Frances smiled, leered, and winked.

"Frances took a rad dose on Murack Five. They had time, so they used a schedule green process to make his new body," explained Tracy.

"And I am so glad to be in the new module. I hated the treatments. Everything was shot in the old chassis. Bernadette is happy about the change too. Some things stopped working sooner than others. Hard on a marriage, if you get what I'm saying." Frances winked at Tracy. "Youthful vigour is making up for lost time."

"You." Tracy shook her head and playfully swatted her friend's chest.

Amberford released a grunting noise and moved to join a group on the far side of the room.

"Don't let Amberford and his bunch bother you. They're young, pampered and want something to rebel against. You're the reservist who led the convict retrieval squad that chased Rowan."

"Guilty."

"That would have been a hunt. I met Captain Chandler during the Murack campaign. Smart man, good friend, worse enemy. Welcome to Humans Inclusive. Tonight, we're drafting a letter to the U.E.S. parliament calling on them to institute a review of the 100-year age limit for medical cloning. For all the good it will do, but we need to start someplace."

"I'll sign it. I'm, well..." Chow looked at Tracy.

Tracy nodded. "Frances knows."

Chow nodded. "I've always believed medical clones get a raw deal. Now I have enough reason to do something about it."

"I've got my mother's proxy." Tracy turned to Chow. "She doesn't attend meetings because her presence is too disruptive, and even less gets done. Plus, tonight, she's having dinner with Admiral Newton."

"Your mother could be a great asset if the extremist fringe wasn't so dominant." Frances led them deeper into the room. "Have you heard much about the series they are making based on Rowan's escape? The dispatches from the premiere praised it dramatically, but some are calling it propaganda."

Chow laughed. "It is propaganda, for our side."

"Captain, surely you can see that emancipating the clones in the set region would be an economic disaster." Minister Lisng, a tall, overweight Milesian man dressed in a blue suit, gestured with his wine glass.

Captain Tansy Denardo eyed the minister who sat across the ornate dining table from her like he was something she'd stepped in by mistake. Her classic Italian features and fit large-busted body were shown off by the dark blue evening gown she'd chosen to wear. Her gold starburst captain's rank pin was displayed on the fabric over her shoulder blade beside a Jupiter commendation which was the image of the planet about the size of the tip of her thumb. The commendation was surrounded by a ring of platinum. Her silver-streaked black hair fell loose about her shoulders, and she was as tall as most of the men in the room.

"Minister, your argument fails on many points. We were discussing medical clones and extending legal equality to them and a meaningful protection of their rights. That has nothing to do with the surrogates the studios generate. Secondly, I do not call for the dismantling of the entertainment industry. I endorse a phasing out of a morally questionable system. Given the short life expectancy of the emotional surrogates, if done properly, there would be no need to integrate them into our society because they would live out their days in the set region, never knowing the reality of their existence.

"Also, if, as you say, the U.E.S. needs the income, then let us show some appreciation to the people who earn the revenue. Starting with using a cloning procedure that would result in a longer life expectancy."

Michael and Marcy, who sat down the table from Tansy, busied themselves with their food.

The dining room was resplendent with a large rectangular oak table. The walls were filled with a desert scene with wildlife moving into and out of the image. The ceiling was a blanket of stars, as seen from the Mojave Desert on Earth.

The table was set for sixteen with fine crystal and china. A pair of waiters in tuxedos stood ready to fulfill the guests' needs. The guests represented a substantial percentage of the most influential people on Gaia.

"But they aren't people. They are clones, and the expense is too much for a, a..." The minister glanced around and focused on Michael. "Help me out here, Mr. Strongbow. You know the realities of studio operations better than anyone."

Mike smiled. "Actually, Minister, with starting the new set region, I've studied the numbers. Using a slower quick-clone process to create the surrogates, when you look at the lower maintenance cost due to the reduction in post-activation cancers and the higher successful activation rate, is more cost-effective over the clone's lifetime. As long as the studio shows some imagination in repurposing the surrogates, there are savings in engineering the surrogates with an average sixty-year operational life. That is close to what was historically the human norm for a long time. The principals in the Kemetic set region will be created with the slower procedure. Only disposable antagonists will be created with a thirty-year or less life expectancy. Unfortunately, the economics favour the faster procedure if you do not expect the clone to be viable for more than twenty years."

"So big of the studio!" snipped Tansy.

"We do have business considerations. With decommissioning Sun Valley, our expenses will be higher than usual for the next few years. I do agree with you regarding medical clones, Captain. S.E.T.E. has a policy that wages are normalized without regard to our workers' genetic origin. Sadly, the U.E.S. doesn't adhere to such a policy. Take the case of Captain Ryan Chandler."

"Who you exploited to make your new show." Tansy scowled.

"He was a willing participant, and we had no way of knowing he had become obsessed with the Rowan surrogate. Unfortunately, John had let the psychological monitoring of his staff slide to the extent of faking the reports."

"I saw Ryan's face, heard his voice. He is in love with Rowan." Tansy's voice brooked no disagreement.

Mike nodded. "He sacrificed everything to prevent her death. What more true show of love can there be?" Mike felt Marcy squeeze his hand.

Marcy chimed in. "I think the point is that Ryan would never have been working for S.E.T.E. in the first place if there was no discrimination against clones. He would have probably been an admiral by now, or, if he left the service, designing and building new and better ships for the U.E.S. We short ourselves when we don't allow members of our society to shine for frivolous reasons."

Tansy ran her finger along her throat and regarded Michael and Marcy.

"But someone has to do the less desirable jobs," objected Minister Lisng.

"Let those whose natural abilities gravitate to that level do them. Should not a society allow all its citizens to rise to the level their abilities permit? Also, we cannot forget that one person's paradise is another's purgatory," remarked Phillip, Tansy's husband, who sat to her right. He was a tall, slender, distinguished-looking brown-skinned man in a classic blue suit.

Lisng glanced from the couple he thought would be his allies to the beautiful ship's captain and her husband, then to the waiters. "Oh, look. They've brought out the chocolate mousse. Admiral Newton, you set an excellent table."

"Thank you, Minister." The bald man with dark brown skin and blue eyes, dressed in a sports jacket and slacks, raised his glass in a friendly acknowledgement.

Tansy leaned closer to Mike and Marcy. "I have to say, you two are a surprise."

Mike smiled. "I'm sorry we haven't had the opportunity to talk before this. Your role in the pursuit of Ryan and Rowan was impressive." Mike dropped his voice. "I'm pleased that you agreed to the use of your image in season two of *Freedom's Run*."

Tansy shrugged. "Several of my crew needed the money you were paying for the permissions, and the bonus for obtaining rights for the entire crew and the log images was substantial. I couldn't deny my people on the basis of my own comfort. Command has its demands as well as its privileges. Besides, maybe *Freedom's Run* will make people think. The clone wars were eight hundred years ago. It's time to remember the lessons learned and let go of the hate."

"Our hopes exactly." Marcy smiled. "Why don't we four continue this discussion after the meal? I'm always interested in finding allies in changing the injustices of the U.E.S."

Tansy let her gaze rest on the handsome couple.

Phillip leaned forward to look past his wife. "That would be lovely. You're a major part of why we accepted the admiral's invitation. I am a huge fan of your music. The way you incorporated flute into felinezoid classics in the Intersecting Rhythms compilation was amazing."

Marcy smiled and leaned forward to look past her husband and Tansy. "Thank you. Mostly, I turned down the volume of the ball bearings hitting the tin roof, then followed the beat."

UNDERSTANDING DAWNS

Farley and Quinta swam through Lake Edgley, keeping to the cover of rock outcroppings and weed beds. They paused, watching the black maw of what was likely a long-defunct mine swallowed by rising water levels. Quinta swam for the surface while Farley sprinted into the opening. He clicked on the diver's flashlight from his utility belt and followed the passage. After five meters, it opened into a chamber with an air pocket at its top. He drew the divers' knife from his ankle sheath and struck the hammer pommel against a rock three times.

Seconds later, Quinta swept past him and surfaced into the air bubble. The chamber was pitch black except for the flashlight's beam, which cast a grey spot on the ceiling.

"The chamber should be stable. The rocks seem to form a dome," observed Farley.

"If that is what you are saying. This is like the meeting halls on Swampla. Only we covered the walls with art, and the sides slope to form shallows. Can you sense Tony?" Quinta closed her eyes and listened to the darkness.

Farley ducked under, letting his gills supply his oxygen, and reached out with his sonar despite the pain. Something moved to his left, where the bottom sloped onto a dry shelf.

Blue light danced over the surface of the water. He heard Quinta yip, then there was dim light above.

Farley surfaced to see the bulbous form of an octozoid floating on the water by the rock slope. On a small 'beach', the twin to Gunther's jammer stood with a line of green lights indicating it was on.

"Tony, is that you?" Quinta swam to Farley's right.

"Mammals! Who else would it be? The jammer unit seems to be working. Or else they haven't had time to kill us yet. What do you know of the plague affecting the felinezoids and otterzoids?"

"Gunther thinks it's a plot development by the controllers. Have you recruited any more pirates?" asked Farley.

"It is difficult without a telepath to impart information. I have spoken to two of my cave mates. They are not convinced but have not reported me. When it is our turn to use the land scuttling equipment, I want to bring them to meet Gunther so that he may impart fuller knowledge. After what I observed with the recovered chamber, I no longer doubt your story."

"What did you see?" asked Quinta.

"Damage to the suits that is suspicious, as if it were deliberately done to make it look like they survived a crash. Also, on the container, the blast damage was too precise. In the life I remember, I worked in demolitions. I know explosives and the patterns they leave. Then the data interfaces we recovered were full of useful applications, but there were no games. Not even stack the crabs. Any one thing might hide in the mud, but together, the hunter becomes plain."

"Any idea what the controllers are using your… people for?" Farley examined the old mine. It was the perfect spot for an ambush. There was only one exit to the lake as far as he could sense, and two other passages lead to unknown places.

Tony swished his tentacles. "I cannot be sure, but my commander has found the contact codes for our supposed ship. That combined with the mobility the scuttle suits will give us—"

"Another try for the FTL telegraph in the escape pod," finished Farley. "You'd think the controllers might try something original."

"My commander intends to gain prominence amongst the species' leaders now that we have a land capacity. For too long, we have done little but salvage bits of our crashed vessel. He feels that he could do a better job against your resistance. He is likely right. The commander was, or so he believes, once a respected captain in the Octozoid Space Fleet."

"Rotten clams on a sunny rock with fish guts and orca-like predator defecation. The last thing we need is competent pirates." Quinta's lips stopped moving long before the translator nanobots caught up.

"I must agree, air-breather. Incompetence on both sides is the only reason this battle has not been resolved." Tony thrashed his tentacles.

Farley rushed in before Quinta could reply. "Gunther has made a portable version of the jammer. When can you have your group at the boat launch at the end of Charles Drive?"

"Where?"

Farley paused to think. "The ramp into the water on the extreme northern end of the lake."

"I know the place. We used to take food there when they came to put their primitive vessels in the water. Tonight, an hour and four minutes after sunset." Tony looked to his jammer. Several of the green lights had turned orange. "You must go."

"We'll see you tonight." Quinta submerged with Farley behind her.

Gunther drove his SUV into the garage. He could feel Jessica, almost smell her, but he kept his mind focused. A lean, olive-skinned man with a thick mane of short, black hair and Mediterranean features walked to Gunther's open window. "What seems to be the problem?"

Gunther could feel Jessica's touch lingering on the younger man's mind. It made irrational jealousy bubble up inside him. He forced it down and kept his voice pleasant. "The front right wheel is grabbing. I think I may have blown a shock."

"I'll get her up on the hoist. There's a coffee shop across the street." The mechanic opened Gunther's door for him.

"I'll stick around for the diagnosis. By the way, I'm Gunther." Gunther stepped from his vehicle and extended his hand.

"Malcom." The mechanic held up his hand, displaying patches of silicone grease and grit. "Wouldn't want to get your clothes dirty. This stuff is murder to wash out."

"Thanks for the courtesy." Gunther moved to the side of the repair bay while Malcom put the vehicle on the lift.

Gunther eased into Malcom's mind as the mechanic inspected the SUV's suspension. Jessica had had doubts about telling Malcom the truth of their existence, and what Gunther found confirmed them. The man's self-image was built on perceiving himself as a hero. The 'monsters' he fought gave him a reason to exist. Gunther shuddered to think what would happen if that was torn from him.

Gunther probed for some way to let him reveal the truth to Malcom, if only for Jessica's sake, but the background personality the controllers had inflicted on Malcom during his creation was too riddled with abuse and guilt. Gunther gave up. The mechanic was happy as a monster-hunting mystic who controlled fire. If he learned that all he felt he accomplished was a fraud, there would be nothing left for him to cling to. Gunther thought back to Armina. A pang of guilt assailed him.

"The right front shock is blown, and the spring doesn't look good. If you like, I can get right on it. Be about an hour and a half, and run seven-hundred and fifty. Provided I don't find anything else wrong."

"Do you have a loaner? I need to get back to the office."

Malcom walked to a set of keys hanging from a hook in

the wall. "She's not fancy, but she'll get you there. Don't take her off-road. Third spot down in the lot at the building's side. Leave your contact info. I'll give you a call when your SUV is ready. I'm done at six today, but you can pick up tomorrow."

Gunther took the keys. "Thanks. I'll pick it up before six." He exited the building into a warm, sunny day and felt emotional gloom. *Too many like Malcom, and this whole rebellion is a wash. Too many like him, and there's no point to it. Am I the greater evil?*

Gunther could feel emotions intrude from the Jessica side of the gestalt. They were sad and resolved but not surprised.

Troy sat in the *Angel Black* control room. He glanced at Gunther's screen, which showed that he was driving down Charles Drive past the Curry Palace, a distinctive small building with a red exterior a hundred meters from the boat launch. Troy did a quick check on the principals from *My Bad Neighbour* as the dive was one of their haunts, but none of them was currently on location, so he didn't have to worry about series contamination. Troy delegated the feed to a secondary screen on the wall behind him but made a mental note to check it regularly. John had berated him for missing an interesting event that came out of the blue the day before. He didn't intend to give the stardusted jerk the satisfaction of attacking him again.

On the main screen, Willa suctioned mucus from Valaseau's airway, then popped open the end of one of her fingers, exposing a USB interface that she plugged into a laptop.

"Just another working girl, with enough computing hardware built in to run a small spacecraft." Troy grinned and put her on a secondary screen opposite Gunther's.

Angel was next for the big screen. She flew over a

decrepit industrial complex. Carl blended into the shadows below her, becoming effectively invisible as he walked down an alley.

Six k-no-ins and Chelaa occupied other screens. Troy adjusted Chelaa's symptoms, dropping the fever so his impending delirium would recede. He balanced the electrolytes, reducing the swelling at the same time.

"For a pirate, he's not a bad sort, and John always overdoes surrogate suffering. Petty sadist," muttered Troy.

"Did you wish to add a notation to the official log?" asked Gene's voice.

"Divine, no! He's still an assistant producer. I'd rather not get canned." Troy focused on his primary screen, failing to notice how Gunther pulled up to the boat launch on Lake Edgley.

The door buzzer sounded. Troy pressed the open button as he focused on the action with Angel and Carl. "Come." He spoke without turning around.

"Hi, I thought I should introduce myself. I'm Ulva. I work the *Freedom's Run* board."

Troy glanced back, then gasped and turned his chair to look at a vision. The mid-twenties woman in the control room's doorway was magnificent. She was dressed in a white, short skirt and blouse combination that showed off her dusky skin to perfection with legs that could inspire one to drive their ground vehicle up a tree, ending in high heels that added to their effect. Her figure was subtle and perfectly proportioned, and her face... He could stare into that face for days and never become bored.

Ulva pushed away from the wall and moved in front of the screen displaying Willa's perspective. Troy turned his chair to face her, putting Gunther's screen at his back. "So... What's your name?" She pitched her voice soft and sultry.

"I... I." Troy closed his mouth and took a deep breath. "I'm Troy." Behind him, the screen for Gunther's perspective filled with static, but Troy didn't notice.

"Troy. I like that name. It's strong. Did you know it was an ancient city on Earth?" Ulva smiled and let her fingers trace along her arm.

"I…" Troy's voice cracked. He cleared his throat. "I did. Homer wrote about it. I've read the *Iliad* and the *Odyssey*."

"I liked the *Odyssey* better. Even though Odysseus was less than loyal to his wife."

To Ulva's right, Carl's perspective was filled with the image of Chelaa as they exchanged data sticks. Angel's perspective had her perched on a nearby roof, loading a pellet into her air rifle. The ammunition was packed with white cream.

"He did sleep around a lot. Twenty years is a long time. Can I get you a coffee or anything?"

"No thanks. I got in early for my shift and thought I should say hello as we might end up working together because of the Rowan thing."

"I… I'd like that, but I don't see how. The cover story Ryan gave Gunther, Willa and Carl seems to be holding up. The rest of them believe she's dead." Troy couldn't pull his eyes away from his guest.

"We'll have to wait and see. It's been a big step for you. Straight out of the media program onto an A-list show. I spent years on *A Cat's Life* learning the ropes."

Troy's slender chest seemed to swell. "I've been lucky."

Ulva leaned against the wall and smiled as she played with the young technician like a cat plays with a mouse. Twenty minutes after her arrival, the static on Gunther's screen cleared.

"It's been nice chatting with you, but my shift is about to start." Ulva stepped towards the door.

"I… You're right. I need to get back to work." Troy glanced at Carl's screen, where he was still talking to Chelaa. He turned his gaze back to his visitor. "Could we maybe… Well, I'd love to talk some more. Could I buy you a coffee?"

Ulva looked at the man she'd been flirting with. Too

young and not her type, but sweet in a just-out-of-school way. She sighed. "Coffee sounds nice. I'll blip you my contact info. We can set a date. I have to run." She swept out the door, leaving a bemused Troy behind her. The sound of a crash came from his primary console. He swivelled his chair to see what was going on.

Ulva stepped inside the *Freedom's Run* control room.

"That was quite a show." Arlene sat in the control chair. The main screen displayed a view of the *Angel Black* control room.

"Mike asked me to distract Troy when he heard that Gunther would be using the portable jammer. One jammer with the excuse of being a telepathy booster is one thing. Too many jammers will attract attention. Can I have the chair, please? These heels are killing me." Ulva stepped forward.

"You've got the legs for them." Arlene stood up and pushed the chair to her subordinate. "Seriously, nice work. I think Troy is smitten. You didn't have to meet him for coffee. Mike may be pragmatic and manipulative, but he'd never pimp his people out."

Ulva sat. "That's better. I hate these shoes. I know I didn't have to meet Troy. I was a distraction, but what's it going to hurt? I feel like I owe him something for manipulating him, and it's coffee, not a marriage. I know it's for the greater good and all that, and it's not like I made promises, but playing the femme fatale isn't me."

"Not Kitoy then?" Arlene grinned.

"That pussycat was a surprise. But you know, I feel for her. She did what she thought was right, and from her side of the war, maybe it was." Ulva scanned the active screens and made some minor adjustments. "If I ever met her, we might become friends."

Arlene nodded. "Ditto, but Rowan better watch out for

that cat. Have you seen her reaction to Ryan?"

Ulva snorted. "No chance. Have you watched Ryan's telemetry? Rowan is who he wants."

"And good on him for that. You might like to review Gunther's telemetry. The relay chip Mike put in the handhelds he gave Medwin's team worked, but it maxed out at three perspectives. I had to kill the telemetry from the octozoids or lose signal from the rest."

"I'll get on it. Doesn't look like there will be much new coming in for the rest of my shift anyway."

"Work on the Ryan and Rowan section. Henry overloads the feeds, and it's a job and a half to trim them."

"How long do you think it will take Ryan to figure out they're still being monitored?" Ulva scanned her charges' telemetry.

"With Kitoy on side, a long time. She can hide the signal. It's only if he comes across the recorder relay system, and it's buried in a part of the ship no one ever goes. Besides, Ryan's got bigger fish to fry. Pikeman wants a fortune for Rowan's treatments." Arlene moved to the door.

"We know it worked out because they're both alive and heading to Murack Five." Ulva brought up the recorded feed from Gunther's meeting with the octozoids and began to skim it.

"The story is in the how. I need to run. My group is having dinner with my parents, and I shouldn't be late."

Ryan and Rowan stepped into Jacques's quarters. The air smelled like the sea with an underlying pang of rotten fish. The octozoid lounged on the far side of what appeared to be a small, above-ground swimming pool that filled most of the three meter by three meter quarters. The octozoid's scuttling suit stood in an open corner beside a ladder that could be used to climb into and out of the pool.

"Ryan, Rowan, I am pleased you have come." Jacques

scooted across the pool and rested two tentacles on the side facing his guests.

Ryan's hand instinctively sought Rowan's now that they were out of the narrow hallway.

"We would have dropped by sooner, but there has been a development." Ryan's voice was resolved.

"I have heard of the ships orbiting Murack Five." Jacques swished two of his tentacles nervously.

"How'd you find out about that?" asked Rowan.

Jacques splashed his 'back' tentacles. "It is a small ship."

"I suppose it was inevitable. If you are going to suggest I turn back—" began Ryan.

"With the loss of the last two cargoes, the aid workers on Murack Five will be trapped in a cave with no crabs. We have no choice but to challenge the shark-like predator at the cave mouth." Jacques reached over the side of his tank and stroked the back side of his tentacle against Ryan's forearm. "It is good to fight the current to feed one's cave siblings. I have invited you to my cave because I have finished my review of my educational records on the crabzoids."

Rowan eyed the octozoid marine biologist. Even in Sun Valley, where the octozoids had been pirates bent on her destruction, she'd found that they had an odd beauty. The way their skin colour shifted and flowed over their bulbous bodies. It was like watching a living oil painting.

"Something is wrong with Star Searcher, isn't it?" remarked Ryan.

"Almost certainly. Do you remember how I said that Star Searcher was a huge crabzoid, and elements of its being must long for division?"

"Vaguely." Ryan moved to the pool's edge and dabbled his finger in the cool water.

"This is not something they would put in the *Space Traveller's Guide to Crabzoids*. Crabzoids are quite private about their spawning rituals. Part of crabzoid nature is a desire to know all things."

"That's impossible. There is too much to know," remarked Rowan.

"Less so for crabzoids because of their structure as hive minds, but still a truth. I believe that Star Searcher has so many subunits that they cannot integrate effectively. Groups of subunits have specialized knowledge that feeds into the whole, but like with a cave that is too small for its population, rivalries break out. I feel that Star Searcher's component units have formed proto-individualities. While they are not separate from Star Searcher, they express independent will at odds with the totality. Similar to the young of your species as they pass through adolescence but are forced by circumstance to share their parent's cave."

"Rebellious teenagers. I can relate." Ryan grinned.

"It sounds more like a multiple personality disorder?" Rowan moved to the edge of Jacques's tank. The smell of rotting fish was stronger closer to the water. She saw several things that looked like crabs moving around the bottom of the pool.

"This is a thing of *Homo sapiens*?" Jacques sounded surprised.

"I took a psychology class in first-year university. It was mentioned. Two or more personalities living in the same body. It also came up in some entertainments. Ryan says they didn't put any false information into Sun Valley."

"The more one learns about other species, the deeper the trench becomes," observed Jacques.

"You think that there are two Star Searchers. One is bad enough," observed Ryan.

"Several, and it makes reason of why you are here, and all that is happening." Jacques inflated and deflated his bulbous body.

"How?" Ryan drummed his fingers on the side of the tank, caught himself and pulled his hand back. "Sorry."

Jacques flicked his back tentacles dismissively. "Star

Searcher holds his school cohesiveness because of the limited space on the station and his will to know everything. In an environment with room to expand, the elements of the individuality would leave, forcing a reproductive cycle. Forming separate individualities that would form hives of their own, taking elements of the Star Searcher individuality's knowledge and experience with them."

"But there's nowhere to go on a space station." Ryan stroked his chin.

"But a large construct or a colony world could supply such a space. I believe the subordinate elements of the Star Searcher individuality have conspired with the sycamorezoid separatists in the Murack system. The separatists would have no use for their out-of-system wealth if they achieved their goals. It must be substantial enough to purchase drift stations or a world suitable for bioforming. Star Searcher's exploitation of your circumstances to send you to the Murack system, timing your transit of the stargate to correspond with when an accident would do the most harm to the dichrostigmazoids. Even the overloading of your vessel that compromises your ability to deal with the blockading ships. They are all the acts of a cunning camouflage predator."

"That miserable piece of sushi!" Henry's voice blurted into the room.

"Henry, you don't call a crabzoid—"

Rowan's voice cut off Ryan's admonishment. "That blasted seafood platter almost got you sent back to the U.E.S. in chains. It tried to get us killed and blamed for destroying a planet and a stargate. It is probably pulling some other stardust with those tree sperm with an attitude right now! Because it can't handle not being the smartest kid in school? Henry's right! If I get my hands on it, I'll eat it with melted butter!" Rowan looked ready to kill.

"Err…" Ryan cringed as Jacques backed into the middle

of his pool. "We'll lodge a complaint with the Republic if we get back." Ryan's voice was soothing.

"She is a tiger-shark-like predator during a tooth moult when given cause." Jacques sounded impressed.

"*Homo sapiens* are the most savage species in the Republic. I'm ready to live down to the reputation. Ryan, there are things you learn fighting pirates. One of them is there is a time to take the gloves off. You know this." Rowan gritted her teeth.

"Take the covers off one's tentacles?" Jacques moved back to the edge of the tank.

"Look up boxing and bare-fisted fighting. You'll get it after that." Ryan couldn't help but smile. One of the many things that had drawn him to Rowan was her fierce protectiveness of those she considered her own.

There was a high-pitched series of pings. The ceiling filled with two boxers in a ring beside an image of a bare-fisted fight.

"How horrid! Rowan, please to be keeping in mind that if we are correct, Star Searcher is a being at war with itself. Only some of the elements will have taken actions against you, and they from a desire to have a place to expand to and grow," said Jacques as the ceiling returned to a sky blue.

Ryan took a deep breath. "Like leaving your family because they disagree with you on moral issues like having yourself cloned to save your life. Stardust! Why do I always have so much in common with the bad guys?"

Rowan moved to Ryan's side and hugged him around the waist. "Because you try to see the best in people and find ways to relate to them. Even that miserable seafood platter."

Ryan sighed, letting the stress flow out of him. "At a practical level, what good does this do us?"

"That is setting the harpoon. The rebel elements of Star Searcher will likely be clustered around specific areas of knowledge. They will not have easy access to many areas of knowledge because it would reveal them to the core personality to access them. Possibly things like masking a communication or the capacities of a decommissioned Earth vessel designed for military incursions will be outside their experience." Jacques smugly swished his tentacles.

"Henry, call Kitoy to the bridge. We have communications to sift through." Ryan squeezed Rowan's waist, kissed her, then headed out the door.

"I was of service?" asked Jacques.

Rowan smiled. "I think so. Since I'm here, why don't I backwash your filter? I'm going to check the UV emitter in the sterilizer as well."

"I did not wish to complain, but it would be appreciated. I did not know you were trained as an engineer."

"Do you know what a lifeguard is?" Rowan moved to the pump and filter unit in the corner of the room.

"One that intervenes in life-threatening aquatic situations. I saw it on an e-entertainment." Jacques moved to the edge of his tank and hauled himself partially out of the water to watch Rowan.

"I worked summers as a lifeguard to help pay for university. Some tech matured early. I can handle a backwash and cleaning for a pool filter. Trust me."

"Oddly, my somewhat savage friend, I do."

A PLAN EMERGES

Ryan sat in the command chair on the *Star Hawk*'s bridge. Kitoy occupied the communications station. He'd dismissed the watch.

"Run it again with maximum gain." Ryan stared at coloured lines that flowed across the main screen.

Kitoy hit a button on her console. "It's weak. Of course, it would be side leakage from a targeted signal."

"Its origin is the stargate, and it fits timewise with how long it would take the sycamorezoid transfer ship to inform the Switchboard Station that their plan failed and for Star Searcher to send a message back, then for the transfer ship to transit the gate and retransmit the message. I'm betting the sycamorezoid aren't pleased about their plan not working."

"Star Searcher is rogered, and not in a fun way." Henry's android mouth twitched into a smile.

"Maybe. That crabzoid has a lot of power and has put itself into positions of authority. Right now, I want things that can help us land on Murack Five. Kitoy, do you see it?" Ryan pointed to one of the coloured lines on the screen.

"It's modulated. I'll try to get a readable signal."

All fell silent as minds, organic and AI, pored over a section of the record of the EM signals in the system.

"That's as good as I can do." Kitoy pressed a button. A series of pops and cracks sounded through the bridge.

Ryan closed his eyes. "It is structured. A code?"

Kitoy adjusted the output. "Henry, access the private code files on my personal computer. Password,

'Mrahissperrau'. It can't be that simple."

"Accessing. Hotty cat, you are a naughty girl. Does felinezoid intelligence know you kept these files?"

"They're all outdated, and after what they did to me, who cares?" Kitoy lashed her tail.

"Mind letting the captain in on it?" Ryan turned his chair to look at his crewbeings.

"It's a felinezoid code from the Murack offensive. Felinezoid intelligence stopped using it before I was expelled."

"Sycamorezoids are not good with codes. Their minds don't work that way. For all their faults, subtle deception isn't one of them. It's part of why they hire other species to fight their wars. What does it say?" Ryan turned back to watch the big screen.

"It's an electronic allegory for sycamorezoid scent marking. I'll translate it to *Homo sapiens* and put it up." Kitoy worked her console.

The big screen filled with *Homo sapiens* text. 'Mixed waste. Burnt plastic, not at fault. Burnt plastic. Sewage. Stop the shipment, or Murack Five will mixed waste. Burnt plastic. Writ of passage, political implications. Suggest you use pirates the burnt plastic food arms in orbit will burnt plastic mixed waste crash ship in south polar. Antiproton breach will end all life on burnt plastic. Mixed waste. Flowers. This individuality sent you the mines for burnt plastic. Mixed waste. Flowers. Transfer, or our deal is off. Message ends.'

"The strange words are how the translator interpreted static," observed Kitoy.

Ryan stroked his chin. "Log this and add it to the files in the notification probe. If we get blown up, I want them to know what happened back at the switchboard."

"Hotty boss, how are we dealing with the mines?" Henry swivelled his chair to look at Ryan.

"Let's keep working on that. A dozen chaffers, and it wouldn't be a problem." Ryan stroked his chin.

"Chaffers?" asked Kitoy.

"Imagine a handsome android structured to simulate a *Homo sapiens* male sprinkling…"

"Henry. Allow me. It will be less embarrassing." Ryan shook his head.

"Killjoy!" Henry sulked.

"They're missiles that explode between you and an attacker, filling space with glittery chaff to refract particle beams. *Homo sapiens* made the chaff out of nanobots keyed to disassemble incoming missiles and mines. They are only moderately effective against missiles because they don't have enough time to work, but they are devastating against mines, if you launch them early."

"Why not make some?" Kitoy kinked her tail.

"We could, but we have no way of getting them in the launch racks. The cargo has us blocked tighter than the queen's chastity belt." Henry smiled as if he'd won a victory.

"I'm going to my workshop. Kitoy, finish out the watch. See if you can find anything else in the background chatter, then check the record during your watches for the duration."

"You should get some sleep," observed Kitoy.

"Too stressed. I need to do something with my hands." Ryan walked to his workshop. Slipping in, he looked at the neatly arranged room. Now that Asalue was wearing his wings, there was room for other projects. An Earth Standard Transport Container and a Felinezoid United Worlds Shipping Container were on the back counter. Ryan moved to them and started removing pieces from the E.S.T.C. Two hours later, he slid the F.S.C. onto runners in the modified E.S.T.C. There was a clicking sound as a mechanical latch locked the smaller F.S.C. into place. Ryan shook the box. It remained stable.

"You made the cat box fit, boss. That should speed up cargo transfers from the United Felinezoid Worlds."

"Loading and unloading cross-species is a pain. When I

get hold of an Otterzoid Standardized Cargo Transfer Module, I want to do the same thing. Too bad the rest of the species have larger modules than *Homo sapiens*."

"Any thoughts on the mines?" Henry's voice betrayed concern.

"None yet. Slamming through isn't an option, and stopping isn't either. If those are line ships in orbit, it won't matter anyway. Henry, I don't have one up my sleeve for this. They've put us in a box with only one way out, and it's full of traps." Ryan sat on one of the stools mounted to the floor.

Henry let Ryan's slow biological processing speed deal with his emotions before speaking. "Hotty boss, you've pulled us out of worse scrapes than this."

"I'm tired, Henry! All I wanted was to rescue Rowan, leave the Republic, and be out of it. But the politicians in the U.E.S. wouldn't let that happen. I didn't want another fight, but it seems that's all I've had since I liberated Rowan. I was willing to leave the U.E.S. and the Republic alone. I'm not a social crusader. Is a quiet life with the woman I love too much to ask?" Ryan buried his face in his hands.

"Yes." Henry's voice held nothing of banter or sexual heat.

"What?" Ryan looked up.

"You are not made for a quiet life, and you know it. What good will being able to nest cat boxes in our fast-loading system be in a system with only human ships? Inside, you know you'll not leave the Republic. The last few years almost killed you. Soon would have. You spent your free time building for a life you could live. Rebuilding the *Star Hawk*, trying to save Joslin, which everyone knew was a lost cause but meant you could avoid romantic interactions. You fell in love with an emotional surrogate because they accidentally made your near-perfect match. Memories selected to make a type that will seek out challenges. A staggering level of compassion and empathy coupled with a harsh pragmatism. Top ten percentile for human intelligence. It's good that you weren't with the studio for her creation, or people would think you custom-made her. When it comes to you fleshies, like attracts like. At some level, you knew she would match you in a way Joslin never could. Do you really think Rowan would be satisfied with routine runs to load up at the ice moon, dump the ice on Geb, rinse, and repeat? She'd go out of her mind with boredom, and so would you. Neither of you is meant for an ordinary life. You and Rowan are meant to do what others dream about. Meant to make a difference."

Ryan sat in silence for several seconds. "I'm going to get us all killed."

"Maybe. But it will be a nova blast of a ride. Now you should get to Rowan's quarters. She has something she wants to show you. I'd like to see too. Hubba."

Ryan smiled as he came to his feet. "You know, Henry. The day they assigned you to the *Star Hawk* is in the top ten best days of my life."

"Of course it is, hotty boss. Look what you got, though you won't take advantage of it."

"And so, the moment ends."

Minutes later, Ryan opened the hatch to Rowan's quarters, and his mouth dropped open in astonishment. The walls and ceiling were a starscape complete with enhancements that made nebulae stand out against the field of black. Rowan lay, clothed in a spring dress, on the bed with her hands behind her head, looking at the ceiling.

"Hi." Rowan rolled on her side and regarded Ryan.

"Hi. This is new." Ryan stepped into the room. The simulated wood flooring was like a raft in the void.

Rowan lay back smiling. "It was sweet of you to mimic my room back in Sun Valley, but it was getting boring. I thought what would give a sense of space, and, of course, space."

"Where is this?" Ryan tried to place the system.

"Outside. More or less. Henry and I made the scan hours

ago. There is a really nice view of the Horsehead Nebula." She gestured to a cluster of hazy stars and gas.

"Very nice."

"I've magnified the planets for effect. To be honest, I may go for a terrestrial environment or set up a random function so the room can surprise me."

Ryan focused on the bed's beautiful occupant and managed to traverse the room without vertigo setting in.

"The bed is the relative position of the *Star Hawk*?"

"Seemed appropriate." Rowan sat up and kissed Ryan, pulling him close. "While I was setting this up, I noticed something." She turned in his arms. Ryan embraced her from behind, kissing her neck.

"Henry, switch to full holographic mode and mark our projected course in blue."

The images on the walls seemed to leap into the room and take on depth. A blue line ran from the bed to a speck of light.

"Henry, magnify and isolate course and blank the sun background. Also, enlarge Murack C-132." Rowan enjoyed her man's embrace as she focused her intellect on the display.

"Do you see it?" asked Rowan.

Ryan pulled his attention away from other pursuits and looked at the display. "It's a comet. Not far off our trajectory." Ryan sat up. "You're brilliant!"

Rowan smirked. "I know. On its current course, it will pass Murack Five at about three light-seconds."

Ryan kissed her. "How big is it?"

"One point two six kilometers radius, hotty boss, and don't stop on my account." Henry's voice issued into the room.

"Can we generate enough pull?" Ryan gazed at the representation of the cometary body.

"If we capture tomorrow at thirteen hundred hours, we can alter its course and follow it in. It should take most of any bombardment those ships can dish out."

Ryan's brow wrinkled in thought. "It can do more than that. We'll need to disperse it before it hits the atmosphere, or it could damage the planet. How close can we get?"

"How close do you want to get?" Rowan shot him a come-hither smile.

"Seriously." Ryan stood up and examined the holographic display.

"We could land on it." Henry's voice intruded from the speaker.

"When we're five hours out from Murack Five. It's cutting it close," objected Rowan.

"I trust our stealth. If this works will depend on how good the commanders of the ships orbiting Murack Five are." Ryan stroked his chin. "Henry, check the waste extractors and any inventory we can reach for volatiles. Call up Pikeman, Krakkeen and Yipya. With their degrees, they'll have backgrounds in chemistry. I need things that go boom. Remind them for use in space and concussive yield. Incendiary doesn't matter. Have them use the medical bay equipment." Ryan stroked his chin.

"I could—" began Rowan.

"Sorry, Row. What you have is equivalent to high school chemistry in this day and age. And I need you for other things." Ryan paced in the room, staring at the hologram of the comet. "We'll use Krakkeen's discarded fruit husks to house the explosives. Turns out lucky I asked him to save them." Ryan stroked his chin. "I think we may have found a delivery system for chaff. How long until we start the manoeuvres to grab that snowball?"

"Twenty-one hours and thirty-two minutes." Henry and Rowan spoke in unison.

Ryan moved to the hologram of the comet and passed his fingers through the light display. "Henry, get on to Tim and explain the situation. Pull the schematic for chaff nanos and have him start making them. The empty food trays should be good for carbon to feed the construction. Tell him to use the energy field of the solar wind impacting the magnetosphere to power them. Set him up in my workshop."

"Shouldn't you—" began Henry.

"Tim's better at nanotech than I am." Ryan smiled. "Tim's one of the best nano-engineers in the U.E.S."

"We have the schematics on file. How did you get them to leave you something like that?" Henry's voice was even.

"Friends in low places and a little blackmail. I'll fill you in someday. I like this. I like this a lot." Ryan seemed to vibrate with a newfound vitality. "Henry."

"Yes, hotty boss?"

"Privacy on."

Gunther watched Medwin and Kendra walk up a short concrete path that led to a small stone house. Solar panels and tulip-blade wind turbines adorned the roof. The garden was done over in climate-appropriate plants with a peach tree in its middle. An old pickup truck sat recharging in the house's side driveway. A canopy projected out from the main roof to shelter the vehicle.

Medwin knocked on the front door.

A fit-looking, older man with short, salt-and-pepper hair answered the door.

Medwin began to speak, holding out a clipboard.

Gunther focused on the older man. The mind he encountered was guarded. Almost closed off. There was a sense of pain and loss. Also, a near unbendable will.

Gunther pushed harder.

The man in front of Medwin gasped and staggered back into his house.

Medwin followed him with Kendra close behind. Inside the house's mudroom, the man collapsed.

Kendra dropped to her knees and checked his breathing and pulse. Both seemed normal.

"Help me get him on his side so he doesn't choke,"

ordered Kendra.

She and Medwin placed the man in a semi-prone position. Kendra was starting a body check when Gunther pushed into the mudroom, dragging his portable jammer behind him.

"Call nine one one," snapped Kendra.

"Give him a minute. I think I understand what is going on." Gunther knelt beside the older man and felt around the back of his neck, finding a place where the skin dimpled in. He pressed hard on the spot. "It's a security feature."

The man's eyes flicked open. He regarded Gunther, then said, "Let sleeping dogs lie."

"Old dogs can guard the yard." Gunther said the words he plucked from the man's mind. Reaching beside himself, he pressed the activate button on his suitcase-sized portable jammer.

The old man's limbs twitched. "The house is clean. I sweep it regularly."

"There are things that make regular security measures ineffective." Gunther helped the older man to his feet.

"What are you, NSA, CIA, CSIS, MI-5, KGB?" The man rambled off the list of agencies.

"None of the above," Medwin interrupted him. "Do we blow his mind, Gunther?"

"I believe we do. Mr. Majors—"

"Allen, please. Mr. Majors is my father. Always has been." Allen led the way into a small but comfortable living room. A sofa, love seat, and lounger stood out from the walls with a central coffee table. A large display screen was mounted on the wall opposite the couch. Aside from a few magazines and books on the coffee table, the room was immaculate. "Excuse the mess. Since... If you've read my file, you know my wife recently passed away."

"I'm sorry." Gunther parked his jammer where its field would encompass them all. "Allen, I have something I must impart to you. If you resist, it will hurt, and your fail-safe blocker will trigger again. To start, everything you know is a lie." Gunther projected his knowledge of the truth into the old man's mind.

Allen looked at his three visitors. "Tea?"

"Didn't it work?" asked Kendra.

"We live on a set in the far future making a fancy form of TV show. Young woman, I've been an intelligence operative for twenty-seven years. That's a slow Tuesday." Allen chuckled. "Besides, I figured it out years ago. I was made to be a spy, remember."

"And you did nothing?" demanded Medwin.

"What was there to do? I'm more machine than human. They haul me in once every couple of years for a tune-up. Without that, I'm dead. Where am I going to go? I figured my show got cancelled because my life slowed down. I had my Martha and my work as the region's intelligence chief. What difference would it have made to make a fuss? And who would have believed me?"

"Will you help us?" Kendra stared into Allen's blue eyes.

"Depends on what you're trying to do. Seems to me, lots of folks can't handle the truth. Might be best to let them be."

Medwin hung his head. "We know."

"I'm a telepath. I can sort out those who can handle it. People outside the set region are trying to reform the system to make a better life for us all."

"And you're agents for these outside forces." Allen laughed. "Some things never change, true believer. It probably beats sitting around waiting to die and sneaking the neighbour's cat treats. I'll miss Fluffy. He's a nice little furball. Slept over a few nights when Martha passed. I don't know if it was him or one of those controllers with more heart than most behind that, but it helped as much as anything can."

"If you'll open your mind, I'll impart all the information you need and when we will meet next. I have to hurry. I can only guess how long our distraction will keep the controllers distracted." Gunther focused his mind on sharing all he knew.

"She is stage four and has been for at least two years. She will not tell you anything." A short man with a wiry build regarded Hilda's face with a sad smile. His sandy-coloured hair sat on his head in a trendy mat style that didn't suit his oval face.

"She can't be that far gone. She's only been in the facility for a few months." Hilda looked down the length of the twin rows of interface tanks. Each transparent tank held a person suspended in a brine solution, with their head hidden by an e-interface. Tubes for feeding and waste removal were connected to the bodies.

"Her husband held out hope far longer than reason dictated. He kept her at home even after she transitioned to stage four. I think he was praying she'd pull her head out of the rig. It is sad when people can't let go. Her husband is that Ryan fellow who stole the Rowan surrogate. I have to say, I admire his taste, and you wear the AS-F appearance well." There was interest in the attendant's tone.

"I'd still like to speak to Mrs. Chandler." Hilda gestured down the hall.

"Only because you'll elevate her package from standard to premium. She'll likely enjoy the New To Experience feature with her husband's exploits about to be made available." The man sighed. "I don't hold out much hope, but if anything could jolt her back to reality, I suppose that would be it." The attendant strode to a tank with a sign on its side reading, 'Joslin Chandler.' A medical readout listed the individual's age and general health data. Below that, another screen listed 'The Station House – general perspective'.

"Can you pull her out? Please." Hilda looked into the tank. Joslin was a woman in her late middle years with a slender body. The isometric routine the system put her body through meant that she'd avoided the muscle wasting her lifestyle would otherwise have caused, and the nutrient brine meant that her skin was nearly perfect.

The attendant pressed a couple of buttons on a control panel, then moved to the top of the tank and supported Joslin's head as the interface canopy lifted off her. A nasal gastric feeding tube came out of her nose and attached to the side of the tank, but otherwise, she had an attractive face.

"What do you want? I was experiencing my show. It is so good that Willow and James are together. They have wanted each other for so long. I don't think it's putting anybody in danger, no matter what that awful Officer Folley says. I really must get back to the show. It is so good."

"Joslin, you have a visitor."

Joslin looked at Hilda, who stood by the attendant.

"Hello, Mrs. Chandler. I'm Hilda Strongbow. I'm a lawyer. I'd like to ask you a few questions about your husband."

"Ryan. He's always pestering me. Won't let me watch a show in peace. It's like he's always there. He says he goes to work and those ridiculous tech restorers' meetings, but I don't believe it. Never…"

"Mrs. Chandler. Did your husband ever talk about Michael Strongbow?"

"Is that the Michael from *Homicide: Life on the Streets*? He is such a nice man and very smart. He—"

"Michael Strongbow, the studio head," Hilda spoke slowly.

"Oh, I don't know. Probably, he's always nattering about something or another, so I'll miss my shows. No respect! It's a power trip for him. I want to get back to *The Station House*."

The attendant shot Hilda an 'I told you so' look.

"Of course. Enjoy your show."

"Hilda, was it?" Joslin focused on Hilda for the first time.

"Yes." Hilda looked almost predatory.

"Tell Ryan he better not disturb me during *Angel Black*.

That awful batzoid has dosed Rowan with a horrible poison, and she could die. Everyone is so torn up about it. I don't know how they'll ever cope without her."

"I'll tell him when I see him." Hilda nodded at the attendant, who lowered the e-interface over Joslin's head and activated the feed.

"Divine." Hilda shook her head.

"Nothing divine about it, but it is what it is. Let's transfer the funds, and I'll upgrade her input package."

They walked away from the rows of tanks holding people trapped in dreams by their own desire.

11
LINING THINGS UP

"**I** have the pull points. Are you sure about these?" Ryan sat at the pilot's station and examined a series of navigational pulls as complex as any he'd ever seen.

"I ran the numbers three times." Rowan stared at him from the navigator's station.

"And I ran them twice, hotty boss," observed Henry.

"Starting a pull against C-132 at two G with a ten-degree deflection towards our starboard. Starting a three G out system pull against Murack Seven and a one-half G lateral pull against Asteroid 286." Ryan worked the controls to make it happen.

"We stay with these pulls for fifteen minutes, then change vectors. As we get closer to C-132, we'll be able to do more of a lateral pull until it is on target for Murack Five." Rowan vocalized for her crewmates' benefit.

Ryan moved to the engineering console. "Grav lasers are in the green. All systems within spec. Kitoy, have there been any more intercepted communications?" Ryan moved to the captain's chair and settled himself.

"Negative. Just normal chatter."

"Tim, how's life support?"

"All systems green. Even the temp in the quarters is holding for once. I want to do an in-depth check. This is too good to be true." Tim spun his chair to look at what appeared to be an uneven dirty snowball on the big screen. "It doesn't look like a comet."

"Give it some time. It should hit its flashpoint in a day or two, then you'll see the tail. It would be pretty if we didn't have to fly through it." Ryan stretched so that his back cracked. "How is the chaff coming?"

"I've converted maybe a tenth of the waste carbon into nanos. You're lucky that I used an assembler like yours in university. The system is slow, antiquated and glitchy. You could do with an upgrade." Tim turned to look at his father.

"When antiproton rains from the sky. If it works, use it. It's what we have. Ziggy, how are weapons?"

"As good as they've ever been." Ziggy looked up from his screen. His skin tone was healthy. The once-tight uniform now fit loosely. The dazed quality had left his eyes, and he was fully in the present.

"Good. Kitoy, Ziggy, finish up your safety checks, then you can go off duty. Rowan, Henry, and I will be tweaking our course for hours. Tim, do your in-depth check, then make as much chaff as possible."

"Thanks. Jacques, Wispy and Asalue said they'd teach Kitoy and me how to play Stop the Dictator," said Ziggy.

Ryan chuckled. "We both know it's harder in real life."

Ziggy smiled, then focused on his shift checks.

Minutes later, Ryan adjusted the pull points. The *Star Hawk* was decelerating to its rendezvous with C-132 while at the same time adding a sideways acceleration to the comet's course.

"Rowan. Put Murack Five up on the screen. Let's see if we can get a better look at our party hosts."

The screen filled with a magnification of Murack Five's equatorial region. A speck the size of an ink dot swung into view on the left side of the image.

"Henry, have you got a compiled image?"

"You know it, hotty boss."

"Put it up."

The screen filled with an image as long as Ryan's hand. It looked like an egg with quills sticking out over its surface.

"Nova blast!" Ryan sat forward in his seat.

"It's like meeting your grandmother at the swinger's

club," agreed Henry.

"I didn't think there were any ankylosaurs left functioning." Ryan drummed his fingers on the arm of his command chair.

"For the primitive in the room? I know an ankylosaur is an armoured dinosaur with a club tail and an, even by dinosaur standards, small brain." Rowan stared at the screen.

"Out of context as a Luba at a Humans Ascendant meeting," commented Henry.

"I always liked the name. It fits them." Ryan sighed. "Know your enemy. At the start of the war in the Murack system, neither side had much in the way of warships. Both planets were newly bioformed and had focused their resources to that end. The sycamorezoids took E.T.S.s—"

"Back it up, oh captain mine. What?" asked Rowan.

Ryan glanced at the chronometer, counting down to the next course adjustment in the bottom corner of the main screen. "We have time. Henry, access my personal files. Tim's award-winning school presentation from grade seven." Ryan's voice reflected pride.

"I can't believe you kept a copy of that. I was what, twelve?" Tim finished his system check. "Environmental green, by the way."

"Of course I kept it. You're my son. It was a great presentation. You deserved that award. Henry, cue it up to the bit on Environmental Transit Ships and play."

The big screen filled with the image of a young boy that may have been Tim or Ryan, standing on a stage in front of a big screen that depicted a collection of bulky-looking spacecraft.

"Because nature is complex, it is difficult to bring everything you need to make a balanced ecology bit by bit. All bio-forming species have adopted the practice of bringing large blocks of the parent environment from their original world. We do this with devices called environmental scoops. They are boxes with life support and grav nullifiers that can dig into a planet and seal underneath themselves. They close around hectares of natural environment, taking land, water, and atmosphere, which they carry to low planetary orbit where space tugs mount them on Environmental Transport Ships. The E.T.S.s take the environmental scoop to the new world, where it is deposited amongst the plants and animals that bioformers have already begun to establish. This fills in the missing parts of the ecology, mostly at a microbial level."

The screen went back to a view of space.

"The E.T.S.s are only good for what they are built for, but nothing else can do their job. At the start of the Murack war, the sycamorezoids had E.T.S.s parked in orbit. As a species, the sycamorezoids were two hundred years out from their last stage-two bio-form." Ryan picked up the explanation.

"Twenty-seven ships, hotty boss," remarked Henry.

Ryan continued. "The sycamorezoids loaded weapons systems, extra antiproton conversion systems, prefab crew modules, and enough outer armour to take a few hits onto the E.T.S.'s frame and made mobile gun platforms. Slow, cumbersome, with enough firepower to pulp a planet. If they could see well enough to hit it given how bad their sensor systems were."

"And that's what orbiting Murack Five?" Rowan stared at the ankylosaur on the screen.

"Tell you, sweetness, if we weren't so jammed up with cargo, the tree sperm wouldn't stand a chance."

Ryan nodded. "The *Star Hawk* was built to slip past worse than this. But don't get cocky, Henry. Against civilian cargo ships, they'd be deadly. If we were fully armed, I'd be tempted to take them on. One at a time, of course. Teach the scum a lesson. But that 'if' creates problems."

"Does this change our plans?" asked Tim.

"No. It means it's a little more likely we will survive. I can be reasonably sure that they can't see us when we cloak. Go get the chaff ready. The mines are now our biggest problem. Rowan, send me the next set of pull points." Ryan moved to the pilot's seat while Tim left the bridge.

Angel swept up and back along the alley, dodging a blast from a kinetic rifle. She flipped in mid-air, brought her air rifle to bear and fired. The pellet packed with lithium grease flew straight, penetrating the skin of her k-no-in attacker. The alien took two steps, then collapsed.

Angel looked down the alley. Carl carried Chelaa, flanked by Fran and a k-no-in chased by three k-no-in and a chameleonzoid. She cracked the breach of her air rifle and loaded another lithium grease-filled pellet before sweeping towards her allies.

She fired, but the chameleonzoid interposed its body with the shot. The pellet barely left a mark on the scaly hide.

A mid-sized car appeared at the end of the alley. Willa stepped out and opened the back door.

Carl sprinted for the vehicle with Fran. He half threw Chelaa into the back seat, then he and Fran piled in. The k-no-in leapt onto the roof rack as Willa slammed the door and dove into the driver's seat before peeling out.

Troy sat in the *Angel Black* control room. He adjusted Carl's adrenaline level, giving him an added push to reach the car.

"Interesting. This I didn't expect," remarked Michael from the back of the room.

"That's why I called you, unc... Sir. The pirates have fallen into a civil war. The otterzoids, about half the k-no-in and the octozoids with the new scuttling suits against the rest. The cast has fallen in with the otterzoids because they want to find a cure."

Michael stared at the secondary screens. Gunther was with Valaseau, examining the felinezoid's blood with a microscope. Farley and Quinta were in the lake, negotiating with the octozoid commander.

"Induce a fever in Fran." Michael's voice held a speculative quality.

"It's out of timetable," observed Troy.

"It will fit. We were going to announce the plague that will expedite the phase-out of Sun Valley in three months. We'll move up the timetable and link it to the plague storyline in *Angel Black*. An alien virus that, while not lethal to humans, causes sterility. Fran can be the transfer vector because she has felinezoid and human DNA. She'll also supply a cure for the felinezoids and otterzoids. We can work that element in in real-time over the next week. Increase Fran's temperature a degree and factor in some congestion, just enough so she'll have Gunther check her out. The other shows will have no idea where the plague came from, only its effects. We'll wrap *Angel Black* within the year."

"Wrapping the series?" blurted Troy.

Michael nodded. "Ratings have been slipping for three seasons. It's still in the top ten, but the series has told most of the stories its format is suited to, and with the loss of Rowan, all projections show a catastrophic failure. The stock of alien pirates is low, and our cloning facilities are fully committed to the Kemetic set region. Add that the kno-in will start dying en masse within a year. Their systems are bioconcentrating the trace amounts of lithium in Gaia's environment. Half of them are on trickle feeds of antihistamines already. *Angel Black* is expensive to make and must be in the top ten to be cost-effective. The show, at best, has two years left in it. This way, we know it is going out and can do the storylines that maintaining the series made impractical. That should let *Angel Black* go out on top instead of fading away. That will be better for the home market and reruns."

"The surrogates?" Troy's voice held concern.

"The primaries have skills that will keep them from becoming tree-planting extras. They'll live out their lives in relative comfort. I'm not sure what to do about the non-*Homo sapiens*. There aren't many left, and that number will sadly drop further. It's good you asked." Michael smiled.

"What do I do?" Troy adjusted Fran's biology.

"Shift gears. The pirate civil war is the principal conflict for the remainder of season eight. We'll resolve the plague storyline over the next two weeks. It was dragging anyways. I only instituted it because we're running out of antagonists. Make certain there are no principal deaths. We'll have to start a storyline to deal with the vilicsa addiction. Give it some thought, and we'll consult. Don't be afraid to start a storyline or two. I'll approve or disapprove going forward. I don't want to miss a potentially good idea."

Troy nodded. "How is Rowan? It sounds like *Freedom's Run* is going to be a hit."

Michael smiled. "I'll let this out because it will be on the news anyway. She is currently en route to Murack Five."

Ryan sat in the command chair, his head leaned back.

"Is that normal?" Tim sat at the navigator's station, running through the general watch checks. Standing, he moved to the environmental station and began the more complex duty officer check.

"It's because hotty boss is doing three jobs, and he'll need to make piloting adjustments in the next hour," Henry spoke softly.

"It must be hard on him." Tim looked at his father.

"During the siege on Murack Seven, there were three days straight that your father only left the bridge for toilet breaks. It didn't become four because the crew told him his smell was impeding efficiency. He'll sleep properly when we make landing."

"Where's Rowan? She's normally at his hip. Lucky bugger." Tim smiled.

"You've made quite a change," observed Henry.

Tim sighed. "I was a fool. Understand, Henry, I remember my mum from when I was little. She was something back then. Back then, she deserved my dad. Back then, she and Rowan would probably have been friends. I'm not sure what happened, but I saw it even before Dad got himself cloned. Mum stopped trying. It was easier to drift through the e-entertainments. I miss my mum. I don't miss the woman Dad took to Gaia, who is probably happier in the e-addict facility."

"Seen it, oh cute one. Lots of crew came back from the wars and crawled into one bottle or another. Men and women I would have killed and died for vanished, leaving hollow shells. Ryan almost went that route, but he's made of sterner stuff."

"You love him. And I don't mean sexually before your overactive libido twists it around." Tim returned to his system checks.

Henry nodded. "Think of me as your uncle."

A tone sounded across the bridge. Ryan started awake. "Status."

"All sectors green. Two-minute warning for pull point adjustment." Henry spoke evenly.

Ryan's eyes darted to the pilot's station. He looked confused, then sighed and stood up. "We need to get more crew."

He sat in the pilot's seat and reviewed the pull point file.

"We need a better pilot for one," remarked Henry.

"Agreed." Ryan adjusted the first grav laser, locking it onto a different asteroid.

"You do pretty well," observed Tim.

Ryan adjusted the next grav pull in keeping with Rowan's instructions. "I can pass, but I'm an engineer. You should see what the *Star Hawk* can do with a real pilot. I've seen her fly through a gap less than a meter to a side at near five per cent light speed."

"I still say Rodriguez had to be an android. No way a human could pull stunts like he did," remarked Henry.

"What happened to him?" asked Tim.

Ryan reached to the back of the pilot's station chair and touched the third plaque down. "Batzoid Pirate Suppression."

"We will never forget." Henry's voice was grave.

Ryan adjusted another drive laser, then moved to the navigator's station. After a moment's hunting around, he changed the view on the main screen. The comet was now sporting a tail of evaporating gasses. A green line marked its desired course, a red line its original trajectory. A blue line marking its current trajectory ran between them. As they watched, the blue line inched closer to the green one.

"Looks good, hotty boss."

Ryan moved back to the captain's chair. "Tim, how is the chaff coming?"

"I've got eighty-seven per cent of the available matter converted into chaff. The nanos are fine. I raided the trash for Jacques's used crab shells. A bit of tape and some hot glue, and they make passable chaff storage containers."

"Less trash when we make planetfall. Henry, wake me two minutes before the next pull point adjustment or if something comes up." Ryan was unconscious in seconds.

Krakkeen carefully lifted a flask of yellow liquid off the heat source.

"I am a medical doctor, not an explosives tech," griped Pikeman.

"As you are fond of informing us." Yipya mixed several fine powders together in a large, transparent beaker.

The medical bay's door retracted into the wall, and Wispy scuttled in. "Hello, I was wondering where everyone had vanished to. It was like the time my sister/father took us to the park. We all decided to play sneak and find. I found a really good hiding place, and no one could find me, but it got really boring because there was no one to speak to and…"

"Wispy!" Krakkeen interrupted the waspzoid. "We're making explosives to help get us past the mines around Murack Five. It is delicate and dangerous work."

"Explosives? Why?" Wispy's voice dropped to a whisper.

"Ryan is diverting a comet that he will use as a shield as we near the planet, but he needs to disperse the comet before it hits the atmosphere to protect the biosphere."

"I wish he'd told me. You are making charges to shatter the comet so the pieces will vaporize in the atmosphere."

"Yes, and we need base materials. What is the status of your waste chamber?" Pikeman demanded in imperious tones.

"Oh. Oh my. I have a bit of crystal. I was trying to hold it until we landed so as not to be a bother. I guess that might be a good thing. I will expel it. I could see where the ammonia might be useful in bomb-making. Oh my, it is such a wonder what can become useful at times. My older sister, Waspilzellic, went on a wilderness expedition as his after-mating excursion. She loved the forest and would often tell me…"

"Wispy." Yipya drummed his claws against the floor. "We could really use the ammonia, now."

Krakkeen held up a large kidney-shaped polycarbonate dish.

"Oh, of course." Wispy took the dish and moved to the corner of the room. A slit in his abdomen opened, and a collection of crystals fell into the tray. "That's all I have."

"It will do, thank you," said Krakkeen.

"How is our captain getting the explosives onto the comet?" Wispy carried the tray to his shipmates.

"He did not say. Henry, do you know?" Yipya poured the powder he was stirring into the empty fruit husks that sat along one of the examination cots.

"He's doing an EVA to plant the charges. If we could reach the missile feeders, we could make rockets, but we're too buggered with nova-blasted cargo to move." Henry spoke through the translator frequency so all could understand him.

"Henry, I must speak with our captain." Wispy waved the arms by his mouth for emphasis.

"Ryan is busy. He…"

Wispy cut off Henry. "I must speak with him. I worked as an EVA technician and have my suit among my personal effects. I also spent over an Earth year helping with the terraforming of Ventec for the tardigradezoids. It was a desert world unsuitable for them until we bombarded it with water ice diverted from the system's Kuiper belt. We had to disperse the water ice in the upper atmosphere to avoid damaging the planet. I have done what Ryan is preparing to do many times. In this, I can help."

Krakkeen tapped his pincers. That Wispy said what was needed without asides or padding spoke to the being's earnestness. "Henry, perhaps you should tell the captain of Wispy's experience. Waspzoids are known for being the best EVA specialists in the Republic."

"I'll pass it on. Be good to get hotty boss off the bridge for a while. He's getting cranky." Henry's voice silenced.

The chemists went back to work. A foul scent filled the room. Pikeman turned up the air circulation so that the intake pumps were a steady background roar. The air cleared.

"You organics are stinking up my atmosphere recyclers." Henry's voice sounded in their heads. "Wispy, Ryan will meet you in the officers' mess. He needs to get some sleep, so make it a quickie."

"A quickie?" asked Wispy.

Pikeman sighed. "It means be brief. Henry, given what we all know of waspzoid mating practices, you could show some sensitivity. Even I found that untoward."

Krakkeen and Yipya shared a look.

"It must have been truly horrible." Yipya turned to the work of making a solution from the ammonia crystals.

Ryan and Rowan sat side by side in the officers' mess. Ryan was sipping a cup of coffee. A muffin sat on a polycarbonate plate in front of him. Rowan had tea and a scone.

Wispy entered the room.

"Captain, Rowan. I have been told you intend to EVA on a comet to place explosives."

Ryan looked up wearily. "That's correct."

"I am a qualified EVA technician. I also participated in the bioforming of Ventec, where we brought ice from the system's Kuiper belt and detonated it outside the planetary atmosphere to disperse it for safe entry. My EVA suit is amongst my personal effects."

Ryan and Rowan both sat up, looking surprised.

"Wispy, that is impressive, but I think between Ziggy and me, we have it covered." Ryan eyed the waspzoid quizzically.

"Do you? Is your plan to lay the charges on the surface and detonate them? That will not work. The blast must be contained. Henry, please put a graphic of C-132 on the wall."

The comet appeared, filling the wall of the mess. "Highlight the water ice in blue, carbon dioxide in red, oxygen in yellow, and rocky matter in brown." Wispy's voice was clipped and lacked the annoying lilt it usually carried.

The image shifted, becoming a mosaic of coloured bands and fields.

"To get maximum dispersal of the cometary matter, you must sink the charges under the surface. The easiest way would be to use a laser drill and vaporize the seam of carbon dioxide that bisects the comet fifty meters above the equatorial line. That will give access to the cometary core. The charges can be set, then the water ice in the neighbouring deposit can be melted to fill the gap, leaving no weak spots for the explosive force to dissipate through. The kinetic force of the detonation will ripple across the solid matter, shattering the natural fracture lines. I estimate you will not have a piece larger than ten meters in circumference."

"We don't have laser drills." Rowan looked at Ryan. "Do we?"

Wispy waved his antenna. "We can use the *Star Hawk*'s particle weapons to do the same function."

Ryan took a breath and let it out slowly. "Wispy, you're on the EVA team. Get me the numbers ASAP and work out contingencies. I'm adding chaff nanos on the surface of the comet. I'll want maximum dispersal for them. Can you work out where to place them?"

"Yes."

The one-word answer left both Ryan and Rowan shocked.

"Wispy, are you all right? You, well... That was to the point." Rowan eyed the waspzoid as if meeting him for the first time.

Wispy waved his antenna slowly. "EVA is dangerous work. Moments count, and I have lost friends. Stories of life are rich and worthy things, but not at the expense of life itself." The waspzoid's tone was resolved.

Ryan and Rowan shared an astonished look.

"Henry, how long before we can land on C-132?"

Rowan checked the chronometer on her wrist. "One day, twelve hours and thirteen minutes," she replied.

"And twenty-seven seconds," added Henry. "Hotty, I love it when you do the math. Almost AI and soft and sexy to boot."

Ryan smiled and took Rowan's hand. "How long do I have before the next pull adjustment?"

"Eight hours," said Henry.

"Adjust the watch. I'm logging six hours sack time. Set a meeting for the EVA team after that and keep scanning C-132. I want to know every centimeter of that snowball."

Wispy made a hissing sound.

"What?" Rowan regarded the waspzoid.

"It was a time that my brother and I went to the polar zone with our educational facility. This was the same brother who tripped over my leg and fell off a cliff, but that was years away. At this time, while not friends, we were at least not ill-disposed to one another. It is funny how sometimes family members can come to odds. There are so many dynamics. In any case, we were to examine the local fauna and take visual images. The educators thought it would teach us how to study the natural sciences. I personally believe, and my father/sister agrees, that the time to teach such techniques is when the male has expressed an interest in the natural sciences because otherwise, they are a waste of time. Wouldn't you agree? I was photographing a buzznik that I found nesting in an ice cliff. The ice was a beautiful shade of blue. The sun on the cliff face sent out little gold flecks of reflection. It was one of the most lovely things I have ever seen, almost as nice as the flower fields of the—"

"Wispy, Rowan and I have to go to bed. We'll talk later," interrupted Ryan.

He and Rowan stood, put their dishes into the collection rack, and then moved to the door.

Ryan paused. "Thank you. With three of us, the EVA will be safer. Your expertise may make the difference."

Wispy waved the little arms by his mouth and dipped his head as Ryan stepped from the room.

THE ACTS OF THE PETTY

John scowled at the control screens before him and moved to adjust the congestion level in a felinezoid upwards.

"Excuse me, sir, but Mr. Strongbow asked me to pass it on. There's a memo on the *Angel Black* board. There are to be no more deaths due to the plague." Troy couldn't help feeling elation at how John sagged in his chair.

"What's the point then?" snipped the assistant producer, once producer and series creator.

"Mr. Strongbow said the plague storyline was instituted to stretch out the supply of antagonists since the cloning facilities are committed to the Kemetic set region. All the shows have been informed that there will be no more disposable antagonists available for Sun Valley."

"Wonderful. What are the fakeys supposed to fight against?"

"You should review the bulletin board. There have been some important changes." Troy slipped from the control room.

John glowered at the surrogates' telemetry but didn't alter any controls. He pulled up the series memo board on the main screen and reviewed it.

"That nova blasted, stardusted, fakey-loving scum!" John jumped out of his chair.

The message filled the screen.

Internal memo S.E.T.E. personnel only.

Be advised that a proposal for wrapping the *Angel Black* series at the end of the current season has been made to the set region administrative committee. The series' high expense, slipping ratings, and a growing repetition in the storylines suggest that a catastrophic failure is imminent. Executive Producer/Studio Director Michael Strongbow believes it is better that such a pivotal and successful series end on a high note. It is the opinion of Mr. Strongbow that doing so will lead to better residual and home market sales that will be more profitable than holding onto an exhausted concept.

All staff from *Angel Black* will be given preferred placement with shows starting in the Kemetic set region. There will be no disruption in the employment of the individuals who made *Angel Black* the hit entertainment it has been.

Further memos regarding the disposition of surrogates will be issued after the Set Region Administrative Committee has decided regarding this proposal.

Thank you for your long efforts in making this much-beloved series. They are appreciated, and you will all be rewarded in keeping with your contributions.

Michael J. Strongbow, Chief Studio Executive Officer/Producer

John stormed back and forth along the length of the control room. Pulling out his handheld, he scanned the memo, then barked, "Connect office of Hilda Strongbow."

"You have reached the law offices of Hilda Strongbow. Ms. Strongbow is currently unavailable. I am her computer,

Christine, and may be able to help with routine matters. How may I be of service?"

"Stardust!" spat John. "Computer, message. This is John Wilson. I'm attaching a memo. That fakey lover is wrapping my show. You have to do something." John closed the handheld, then, red-faced and fuming, threw himself into the controller's chair.

"No deaths from the plague, he says. I'll show him. Let him try and do a controlled wrap of the show with the principals dead."

John brought up the screen for Hurast, the chameleonzoid pirate commander, and released a drug that blocked inhibitions from the alien's control pack. He then increased the hormones associated with aggression. "If Michael wants to end my show, I'll end it for him! I'll kill every one of those fakeys before I let someone steal them. Sun Valley will burn." John grumbled.

Hurast, the pirate commander, moved back and forth across a boxy room with a large window overlooking an abandoned factory yard. She felt her rage build. Moving to a metallic office desk, she pressed a red button at its corner. A k-no-in entered the room. The mammal began to pant in the heat of the chameleonzoid's preferred environment.

"We have tolerated the *Homo sapiens* defenders too long. With the rebellion against us, we cannot be circumspect in our dealings with them. The *Homo sapiens* government could hardly pose more of a problem than the defenders. I am instituting a policy of total war."

"Yes, Commander!" The k-no-in glanced from side to side.

Gunther pushed the needle into Fran's arm.

"You are good at that." Fran watched her blood fill the collection tube where she lay on Gunther's couch. Carl stared out the front window.

"I had a nurse who taught me. There is no excuse for it being worse than a pricking sensation. How do you feel?" Gunther pulled the needle out and put a cotton ball over the puncture site.

Fran sneezed. "Tissue, preese."

Gunther passed her the box, and she blew. Gunther took the tissue before she could put it in the garbage and deposited it in a plastic bag. "I need a mucus specimen. You were saying."

"I'm sore and sniffly, and my chest is congested but no worse than a cold." Fran slumped on the couch. "And dizzy. Could you stop the room from spinning? This is worse than that time I got drunk in grade nine."

"When Rowan and Carl set up the tent in the backyard and pretended you were having a camp-out so you wouldn't have to face your parents?" Gunther chuckled as he stowed his blood-taking kit.

Fran smiled. "You knew?"

Gunther shrugged. "Young people make mistakes. It's how they learn. Willa and I always thought your folks were too strict. Good people, and they loved you, but you needed more freedom to be young."

"I still miss them." Fran's voice was sad.

"You always will. Missing them means you remember, which means you still have them in a way." Gunther took Fran's hand. Her skin was warm to the touch.

"Am I going to die?"

Gunther took a slow breath. "If it is what the aliens have, and I think that likely. Your symptomology is less severe. Your body seems to be putting up an effective fight against the disease. Most of your DNA is *Homo sapiens* with only a little felinezoid. I think you'll be fine. You may even supply a cure for the felinezoids and otterzoids."

"Only Toronk and Quinta. For what the pirates did to my parents, those alien scum deserve to die."

Gunther sighed. "And many who die deserve life. Can you give it to them?"

"No fair quoting *Lord of the Rings*, Gandalf." Fran closed her eyes.

"We'll talk about it. Now lay back. I'll get you some chicken soup." Gunther stood up.

"My friend, the MD, and that's the best you can do?" Fran smiled up from the couch.

"Gunther, over here." Carl beckoned from the window by the door.

Gunther joined him. A van had pulled up on the street and stopped.

"It could be a delivery," observed Gunther.

"At this time in this place?" remarked Carl.

A man carrying a box left the van and approached Gunther's door.

Gunther focused his mind on the man. "Crap! Get Fran to the basement."

Carl raced to comply as Gunther focused on the delivery man. The delivery man walked in place several steps and then set the box down.

'They'll fix me up right good for this.' Gunther could hear the man's stream of consciousness. *'Now to arm it and get the nova blast clear before someone jiggles it. I need my fix.'*

The addict pressed down on one corner of the box. Gunther could hear a click through the man's ears. The pirates' slave stood and mimed pressing a button in the air at doorbell height. Gunther projected the sound of a doorbell into the illusion. The delivery person hurried back to their van and drove off, thinking of his next fix.

I wish Quinta was here, Gunther thought as he released his link to the man.

'Are you all right, Daddy?' Jessica's thought intruded into Gunther's mind. The desire to merge hit him like a brick.

'A bomb, I think. We shouldn't communicate like this.'

'Then keep your emotions under control, Papa. Your worry basted through me like a cannon. It makes it hard to pay attention in class.'

'Sorry. I... any thoughts?' Gunther projected his situation into her mind.

'You can't leave it, someone is bound to pick it up, and the vibration will set it off.'

'I'll try hitting it with something thrown from behind cover.'

In a classroom halfway across town, an elderly professor in a tweed suit focused his attention on Jessica. "Miss Safehaven, as you seem bored with the lecture, I can only assume you have fully understood its contents. Please tell me, what are the most glaring shortfalls of the classical Freudian model of psychology?"

Jessica felt a wave of embarrassment as she stood, then Gunther took her voice. "The largest failing of the Freudian model, in my opinion, is its limited motivational base. The basic concept of dynamic tension between elements of the psyche that stand in opposition has validity. Still, it is too limiting to reduce the core motivations to Eros and Thanatos with additional social overlays, as is indicated by the superconscious. It is also limiting to think that there would not be times when an expanded id would be in alliance with the superego. The defence of offspring is a case in point. In societies that value material wealth and the garnering of possessions conducive to survival, the superego and id would find common cause. Many of these factors become obvious if you expand the motivational bases of the Freudian model out of a sexual drive into what could be termed an animal drive. These elements can be observed in the behaviours of other higher-order mammalian species. From that, assumptions can be made about what they would be in humans."

Jessica felt herself take a breath, but the prof held up a liver-spotted hand.

"Young lady, I apologize. Your insights are well taken. You've obviously read Doctor McPherson's book from the auxiliary reading list.

"Now, class. I will move on to the next psychological school of thought, the Jungians..."

'Thanks,' Jessica thought the word into the gestalt, then focused on her class.

Gunther opened his front door and stepped onto his porch. He picked up an ornamental rock and threw it at the box, hitting the dirt behind his trash bins before it impacted.

An explosion left a blackened spot on his front yard and a speckling of shrapnel against the wall and door of the house. The front window shattered inward, and the trash cans Gunther sheltered behind fell over him, their sides peppered with holes.

"Unauthorized series crossover in effect. Impending *Police on the Street/Station House/Angel Black* crossover," warned the studio computer.

"Neighbours called it in, did they? Good! Let Strongbow explain why his stolen show is peeing in other people's pools." John rubbed his hands together as he looked for other ways to sabotage the set region.

Ryan adjusted the pull as Rowan re-checked the numbers. The entire bridge crew were at their stations.

"C-132 is on target for Murack Five," announced Rowan.

"Isaac Newton can take it from here." Ryan leaned back.

"The comet is a little over speed." Rowan rechecked her instruments. "It's accelerating. It's on course, but... Wait... A hair off."

Ryan sat forward in his seat as Rowan and Henry

reworked the numbers.

"The impact will be in the western, south polar region instead of the eastern north polar region." Rowan sounded frustrated. "I thought I accounted for all the pulls."

Ryan buried his face in his hand. "You probably did. Why are some fanatics competent? It would be nice if stupidity applied to all areas of their lives. Rowan. Run the numbers. Will the comet impact near Kangra-la if its acceleration and course remain constant?"

Rowan fell silent as she worked the problem, then went pale. "Almost a direct hit. It doesn't make sense. The odds against it are enormous." Rowan kept rechecking her projections.

Ryan scowled and moved to the captain's chair.

"Hotty boss, if they got caught doing what we think they're doing..." Henry's expression matched Ryan's as much as his mutilation allowed.

"What do you think they're doing?" asked Tim.

"Using the comet as a planet buster. They tried to blow up a stargate and murder a world. Using a planet buster when it falls in their lap is not a stretch. If the sycamorezoids were caught, they'd blame it on the pirates and/or us. The damage would be done. They might not even be caught out if Star Searcher can fob it off as a natural disaster."

"But you lined the comet up for the impact," gasped Ziggy.

"And slowed it down," countered Rowan with a note of distress.

"It's projectile weapons ballistics, Ziggy. Mass times velocity equals destructive potential. The size of C-132 at the speed we left it, even if we didn't blow it up, would be, at most, a city killer, and we were bringing it in on a dead zone of the planet. Blow it up, like we intend. The bits will be steam and dust before they hit the ground. Speed it up and change the target. It could depopulate Murack Five." Ryan stared straight ahead.

"The fools are counting on the Republic not caring enough to investigate. The sycamorezoids would blame us if the Republic checked since we lined the comet up. They'd bomb humanity back to the Stone Age. And it's my fault." Rowan's voice cracked.

"Not your fault. You had a good plan. I should have seen this possibility." Ryan sighed.

"Even if they don't blame us, the Republic will blame the pirates to avoid having to revert the sycamorezoids back to their Stone Age." Kitoy lashed her tail.

"Rowan, focus the scanners along the comet's course to Murack Five and magnify."

The image on the screen filled with a field of brown and blue. What looked like a fuzzy, golden egg dominated the middle of the screen.

"They aren't moving relative to the planet," remarked Rowan.

"If you check, sweetness, you'll find a stream of cometary matter flowing towards them." Henry sounded disgusted.

"Kitoy, prepare a communication. Include all the data and evidence we have thus far, including the telemetry of that ship pulling the comet in. Send it to the dichrostigmazoid with instructions to forward it to the Republic and..." Ryan considered for a moment. "It's in their own self-interest, and Star Searcher could block Republic channels. Yes. Send it to the UES as well. If this hits the air recycler, they'll at least be able to mount a defence."

"It does make a sick kind of sense," observed Ziggy. "The sycamorezoids want everyone out of this system. They want to be pure without the contamination of the other species. If the kangazoids were wiped out by a natural disaster, that's one problem solved."

"I had a body die to save those wallabies. I'll be nova blasted if I let some tree-sperm kill them now!" Ryan moved to the captain's seat, his face becoming hard. "And I'm getting nova blasted tired of running away from bullies!"

Henry swivelled in his chair to watch Ryan with his android eyes. His captain and friend had become a thing of cold purpose. Every move, every shift of weight, was calculated. An expression straight from humanity's savage past appeared on his face. "Oh, stardust! King Arthur has taken his throne. Somebody is going to die!" Henry's tone was expectant.

Ryan ignored the AI. "We proceed as planned. If the explosives work, the pieces will dissipate in the atmosphere. Henry, access the grav pull limits for an ankylosaur and put them in Rowan's active files. Rowan, work out pull points. I want to force them to commit all their power to maintaining a false Lagrange point for themselves between the comet and Murack Five. We'll start pulling back on the comet as soon as we plant the charges and chaff. At the last moment, we'll divert all grav lasers into a braking manoeuvre to drop our speed for atmospheric entry. Work out our deviation to cut along the planet's curve while we equalize with rotational speed. We can let ourselves fall as long as we miss the dirt. You don't need to be tidy. We'll let the ankylosaur's grav lasers pull the comet into them, then blow the charges when they collide. That will make a matter cloud to take out the mines and drive them towards the planet. A six-hundred-kilometer fall onto a hostile environment should deal with them."

"What about the other ships?" asked Kitoy.

"They aren't built to enter atmosphere. If they try to manoeuvre in the cloud of stardust blowing the comet will cause, their grav laser ports will be clogged in seconds."

"Aye, Captain. Is any of this safe?" Rowan turned to her controls.

"Stardust, sweetness. Most of this isn't even legal," observed Henry.

"Tim, build up our stores of liquid nitrogen. We may need to use them as a heat sink. You can drop internal air pressure to sixty-nine kilopascals and bring percentage oxygen to thirty so long as everyone aboard can handle it. Consult with Pikeman and Yipya. Kitoy, ship-wide announcement. No combustion or unnecessary heat sources until after landing." Ryan leaned back in the command chair, stroking his chin and watching the sycamorezoid ship on the main screen. "They want this comet? I'm going to shove it straight down their throats."

Gunther and Willa sat at their kitchen table as police technicians scoured their living room for shrapnel. The front windows were bits on the floor.

"This is good tea," remarked the brown-haired, friendly-looking, middle-aged detective who sat opposite them with a cup in his hand.

"We enjoy a good cup. Dave, was it?" asked Gunther.

The detective nodded.

"I'm at a loss as to what happens now. I should call my insurance agent. Will I need a police report?" Gunther played the shocked homeowner focusing on minutiae to avoid the enormity of the event.

Dave smiled. "You have got to be kidding. It will be hours before the collection teams finish. Days after that, before the analysis is done. You're lucky that your guests were in the basement. You have some interesting equipment down there."

"My husband does a little practice as a GP on the side." Willa stared through the door at the devastation.

"Just to keep my hand in. I'm primarily a psychiatrist. The electronics, they…" Gunther allowed a hitch to enter his voice.

"They were our daughter's. We haven't had the heart to…" Willa trailed off.

Dave reached across and patted Willa's hand. "I am sorry for your loss. For now, I'd suggest boarding over the windows. Do you have any idea who may have done this?"

Gunther sighed. "I do have potentially dangerous patients. When dealing with an ill mind, predicting behaviour can be difficult."

Detective Dave O'Brian nodded. "It is a good thing that the bomb destabilized."

Carl settled Fran in his bed with a hot cup of herbal tea. The police had kept the interview mercifully short, and Willa had lent him her car so that he could look after Fran.

"Thank you." Fran snuggled in amongst the blankets, her back propped up with pillows.

Carl regarded her. "Fran... I planned on taking you to the botanical gardens to do this, but... We could have died today, again. I... Stardust, with all that's going on in our lives, this will probably seem silly. I don't want to lose you before having you. If that makes any sense. Will you?"

Carl pulled open his dresser drawer and took out a ring box. He opened it to reveal a gold band with a small diamond. He held it towards Fran.

Fran's face contorted as she released a tremendous sneeze. She hurried to grab the box of tissues on the bed's headboard and spent the next thirty seconds blowing her nose red and wiping at her watering eyes.

Carl waited, holding the ring box.

"Picked a nova blasted time." Fran reached up from the bed and grabbed his arm, pulling him towards herself. She kissed him, then took the ring and slipped it onto her finger. "The answer is yes."

They kissed. Fran pulled away and sneezed.

There was a crash from the living room. Carl jerked up. His skin instinctively camouflaged. Fran fought to still her sniffles. Carl crept from the bedroom into the living room. Two k-no-in had pushed into the room from the building's hallway.

Carl felt his rage build. Unthinking anger coursed

through him as his adrenaline and other stress hormones peaked. His mind screamed in fury as he mentally reached for help.

'What's going on?' Gunther's voice demanded in Carl's mind.

'K-no-ins in my apartment. How dare they?' Carl saw red and was about to charge into battle.

'Think,' ordered Gunther's thoughts. *'I'm sending help.'*

'Think? They are invading my home!' It was all Carl could do to keep from shouting the words.

'Think, the studio can control our emotions, not our thoughts.' Gunther tried to soothe the younger man's mind from blocks away. *'Fight smart, not angry.'*

'I can help.' Jessica joined the gestalt, and Gunther's power grew exponentially, as well as his desire for the younger woman.

Carl found that he could think through his emotion as the k-no-ins moved towards the open bedroom door. Still seeing red, he raced to his dresser and wrenched open a drawer, grabbing a Bowie knife. He pulled it from its sheath, revealing that the blade glistened with a coating of lithium grease. The first k-no-in filled the doorway and pointed a kinetic rifle at Fran. Carl lunged, driving his blade into the alien's throat.

K-no-in blood soaked Carl and sprayed across the room. The k-no-in stumbled back. Carl leapt over his enemy, landing on the back of the second k-no-in. The pirate bucked, making Carl's slash go wide. Fran appeared in the bedroom doorway. Mucus dribbled from her nose, but her claws were extended and covered with lithium grease. She leapt while the k-no-in tried to buck off Carl, who had locked one arm around his enemy's throat and was ready to drive his blade home. Fran swiped her claws down the alien's side, drawing blood. Carl drove his knife home with adrenaline-induced strength. The first k-no-in stumbled to its feet, gasping for breath and spraying blood in all directions. It raised its rifle towards Fran. Carl saw the move and, bracing himself against the second k-no-in's back, leapt, clutching the gun's barrel. The rifle fired, blowing out the living room's outer wall.

Fran stumbled and fell to her knees. The second k-no-in stepped towards her and grimaced. The blade in its shoulder shifted, then dropped out, accompanied by a gout of blood. Its throat began to swell.

Carl jerked the kinetic rifle from the hands of his fast-weakening foe and threw it into the kitchen at the far side of the living room. The k-no-in tried to bite Carl, who stepped back and drove his foot into his opponent's throat.

Between the blow and the anaphylaxis, the k-no-in collapsed.

Carl turned to see the second k-no-in looming over Fran. He charged, hitting the unbalanced, dying alien in the side, driving it towards the missing wall. The alien teetered on the edge, then fell.

Carl rushed to Fran, who was stumbling to her feet, leaning against a wall.

"The bodies?" she breathed.

"You first." Carl helped her back to bed.

"The police. They're going to find out." Fran settled under the covers.

"I think the days of secrets are over." Carl looked at the dead k-no-in in the living room.

"What a mess." Fran closed her eyes. Carl rushed to take a shower to the sound of sirens. He was wrapped in a towel free of his coating of alien blood when he met the police at the shattered door.

⊂═══◇

Farley moved from the threadbare couch in his one-room apartment to the kitchenette and picked up his beeping landline. "Hello."

"Ris Farley?" asked the gravelly, heavily accented voice.

"Grell?" Farley struggled to understand the k-no-in's

Homo sapiens speech.

"I no reach Carl. Pirates plan poison Lake Edgley. Pirates get poison now. Meet me Cumberbatch Drive, stop r-em. R-urry!" The line went dead.

Farley hit the speed dial for Gunther, but it went to voice mail.

"Quinta, we need to get to Lake Edgley. Grell says the pirates are going to poison it. All the drinking water for Sun Valley comes from there." Farley grabbed his car keys as Quinta used a remote to shut off the television.

Minutes later, Farley and Quinta joined Grell, the k-no-in double agent, behind a boathouse by the parking lot of the pier at the end of Cumberbatch Drive. Between night and shadow, they were as good as invisible from the dimly lit parking lot.

"Me contact octozoids. Poison lake, they die." Grell shifted the mass of his bulky six-limbed form.

A box truck pulled up by the dock. The driver, a *Homo sapiens* woman, stayed in place while three k-no-in, two chameleonzoids and three human slaves started unloading barrels marked with the skull and crossbones poison symbol.

"It looks like it's just us. Hard and fast. Try to get them close to the water," ordered Farley. Farley charged the pirates with Quinta on his back and Grell at his side.

One of the chameleonzoids glanced up, paused, then snapped, "Kill them," alerting the rest of his group.

One chameleonzoid and two k-no-ins lifted kinetic rifles. The humans rushed forward, brandishing clubs and knives.

Quinta's brow wrinkled in concentration. The chameleonzoid's rifle jerked to one side and fired into the back of a k-no-in. The blast tore the dog-like alien in two. The distraction bought Farley and Grell the time they needed to reach their enemies.

Grell grappled the gun of the other k-no-in. Farley placed Quinta on the ground and threw himself at the armed chameleonzoid as it brought its weapon to bear on Quinta.

The human slaves surged forward with clubs raised. An invisible line of telekinetic force sent them sprawling. The remaining aliens rushed to dump the barrels into Lake Edgley.

Farley and Grell took hits from clubs as the slaves regained their feet and joined the fray.

Quinta was driven across the parking lot to the dock by a series of kinetic rifle blasts that she barely managed to deflect.

There was a creaking sound. Two octozoids in scuttle suits climbed onto the dock. They rushed forward, then reared up on two of the suit's legs and pummelled the chameleonzoid that was trying to push the barrels into the lake.

The human slaves abandoned their attack on Grell and Farley and rushed to the defence of the chameleonzoid. Spitting blood, Farley stopped pushing against the chameleonzoid with the kinetic rifle and dragged the off-balance reptile towards the lake. The chameleonzoid realized its peril and tried to stop its advance but was off balance. Farley threw all his weight backwards while clutching the alien's wrists. They both stumbled into the water by the pier.

Tentacles entwined the chameleonzoid, dragging it under.

Farley let his gills expand, flooding his battered body with oxygen, then pulled himself onto the dock.

Grell had wrestled the rifle from the other k-no-in, and they were snapping at each other with their fangs. Both bled from several wounds. Quinta was on the dock with a human slave swinging at her with a club. It impacted. Quinta let out a yelp of pain. Farley tackled the human and drove him into the water. They grappled until tentacles closed around the slave's neck and arms. The bulbous form of Tony carried the addict to the bottom.

Farley felt exhausted. He raced to the landward end of the pier and surfaced in time to grab a slave who was about to tip a barrel into the lake. Farley forced the slave's face into the liquid. The poison sloshed, burning Farley's forearms. The slave fell back, screaming. The skin of his face peeled away to the bone, his eye sockets empty.

Farley dove into the lake and came up on the other side of the pier. His arms blazed with pain. The octozoids in the scuttle suits had managed to drag two more slaves into the lake. The remaining chameleonzoid clambered onto the truck, which sped away.

Farley rushed to Quinta's side.

"Farley." Her voice was a whisper.

"Quinta. They're gone now."

Quinta's nostrils flared. "Good for them. I was about to toss them in a net and pull them to shore."

Farley went to touch Quinta's side, but the burns on his hands stopped him. "Gunther will fix you up."

Quinta nodded.

Tony surfaced by the dock. "Mammal. The commander wishes me to tell you that he respects your actions. The alliance is agreed to. If that," Tony waved a tentacle at the barrels of poison, "had gotten into the lake, it would have killed us all."

Farley nodded. "Wouldn't have done the Sun Valley's water supply any good either."

"We have called your healer. He says he is coming. We will call the *Homo sapiens* authorities to take the poison when he has removed you."

Grell stumbled up the pier, limping on two of his six legs with bleeding puncture wounds from his enemy's fangs on his shoulders. "We won," he said, using the translator nanobots.

"Barely," agreed Farley. The world was descending into shades of grey.

"Whether you pass the breeding exam by one per cent or by ten, you will have young." Grell settled painfully by Farley. "Susan will not face poison water now. It is good."

Farley was conscious enough to see Gunther and Willa run down the pier.

13

EVA

The *Star Hawk* slipped through the gas and dust forming the comet's tail to the centre of the flow. The disruption in the tail was no more than a minor variation in light that could have been a rock breaking away from the comet.

"Shifting vector. All grav lasers bottom, rotating pulse mode point zero five G pull," announced Ryan.

The *Star Hawk* faced its flat bottom to the comet as the grav laser ports cycled sequentially so none would get clogged with matter.

"Contact in ten seconds. Terrain within tolerance." Rowan riveted her attention to her instruments.

Ryan pressed a button on his console. Ports opened on the *Star Hawk*'s bottom, allowing its telescoping landing legs with their three-clawed feet to deploy.

"Legs down and locked. Henry, what does engineering say?" asked Ryan.

"Down and locked, confirmed," Henry spoke from the computer station.

"Two seconds to contact." Rowan scanned her instruments. "Contact."

A shudder ran through the ship, then another and another.

"All legs down. Deploying low gravity grapplers." Ryan pressed another button on the pilot's station. The *Star Hawk* shook as spikes on its legs drove into the rocky ice ball below. Ryan locked down the pilot's station, then raced to engineering and reviewed his checks. "Engineering confirms landing legs down and locked. All systems are green. Ziggy, can you target that CO_2 seam Wispy highlighted?"

"The upper port gun can get it." Ziggy bit his lip as he worked his board.

"Henry, do you confirm?" Ryan stood and stretched.

"I confirm." Henry closed his android eyes and focused his attention on the targeting system.

"Ziggy, take the first couple of cuts, then hand it off to Henry. We'll need you for the EVA."

"Finally, something I know how to do." Ziggy worked the gun, passing its beam back and forth along the seam of CO_2. On the big screen, the CO_2 erupted from the comet in a cloud that was swept up into the cometary tail.

Rowan stood and rushed into Ryan's arms, kissing him. "I know it's inappropriate. Let it slide, and be careful."

Ryan cupped her cheek, his steely demeanour falling away for a second. "I have someone worth coming home to. I'll see you after the EVA." He kissed her, then left the bridge.

"He'll be all right. Ryan knows his way around an EVA," soothed Kitoy.

"I'll keep an eye on him," added Ziggy.

Rowan nodded. "Most dangerous part of space travel is all." She returned to her station.

Ryan moved to the top airlock, where he found Wispy in a suit resembling a sausage with six downward-directed legs and two forward-directed arms. Each limb ended in pincers. The front of the suit looked like a fishbowl with Wispy's insect-like head inside.

The taped-together crab shells and explosive-filled fruit husks sat in a pair of plastic boxes beside the waspzoid.

"Captain." Wispy spoke the one-word greeting, then stared at lines of squiggly script projected onto his helmet.

"Wispy." Ryan opened the closet by the airlock and extracted his spacesuit. He was half-dressed when Ziggy walked up the corridor.

"The trench should be dug by the time we're ready to exit." Ziggy took out a suit and inspected it before donning the first piece.

"I will take the explosive charges into the trench while Captain Chandler distributes the chaff containers. Zygmunt will stand as safety officer. Remember to keep your lines attached and watch for volatile regions. If you stay to rock and water ice, you should be safe for this approach. Avoid other surfaces. This close to the sun, they might vaporize, and your grapples could come loose." Wispy repeated the briefing he'd given during the meeting that convinced Ryan that the waspzoid's experience made him the best candidate for mission leader.

Ryan put on his helmet and ran the safety checks. Finally, he checked the radio. "Wispy, do you copy?"

"I copy. We will check with the control hub when we exit the craft." Wispy shifted position. "Captain, if you would do the mutual inspection and radio checks with Zygmunt, I will exit the ship first. I do not think you will fit in this airlock with me."

"Agreed. Wait on the hull until we join you." Ryan finished his safety checks and inspected Ziggy's suit while Wispy clambered into the airlock. The inner door sealed.

"Radio check?" Ziggy's voice came over the channel.

"Reading you loud and clear. Over."

The two *Homo sapiens* had finished checking each other's suits when the inner airlock door opened. They entered a circular chamber big enough to hold three *Homo sapiens* in EVA suits. The hatch closed. There was a hiss as the air drained, then the eerie silence of hard vacuum. If they listened, they could hear the beating of their own hearts.

"EVA, what are your statuses, over?" asked Kitoy's voice.

"Ryan, check, green across the board. Over."

"Zygmunt, check, green across the board. Over."

"Telemetry confirms. Over," said Kitoy's voice.

Ryan and Ziggy climbed through the *Star Hawk*'s top

hatch and stood on the hull beside Wispy. "Radio checks. Over," Wispy's voice demanded.

"Ryan, reading loud and clear. Over."

"Ziggy, loud and clear. Over."

"Bridge is reading all of you loud and clear. Over." Kitoy's voice came into their suits.

"Tie off. Over," ordered Wispy.

Ryan and Ziggy bent down and connected monofilament cables on spools attached to their suits to clips by the airlock's pressure door. The camouflaged outer hull panel was retracted under its neighbouring plate, revealing the pressure hatch.

"You may lose contact with me when I enter the crevasse. If I am not back in two hours, you will know something has gone wrong." Wispy picked up the box of bombs and hugged it to his suit's chest with his two middle legs. With the grace of a premier ballerina, he leapt from the back of the *Star Hawk*. His monofilament safety line spooled out as he flew over the comet. Firing small puffs from his suit, he descended into the narrow trench cut by the *Star Hawk*'s lasers.

"Graceful. Over." Ryan picked up the box of crab shells packed with chaff and walked down the hull of his ship. Coming to the edge, he leapt forward, letting his safety line spool out. When six hundred meters had extended, he stopped the reel mechanism and felt the jerk as his momentum was arrested. A puff from his manoeuvring jets, and he was on the comet's surface.

"Computer, boot cleats activate, walking mode." Spikes pushed out of Ryan's boots, driving into the ice beneath him.

"*Star Hawk*, Ziggy, I'm on surface six hundred meters out. I've found a patch of water ice to land on. Over." Ryan lifted his right foot, and the computer locked the left cleats into place as he took a step. When the right foot was firmly planted, those cleats deployed, and the left retracted. The comet boiled into space around him. Three steps took him to the edge of the water ice he stood on. Using an arm-mounted laser cutter, he vaporized a hole in the seam of CO_2 ice ahead of him and deposited one of the shells in it. Retracting his cleats, he hopped parallel to the comet. His safety line pulled him in an arc with the *Star Hawk* at its centre. The arc more or less ran along the edge of the comet. Spotting a rock pile, he fired a small thrust, stalling himself and landing. He pushed the second chaff load under a rock, then repeated the procedure.

Ryan had only two crab shells left when he landed to find the ground shattering beneath him. His safety line jerked taut and tore through the thin layer of ice, swinging him face-first into the side of an ice cave. The impact winded him.

Ryan gasped. "*Star Hawk*, do you read? Kitoy, do you copy? Ziggy, do you copy? Over."

The only answer was static.

"Wonderful." Pushing back from the ice wall with his legs, Ryan calmed himself. All was silence except for the sound of his own heart. "Computer, diagnostic heads-up."

Ryan's faceplate filled with readings, all in green.

"Next page."

The second page was as green as the first.

Ryan sighed as the routine steadied his nerves.

Pushing himself around, he glanced to either side of the ice cave he found himself in. It ran parallel to the course he'd been following above.

"Close enough, and I'll need my hands." He threw one of the crab shells to his right, where it impacted the end of the cave after about thirty meters. He threw the last shell to his left, where it smashed into a pile of smoking CO_2 snow after about forty meters. Extending his cleats, Ryan walked up the wall. The low gravity offered no more resistance than a breeze. The safety cable rewound slowly, then disappeared through the ice. He directed his laser cutter in front of his feet. The chamber filled with steam as ice crusted on his suit. Minutes passed as the passage through the ice grew deeper, then all the steam and ice particles exploded outwards. When he could see clearly, a hole about two meters deep opened at his feet. Ryan grabbed the inside of it and flipped himself over. Pressing on its sides, he crab-walked upwards. The safety line caught, and he let out more.

"I'm halfway down his line. Over." Ziggy's voice filled the channel.

"You'll probably have to dig him out. I haven't been able to raise Wispy. Hurry. Over." Kitoy's voice was stressed.

"Take your time. I found an ice cave. I'm back on the surface. I'm melting my safety line free, then it's back to home. Over."

"Confirmed, Captain. You had us on the wrong end of the stampede here. Over," remarked Kitoy.

"Roger, Captain. Do you need me, or should I head back to the barn? Over." Ziggy sounded relieved.

Ryan played his laser cutter over the ice where his safety line was snagged while pushing away from the comet. The line freed, and he found himself floating.

"Ziggy, take it home. I'll be right behind you. Over. Computer, begin winch in manoeuvre ten centimeters per second, pull for one second, pause for two seconds, then resume reel at the same rate." Ryan hopped up as the reel system on the monofilament cable activated.

As he rose from the comet, the *Star Hawk* came into view. He looked under the ship where the support legs were extended to different degrees, compensating for the unevenness of the terrain, keeping the ship level.

His altitude increased as momentum carried him in a slow drift forward. The winch collected the slack safety line without adding to the pull. Ziggy flew ahead of him using the same technique.

"How's Wispy? Over." Ryan admired the view as the gossamer sheet of gasses boiling off the comet flowed over the stars, turning them into glowing nimbuses of refracted light.

"No word, and his two hours are up. Over," replied Kitoy.

Gas blasted out of a fissure on the comet's surface, hitting Ryan, driving him up in an uncontrolled spin. His tether line snapped taut.

Wispy drifted over the trench, then released the slightest puff of gas from his suit's control system. The mental discipline that stopped his mind from wandering was enormous and foreign to his species but essential for the dangerous work of an EVA.

He sank into the narrow crevasse. Walls of ice rose to either side of him.

"Suit, mark current level. Measure and announce at… convert *Homo sapiens* measurement. Four hundred and fifty meters."

A rich female voice replied in the waspzoid language. "Three hundred and twenty-one point three two one six braknell."

"Announce descent at three hundred and twenty-two braknell." Wispy watched his lights glisten off the ice, turning it into shining walls of blue-tinted diamonds. The forces of billions of years had sculpted flows and patterns that drew his eyes. The silence was absolute save for the beating of his hearts. Time passed, and the canyon narrowed until it was too thin to accommodate him. Putting his legs out, he stilled his descent.

"Suit, current depth from mark."

"Three hundred and sixteen braknell."

"Close enough for explosives." Propping the box against the ice walls, Wispy pulled out a bomb, then placed a detonator from a pouch on one of his utility belts onto the side of the fruit husk, activated the timer and dropped it.

Feather-light, it drifted into the narrowing canyon, then hovered in space.

"One does not get a better placement than the absolute

centre," Wispy remarked to himself. He prepared another bomb and scuttled several meters up the canyon, dropping it to lodge in the deepening crack. He repeated this until all the bombs were planted, then scuttled up the canyon several meters. Attaching a diffuser to his suit's laser torch, he played hot light over the ice, which melted. Half of it flashed into steam and escaped, but the rest flowed into the crack and solidified, encasing the bombs.

"Suit, reel me in, five brak per second. For two seconds, then pause for two seconds, then resume."

Wispy set his legs to fend off the uneven crevasse walls and felt himself accelerating upwards. Momentum carried him against the comet's minuscule gravity. A tremor ran through the walls, then they closed around him, crushing against his back and front, jamming his legs so he couldn't move.

"Winch tension exceeded. Halting retraction," spoke the suit's monotone voice.

"Sister/father mating male with defective genes!" Wispy swore.

"*Star Hawk*, Zygmunt, Ryan, can anyone read me? Over." Wispy spoke into his transmitter. Static was his only reply.

"Thrice-hatched female with unsavoury habits and a shrivelled stinger." Wispy sagged in his suit and started trying to work a leg free of the ice.

⚕

"Computer, stabilize spin," Ryan barked into his helmet as he tumbled in space at the end of his safety line.

Jets fired from his support pack, and he stopped spinning.

"Computer, resume winch manoeuvre." Ryan took deep breaths to keep his stomach down. Directly below him was the *Star Hawk*.

"Ryan, what happened? We show you forty meters above the ship. Over," demanded Kitoy.

"Confirm. I have visual. Over," stated Ziggy.

"I'm all right. A gas vent hit me. This snowball is getting interesting. I'm heading straight down on the *Star Hawk* now." Ryan kept the safety line slack, so it added no momentum, and twisted so that his feet were beneath him. He landed with no more impact than jumping off the bottom step of a flight of stairs. Ziggy helped stabilize him.

"Any word from Wispy? Over." Ryan scanned the ice field.

"None. Over." Kitoy's voice betrayed concern.

"I never thought I'd say this, but I'd pay good money to hear his voice. Ziggy, you and I had better see what's wrong. Over."

"Affirmative. Over."

"*Star Hawk*, this is now a rescue mission. You'll likely lose our signal when we go down the trench. Over."

"Confirmed. Over."

Ziggy and Ryan lined themselves up with where Wispy had entered the trench and leapt, letting their safety cables play out, being careful not to cross each other's paths. They fired bursts of gas, stalling their forward momentum and pushing themselves to the icy ground at the edge of the trench.

"Ziggy, stay here and relay messages. Hopefully, we can keep a communications line out of the trench if we do that. Over."

"Yes, sir. Over." Ziggy set the grapplers on his boots and leaned over the chasm.

Ryan stepped off the lip and let the almost non-existent gravity pull him down. His suit lights sparkled off walls of water ice speckled with occasional rocks. He fell deeper and deeper. "Wispy, can you hear me? Over." Ryan repeated the call. "Wispy."

"I hear you. I am gratified you held to the two-hour limit. Over."

"Where are you, and what happened? Over."

Lights blinked three meters down the chasm and two

meters along its length. Extending his arms, Ryan pushed his hands into either side of the gorge, stalling his momentum, then slowly pulled himself to Wispy's side.

"I will begin by saying the charges are planted and armed. I was ascending the shaft when the ice walls shifted. I am stuck. The arms and legs of my suit are pinned. I've been trying to melt my way free, but I am not at an angle to effectively use any of my tools. Over."

"I'm here now. Over." Ryan examined how the ice pressed in on Wispy's suit. "Wispy, it looks like you're bracing the wall. When I cut you free, we'll have to move fast or be crushed. Are you getting this, Ziggy? Over."

"I'm reading both of you. Over."

"Tell the *Star Hawk* we'll blast out of here as soon as Wispy is free. The ice plate they're on might shift. They're to retract the landing legs and hover free of contact with the comet. Once we get in, execute the distancing manoeuvres immediately. We're behind schedule. Over."

"Got you. I will relay it to Kitoy. Henry is setting up to pilot. Over."

"You ready, Wispy? Over."

"Ready, Captain. Over."

Ryan activated the laser cutter on his suit's forearm and started melting the ice around Wispy, freeing his most forward arms first. With the manipulator arms free, Wispy activated his laser cutter and began melting the ice in front of his chest. Minutes passed as the area filled with steam that froze almost as soon as it was created. There was a loud cracking sound.

"Now!" snapped Ryan.

Rockets fired on both EVA suits. Wispy tore free of the walls. Both sentients shot upward as the walls of ice slid together. The sentients blasted out of the crevasse as it silently slammed together. Ryan and Wispy stilled their jets and jerked up hard against their safety lines. Turning, they saw Ziggy cranking towards the *Star Hawk* in open space. They followed his example.

"*Star Hawk*, mission accomplished. We are coming home, over," said Ryan.

Minutes later, Ryan and Ziggy sat on the hull of the ship, their safety lines winched short as Wispy was decontaminated in the airlock. The hatch opened, and the two *Homo sapiens* slipped into the confined space, closing the hatch behind them.

"We're in. Button her up and proceed to pull point. Over," ordered Ryan.

Outside the ship, the armoured, camouflage-capable, outer hull slid over the access port. Inside the airlock, Ryan and Ziggy's suits were subjected to a barrage of lethal environments designed to kill any hostile life forms and burn away toxins. Both men breathed sighs of relief.

FIXING A MESS, MAKING A MESS

14

"**G**et him out of here and stay with him. Give him an hour to clean out his office, then he's banned from all S.E.T.E. property," snapped Michael as two muscular, uniformed studio security guards dragged John out of the *Angel Black* control room.

"You want to kill my show! I've helped you. You nova blasted fakey lover. Try to make Sun Valley work with the fakeys knowing there are aliens. You won't keep those fakeys in the dark now." John was frothing at the mouth as he was dragged from the room.

The door closed. Mike looked at the stream of complaints and cautions scrolling down one of the auxiliary screens. The inter-control room audio feeds were muted, but the message pending lights were all lit.

He closed his eyes as his mind raced. He'd only become aware of John's activities when the other producers called him to complain about series contamination. He couldn't know all John's actions until he reviewed the quick log, and Michael didn't have that kind of time. He took a breath, then, with the air of a virtuoso pianist sitting before a concert hall, settled himself in the controller's chair.

"Gene, priority voice interface. Reset all *Angel Black* characters, primary, secondary and antagonists, to default. In five minutes, reset felinezoids and otterzoids to stage two plague status.

"Interface with *The Station House*. Audio link. Stan, John

went nuts and made a mess. I'm trying to fix it. Enhance all your surrogates working on the toxic waste by Lake Edgley. That is not a sanctioned part of any show. Book a vehicle to get those nova-blasted barrels back to the toxic waste disposal facility as soon as your surrogates contain them."

"Thank the Divine. I didn't know what the nova blast was going on. That stuff is bleeding deadly." The voice on the intercom sounded harried.

"Will what has spilt into the water already be a problem?" Mike scanned the screens for the *Angel Black* primary characters.

"I'll pull up the reference."

Mike turned back to the main screen, adding a coagulating factor to Quinta's blood from her inbuilt control pack to halt her internal bleeding. He shifted focus, decreasing the congestion building in Farley's lungs and dropping his blood pressure so that he didn't stroke out. A few actions later, the artificial blood in Farley and Quinta's control packs was in their system. "Gene, maintain Chelaa in good health. Quinta needs him."

"Michael, I looked it up. At the dilution factor of what got in the lake, it should be all right." Stan's voice came from the intercom.

"Thanks, Stan. Let me know if there are any problems. Gene, close the line."

Michael examined the complaints board and snarled. "Gene, connect me to the *Freedom's Run* board. Ulva."

"Michael." The young controller sounded surprised.

"Take over Fran and Carl. Work on Fran's symptoms. Try to make it look like a natural recovery. Keep an eye on all the *Angel Black* principals. I need oversight in case I miss something. None of the principal characters dies if we can help it."

"Yes, sir." Being an army brat, Ulva knew when to obey an officer.

In the set region, Hurast stormed across her office in a fury. She stopped and swayed on her six reptilian legs. Her heart slowed, and the rage receded. Her k-no-in aide rushed in.

"We received word. The plan to poison the lake failed. All but three of the personnel are dead. The raid against the defenders' dwelling also failed. The *Homo sapiens* authorities have found bodies and recovered a kinetic rifle. The *Homo sapiens* law enforcers are examining the remains of the explosive device we used against the telepath."

"Relax, Graa. The last matters little. We used only locally available components. So many dead so swiftly." Hurast slapped her reptilian tail against the wall in dismay. "Call back our other assault teams. We must rethink our strategy."

"Ma'am, the five k-no-in and six slaves you sent to attack the octozoids in their cave. We have had no word from them." Graa hung his head and tugged at his fangs with his hands.

"What have I done? What madness possessed me? Cancel all missions. We must regroup. Open the communications channel with the octozoids. I will speak to their commander."

"Yes, Commander." The k-no-in left the room.

Hurast straightened her toppled desk. "What madness took me?"

Mike pulled up a graphic on one of the auxiliary screens. On the main screen, Gunther had started an IV on Farley and was preparing to perform a peritoneal lavage to lessen the concentration of toxins in his system. On the screen beside Gunther's, Willa was racing to collect Chelaa so he could treat Quinta.

Carl and Fran occupied auxiliary screens. They both sat in police interrogation rooms. Fran had used tissues on the desk in front of her and was wrapped in a blanket.

The graphic in front of Mike was a brown file folder with 'Top Secret For Your Eyes Only' in large red letters across its front.

He pressed a key and filled the first box with a picture of a k-no-in.

To I.I.B. Director Sun Valley cell, Allen Majors.

Immediate attention.

Genetic experiments to create a more effective canine variant for use in security and assassinations. Intelligence suggests that the...

Mike paused. "Gene, list old Earth states." The screen filled with hundreds of names and scrolled with more.

"Stop. No one ever uses Wisconsin. It will do." Mike resumed typing.

...Wisconsin Separatist Front has been developing a creature for use in covert operations. The general populace must be kept unaware of this ability in the hands of a hostile splinter group to avoid panic. You are instructed to confiscate all evidence of this weapon's existence. The central I.I.B. lab will arrange for pick up within two days. All witnesses will be encouraged to silence with means reflecting your best discretion.

Intelligence Interagency Bureau Director.

Admiral Shawn More.

Mike scanned the security memo. "Gene, send this to Allen Majors in the set region, security scramble three.

Then get me a voice channel to Allen Majors and put the keywords up on screen five."

One of the side screens filled with text. 'Identifier - CASINO ROYALE, JASON BOURNE, BOND.'

'Acknowledgement – Q, UNCLE, RED.'

Michael rolled his eyes as an old-time phone ringing came through the speakers. "Hello, Majors' Extermination. If you've got bugs, we've got you covered."

"Mr. Majors, this is the *Casino Royale* calling. My friend *Jason Bourne* recommended you as someone who was *bond*ed to work on my kind of pest problem." Mike waited.

"I have quite a *Q* right now, but I could put back a job I'm doing for my *uncle*. He'll see *red*, but I can do it."

"Commander. I am the Chief Director of I.I.B. I have sent you a file. Encrypt A. Shift 13. You must do everything in your power to deal with the situation. End communication."

Mike pressed a button that closed the line and moved on to dealing with the next disaster.

Allen sat at his desk in the nondescript office. Outside, the employees of his extermination business were putting equipment away for the night. Two-thirds of them had no idea who they really worked for. The third that did were as skilled in dealing with insect infestations as human ones.

He closed and locked his door, then moved to his desk, pulled out his drawer, and pressed a hidden button. His cybernetics twitched as the anti-surveillance field swept over him, then he turned on his computer.

In his e-mail was a message from a lawyer named Fritz Blunt saying that a long-lost relative had left Allen a fortune and requested his banking information. He opened the attachment. His screen filled with gibberish. He ran a file hidden on his hard drive under five subheadings. The screen resolved to a picture of a six-legged beast and a jumble of nonsensical letters. Allen typed in shift 13.

Each letter in the text moved thirteen places clockwise in a loop of the alphabet. The message became comprehensible. He read it twice, then erased the file.

Opening his office door, he called out. "Theodore, William, Abdul, put on your good suits. A grateful client is treating us to dinner at the Skyfall."

Three of his employees passed their tools to the others and moved to the locker room.

Allen pulled a tube out of his desk, squirted the contents into his hand and rubbed it into his hair, which became a sandy brown colour. He wiped off his hands and started to change clothes.

Ryan piloted the *Star Hawk* to a position behind C-132, then activated the bow grav laser, pulling against the comet while at the same time using the stern grav lasers to latch onto masses out-system to slow the ship's momentum. The ship shuddered.

"The comet is slowing." Rowan watched her monitors. "The impact site is shifting north away from Kangra-la. Wait. It's speeding up again and pulling back to the collision."

"Expected." Ryan upped the pull, maintaining the *Star Hawk*'s deceleration while slowing the comet.

"The comet is deviating again. It's correcting." Rowan watched her monitors.

"Is this going to damage the ship? It's like being the rope in a tug of war," asked Tim.

"The *Star Hawk* was built to slip past enemy blockades. Do you think this is the first time someone has pulled a stunt like this? My girl will take it with integrity to spare." Ryan spoke without taking his eyes off the piloting board.

"I'm picking up sycamorezoid chatter. They aren't even bothering to encrypt it," stated Kitoy.

"Translate it and put it on." Ryan adjusted his pulls,

forcing the sycamorezoid ship on the far side of the comet to commit more power to its pull to keep the comet on its destructive course while slowing the *Star Hawk* so that the distance between it and the comet increased.

A deep, guttural voice sounded onto the bridge. "It makes no sense. It must be the *Homo sapiens* ship pulling against the comet."

"It makes no difference. It is one small ship. They cannot match your pull."

"Can we locate the ship? Missiles would deal with them."

"We might locate their line of travel, but they could be anywhere along it for ten light seconds and charting the deviations would take our computers hours. These ships are seed pods in a winter wind."

"On that, we agree. The comet has slowed again. I am committing more power to its acceleration, but I am nearing my maximum pull."

"Understood."

Seconds passed as the tug of war continued. On the big screen, Ryan watched as a second ankylosaur took position in a parallel spot to the first. The comet accelerated as the second ship hovered still against the backdrop of Murack Five.

"This is better than I hoped." Ryan committed more resources to pulling back on the comet while maintaining his ship's deceleration.

"Hotty boss. We only have a couple of g of pull left in us," observed Henry.

Ryan raced to the engineering station and checked his systems.

"We'll do one more g, then leave it stable for... Rowan, how long before release?"

Rowan ran her numbers. "Five minutes if things stay constant. They'll have time to retarget on Kangra-la."

"Can't be helped. The kangazoids are going to have interesting skies tonight. With luck, none of it will reach the ground." Ryan returned to the piloting station and once more adjusted the pull. The *Star Hawk*'s speed relative to Murack Five dropped steadily as the comet pulled ahead.

Ziggy entered the bridge. "Both suits inspected, recharged and stowed, Captain."

"Thank you. Take gunnery. We may have some shooting to do."

Ziggy hurried to his station.

"Kitoy, call general quarters."

"Aye." Kitoy's voice echoed through the ship. "General Quarters, all aboard to emergency stations, brace for high g manoeuvres."

The comet accelerated.

"It's on a collision trajectory with Kangra-la," stated Rowan.

"Tim, be ready to dump heat into the built-up liquid nitrogen. Keep our internal temperature as close to norms as you can and restore our atmosphere to standard to accommodate the expanding nitrogen. The hull can take the heat, but I'd rather not be baked in the can. Everyone, when Tim does that, you'll need to pop your ears. Gum chewing is now permitted on the bridge." Ryan tightened the straps of his safety harness.

"Don't leave the gum stuck anywhere when you organics are done chewing. Cleaning up after you when you aren't disgusting is bad enough," added Henry as the rest of the crew strapped themselves in.

Minutes passed.

"Now," said Rowan.

Ryan stopped pulling against the comet and directed the gravity laser's full power into stalling the *Star Hawk*'s forward momentum.

The comet accelerated ahead under the effect of the ankylosaurs' grav lasers.

The *Star Hawk* shuddered as the inertial dampers reduced the effect felt by the crew by a factor of ten. Two point five gs of force pulled on them as they watched the main screen.

The comet blasted forward.

"What is going on? Full forward velocity, brace for—" The guttural voice of the sycamorezoid captain blasted out of the speakers.

The comet eclipsed the view of the ankylosaurs. The bow of one of the large, clumsy ships poked into view. The comet slammed into it, spinning it up and around, so it lay a wreck on the comet's surface.

"Five," announced Ziggy, who watched a timer on his board. "Four."

Escape pods started blasting away from the ankylosaur on the comet's side.

"Three." A host of escape pods came into view from the comet's front.

"Two." Explosions sent showers of various types of ice into space as the comet started impacting mines.

"One." The ankylosaur the crew could see erupted amidship as it attracted some of its own mines.

"Now!" In silence, the comet burst asunder, flying out in a nimbus of ice and rock. The ankylosaur on the far side became visible as it hurtled towards the planet beyond. Escape pods blasted away from it. Flashes of light filled the sky as the cometary matter impacted the mines. A piece as big as an oceanic cargo vessel slammed into the side of one of the ankylosaurs, accelerating the battered hull along its orbital access. The other ankylosaur hit the atmosphere along with a barrage of cometary materials. Streaks of light filled the screen.

"Targeting centre of blast," stated Ryan. The *Star Hawk* sped forward, still dumping momentum.

Mines exploded as the cometary matter sped out to orbit Murack Five. Where the comet had been was a hole like the centre of a giant doughnut made of powdered sugar.

"Distress, distress, distress," blared through the speakers in the sycamorezoid's guttural tones.

"Kitoy, kill the external audio." Ryan fought against gravity to pilot the ship. "Killing aft pull. Cycling pull to starboard fore at eleven gs."

"Ten degrees to entry window. Entering thermosphere," announced Rowan.

The *Star Hawk* shifted its momentum to glance across the planet's curve. The remaining ankylosaur rounded the planet, using its gravity lasers for maximum acceleration. It hit the expanding cloud of debris. A second later, it slowed its acceleration. Five seconds later, it was dead in space.

"Grav drive efficiency decreasing. You've made a real mess out there, hotty boss."

"Come on, girl. I'll give your ports a nice cleaning when we hit ground. If we don't hit ground," muttered Ryan.

"Two degrees to entry window," said Rowan.

Flames licked over the main viewscreen as the *Star Hawk* shook and bucked.

"Entering the mesosphere," announced Rowan. "Angle is good. We should miss the ground, I hope."

"Internal temperature rising. Compensating," announced Tim.

"Activating anti-grav at zero net attraction. Initializing scram jets for braking manoeuvre. We're coming in hot," said Ryan.

"Stardust!" Rowan and Henry swore in unison.

"What?" Ryan worked his board to let the atmospheric buoyancy still the ship's fall.

"Piece of comet as big as a house. Missed us by fifty meters," explained Rowan.

"Will it impact the surface?" Sweat beaded on Ryan's brow as the bridge became uncomfortably hot.

"Internal atmosphere restored to norms. We're thirty degrees Celsius and rising," observed Tim.

Rowan quickly ran the numbers. "It will impact the ocean, but it will be small. A minor tidal wave well away from Kangra-la."

"Thirty-five degrees Celsius," announced Tim.

"Entering stratosphere." Rowan looked to the main screen, which showed a sunrise approaching at an impossible speed.

The sun flashed across the viewscreen as they transited to the plant's day side.

"Entering troposphere." Rowan's voice held fear.

"I told you to wear your brown slacks for this. Killing anti-grav. We'll let the planet pull against our momentum." Sweat poured off Ryan.

The *Star Hawk* blasted over the ocean as it ascended relative to the planet.

"Henry, record surface rad levels. I'll review them later." Ryan watched the screen.

Physics behaved as it always does, and in minutes a much slower *Star Hawk* popped into the stratosphere as a series of sonic booms shook Murack Five.

"Internal temperature forty degrees Celsius and dropping," announced Tim.

"Henry, take the pilot's board." Ryan stood and moved to the engineering station. "Grav laser ports need a clean, but aside from that, we're in good shape," he announced as he returned to the pilot's station.

"We are dropping towards planetary surface," observed Rowan.

Ryan reduced the *Star Hawk*'s gravity profile, slowing their fall. "Rowan, plot an atmospheric course to Kangrala." Ryan stared at the main screen. They were transiting to the planet's dark side. The upper atmosphere was alive with streaks of light. "Do it in the mid-troposphere. I don't feel like getting bonked on the head."

PROBLEMS ADDRESSED

Mike slipped in the back story of Fran's mother being a researcher who'd worked for the Wisconsin Separatist Front who was in witness protection.

"That should knit up the bombing. The Sun Valley authorities will pass it back to the national level, a.k.a. S.E.T.E. administration," Mike explained to Troy, who'd come in for his shift and found Mike neck-deep in the bedlam of fixing John's mess. Fetching a second chair had been his first task. Then, as Troy did the routine monitoring and reviewed the complaints file, picking out the items still to be dealt with, Mike kept up a verbal stream of consciousness, educating the younger man.

Outside, day had turned to night.

"Farley isn't doing well. I don't think he's going to make it," Troy warned as he watched the surrogate's board.

"I have Ulva dealing with it."

Allen got out of the black SUV he kept in a secret room of the sewage treatment plant. He was in a black suit and had a nine millimeter pistol in a shoulder holster. His three special employees got out with him. They were all similarly dressed, and each had changed their hair colour and wore dark sunglasses. The broad, concrete steps that led up to the glass and aluminum doors of the Sun Valley police station stood in front of them.

Allen took pleasure in ignoring the no parking sign. The

government plates on his vehicle almost guaranteed he wouldn't be ticketed and that if he was, he could burn it in front of the local cop with the audacity to do so.

"Come on." He led the way up the stairs and through the doors into a clean, modern-looking lobby, by early twenty-first century standards. Citizens stood in lines to talk to various uniformed desk personnel. He strode across the room to a counter where a desk sergeant was busy taking information from an elderly woman.

Allen pushed ahead of the woman. "Sorry, ma'am. Government business." He held his identification card out to the sergeant. "I need to talk to your watch commander. Now!"

The sergeant glanced at the identification, then Allen. "Aren't you the exterminator?"

"Twin brother. Now, the watch commander." Allen played the role to the hilt.

The sergeant looked at the ID again, then pressed a button on his desk, releasing an electronic lock on a door beside his workstation. "I'm sorry, ma'am. I'll be right back." He spoke to the elderly woman, then guided the government agents down a narrow institutional hallway.

They came to an area where doors lined the hall. The sergeant stopped at the door labelled 'Deputy Chief of Police Gordon Bullock'. The sergeant knocked.

"This had better be important!" snapped the muscular middle-aged man in a cheap suit who pulled open the door. His vaguely Asian features were drawn into a scowl.

Allen held up his identification. "I believe you have stumbled into a case under our jurisdiction."

"What... Who?"

"The attempted poisoning of your water supply, the bombing of the psychologist Gunther McPherson's home, and the attack on the apartment of Carl Perez by... creatures, are linked to the Wisconsin Separatist Front. A terrorist group my agency has been pursuing. I can answer your questions while my men secure Carl Perez and Fran

Maize."

"What do you intend to do with Carl and Fran? From what I can see, they are the victims here."

Allen nodded. He liked the Deputy Chief. The man's first instinct was to protect the innocent. "We'll debrief them, then take them to the young woman's apartment. I hear she is feeling poorly."

Gordon eyed Allen.

Allen relaxed his posture, allowing his chest to expand. "We're on the same side. I'm sorry if I came on strong with your sergeant. Time is of the essence."

"Come in. Do you want a coffee?" Gordon stepped out of his office doorway.

"No, thank you." Allen smiled. "I'd be up all night. Not that that will make a difference."

"Hear that. The city has gone insane." Gordon settled behind a large metal desk and smoothed his short grey hair. "Take a seat." He indicated a simple plastic chair on the other side of the desk.

"Thank you." Allen sat.

"So, what is happening?" Gordon leaned his elbows on his desk.

Allen shared his cover story. "Years ago, the young woman's mother worked on a project for the Wisconsin Separatist Front. She turned state's evidence in exchange for witness protection. That is when she and her family moved to Sun Valley. The W.S.F. recently completed a genetically enhanced attack dog. They couldn't risk detailed knowledge of its construction falling into our hands. The W.S.F. fears that Fran might know where the records her mother held back from us as a form of insurance are. The bomb was meant to target Miss Maize, as was the attack on her boyfriend's apartment using the bioweapon. My agency stopped the poisoning of the Sun Valley water supply and the attack on Mr. Perez's apartment. We lost one of our weapons during that battle. Have you found it?"

"The thing that blew out the wall?" Gordon drummed his fingers on his desk.

"It was set on low." Allen was deadpan.

"Oh-kuni-nushi, protect us from the folly of man!" Gordon sat back in his chair.

"I'll need it returned. I also need your people to stay mum about the genetic construct and kinetic rifle. Let people know that a combined task force of government agencies stalled a terrorist group."

"I'll tell my men, but there will be rumours."

"Rumours happen. My people will leave chemical residue from a common explosive around Carl's apartment. Have your forensics people do a sweep tomorrow afternoon. I'll be taking the genetic constructs and the kinetic rifle immediately. Have your people package the rest of the evidence. My people will pick it up in the morning." Allen leaned back and examined the ceiling.

"Fine. That closes three of my headaches. If you'll excuse me. There was a chemical spill in the industrial sector. Something that is making the people exposed loopy. I've had dozens of reports of monsters on the loose." Gordon looked at his computer screen.

Allen thought for a moment. "It could be another W.S.F. operation."

⚬━━⊰⊱━━⚬

Mike sat in the control room. "Gene, remind me to up Allen's on-set pay. He just planted a seed that makes sense of Hurast's behaviour and covers most of its consequences. By tomorrow the *Sun Valley Gazette* will have it all explained away."

"What are you going to do?" Troy watched through Gunther and Willa's eyes as Farley was loaded into what looked like a Sun Valley ambulance. Ulva was dressed as one of the three attendants. The doors closed, and the vehicle sped away.

"I'll circulate a story that an explosion released a toxin into the air. Gene, run the list of what they had in the twenty-first century that could go airborne and cause mental effects in *Homo sapiens*. Cross-reference what you get against chameleonzoid physiology, looking for mental effects." Mike leaned back in his chair, reviewing the next section of the quick log from John's outburst.

> Quinuclidinyl benzilate – *Homo Sapiens* = deliriant/hallucinogen – chameleonzoids = Rage Inducing – stockpiled as a weapon by various nation-states – powder suitable for atmospheric deployment.

Appeared on the screen beside the one Mike was reading.

"Perfect." Mike typed up a news dispatch about an accident at a military storage facility that released the hallucinogen. "Now Hurast can explain why she decimated her forces. It will also cover the random alien sightings by surrogates. The simplest trick to dealing with the multi-use nature of the set region is to give the populace a plausible scenario. People resist having their view of reality challenged." Mike went down the screen of complaints, removing a dozen of them.

"My mind's made up. Don't confuse me with the facts," Troy reflected.

"Exactly. It works in the real world as well. Look at politics." Mike sighed.

"What about Willa and Gunther? Will they accept the story of us taking Farley to a government lab for treatment?" Troy adjusted Quinta's control pack, letting a trickle of painkiller enter her system.

"That was for the *Angel Black* fans. I can't keep it from you, but it goes no further. Willa and Gunther know the truth about Sun Valley. They are part of *Freedom's Run*, as are the rest of the primary *Angel Black* cast members."

"Stardust!" swore Troy.

"Sun Valley serves a purpose in a larger game than entertainment. Watch Quinta. Otterzoids are sensitive to painkillers. You don't want to OD her."

Croell watched on the main screen of the *Mary* as C-132 blasted out in all directions, destroying two of the three large vessels orbiting Murack Five. Zandra's tongue flicked from her snake-like mouth as she lay her serpentine neck along her husband's. The red of her scales contrasted with the black of his. She could feel tension in the stiffness of his muscles.

On the screen, the *Star Hawk* blinked out of stealth and careened towards the planet, slowing at twenty-five g's.

"My husband. Ryan. He…"

"With a largely unarmed vessel, outnumbered and outgunned by a prepared foe." Croell couldn't tear his eyes away from the forty-second-old images. He shifted on the cushions he'd stacked on the space yacht's command chair in the middle of the horseshoe-shaped bridge so that the chair's arms didn't dig into his chest as much.

"He will burn up in the atmosphere. He is moving too fast." Zandra's voice was guardedly hopeful.

"We will soon know, but I will not underestimate that *Homo sapiens* or his ship. Look, the third pirate vessel."

On the screen, the third ankylosaur came into view. It sped towards the *Star Hawk*'s approach, slamming into the expanding cometary materials. It stopped accelerating. Jets of chemical propellant shot out, pushing the ankylosaur into a higher orbit. Orbital mines exploded across the screen, making flashes of light.

Seconds later, a streak of light larger and brighter than the others appeared in Murack Five's atmosphere and arced around to the day side and out of sight.

"I can only hope he burnt up. I do not relish facing him in the performance of our geasa. He has proven too skilled, too often," commented Croell.

Zandra rubbed her neck against his. "If he is alive on the ground when we arrive?"

"It changes nothing. We must bring the body of Rowan before John to fulfill our geis. Then there is the matter of our obligation to Hunoin. I can only ask of the Great Flyer of the Skies that Ryan be less skilled on the ground than amongst the stars. At least once he has left Ryan's ship, Pikeman will no longer be under his protection. Dispatching with that geis should be simple. When we die, we must be pure before the Great Flyer of the Skies. It is sad that our geis puts us at odds with Ryan and Rowan. If it did not, I would wish to call them friends."

Zandra flicked her tongue. "At least they have cleared the mines from our path."

"Yes. Luba, adjust our approach deceleration and vectors so we will enter on the dark side of the planet when the pirate vessel's orbit has carried it to the bright side. Against these pirates, Ryan and I have a common cause. I am sure he would not begrudge us a safe landing laden with relief supplies as we are. Ryan seeks to harm none other than his target."

What looked like a beautiful woman of mixed Asian-Caucasian descent sat at the pilot's station. "Adjusting course and deceleration."

"Luba, set scanning to detect any high-altitude objects in the Murack Five atmosphere."

"Scanner acuity is inadequate for visuals of such objects at this distance." The Luba bot spoke without inflection.

"An observation of movement is enough." Zandra watched the screen as the ankylosaur swung back and forth across its orbit using chemical jets. "Husband, what are they doing?"

"Collecting survivors. When I see Ryan, I must tell him of

this. Knowing there were survivors will be a comfort to him. What a vengeance proxy he would have made, and to think, a *Homo sapiens*." Croell flicked his tongue. "I shall have to write a symphony to his honour."

They watched the screen as flashes from cometary debris and exploding mines dotted the atmosphere of Murack Five. A dot cut a course across the planet's night side towards Kangra-la.

"He made it," observed Zandra.

"Space Mink. The felinezoids named him well. Luba, how long until we enter orbit around Murack Five, and how long after that for atmospheric insertion?"

"Twenty-seven hours, thirty-seven minutes and ten minutes, respectively," spoke the robot.

"Your reprogramming of John's toy is masterful, my love." Croell slipped out of the command chair.

"We do what we can. Where are you going?"

"Quarters. The bed is the only comfortable spot on this *Homo sapiens*' toy."

Zandra flicked her tongue and puffed her wings as much as the bridge's confines allowed. "I'll join you. Twenty-seven hours is a long time, and we must not let things distract us when it is time to act."

Croell flicked his tongue. "With one wife like you, I need no others."

"I will enjoy exclusiveness while I may, my husband. Males do have their limits." Zandra tucked her wings and left the bridge.

Ryan increased the *Star Hawk*'s specific gravity by reducing the antigrav, allowing the ship to drift downward. The scram jets barely turned over to counter the wind so that the ship stayed stationary relative to the ground, save for its descent. The colossal triangle carved from the glacier that was Kangra-la stretched out before them. They were just down from its inland point. The ice walls to either side rose, blocking the wind. Ryan killed the jets and deployed the landing legs.

"Legs read down and locked, hotty boss," said Henry.

"Put main screen to bottom," ordered Ryan.

Rowan adjusted the view screen. They all watched as the *Star Hawk* settled on a rocky barren.

Ryan killed the anti-gravity. The *Star Hawk*'s mass settled fully on its landing legs. "Put the screen forward. Everyone, lock down your stations."

On the main screen, sentients of several Republic species shuffled from a crude village of emergency shelters. Beyond the village, kangazoids were abasing themselves in a fallow field. Past them was a configuration of woven branches that mimicked the shape of the *Star Hawk*.

"What does that look like to you?" asked Tim.

Ryan sighed and continued the pilot's after-flight checks. "Trouble! Pilot's station checks green." He stood and moved to engineering.

"Computer is green as sexy little otterzoids," said Henry.

"I have a message coming in," announced Kitoy.

"Put it on."

"Thank the Divine, this is Murack Five Relief Station Alpha, Director Muperr Trapsetter speaking. I can only hope you are the supply vessel."

"Kitoy, put me on. Murack Five Relief Station. This is the *Star Hawk*, Captain Ryan Chandler speaking. We have relief supplies. We'll be out as soon as safety checks are done. Until then, please keep your people back. The trip in was... eventful. We may have something stuck on our hull."

"Affirmative, I'll pass the word. Was the light show your doing?"

Ryan rubbed the back of his neck. "There will be time for stories when we're face to face. I'll climb down and talk to you."

"Why climb?"

"We're full of supplies. The only stardusted hatch I can get to is top."

"*Star Hawk*, you don't know how happy that makes me. Do you have medical personnel aboard?"

"Blair Pikeman, a *Homo sapiens* medical specialist with experience in other sentient species, and Yipya, a k-no-in veterinarian."

"Can you send them immediately? I have beings in desperate need."

"Understood. We'll expedite matters. Kitoy, kill the signal. Call Pikeman and Yipya. Tell them to prepare emergency packs and be ready to climb down the ship's side. Engineering checks done. All green except for the grav port cleaning."

"Navigation green across the board," added Rowan.

The others finished their checks in sequence.

"Pikeman is saying he isn't a chimpanzee and won't climb," relayed Kitoy.

"Tell him he can climb down or be carried down, and Wispy might drop him!" Ryan took a breath. "I'd like to sleep a good eight hours, but it sounds like the folk out there are very happy to see us."

Rowan adjusted her screen to show a pair of k-no-in close against the *Star Hawk*'s side. The ice wall cast a long shadow, but towards the valley's wide end, the sunlight was a quarter of the way down the western wall.

"I thought I told those fools to wait," snapped Ryan.

"Desperate people don't always hear that well." Rowan shifted the shot to a mixed crowd of *Homo Sapiens* and felinezoids shuffling towards the *Star Hawk*. As the image closed, Ryan could see that they all looked malnourished, the felinezoids worst of all.

"Right. We unload enough rations to feed the camp today. Medical supplies, if we can reach them, then we sack out. We'll only have three hours of sunlight at this latitude and time of the year. I don't want anyone working tired and in the dark." Ryan moved to the bridge door.

Minutes later, Ryan secured a rope to the lockdown clips on the top airlock and tied its other end to the bag and dolly that contained the portable loading ramp.

Wind whipped around him, cold enough to numb his fingers. Hand over hand, he lowered the ramp dolly until it vanished over the side. He released rope until the line was slack and then let it drop. Using another length of rope, he secured a pair of grav lifters on his back. The long tubular devices were just under his height, each as thick as his wrist. Stifling a yawn, he started down the line. The temperature increased as he dropped into the ice canyon.

Reaching the ship's edge, he climbed down the rope the last three meters to the rocky ground. Here it was as warm as a pleasant spring day.

"Captain Chandler," greeted Muperr Trapsetter. The felinezoid was tall, even by the standards of his species. His tabby-stripe fur was patchy, and you could count his ribs. His gold sash of office was grubby, and his eyes rummy.

"Yes. Director Trapsetter, I presume. Excuse me." Ryan pulled his handheld from his pocket and folded it open to cover his shock at the director's appearance. "Henry, tell the others to come down if they can handle the rope. Otherwise, to wait until I get the cargo ramp set up. Open the hangar bay doors and the cargo transfer hatch and extend the link rails."

Above Ryan, a hatch in the left stern of the ship opened. A set of four rails forming the corners of a cube over a meter on all sides extended. There was the sound of hydraulics as the hangar bay ramp descended.

A dark shadow bounded from the upper surface of the *Star Hawk*. A second later, Krakkeen landed on the rocky ground. He had four grav lift tubes strapped to his back.

"It is so good to move," announced the spiderzoid.

"This is Krakkeen. He's an exo-botanist and one of the best packers in the galaxy." Ryan smiled to see the spiderzoid capering like a child let out to play. "Krakkeen, we'll need your help unpacking the hangar bay. Anything in the way that's for the auxiliary sites, put to the ship's port. Anything for the main camp put to the starboard. Get the food directly to the mess. Does that suit you, Director?"

"My people will help as we are able." The felinezoid swished his tail, which caused fur to fall out in a haze.

There was a scrambling noise from above. Rowan lowered herself to the ground by the rope. "I guess some of us haven't been out of the trees for as long as others," she quipped.

Ryan smiled. "Go help Krakkeen get the hangar bay started. It should go smoothly once we get the bits he suspended for the flight."

Rowan nodded and jogged towards the front of the ship.

"She is your crew?" asked Director Trapsetter.

"Navigator and trading officer." Moving below the tracks, Ryan unfolded and attached the loading ramp he'd lowered from the *Star Hawk*. He then grasped two grav lifts and walked up the ramp.

As this happened, Wispy hurtled off the ship onto the side of the ice canyon, then leapt, doing a barrel roll before landing in front of the hangar bay's ramp.

"The loading ramp is set up. Somebody, bring me the rope. I'll tie off this end," yelled Ryan as he positioned the grav lifts in front of the tracks. "Henry, the first E.S.T.C., please."

The meter-cubed E.S.T.C. came along the trackway and slid onto the grav lifts. A k-no-in female with stunted white fangs walked up the ramp and waited as Ryan pulled the cargo unit away and turned it so she could grasp the lifts. Ryan took a moment to scan the box. "Heater parts."

The k-no-in grunted and moved down the ramp. A rope dropped beside Ryan, and he tied it to the loading ramp's railing. Ziggy descended the side of the *Star Hawk* with two grav lifts strapped to his back. Ryan took the lifts and positioned them. "Henry. I'm ready for the next module."

A second E.S.T.C. slid out of the *Star Hawk*. Ryan

scanned the bar code on its side.

"U.E.S. ration packs. Ziggy, get these to the mess."

A high-pitched squeal of joy sounded above as Asalue leapt from the edge of the *Star Hawk*. The batzoid's cybernetic wings unfurled. He awkwardly glided to the ground, landing in front of the stone wall surrounding the relief workers' village. He folded his wings and jogged back towards the *Star Hawk*.

Kitoy was the next down the rope with grav lifts. Another box was dispatched to the mess.

Pikeman was next, carrying a pack of medical supplies. He vanished down the ramp as an emaciated *Homo sapiens* woman in tattered clothing mounted the ramp with the grav lifts the k-no-in had taken. She descended with an E.S.T.C. of solar panels.

Yipya came down the rope with three huge field medical kits strapped to his body.

"I am prepared to do what I may for the sick and injured," announced Yipya as his feet hit the ramp.

"Director Trapsetter will tell you where to go. Look for the tallest felinezoid you've ever seen." The sun reached the corner of the eastern ice wall, flooding Kangra-la with a dazzling radiance. Ryan paused to look out over the refuge. Villages of small huts dotted the ground. Kangazoids still crowded the nearby fields, heads bowed. Several relief workers had strung a rope marking how close the kangazoids were allowed to come.

One of the relief workers brought a battered pair of grav lifts Ryan didn't recognize, but they worked, so the k-no-in departed with a case of rations.

Krakkeen bounded to the open hangar bay and scrambled up to the line of goods he'd secured over the hatch. Thrusting the grav lifts into a Felinezoid United Worlds Standardized Shipping Unit, he lowered the cat box to the ramp. Rowan caught the lifts, increased the anti-grav and guided the box off the ramp. She checked the bar code with her handheld and then moved the item to the ship's starboard side.

Krakkeen looked down as a felinezoid passed him a fresh pair of grav lifts. He moved on to the next container. Wispy appeared on the ramp. He lifted three crates from a stack and carried them to the ground.

Yipya followed a small, emaciated felinezoid female with patchy cougar-tan fur into the relief workers' village. Everything was worn, and there was the smell of sickness. The housing consisted of boxy emergency shelters. A single larger building dominated the middle of the compound. It was constructed of polycarbonate linking bricks, but dirt and mould stained the outside. At the end of the village's single street, an atmospheric heater hissed and released an unhealthy ozone smell.

"In here, please." The felinezoid opened the door of one of the emergency shelters.

Yipya squeezed through the narrow door into a chamber three meters long by three wide. The back was dominated by a waste collection system with a fold-down sink above it. To his right was a cot just over two meters long. A felinezoid male lay on it. His breathing was laboured, and his cougar tan fur had fallen out in mats.

"Please help him," pleaded the female.

Yipya studied his patient. The k-no-in was a vet, and he had sadly seen the like of this before. "You haven't been feeding him right."

"We ran out of rations six months ago. We've..." The female felinezoid stopped mid-sentence and lashed her tail. "We had to make do with native food. It is not as bad for the k-no-in. They are close to this miserable place's biochemistry. *Homo sapiens* can eat practically anything, but even they are having problems. For felinezoids and otterzoids, we have been starving from a lack of key nutrients and poisoned by trace elements in the foods we can eat. We ran out of vitamin supplements months ago. It has gotten worse since then." The female's voice held pleading.

"Bad breeding!" swore Yipya as he opened his pack and prepared an injector. "I am going to give you both a general nutrient shot. Then I want you to go to the mess. If there are any felinezoid rations, get a pack and feed him a tenth of it immediately. An hour after that, feed him two-tenths, then an hour after that, three-tenths, then four. Take a pack for yourself and eat half of it now and half when you are hungry again. If anyone tells you not to, tell them I have ordered it. I will check on your…"

"Mate. We signed up to help together. I wish we never had. We wanted to honour my brother who died during the war here." The female gazed lovingly at the stricken male.

"I will check back on your exclusive client as soon as I am able." Yipya tapped his leg claws on the floor.

"Thank you." The female's nose was running as Yipya injected them both.

"Show me to the next patient and send someone else to be my guide. You will be busy caring for your client."

The female looked at the k-no-in with adoration and led him from the shelter.

Pikeman slipped into the emergency shelter and practically gagged with the stench. A grey-skinned *Homo sapiens* lay on the cot. Her leg was missing from the knee down, and bandages were wrapped around her chest.

"What happened to her?" Pikeman knelt beside his patient and began cataloguing her injuries.

"She was collecting microflora samples, and a Grauall attacked. They're like a six-legged polar bear," explained a thin man who looked to be in his middle years. His clothing was patched, ragged, and dirty, and his dark skin had a shallow grey quality. "There aren't many large predators left, but a few have held on because their forebears were in hibernation during the worst of the radiation. They are always hungry and vicious. By the time I drove it off, her leg was gone. Our primary medic died last year. We did our best, but we're out of almost everything."

Pikeman tried not to breathe. The smells of rot and infection permeated the shelter. "I will start with a broad-spectrum antibiotic. I will also use a sealant on these wounds. When my equipment is ready, we will see about regenerating the leg. I will start an IV to hydrate her and get some sugars and electrolytes into her system. When she regains consciousness, feed her a quarter of an M.R.E. Two hours later, wake her and feed her a half. Two hours after that, repeat the half ration, then two hours after that, three quarters, then two after that a full ration. I will be back to check on her as my duties allow. She is fortunate I was not a day later. Even I cannot raise the long dead."

The last rays of sunlight reflected off the bottom section of the eastern ice wall of Kangra-la. Ryan pulled down a final E.S.T.C., scanned its bar code and walked it to the village's common building.

He saw his crew slogging in the same direction and joined them. Ziggy yawned, and Kitoy followed his example.

"How much to go?" asked Tim.

"We've gotten through maybe an eighth of it. They need every box and more from the looks of things. This is horrific!" Ryan scanned the squalor of the village.

Rowan moved to his side and pulled his arm around her. He paused to look at her and pulled her into a hug.

"We're here now. We'll make it right." A shudder ran

through him.

Rowan backed off to regard him. "It's all lost on you."

"What?" Ryan regarded her.

"I'm standing on an alien planet." Rowan reached down and picked up a rock the size of her fist. "I'm holding an alien rock. Okay, I thought I was on Earth, but I was really on Gaia, and I've been on spaceships and a space station as big as a small planet, but this." She tapped the rock. "You grew up knowing it was a possibility. I was created knowing it wasn't. Even after the pirates attacked, I never thought I'd visit alien worlds."

"Rowan, I love you, but not now. Please, not now." Ryan tried to push his dread and fatigue aside.

"What?" Rowan looked shocked.

"This." Ryan waved around him. "This is Murack Five. All the death. All the…"

"You seemed all right," observed Rowan.

"As long as I can bury myself in doing something, I can hide from it, but my guts knot up every time I stop. I feel like I have a fever, and an icy claw is gripping my heart. I have palpations, and dread is running up my spine. I don't know if I can do this. All I want is to run back to the *Star Hawk* and blast into orbit."

"And here I am asking you to drop everything and hold me up over something no more important than losing my virginity. Reality check, Rowan." Rowan shook her head. "You need to look after yourself right now. Some things you think will be huge, life-changing, then the next day, you get up, shower, dress and nothing has changed. I know you're hurting right now, but I think this might be like that. I'm here for you no matter what."

"Thanks. I know it's foolish, but the dread won't go away." Ryan hugged himself.

"Do you know what I dread? I dread that I will wake up and discover that this was all a dream. I don't want that. Not anymore. You gave me so many gifts, gifts of life and living. It's time I gave you a few, so think of me. Whether

I'm holding your hand or a planet away, I'm here for you."

Ryan took her hand. "You are a dream. I'm sorry I had to bring you to this nightmare." He glanced around again.

Rowan saw what her fatigue and self-involvement had kept her from noticing. The hard line of Ryan's mouth, the tension in his stance. He was fighting to hide his anxiety because he was the captain, and the captain must be strong.

"Murack Five isn't as bad as I feared it would be. Getting here gave me time to brace. I still want to get away." Ryan forced himself to breathe.

Rowan hugged him. "We will, and I'm here."

Ryan forced a calm demeanour. Hand in hand, they entered the common building where beings of three species ate in absorbed silence.

DIVINE DUTIES

16

Ulva rode beside Farley in the ambulance. They cut through the streets of Sun Valley and out past farms and forests. The road came to an end on a field of flat rock. A hum ran through the ambulance as the anti-gravity kicked in and small jet engines hidden around the back activated.

"Quinta?" whispered Farley.

Ulva lay her hand on his brow. "She's all right. Gunther is looking after her."

"G-g-g-good." Farley lapsed back into unconsciousness.

"How is he doing?" Ulva wiped sweat off her hand onto the leg of her uniform pants.

The lean, pale-skinned, twenty-something ambulance attendant beside her glanced at Farley's readouts. "Not good. The lavage lowered the toxin level, but not enough. Ask me, this isn't worth the cost. Farley is a joke. Without Rowan, he isn't important to the series. I could see it if it was one of the good characters. But Farley?"

Ulva looked at the ambulance attendant with distaste. "He's a human being."

"Oh, you're one of those. We'll agree to disagree. I've been told to keep it alive until I hand it off to the studio medical engineers, and that is what I'll do." The ambulance attendant adjusted an instrument. "I've upped the number of anti-toxin nanobots in his system. It's not good to have so many, they can clog blood vessels, but he won't make it to the studio facility if I don't."

Ulva leaned over Farley. "You hang on. We'll fix you up."

The ambulance attendant shook his head. "Why are the hot ones always nuts?"

Mike leaned back in the controller's chair and sipped a coffee. On the secondary screen in front of him, Allen unloaded a k-no-in corpse from the back of his SUV into a walk-in freezer hidden in one of the sewage treatment plant's buildings. With no one to see, he used the strength of his cybernetics to lift the alien body.

A light flashed on Mike's console, and he pressed a button.

"Go ahead, Stan. I'm wrapping up. Troy's in the WC." Mike spoke to the air.

"*The Station House* team have got the toxins back in the facility. The water toxicity is within tolerance. James, my watch commander, has been briefed about the terrorist group by Assistant Commissioner Bullock. He'll tell the rest of my guys. They should take care of telling the press. I have to say, the Wisconsin Separatist Front was inspired! Fits with the period. They always had some bunch trying to screw things up back then."

"Inspired... maybe. It will take a *Cyborg Spy* miniseries to wrap the mess up. Fortunately, most of the equipment we'll need is in storage, and the principal surrogate has been underutilized, but it's still going to cost, and I don't have anybody free to run it."

"I always liked that series. A revisit with Sun Valley being decommissioned might be a money-maker. Have you thought of asking Frank to come back and run it?"

"He's happily retired." Mike fiddled with one of Fran's controls to promote pleasant dreams.

"Not so happy. We stay in touch. His grandson got in with a bad crowd. He pulled his head out of his backside, but not before crashing his father's land vehicle through Frank's house. Between legal fees and repairs, it wiped out a big chunk of his savings. I could ask him if he'd like to come back for a revisit. A bunch of the other guys from that era would probably come back, at least part-time, to bump up their savings and keep their hand in."

"No harm in asking. It will be one less headache for me. Between Sun Valley closing, the Kemetic region opening, and *Freedom's Run*, I'm swamped. I'm not certain how I'll keep Sun Valley profitable while it times out." Mike leaned back and closed his eyes.

"You open to a suggestion?" Stan's voice was quizzical.

"Shoot."

"Go through the cancelled shows and use phasing out Sun Valley as an excuse to revisit anything that seems suitable. Most of your best talent will shift to the Kemetic set region anyway. Not anything too grandiose. A bunch of half-seasons that let people touch base with old friends. Use as many retirees as you can. Most who've been out of it for a few years would probably like to relive the glory days. Pair them up with students fresh out of college. It would be a good learning experience and could bring on the new crop of talent."

Mike smiled without opening his eyes. "Stan, you just got *The Eyes of Pharaoh* approved. That is a great idea. I don't know why I never thought of it."

"Hard to see the beaver dam when you're chin-deep in the swamp. My controller is giving me the stink eye, so I should go."

"Dad! I am not giving him the stink eye, Mr. Strongbow. It took both of us to keep things from going haywire. Oh yes, I didn't get to tell you how much I loved *Freedom's Run* at the launch. I always thought Rowan was underutilized on *Angel Black*," spoke a female voice.

"Thank you, JoAnn. I'll let you go now. I have calls to make." Mike closed the line as Troy entered the control room.

"The place is buzzing about John going off the deep end." Troy moved to his chair and scanned his boards. He adjusted Willa's system, pushing her into a deeper sleep.

"Gunther will have to get up soon for work," observed Mike.

"He can. She needs her sleep. She forgets she's partially organic and relies on her cybernetic systems too often." Troy spoke with a note of affection.

Mike nodded. "You're getting it, my young apprentice. I'm going to my office to lie down. When it's a decent hour, I have some calls to make."

"You idiot!" Hilda glowered across the metal desk of her tiny office. Screens with lists of presidents and case law filled the walls.

"But he..." John stood facing her, wearing the same clothing he'd worn when he was expelled from the S.E.T.E. grounds.

"You have ruined everything." Hilda stood up and started to pace.

"He was killing my show!" John's jowly face flushed red.

"And none too soon, I'm sure. John, we could have fought him on cancelling *Angel Black*. Gotten fan petitions going."

"He has no right!"

"Wrong. With Sun Valley being decommissioned, shows will be phased out. He has every right. If we could prove your show was picked for phase-out with malicious intent, we could have had a case, but I'm sure Mike will have all his ducks in a row. We won't have any sympathy with the public after your stunt. Trying to decimate Sun Valley years early will hit them where they live. People obsess about the shows, and you tried to kill their escape. May as well steal a junkie's fix and then ask them for a loan. Most fans will applaud your expulsion if they pull their heads out of their fantasies long enough to become aware of your actions. Mike is sure to let what you did out to at least the entertainment magazines and trades. If he can play himself up as the hero who saved the studio, all the better for him. You have vilified yourself. If your tantrum had worked, all the Sun Valley storylines would be cancelled. The studio profits would plummet, but with the Kemetic set region less than a year from start-up, they'd rebound. All the major investors will know that and cleave to a known quantity to ensure their investments. The goal was to vilify Michael in the public eye. You handed him a hero moment."

"What are you going to do about it?" demanded John.

"Me?" Hilda took a breath. "I will work on my other cases and wait until I see what officially is being done about your bone-head manoeuvre. Then if I can't see a way to salvage this mess, I am washing my hands of you."

"You can't." John slammed his fist into the top of her desk.

"I can. And I'll tell you this much. If I do keep you on, you will do what I say when I say it, and that is that. Maybe I can twist it around that the stress of Michael's abuses drove you to your actions. That his long-standing harassment and cruelty as an employer shattered your mind. That you are a poor, abused victim of a megalomaniacal, petty dictator."

"You're going to say I'm insane," John blurted.

"As things stand, the truth is the only card we have left. The only deception will be to blame it on Mike."

Ryan awoke in Rowan's bed. The starscape on her walls had been replaced by a springtime woodland glade. A deer moved into view and started grazing. He rolled over and put his arms around Rowan's sleeping form, letting her warmth push back the impending cold of his anxiety. She nestled into him, warm human flesh against warm human flesh. The panicking ape within settled.

"Hotty boss, you awake?" whispered Henry.

"What is it?" Ryan spoke softly.

"Director Trapsetter has been calling for over an hour. He wants a face-to-face."

Ryan kissed Rowan's shoulder. She stirred in her sleep. "If he's willing to climb up to the top hatch, give me a half-hour and guide him to the officers' mess. If he isn't up to the climb, tell him I'll meet him in the town hall in an hour. How long have I been out?"

"Ten hours."

"It's still night. What is the blasted rush? There has to be enough rations left for breakfast."

"He'll meet you in the mess. He's worried about the auxiliary posts."

Ryan nodded, stroked Rowan's side, kissed her shoulder and eased away from her. "I'll do a nano-clean and grab a fresh uniform before the meeting. Brief me on everyone's status as I de-stink myself." He rose from the bed and strode to the washroom that occupied half the wall opposite the quarters' entry door.

"Kitoy, Tim, and Ziggy are all sacked out. Sadly, not together."

Ryan relieved himself into a toilet reminiscent of what you would find in a twentieth-century commercial aircraft. "Give Tim and Kitoy time."

"You matchmaking, my sexy captain?"

"The man I raised is coming through the dross my parents and Earth covered him in. And my boy is no fool. Kitoy has issues, but who doesn't? I could do worse for a daughter-in-law."

"Funny universe, isn't it?" observed Henry.

"Insane, but it's all we got. How about the rest?" Ryan moved to the small sink built into the wall opposite the toilet and opened the mirrored cabinet above it, extracting what looked like a mouthguard. Popping the device into his mouth, he bit down. Thousands of microbots swarmed over his teeth and mouth, removing dirt and bacteria while repairing damage to the enamel and gums.

"Pikeman and Yipya are still treating patients. For all he's as appealing as herpes, Pikeman is dedicated. Trapsetter has had abandoned shelters cleaned out for them. They both called in for more medical supplies. Asalue has been flying rations to the auxiliary relief station on the coast of Kangra-la. He's tippy as a ground pounder on leave, but he's getting better with each flight. We did a good thing there."

The oral hygiene device let out a beep, and Ryan removed it. Rinsing it off in the sink, he put it back in the cupboard. "Losing some memories seems to have improved Pikeman. He and Yipya must be exhausted. Unfortunately, the way we're packed, we can't do much about how we offload. They'll have to make do with the supplies we can get to them. They can thank Star Searcher for that."

Ryan moved to a human-shaped depression in the wall opposite the WC's entry door and pressed his front into it, then pressed a button by his hand. Millions of flea-sized microbots swarmed out, covering his front, removing dead cells, dirt, excess oil, and harmful bacteria.

"Trapsetter would like to. I'm chatting him up with a separate ram segment. They've had problems with that crab.

"Krakkeen and Wispy have kept up with unloading the hangar bay. Along with a rotation of the relief workers. They've almost made a passage to the lift. They get that done, and I can get maintenance drones on the hull to scrub the grav laser ports and help shift cargo."

The microbot cleanser beeped.

"Good." Ryan turned around and pressed his back into the depression in the wall, then pressed the activate button again. The microbots swarmed out to do their job. "How many of the E.S.T.C. do you still need to offload before you can shuffle and sort on the rails?"

"Twenty more, and I can start. Thirty would be better."

"We'll need to sort the units for the auxiliary sites. Once we clear most of the hangar bay, we can toss the units for the auxiliary sites back in and do the rounds. Have the team focus on clearing one of the hangar's cargo rail ports. That will save us setting up the ramp at the auxiliary sites. I'd like to get those k-no-in aquatic habitat containers out of the bomb bay ASAP. They'll be the slowest to deploy, and we can drop most of them while Kangra-la is in darkness. I'd rather work with natural light. It's safer for unloading."

The cleanser beeped. Ryan stepped away from it into Rowan's quarters. She still slept. He paused to look at her. "Hard to believe that four months ago, she was a thing of fiction, a sensory input, a fantasy." Moving to Rowan's closet beside the WC, he opened it and pulled out his bathrobe. Donning it, he left the room for his quarters.

The captain's quarters were barren, with a standard roll-down couch/bed against one wall. General maintenance robots displaced by the cargo on the rail system littered the floor two deep, leaving a narrow passage to his closet and one of the end tables by the couch/bed, which was rolled up into its former position. Storage boxes were stacked along the couch/bed's top.

Tripping over the maintenance robots, Ryan retrieved his clothes and dressed. He scanned the boxes on his bed and shifted one so a scanner in the wall could read its bar code.

"Henry, what's in this one?"

"Felinezoid M.R.E.s. Two dehydrated buffalo-like herbivore and rara greens with blood powder hot beverage. Just add hot water. Two trout-like fish and praamasii root with dehydrated blood powder beverage. Just add water. Two—"

"Enough. It will do. Is the director on board?" Ryan started towards the mess, carrying the crate.

"Climbing down from the airlock as we speak. Nice tush if you like them skinny. I'll guide him in while you do the cooking."

Minutes later, Ryan pulled a food tray out of the reconstitution system and pushed it in front of Director Trapsetter.

"You are most gracious. I am sorry to have hurried you, but the situation is dire." Trapsetter pulled back the lid on the felinezoid M.R.E. and inhaled deeply before gulping half the reconstituted blood.

"Malnutrition. The supplies I brought will help with that." Ryan sat and opened a *Homo sapiens* M.R.E. revealing scrambled eggs, coffee, toast and jam.

Trapsetter nodded as he pulled on claw sheaths and sliced into his reconstituted buffalo-like herbivore. He chewed, then swallowed, obviously relishing every bite. "I never thought I would enjoy ground forces rations."

"It seems to be one of those things that is universal. Henry tells me you're concerned about your secondary stations. As soon as I have room to move around in my ship, I intend to do short hops to them, then come back here and finish unloading. Are your stations in the same places as your last report?"

"Yes. There has been little progress over the last year. We needed equipment. I know pirates took the other shipments. Has the Republic dealt with them?"

Ryan took a moment to swallow. "Inasmuch as I'm part of the Republic. A lot is going on."

Trapsetter swallowed and spoke in a serious tone. "Star Searcher is taking bribes from the sycamorezoid separatists."

"I suspect." Ryan bit into his toast.

"As do I. There is evidence in the lost resupply vessels and the obviously deliberate mistakes in the shipments. Even things as simple as lost mail. The dichrostigmazoids have tried to keep our lines of communication open, but all too often, they haven't received our messages to relay, or their signals have gone missing at the Switchboard end." Trapsetter popped a limp shoot of rara green into his mouth. "I must be vitamin deficient. I hate rara, and this isn't bad."

"*Homo sapiens* have a saying: hunger is the best spice." Ryan sipped his coffee.

"I will remember that. What do you intend to do about Star Searcher when you return to the Switchboard Station?"

Ryan used eating a forkful of eggs to give himself time to consider.

The door to the mess opened. Kitoy walked in. Trapsetter stood up as his tail went rigid.

"Hello, Director," greeted Kitoy.

"Hello, and please call me Muperr. Kitoy, wasn't it? I'm sorry we didn't have time to become acquainted yesterday."

"Too much work, too little time." Kitoy flicked her tail in a gesture both flirtatious and dismissive.

"Sadly true. It is so rare to find time for the important things."

"Like?" Kitoy practically purred.

"Appreciating beauty, enjoying the company of interesting beings, embracing pleasures." Muperr puffed out his chest and tried to make the best of his patchy fur and dirty gold sash of office.

"I find one can always make time for such things." Kitoy swished her hips and tail.

Ryan focused on his meal as the felinezoids conversed without using the translator nanobots. He managed to catch every seventh or eighth word.

Kitoy turned to Ryan. "Morning, where's Rowan?"

"Still sleeping. I didn't want to wake her. I loaded some felinezoid M.R.E.s into the cabinet. They're on the left side."

"Thank you. I'll review the communication logs after I've eaten." She looked at Muperr. "I find that communication is essential." She turned back to Ryan. "What's the situation in orbit?"

"Hey, hotty cat. One ankylosaur has survived. They've been picking up the escape pods."

"With luck, they'll leave to drop survivors when we're ready to depart. Keep an ear out for a sycamorezoid response and our shadow," ordered Ryan.

"Shadow?" asked Muperr.

"There is a space yacht bringing more supplies. They were following us in," explained Kitoy.

"That is wonderful, but... Captain, I have become adept at reading *Homo sapiens'* non-verbal communication. You do not look happy."

"There's a batzoid honour geis coming along with that other ship."

"Meat rot! You do have interesting problems. Though I may be able to detract from your batzoid problem. Those in the relief effort have immunity from all but Republic legal entanglements. Even the Batzoid Theocracy has agreed to this. Geasa are paused until after the term of service of whoever they are against." Muperr's eyes lingered on Kitoy as she went to collect her rations.

"I've heard that, but you know batzoids and the laws of other species. Still, it may help." Ryan sipped his coffee.

"I am glad I could lessen a burden because I sadly must add one."

Ryan finished the last of his food and rested his forehead in his hands. "Of course you do. What is it?"

"In short, Captain, you've been promoted to godhood."

"What!" Ryan felt the food in his stomach turn to rock.

"Knew you'd get there someday. Don't forget your old friends." Kitoy settled with her food tray.

"This isn't funny. The cultural contamination..." Ryan shook his head.

"The kangazoids were contaminated when we got here. The gopherzoids were not as good at keeping their distance as we might have hoped." Muperr watched Kitoy as she ate. His tail lashed, sending out a puff of loose fur.

"The famine made things worse. Before you say

anything, hear me out. If the aid workers die, the kangazoids die. We needed to eat. We… we did what we had to. One of those actions was to set up a system of tithing. The local foods are imperfect, but they are better than nothing."

Ryan sighed. "Desperate times. But what does it have to do with me?"

"We don't have translator nanobots for the kangazoid. The neuro-mapping hasn't been done. What we have managed is an audiovisual translation system. Their language is simple, combining perhaps a hundred and fifty words and an additional seventy or so gestures. We've been recording their mythology for the anthropologists."

Kitoy swallowed a bite of some kind of fish. "Asalue and Wispy will be happy about that."

"The batzoid and the large bug-like being?" Trapsetter pushed his tray away.

"Wispy is a waspzoid. The only one physically capable of sharing an environment with us. Would you care for another meal?" asked Ryan.

"I would, but it would be ill-advised after my recent forced fast. As I was saying, we have been recording the kangazoid myths. In the beginning, the earth lords lifted the kangazoids from the ground and made all good things."

"The gopherzoids." Ryan nodded.

"Then there are stories about natural phenomena and various animals. What matters is this one. It came to pass that the kangazoids became wicked and cruel. They killed the prey but did not eat the meat. They tore the plants from the soil and planted nothing in their place. The great Gramplik, their creator goddess, who looks suspiciously like a gopherzoid, decreed that they should be removed from the land of rivers and fields, their world."

"Fairly standard mythology from what I know. How the nova blast did I end up a god to them?" Ryan felt his ire building.

"This is it. Crach, the crippled god of mercy—you only

have four limbs—begged his mother, Gramplik, to let him save those kangazoids who were virtuous. Gramplik agreed. Crach came to the virtuous in his great sky raft and brought them to a place of safety where they might live. He then left, charging his servants to look after the kangazoids until his return, when they would once more occupy the land of rivers and fields.

"This is where we embellished the myth. The kangazoids already made offerings to their gods. We became the gods' servants who transported their offerings to the divine."

"And the statue of the *Star Hawk*?"

"They made that before we started taking tithes. Typical cargo cult. 'Crach' is as close to Captain Ryan Chandler as they can pronounce. They must have heard your name when you were saving them."

"It's a mess. Hopefully, they'll forget it before they develop writing." Ryan drummed his fingers on the table. "Frankly, it's not my worry today."

"There is a new twist. The kangazoids are saying that Crach has returned riding on the flames of heaven to restore them to the lands of their mothers."

"If anyone deserves the promotion, it's you. I pray you hear me, oh divine one." Kitoy flared her nostrils and hissed in a felinezoid laugh.

"Captain, given what you faced in rescuing the kangazoids, there was little you could do to avoid contaminating their culture. Do not blame yourself. I have learned that in desperate situations, you do the best you can." Muperr stared at the table with a haunted air. "And I am sorry that we capitalized on that contamination, but the survival of all involved depended on it."

"What's done is done." Ryan leaned back in his chair, looking resolved.

"Oh, divine, hotty boss, lord of mercy, four-armed master of—"

"Henry! You're going to need me to fix your hips someday. Think carefully about what you say right now!"

menaced Ryan.

"Fine, my sexy captain. I wanted to tell you that Wispy and Krakkeen have cleared a path to the primary lift. Isn't the news divine?"

"That's heavenly," chimed in Kitoy.

Muperr fought not to flare his nostrils at the expression on Ryan's face.

"Henry, wake everyone up and get ready to start unloading. We'll start when there is enough external light to see clearly. Kitoy, go to the bridge. Tell Pikeman and Yipya they have access to the medical bay. Then find Asalue. I want an update on the auxiliary village he's been visiting. Also, check with Wispy and Krakkeen that they aren't overdoing it. I know their sleep cycles are different, but I don't want them pushing themselves."

Muperr made a sneezing sound that caught Ryan and Kitoy's attention. "Pardon me, Captain, but Wispy and Krakkeen, not to mention Pikeman and Yipya, are my responsibility now."

Ryan looked at the felinezoid director, who towered over him.

"Your point is well taken, but we need to get the work done and not have any more injuries. I've had more experience with their capacities and limitations than you have. Thus, I ask for your indulgence." Ryan spoke slowly and softly.

Muperr found himself happy to oblige and had a sense he somehow gained a measure of dignity by siding with the *Homo sapiens*. "Of course, Captain. Now is not the time for a petty territorial squabble, especially when we are in accord."

Ryan smiled, touched his fingertips together and bowed where he sat. "Mraperrhistik."

Muperr returned the gesture, showing that his claws were sheathed. "Pramishass."

Ryan stood up. "I need to check some things on the bridge. When we lose the light at Kangra-la, we'll start the circuit of the auxiliary stations. Muperr, please feel free to take a couple of extra ration packs." Ryan left for the bridge.

"He was saying 'thank you', wasn't he?" asked Muperr when the door closed.

"His accent is horrible. But he tries." Kitoy swished her tail.

"He is like most legends. Both less and more face-to-face. I'm glad to meet the Space Mink as a friend," remarked Muperr.

"You'll get used to him. He's not always so stiff-tailed. Murack Five tugs his whiskers." Kitoy flicked her tail.

"That is common for those who were here for the disaster." Muperr's nostrils quivered.

"You served?" Kitoy let her eyes rake over the director.

"Ground forces pack leader for the southeastern continent. I was lucky enough to have set up my command base in the lee of a mountain range. Most of my troops weren't so fortunate." Muperr looked at the table, and his tail drooped.

"I'm sorry. Where do you come from originally?" Kitoy rushed to change the topic.

"I was born and raised in a small city, Ssssmaaa, on Mruu." Muperr forced his nostrils to flare.

"Really. I'm from Ssssmaaa. Go Hunters!" Kitoy swished her tail.

"You're a Hunters fan?" Muperr looked up, his eyes going wide and nostrils flaring.

"My father used to take me to the games." Kitoy's pupils dilated.

"Did you ever eat at the Snagged Tooth? It was a little den of a place by the stadium." Muperr sat straight in his chair.

"Juiciest goofla on the planet. Free bibs with every order." Kitoy made the nasal hiss that served as a felinezoid laugh. She shook her head, then sighed. "I need to get to the bridge. When things are more settled, we should talk about Ssssmaaa. I miss home sometimes. Henry, please guide our guest to the hangar ramp. No reason to scramble up and down from the top lock anymore." She stood, scooped the food trays into the recycler and left the room.

MORTAL HANDS

Farley opened his eyes. He lay on a soft surface. Tubes came out of his arms, legs, and a slit in his belly. The room seemed to spin around him.

"The fractional blood dialysis has removed the toxin. We've put stem cells into the burns on the forearms. There will be scarring with only one treatment, but he should regain full use of his hands. If he survives. The congestion around his heart is worrying. I've manipulated his electrolyte levels to lower that and added generic stem cells to his kidneys and liver to restore function. They'll probably outlast the rest of him. I'd say the odds are about ninety per cent for survival and seventy-five for regaining full function. I also took the liberty of halting a rejection process against his gills. The membranes in his eyes protected the cornea from the toxins, but the membranes will have to be replaced when he is stronger."

"Thank you, Doctor."

Farley turned his head to see a beautiful dusky-skinned woman talking to a medium-built man with brown hair and a pronounced nose. The man was dressed in surgical scrubs.

"Ulva, does Mr. Strongbow know how much this is costing? It seems a lot for a B-list character on a show past its prime," remarked the doctor.

"Michael said spare no expense." Ulva leaned close to the doctor. "I think he has plans for Farley."

"Mr. Strongbow knows best, I suppose. I need to set up a scheduled intervention on Jessica from *Defenders of the*

Crystal. Something went flooey with her control pack, and the total stock of blood coagulants and painkillers was lost. I'll be in room two if you need me." The man left the room.

Farley feigned sleep.

"Don't you listen to him. You did well stopping them from poisoning the lake. You saved Quinta. John built you to be a joke, and that's all most people see, but I see how hard you try. How hard it is for you with a power that only becomes useful once in a while. That thing with Angel was all John. He's off the show now. Mike will do right by you. I wish I could really talk with you. Tell you it will be all right, but this will have to do. Sleep easy, Farley, and get well." Ulva stroked his hair, and a large clump fell out in her hand.

Gunther spat the regulator from his mouth and floated in the same cave Farley had met Tony in. Blue lighting danced across the surface of the water.

"What have you done?" demanded an octozoid half again as large as Tony.

"Commander," a high-pitched squeal that hurt Gunther's ears followed. "This *Homo sapiens* has secrets to impart. All will be clear if you will open your mind." Tony hovered under the surface of the water.

"I would not do this but for the actions of Farley. He fought with much courage. I respect him. I feel it wise to make common cause with you defenders."

"Thank you, Commander... May I call you Napoleon? I cannot produce the sounds of your name."

"I have read your history. You honour me. Proceed with your information."

Gunther telepathically imparted the truth of Sun Valley.

"And you feel all this to be true?" The octozoid commander swished its tentacles.

"Yes." Gunther let his flotation vest support him.

The octozoid commander wrapped its tentacles tightly around itself. "Then there is no charge of mutiny facing me should I return to Buuuk."

"Everything is fiction." Gunther felt the turmoil in the commander's mind.

A stream of bubbles rose from the top of the commander. *"Homo sapiens*, Gunther. This is doom to my crew and me. The controllers will not extend our lives even if they can."

"They might if we can make a strong case. The studio head seems to want to help us."

"One sentient manipulating the cave's spawning to change." The commander unwrapped itself and flicked its tentacles. "He may make a place for his own kind, but for such as I and the other pirates... We were created as villains, and we have done things that mark us as such. We will be allowed to die. Perhaps in comfort, I do not expect more than that."

"I'm sorry."

The commander held up a tentacle. "There is peace in this truth. Many regrets and obligations may now drift on the current. I have no cave siblings to be shamed by actions I never took. I will continue our alliance on the 'show'. I will help you recruit from the other species. The struggle for dominance with Hurast will continue, but now I will certainly be victorious."

"Why?" asked Gunther.

"Because I need not look to a future. I can spend all my long-term resources today, for there is no tomorrow. There will be no spawnings. I suspected that would be the case because there have been none. I thought it was some deficiency in your world or of this location. I had hoped that your seas would better suit my kind. Now I know the fault is in the bodies we inhabit. There is no ship orbiting Jupiter to reinforce us. Though I suspected that they would have left already. The window for accessing a moving stargate from a system rarely extends for eight years."

"I'm sorry." Gunther felt a deep sadness in the commander. The pain of those who long for children and are denied by fate. He thought of Rowan, his daughter and for all she was technically adopted, it made no difference to their love. He could only pity the octozoid.

Rowan pulled an E.S.T.C. to the heater unit at the far side of the relief worker's village, lowered it to the ground, and extracted the grav lifts. "This is supposed to be spare parts for the heater units."

The slender, unkempt, fortyish *Homo sapiens* working to remove the unit's housing looked up at her. His blue coveralls were filthy. "Thank you. We've barely kept the units operational. If they go, this valley will freeze. Of course, it might not make much difference."

"Why?"

"We're almost out of antiproton. Originally the plan was to shift to safe energy forms, solar, wind, tide, that sort of thing. But with the lack of shipments, we haven't been able to set them up. The antiproton unit that was the short-term solution is down to one per cent. Is it true your captain is the Ryan Chandler? The one who made Kangra-la."

"Yes." Rowan started unlatching the panels on the box of spare parts.

"Cloned?" The question was deadpan.

"Is that a problem?" Rowan straightened and shifted into a defensive posture.

"Not anymore. Half the *Homo sapiens* on this rock are clones. I've learned what a fool I was. Did you hear about the dirty bombing of the set region on Gaia?"

"I must have missed that one." Rowan took a step back.

"There were six squads. We all had dirty bombs. We were going to strike a blow against the fakey menace. What idiocy! My team got caught before we were close. The court gave me a choice because they needed an engineering tech for the relief effort. Ten years on Murack Five, or twenty years on a terraforming farm. Boy, did I choose wrong!" The man hung his head. His limp, salt and pepper hair fell into his eyes.

"Are there a lot of people from your old group here?" Rowan glanced around nervously.

"Three left, and we've all grown up. Clones are people. My wife is a clone. My best friend is a k-no-in. A felinezoid saved my life. Humans Ascendant are fools! It's easy to be blind when you're raised knowing nothing else! The H.A.s that didn't figure that folk are folk didn't last. In a place like Murack Five, you need to rely on the sentients around you, and you can't do that and hate them."

Rowan's posture relaxed. "I came in with a lot of different species. I think everyone saved our bacon at one time or another."

"Way it should be. By the way, name's Kikkuli. Oh, stardust, will you look at that?"

Rowan leaned forward and gazed through the open panel at a mass of crumbling ceramic. "What is it? And it's Rowan."

"Rowan, pretty name. The heat dispersal core is shot. If this one is gone, the other heaters won't be far behind. Even if the crab sent all the replacement units we ordered, we wouldn't have enough to do all Kangra-la. Nothing for it. Could you pass me the one from the E.S.T.C.?"

Rowan moved to the box and looked at the parts in their mushroom-foam niches, pulling out what looked like a ceramic tube a little under a meter long.

"This?"

"Thanks." Kikkuli threw a line of switches to one side of the open panel and pulled the ceramic rod out of a pair of clips.

Rowan hugged herself as the temperature dropped. "Is there any way to repair the heat dispersal cores?"

"Not without a nano assembler. Ours burnt out two years ago. I checked the inventory. There's none in the cargo." Kikkuli pushed the replacement ceramic tube into the clips, then flicked the switches back on. Heat poured out of the device.

Rowan smiled. "What would you need if you had the nano assembler?"

"The old units and some calcium. Probably be enough to use the old ones and strip a couple for materials. But it's a moot point." Kikkuli stood up slowly.

"Kikkuli, let me talk to my captain. I think we may have made your day."

The tech's brown eyes lit up. "You have a nano assembler?"

Rowan smirked. "You don't know much about a Hawk class, do you? Miracles are their specialty. I'll talk to Ryan. You talk to your people. Find out what you need. I'm sure Ryan will do what he can."

"Divine bless you." Kikkuli closed his eyes on tears.

Pikeman yawned as he sealed the wound on the stump of the woman missing her lower leg. "I will need raw materials to regenerate your limb. Preferably from a U.E.S. source so that the mix of micronutrients and amino acids will match your biology."

The woman lay on a treatment cot in the *Star Hawk*'s medical bay. An E.S.T.C. sat open on the floor, and boxes of medical supplies covered the central treatment cot.

Yipya worked on a felinezoid female on the other open cot.

"I don't know where, outside the ration packs, we could get U.E.S. nutrients. The local biology lacks elements necessary for our species," observed Pikeman's patient.

"If you will be excusing me, Samantha?" Yipya injected his patient and absently petted her shoulder.

"Yes." Pikeman sounded sharp.

Yipya curled his lip, baring a fang. "Samantha, what have

you done with your dead?" Yipya refocused his attention on his patient, smearing ointment onto open sores.

"Innovative," remarked Pikeman.

"I don't understand?" Samantha looked nervous.

"I assume you have proper disposal for your dead so they will not contaminate the local environment." Pikeman finished putting a regenerative gel into the last of Samantha's wounds. Her infection was broken, and her dusky skin had lost its grey quality.

"Procedure is to bag them and put them on the ice to freeze with the intent of shipping them out with the supply ships." Samantha bit her inner lip. "My wounds feel much better."

"Of course," snipped Pikeman. "As to your leg. My nano-system can reduce the biological components of dead flesh to base proteins that stem cells can use to replicate your limb. I'll have to print off an intercellular matrix to support the living elements. I could do it even with the antiquated equipment in this joke of a medical bay. When my equipment is set up, it will be simplicity itself."

"You want to feed our dead to stem cells to make me a new leg?" Samantha sounded nervous.

"It is the final gift one can give to their species kin. All k-no-in gift their bodies to the betterment of their fellows," remarked Yipya.

"Long ago, many *Homo sapiens* did the same. It will have to wait. I want you healthy before I take cells for a stem cell culture. You will rest here for twelve hours, then I will revisit your condition. I am going to sleep in my shipboard quarters. I may as well be comfortable before I am consigned to that disgusting crate in the village." Pikeman left the room.

"He is brilliant at what he does." Yipya inspected his patient's teeth. "Someone has not been taking proper care of your teeth. Your own... pardon me, you should know better. It will take a while to generate the nanobots and containment guard to deal with this, but we'll fix you."

"I'll trade you the vet for the *Homo sapiens* doctor, Mrapp." Samantha relaxed with the change of topic.

"No deal." Tension seemed to flow out of Mrapp as she shared a look with Samantha.

Ryan passed the grav lifts supporting an E.S.T.C. to Rowan.

"How do they look?" He gestured towards the relief village.

"The relief workers? Better than yesterday. Though they're burning through the rations." Rowan looked down the valley. Kangazoids still crowded the fields by the rope barricade. The sun was about to vanish across the western ice wall. "Can you fix the heating cores?"

"It's a matter of time. Muperr gave me a list of repairs that are beyond their equipment's capacity. They need a nanobot assembler and the power to run it."

"Can we stay longer to help them?"

"Muperr does have the authority to authorize wages, but..."

"You want to get out of here." Rowan released the E.S.T.C., which drifted feather-like to the ramp on the grav lifts, and moved so she could hug Ryan.

"Henry thinks we'll never reach Geb. At this rate, we'll lose the access window the stargate being towed by the system creates before we have the chance."

"As far as that. I kinda like being in the Republic." Rowan blushed. "It's a rush to deal with the other species."

Ryan held her closer. "I feel like I'm going into battle every second. The stress is killing me."

"You'll do the right thing. You always do." Rowan rested in his arms, laying her head against his shoulder.

"Hate to break up the snuggle fest, oh hot and cuddly divine saviour," quipped Henry's voice from Ryan's handheld.

"Henry!" Ryan's voice was disgusted.

"Wanted to tell you that the ground crews have cleared the port hangar bay hatch to the rail system and reloaded the E.S.T.C.s for the auxiliary stations. Isn't it divine?"

"Henry, are you familiar with the nickname 'Stubby'? Something to consider for after you're… *fixed*," said Rowan in a no-nonsense voice.

"Just funning, oh sexy captain's mate, divine mistress."

"Recall the crew. We're running out of light here anyway. Have Kitoy clear it with Muperr. Ask Asalue to join us. I'd like someone to do a detailed flyover of the areas with low rad. We'll be back in a few days, lighter and less cluttered. Tell Wispy and Krakkeen to pull their shelters and some rations. They should stay with the relief workers. These people need muscle to get back on their feet, and strength is one thing those two have in abundance."

"Sending out the calls." Henry's voice went silent.

Rowan moved to her cargo container, increased the antigrav on the lifts and towed it away from the ship.

"Henry, button up the exterior cargo transfer port and do a pressure check. How is cleaning the grav laser ports coming?" Ryan watched the rail retract into the ship. The hull closed over the hole. There wasn't even a seam to show where the port had been.

"Pressure checks good, oh divine one. I've finished thirty-two per cent of the grav ports. They are crusty."

"Pull in your maintenance robots. We'll redeploy when we land. We won't be using the grav laser for the planetary flights anyway."

"Staying low?" asked Henry.

Ryan descended the ramp and then began the process of dismantling it. "There's still an ankylosaur up there. I want a good shield of air between us and anything they could launch at us. Besides, it's better for scanning."

"Looking for something?"

Ryan nodded, trusting Henry's external sensors to 'see' it. "The need here is greater than what I can give. That has to change, and I've said it before. I'm tired of running away."

"Still saving the kangazoids?" Henry's voice lacked its usual banter.

"They need us. We caused this, and we need to make it right." Ryan watched as the surface of the ramp rolled itself down the poles.

"The wallabies could have picked worse, boss."

"It's an obligation I don't want and a title I don't deserve. I'm a man, not a god. But once you receive a title, you try and live up to it. Lieutenant, Commander, Captain, I think I've managed. I can't live up to God. I've always done the best I could. My ego doesn't need the adoration, but the kangazoids are looking to me, and to disappoint is to let them die."

⊂══◆⊷

Michael looked at a long list of cancelled shows on his office's wall. "Gene, eliminate all shows where the principal characters are non-active."

The list dropped to less than half its length. The font size increased to fill the wall, becoming legible.

"Eliminate those where all the showrunners are active with current shows."

About a third of the list dropped off. The titles became easy to read.

"Eliminate all shows where all showrunners are dead."

Two shows dropped off the list.

"Gene, start a file for *Tales of a Country Vet*. Collect contact information for the showrunners who are currently available."

On the side wall, a list opened with credits for the show. 'Terry Monk.' Mike read the name. "Gene, put up the studio ident picture." Mike looked at a gawky man with a bird-like quality and thinning brown hair. "Why don't I recognize him? We must have had overlap. Wait... Gene, pull a recent picture from the web."

The image changed to a slender, elegant woman of late middle years with long dark hair, wearing an evening gown. "Right, Terry Monk, now I remember. Gene, track down her contact information and add it to the file. Find out what she's been doing since she left the studio. Make some quick notes. I'll call her later."

Mike turned back to his main screen. "*Days of My Youth*. Gene, delete it. Never thought much of it. *Spooky Investigations*. That could work if we can find the right dog. Nice tie-in possibilities to *My Psychic Sister*. A good way to pass the torch. Start a file for it and locate the showrunners."

Mike kept scanning the old shows.

DELIVERY

18

The *Star Hawk* drifted down towards a large ice shelf by five black domes, each topped by a tulip blade wind turbine. Seven otterzoids rushed out of the domes and gawked at the heavy lander. Ten boats reminiscent of the reed boats of the ancient Egyptians on Earth lined the shoreline.

Ryan adjusted the pilot's station as the *Star Hawk*'s landing legs set down. "Rowan, how is the ice holding?"

Rowan scanned the navigator's sensors. "It's taking the weight. If you don't want to get wet, ease into the displacement. The bow end has water under the ice."

"On it. I'm leaving her stern heavy." Ryan bit his lip.

The *Star Hawk* settled. Brilliant sunlight reflected off the glaciers and sparkled on the sea. A kangazoid village could be seen a short way up the ice valley. Maybe fifty kangazoids were clustered around the seaward gate of a piled stone palisade. They watched the *Star Hawk* settle on the ice with reverence. Several of them hopped closer.

Ryan let the ship's weight rest on the stern section, then eased back on the bow's antigrav.

"Stop it there. The ice is cracking. Ninety-five per cent of ship's mass supported." Rowan began locking down her console.

"It will do. Henry, open the hangar bay ramp and the bomb bay. Quick checks on all stations. Kitoy, call Asalue to the hangar ramp. He can make the introductions."

Minutes later, Ryan and his crew, with Asalue and Jacques, wearing his scuttle suit, stood at the base of the hangar ramp in front of seven otterzoids draped in grubby garments reminiscent of dog coats. The otterzoids' eyes were sunken, and their pelts were dull.

"It is a fine fish to have you here, Captain. Asalue's delivery of M.R.E.s was fresh water in a muddy stream, but they have only begun the process of restoring us. We thought ourselves abandoned." The foremost otterzoid of the group was a female who walked with a pronounced limp.

Everyone cringed as words slammed into their minds. "I can't, I can't. They scream. Fishy thoughts, fishy thoughts." Images of underwater shoals and plants, along with smaller fish and the thought of hunger, cascaded through their minds.

"What the nova blast?" demanded Tim.

The otterzoid leader groomed her muzzle in embarrassment, stopping when her hands came across an open sore. "That is Quast. The lack of key nutrients has affected him more than most. He hears all the thoughts around him, and his mind is confused. With proper food, he will recover."

"Coopla, we have medical personnel aboard. They're on a sleep cycle, but..." began Asalue.

"There is no need. My speciality rating is as an otterzoid healer. I have injected Quast with the nutritional supplement you brought, and he has eaten as much seaweed as is good in a short time. Thanks to you, Asalue, he is in no danger of dying, though it was close. Time and nutrition are the only treatments. Olist is trying to silence his outbursts, but it is difficult. Non-otterzoids are at greater risk of intrusion. For this, I am sorry."

"Was the image I saw the local habitat?" Jacques walked up in his scuttle suit.

"Yes. A fish-eye view. You are the marine biologist?" asked Coopla.

"Yes." Jacques moved one of his scuttle suit's legs in a welcoming gesture.

"Your insights will be welcome. To be honest, we have not gone beyond the sunlit zone. Our diving equipment is old, and I do not trust it."

Ryan let his eyes quest over the ice to where a crowd of kangazoids stepped onto the beach. "Let's get unloaded. Rowan, start on the hangar bay. Tim, Kitoy, you're with me at the bomb bay. Coopla, I'll need someone to tell us where to put the marine seed habitats."

"Of course, Captain. Qallsip, join the captain's party. Follow the planned dispersal."

Ryan led the way under the bomb bay. Clambering up a ladder built into one of the support legs, he placed a pair of grav lifts against the base of a k-no-in aquatic habitat module. Undoing the ropes securing the module one-handed, he released the power transfer clip and let the module drift down. Kitoy and Tim caught the unit, and Qallsip scanned its side with a handheld before leading them away. Ryan climbed to the ground and jogged to the circle of five dome-shaped otterzoid emergency shelters. A female otterzoid looked up at him from the arched entrance of one of the domes.

"It is a fine fish in clear water to meet you." The otterzoid moved sluggishly, and large patches of her green fur had fallen out. She still made a splashing motion with her paws.

"It is good to meet you as well. I was wondering if you had anything like a step ladder. We're short on grav lifts." Ryan regarded the invalid.

She made a splashing motion with her paws. "There is an ice cave behind the village. We keep our tools there."

"Thank you." Ryan jogged through the village. A methane composting septic system, tied to a fuel cell and algae generation tank, was in a pit on its far side. Beyond that, an open hole in the ice loomed. Inside, amongst a jumble of tools, basic and advanced, he found what looked like a flight of steps with support rods to brace them.

"Some things are too useful to let time affect them."

Ryan hoisted the steps up and carried them back to the *Star Hawk*. He'd only placed the steps when Kitoy, Tim and Qallsip returned.

"We deployed the unit and left it by the hangar bay ramp," explained Qallsip. "The microorganisms should divide quickly and restore the stream before the spawning run."

"Good." Ryan climbed the stairs to place the grav lifts under the next aquatic normal flora tank. In minutes, Qallsip, Kitoy and Tim guided the tank across the ice while Ryan slung a harness of ropes around the next unit and lowered it to the ice.

He was dropping the fifth module when the rest of his team returned with the grav lifts. They took a module and vanished. Ryan was lowering the next container when his mind filled with an agonized scream. Teeth bit into his side, tearing through his scales. A jumble of wheeling, dimly lit visual images, then a flash of light and nothing. His mind reeled as he lost his balance. The tank crashed to the ground. Ryan slammed his head against the tank's side as he fell and sprawled on the ice below.

Rowan was the first of the *Star Hawk*'s crew to come to her feet after the mental scream. She glanced around. Her shipmates were all unconscious or staring with bewildered expressions. She stepped off the ramp and looked at the area under the bomb bay. In the evening twilight, Ryan sprawled in a puddle of blood on the ice.

"Henry, wake Pikeman. Ryan's hurt." She glanced over her comrades and saw that they were now conscious. She grabbed the emergency medical kit beside the ramp and sprinted toward her lover.

"On it," Henry's voice replied from the handheld in a holster at her waist.

Skidding to a halt beside Ryan, Rowan checked his

airway, breathing and circulation.

"He's still alive." She checked his pupils. "Pupils equal and reactive to light." Her hands explored his head and upper spine. "Deep scalp laceration, severe bleeding but the skull and spine feel intact." Her hands came away coated with blood. She ran the rest of his spine, finding no signs of breakage or deformity, then eased him onto his side. A mix of drool and blood poured from his mouth.

Kitoy arrived carrying a grav stretcher. Rowan opened the med kit. About a third of it was alien to her, but she did recognize pressure dressings. Extracting one, she unwrapped it and put it against the wound in Ryan's head, using its built-in gauze wraps to secure it.

"I don't feel any spinal deformities or breaks, but I can't be sure. Where the nova blast is Pikeman?" snapped Rowan.

Kitoy set the stretcher by Ryan, then pulled out a boxy device from the med kit and folded out her handheld's screen. She spoke a command in felinezoid and then passed the device over Ryan while holding the screen up for Rowan to see.

"You know *Homo sapiens* anatomy better than I do." Kitoy looked at Ryan with concern.

"First chance I get, I update my first aid." Rowan examined the images on the screen. "Nothing is broken. Let's get him on the stretcher. Where the nova blast is Pikeman?"

"Dad! What the stardust happened?" Tim raced up.

"He fell when the telepathic blast hit. Help us roll him onto the stretcher. Support his head. Kitoy, take his feet. Try to roll him slow and steady." Rowan looked at the two grav lifts with a canvas spread between them.

Together they rolled him onto the stretcher and put him on his side. Immediately a display of his vital signs appeared on one of the support bars. "Pulse eighty, blood pressure 125/85, respiration 11, temp 37.3." Rowan ignored the more advanced telemetry that she didn't have the background to interpret.

"His blood gases look good, and his EKG isn't bad. The EEG is a little off, but that fits with a head injury," commented Tim.

Ryan groaned and opened his eyes. "When will this nova-blasted planet stop trying to kill me?"

"Don't move," Rowan, Kitoy and Tim spoke in unison.

Rowan retrieved a survival blanket from the emergency kit and covered him. "Pikeman is coming."

Ryan closed his eyes. "Wonderful."

Pikeman strode up, pulled out his handheld, and scanned Ryan.

"No fractures. Laceration to the back of the head. Strained muscles and the beginnings of an inflamed sinus. A mild concussion." He focused the handheld on Ryan's skull and pressed a button on the screen. "No intracranial bleeding." Pikeman looked up. "You are lucky, Captain. Sleep for ten hours to let your body get over the shock. The stiffness and bruises can remind you not to be so foolish in future! Miss McPherson. Wake him hourly for the next four hours and ensure he is oriented to time, person, and place. Do you know how to do that?"

"Yes." Rowan stared at Ryan, taking in every line of his face.

"If he gets any of the questions wrong, wake me. I'm going back to bed." Pikeman marched back to the hangar bay ramp.

"I think he likes me," observed Ryan.

Rowan sighed. "Doctor's orders. To bed. Now!"

"A wonderful invitation, but I have a headache. I need to check on the unloading and—" Ryan struggled to his feet to find himself staring at three determined expressions.

"Now! We can move boxes without you." Rowan's tone was like a mother admonishing a foolish child.

Ryan felt his ire rise. A throb of pain from the back of his head silenced his reply. "Make sure they deploy those aquatic habitat units before the power storage runs down."

Ryan started towards the hangar bay.

Rowan glanced at Kitoy, who flicked her tail in Ryan's direction. "We have this." Kitoy started packing away the emergency gear. Rowan raced to Ryan's side and took his arm in case he stumbled.

Henry closed the bomb bay doors. "I read full seal. Pressure check is green," he remarked through Ziggy's handheld.

Ziggy walked the length of the hatch, looking up into the spotlight of a flashlight's beam at what looked like uniform pieces of hull. "Visual inspection confirm. The seal and camo are good."

"Good environmental seal." Tim's voice came through the handheld.

"Better come in and get some sleep. If I know hotty boss, he'll want to hit the next post as soon as it's daylight for them. That gives us about eight hours."

"Did Coopla mention she wants to come along? She's heard there are sick and injured otterzoids at the other coastal installation."

"She didn't get to Dad before the fall, but Rowan and Henry green-lit it. I set her up in Wispy's old quarters. When I think about what I went through to adjust that environment to hot and dry…" Tim's voice was resolved.

Ziggy stepped out from under the *Star Hawk* and looked up. A triangle of coloured lights drifted overhead. Something dark blocked the stars between the lights.

"*Star Hawk*, you seeing this?" Ziggy jogged to where he could watch the lights move up the length of Kangra-la.

"Affirmative. It's the *Mary*." Rowan's voice came from his handheld. "Get in quick, Ziggy. I want to button us up before they set down in case Croell decides to do something cute, and I have to check on Ryan in fifteen minutes."

"See, hotty. I told you you'd be as paranoid as Ryan and me sooner or later," remarked Henry.

"Polymer prat!" Rowan's voice was more amused than annoyed.

Ziggy ran back to the hangar bay. The ramp closed behind him.

Gunther stood beside Fran's bed in a modest but homey room. A dream catcher hung in the window, and a long pipe with hawk feathers was in a rack on the wall beside a pair of beadwork pieces. A blood collection bottle slowly filled from a tube in her arm.

"Are you sure you are fully recovered?" he asked.

"I'm fine, Gunther. Fever's gone, runny nose a thing of the past. Will this be enough for Toronk?"

"It will be enough. I'm going to test it on Valaseau. I'd be more comfortable if you and Carl would move in with Willa and me until the pirates resolve their internal dispute."

"We can't stop living. We all found that out over the years. I hope those alien scum wipe each other out." Fran leaned back in her bed. "Where is everybody?"

Gunther looked at the floor. "Quinta is recovering in the infirmary. The federal government took Farley. I couldn't treat him."

Fran looked at Gunther in surprise, then heard his voice nearly devoid of emotion in her mind. *'The one who took him was a controller from* Freedom's Run. *It was his only hope.'*

Gunther spoke aloud. "Angel is sitting with Valaseau. Toronk is in their apartment going stir-crazy. The sooner I can make a serum, the better. Are you sure you won't help the other felinezoids and otterzoids?"

Fran took a breath. "Pirates killed my parents. I can't say yes. I can't, but what you do after you take my blood, I can't control. Just don't tell me about it."

Gunther moved to the edge of the bed and kissed Fran's forehead. "Understood."

Willa sat on a battered couch in Fran's living room. Afternoon sunlight streamed through the second-storey windows. A coffee table book on the indigenous nations of North America sat on the pressboard coffee table. Boxes of Carl's possessions were stacked against the wall.

"They're going to tear down the building. The blast knocked it off its foundations. Everyone is scrambling to find places. With Fran and I combining incomes, we may be able to buy a house. What's left of her parents' insurance will make a down payment." Carl paced, pausing periodically to check out the window.

"I'm glad things are working out." Willa smiled.

"That means a lot coming from you." Carl stared at his ex-lover. "It was always just a dream."

Willa smiled. "A pleasant dream, but a dream. I love my husband."

Carl stared out the window. "Stardust!"

"Problems?" Willa came to his side.

A panel van pulled up in front of the building. Three *Homo sapiens* climbed out.

"Vilicsa addicts," remarked Willa.

"Get Gunther and tell Fran to get ready. I'm going to check them out." Carl slipped out of his clothes and blended with the walls. The door opened and closed with no more than a shadow to be seen.

Carl moved down the hall onto the stairs, then into his building's lobby. The three *Homo sapiens* entered. One kept watch at the door while the others mounted something the size of a pencil eraser end in the upper corner of the room. The three then moved to the stairs and ascended, putting another device directly in front of Fran's door.

"The masters will double our dose," whispered one of the slaves.

"I'll be happy if they keep it steady. Have you seen Keith? He is suffering. Hurast is heartless."

"Shh. These systems are live. They could be listening," hissed the third.

They started towards the stairs. Carl pressed himself against the wall as they passed, then followed.

"Way I hear it, bosses can't afford to lose any of us. The bunch that went to attack the octozoids got wiped out, and with the felinezoids and otterzoids sick and like to side with the rebels if they survive, Hurast needs every pair of hands she can get."

"We better hope that someone knows how to make vilicsa at the end of this, or we're all goners."

"You sure no one's ever gotten off it? My brother got hooked on smack. He managed to get clean."

"Heroin isn't vilicsa. The alien stardust don't let go."

The three descended the stairs, exiting the building. Carl crept back to Fran's apartment.

Pulling on his clothes, he willed his skin back to a human shade. "I think I saw a cockroach. We'll have to call an exterminator." He gestured offhandedly to the door.

"I thought I sensed a bug," agreed Gunther, who had left Fran's room.

"There is a lot of misinformation about bugs going around." Carl smiled.

"Yes. I'll take this to the hospital lab to work on it." Gunther picked up a cooler containing the bottle of Fran's blood.

POETRY RECITAL

Ryan tried to ignore his headache as he let the *Star Hawk* rise on the air until it topped the ice walls surrounding Kangra-la. The rising sun was a dim glow over the glacial plain.

"Rowan, scan the *Mary*. What are they doing?"

"It looks like they are going through decontamination. The relief workers are snug in their beds. Most of the kangazoids have returned to their villages. Krakkeen has put up something that looks like a tent on stilts. It's the tallest thing in the settlement."

"That would be a spiderzoid emergency shelter. Hopefully, unloading will keep Croell and Zandra busy until we're done. Give me directions to auxiliary base two."

"Set course north by northeast at eight kilometers altitude."

"Setting course. Activating scram jets for atmospheric flight." Ryan caressed the piloting board, and a shudder ran through the ship. "Everyone, start on your checks. I'll want status when we set down."

Minutes passed before Ryan stilled the scram jets and let the *Star Hawk* drift forward and down. Below, a river flowed into the sea through a depositional delta. A broad valley resplendent with flowers, grasses, and trees stretched out around the river. Marshlands full of reeds dotted the river's banks. Seven otterzoid emergency habitats formed a ring on the delta. Two broad channels spilt into the sea ten meters past the otterzoid dwellings. Two hundred meters further inland, there was a barren of rock with tufts of grasses and small patches of flowers. Beside the barren was a huge, sand-coloured, boxy vehicle. Two hundred meters further up the valley were ten *Homo sapiens* emergency shelters positioned several meters above the river's current level on one side of the flow. Four more boxy vehicles dotted the valley on the other side of the river.

"Rowan, outside radiation level?" Ryan's voice reflected fatigue.

"Six millisieverts annual. The scans show safe levels for a hundred k in all directions."

"Kitoy, anything?" asked Ryan.

"Dead air. Maybe they're asleep." Kitoy scanned the contact frequencies.

"We can hope." Ryan worked his controls.

The *Star Hawk* settled on the rock barren.

"Stations report?" Ryan locked down the pilot's station and moved to the engineering board.

All stations reported green.

Ryan settled into the captain's chair and looked at the main screen as the image circled the ship. Outside, the sun was cresting the eastern horizon.

"Ziggy, Rowan, with me. Kitoy, have Coopla meet us at the loading ramp. Keep the bomb bay buttoned up for now, and be ready to scamper. We'll go to the otterzoid village. Call Asalue and have him load himself up with *Homo sapiens* M.R.E.s. He can fly to the *Homo sapiens* settlement and drop off breakfast. Wake Pikeman and Yipya. We're likely to need medical." Ryan stood up and led the way from the bridge.

When they stepped out of the ship, towing Otterzoid Standardized Cargo Transfer Modules on grav-lifts behind them, Rowan noticed how warm the air was. There were the smells of rotting vegetation and a salt inland breeze. An insect of some kind leapt as they followed a footpath through the delta.

A house cat-sized creature with four legs ending in

clawed feet, two wings and a sharply pointed snout full of small white teeth burst from a grove of reeds and flew after the insect, snapping it up.

"Somebody had breakfast." Ryan walked towards the circle of otterzoid shelters.

Rowan and Ziggy pulled O.S.C.T.M.s as they followed their captain. Coopla had a medical kit in pouches on her back.

As the *Homo sapiens* walked, a feeling of anxiety grew in all of them. Rowan's stomach gurgled despite her having eaten not long before. Ziggy kept hugging himself as if he were cold. Ryan had to fight to keep his hands away from the bandage on his scalp.

Reaching the outskirts of the otterzoid encampment, Coopla pushed inside the closest dwelling, emerging moments later. "Two here, alive, but barely. I've given them nutrient shots. I will continue their treatment while you examine the other huts." She vanished into the shelter.

"Kitoy, we'll need more otterzoid ration packs. You and Tim get on that ASAP. Get Yipya and Pikeman out here with otterzoid nutrient shots. The log listed this station as having twelve inhabitants." Ryan spoke into his handheld.

"Received. We'll be right there."

Ryan felt an insane thrill of hope run through him, coupled with a clawing pain in his belly. Random things flew through the air, pelting his group.

"Captain!" Ziggy fell to his knees, clutching his head and his belly. "The hunger!"

"Stardust!" Ryan swore and clutched his head as he doubled over.

Rowan gritted her teeth and started reciting.

"'There are strange things done neath the midnight sun by the men who moil for gold.'

"Ryan, you and Ziggy, get out of here! Keep everyone back. I'll help Coopla. Run!

"'The arctic trails have their secret tales that would make your blood run cold.'"

Ryan began reciting.
"'In Flanders fields the poppies blow
"Between the crosses, row on row,
"That mark our place; and in the sky
"The larks, still bravely singing, fly
"Scarce heard amid the guns below.'
"Ziggy, remember your training. Telepathic assault." Ryan helped his crewman to his feet, and they stumbled from the village. Clods of dirt and twigs pelted them.
"'We are the Dead. Short days ago
"We lived, felt dawn, saw sunset glow,
"Loved and were loved, and now we lie,
"In Flanders fields.'"
Ziggy gasped and started speaking.
"'Half a league, half a league,
"Half a league onward,
"All in the Valley of Death
"Rode the six hundred.
"Forward, the Light Brigade!
"Charge for the guns!' he said.
"Into the Valley of Death
"Rode the six hundred.'"
Ryan and Ziggy staggered towards Kitoy, Tim and Yipya, who were towing cargo from the *Star Hawk*.
"Go back. Don't approach the village," shouted Ryan.
"What?" asked Kitoy.
"'Forward, the Light Brigade!
"Was there a man dismayed?
"Not though the soldier knew
"Someone had blundered.
"Theirs not to make reply,
"Theirs not to reason why,
"Theirs but to do and die.
"Into the Valley of Death
"Rode the six hundred.'"
"Nova blast!" hissed Kitoy. She started reciting as she moved to Ziggy's open side and helped Ryan half carry him

back to the ship.

"'There was a leopard spot from the south lands.

"Who liked to play with her strong hands.'"

The translator tried to cope with the felinezoid limerick.

Everyone left the crates they were hauling on the grav lifts and rushed to the ship as random items pelted them.

Ryan kept reciting.

"Yet still the heroes battled on though hope was truly gone.

"Let their courage and valour true never be forgot.

"They paid a price in blood and tears that their fame begot.

"Nine serpents slain at cost in blood, only one remained.

"The *Thor*, a shattered wreck, did glow her fusion room in flames.

"Mjolnir lost, no missiles left and still one snake remained.

"No choice had they for their next act to guard their kith and kin, heed not the words which say them not, give honour to their names.

"The *Thor* with three who still drew breath within their armoured suits.

"Did set its course and charge the foe who fled with their pursuit.

"In victory in that ancient lay Thor poisoned, he did stride, like a giant took twelve steps before he fell and died.'"

Rowan stuck her head into the second shelter.

"The northern lights have seen queer sights. But the queerest they ever did see…"

The shelter held two otterzoids and Coopla.

"Give me a hypo." Rowan continued reciting.

Coopla startled. "No. You are too vulnerable. Get out of here! It is too dangerous."

Rowan interrupted her reciting. "I have an edge.

"Now Sam McGee was from Tennessee, where the cotton blooms and blows.

"Why he left his home in the South to roam 'round the Pole, God only knows.

"He was always cold, but the land of gold seemed to hold him like a spell;

"Though he'd often say in his homely way that he'd sooner live in hell."

"Fine. Pull ration packs. One pack for two otterzoids. Follow me through the shelters and feed any who live. I'll keep up with the injections." Coopla shuffled to the shelter's door.

Rowan rushed to the otterzoid shipping unit that contained the M.R.E.s and practically tore it open. Random objects flew towards her as she worked, but her telekinesis deflected them. Grabbing a pack, she pulled its warming tab and entered the first shelter.

"On a Christmas Day we were mushing our way over the Dawson trail.

"Talk of your cold! Through the parka's fold it stabbed like a driven nail.

"If our eyes we'd close, then the lashes froze till sometimes we couldn't see;

"It wasn't much fun, but the only one to whimper was Sam McGee."

The otterzoids before her were bone-thin with patchy coats spotted by weeping pustules. They looked up with rheumy eyes. Her voice caught as their sense of need permeated her. She forced control as she peeled back the food tray's cover and started hand-feeding bits of fish and seaweed to her charges.

"And that very night, as we lay packed tight in our robes beneath the snow,

"And the dogs were fed, and the stars o'erhead were dancing heel and toe,

"He turned to me, and 'Cap,' says he, 'I'll cash in this trip,

I guess;

"'And if I do, I'm asking that you won't refuse my last request.'"

The tray emptied. The two otterzoids slumped down on their sleeping mats. Their eyes closed. Their breathing became regular. Rowan rushed to get a ration pack for the next shelter.

Rowan was on the fifth shelter when she reached the poem's end.

"Since I left Plumtree down in Tennessee, it's the first time I've been warm.

"There are strange things done in the midnight sun
"By the men who moil for gold;
"The Arctic trails have their secret tales
"That would make your blood run cold;
"The Northern Lights have seen queer sights,
"But the queerest they ever did see
"Was that night on the marge of Lake Lebarge
"I cremated Sam McGee."

"T-T-T-T-Thank you," whispered the male otterzoid she had fed. The sentient plummeted into sleep.

Rowan hurried to get another ration pack. The mental intrusions were less severe, and the number of projectiles she had to deflect had dropped. Coopla limped out of the first shelter and moved to the second.

Rowan started reciting again.

"She walks in beauty, like the night
"Of cloudless climes and starry skies;
"And all that's best of dark and bright
"Meet in her aspect and her eyes:
"Thus mellowed to that tender light
"Which heaven to gaudy day denies."

When the final hut was fed, Rowan watched Ryan and Kitoy tow O.S.C.T.M.s that had been abandoned on the trail into the common.

"A twinkling light upon a sea of velvet black I see.
"My lover is so far from me upon that darksome sea.

"In all of time and space I know, she is the one for me.

"My heart it will set sail, upon that velvet sea.

"A thousand years before the light that touches her I see.

"In the darkness I must wait, tis sadness all to me," Ryan recited.

"He flicked his tail and started to wail as his mast did bend in the wind.

"And so the great sailor just could not impale her. And she let out her scent on the wind," Kitoy chanted.

"You can stop. They're asleep." Rowan moved into Ryan's arms.

"Are you all right?" Ryan held her.

"It wasn't easy. My dad taught me how to defend myself. You're a surprise." Rowan spoke without breaking the embrace.

"Telepathic defence is part of military training for most species. If it wasn't, otterzoids would be running the Republic by now."

Coopla emerged from the shelter and moved to the edge of the group. She rose on her hind legs and stared at Rowan. "It is time to put the fish over the dam. This is the worst case of malnutrition I have ever seen. You should not have been able to stay anywhere near this place. I wanted to swim away. What is the 'edge' you said you had?"

Rowan moved from Ryan's embrace.

"Coopla, it is a private matter," began Ryan.

Rowan held up her hand. "I have otterzoid DNA."

Coopla dropped onto all fours. "Rotted clams! You permitted this violation?"

"I permitted nothing. It was done to me." Rowan looked down at the otterzoid healer.

"I have heard rumours of such things." Coopla looked around the village. "Are you the only one?"

"My father as well. I don't know of others."

Coopla turned her back. "I must get on with my patients.

Feed the stricken as before. When they are no longer in danger of dying, as sure as the stream meets the swamp, we will discuss this violation, *Homo sapiens*." Tail in the air, the otterzoid healer entered the next shelter in the circle.

"I don't think she's pleased. Doesn't S.E.T.E. sell shows to the otterzoids?" Rowan started towards the food containers.

"They do. I'm guessing she's been deployed here for over eight years." Ryan stroked his chin. "When *Angel Black* first hit the open market, the otterzoids had protests. Some extremists hated that anyone but them might have strong psychic abilities. They settled down when they figured out you were unique."

Rowan shook her head, pulled out a food container and moved to the first hut.

"Any dead?" asked Ryan.

"Two, missing. I haven't seen any bodies. How are things with the *Homo sapiens*?"

Asalue overflew the *Homo sapiens* shelters. Each shelter was nine square meters with a sloping roof of solar panels oriented to the north and twin tulip blade micro turbines rising on posts from its back corners. He performed a slow turn. He felt like he had when he first learned to fly. Unsure of how to use his wings but thrilled to embrace the skies. He flicked his tongue. He had flight again, and that impossible dream was worth any inconvenience.

Tilting his wings, he stalled his momentum and descended to the ground beside the collection of survival shelters. He landed, ran several steps and surveyed the grubby street of hard-packed earth that connected the buildings. Bits of garbage littered the ground. A waste treatment facility/energy generator was at one end of the village. One of the shelter's doors opened, and a k-no-in climbed out.

"I have relief supplies. Why didn't you reply to our hails?" Asalue eyed the k-no-in.

"I was sleeping, and the shelter's radio doesn't have an auto page function. Well, at least not anymore. I am Flower. Are those ration packs you're carrying?"

"Yes. I was sent ahead by—"

"Give me one. My friends are starving to death." Flower rushed forward.

Asalue resisted the urge to fly away. He opened the pack closest to his hand and extracted a *Homo sapiens* M.R.E.

Flower snatched the meal from the batzoid's hand and pulled its heating tab. "Dump your packs and pick a hut."

"Don't feed a whole meal to anyone. It could make them sick." Asalue worked the buckles securing his packs.

"The fact that I'm not hideous does not make me stupid!" Flower vanished into a shelter.

Asalue dropped his packs in a pile, then, taking an M.R.E., entered one of the shelters.

The air inside stank of unwashed humanity. A man lay on the cot that filled one side of the shelter. Filthy blankets covered him. His brown eyes opened at the sound of Asalue's entrance.

"I have come to help." The batzoid anthropologist opened the M.R.E. and lifted a piece of some nondescript orange vegetable out of one of the tray's compartments.

Nearly an hour later, the *Homo sapiens* living in the settlement had been fed. After eating, the relief workers fell asleep. Asalue emptied the packs he'd brought, stacking their contents against a shelter's wall. There was enough for two complete meals for the beleaguered community.

Flower stepped out of the last of the shelters. "I apologize for my rudeness earlier."

"No need. Haste was important. I am Asalue, the new anthropologist. Captain Chandler asked me to help with the food distribution."

"I thank you for that. I..." A shudder ran through Flower's hulking form. "I have grown fond of my fellow aid workers. It brought me great sadness to watch them starve."

The batzoid version of a handheld on Asalue's belt beeped. He opened the device. "We are on our way. Is it safe?" asked Yipya's voice.

"Yipya, I thought you'd be with the otterzoid encampment," said Asalue.

"Coopla is an otterzoid healer, and there is a danger there that requires specialized training. Ryan felt I could be of more service with the *Homo sapiens*."

"The survivors have been fed, but there is still much to do."

The screen went blank. Looking up, Asalue saw Yipya, Pikeman and Ziggy walking along the trail to the landing field, each hauling an E.S.T.C.

"This Captain Ryan Chandler, was he the captain of the *Star Hawk*?" Flower rose to her full height to better see the approaching sentients.

"Was and is. Ryan bought the ship when it was sent for scrap and has restored it as a cargo vessel. He is a remarkable engineer." Asalue flexed his wings. "I wish I knew what the problem was at the otterzoid encampment."

"Otterzoid abilities react violently to malnutrition. Most likely a defensive reaction to keep predators away when the otterzoid is in a weakened state." Flower nodded sagely.

"I've experienced the effect at the first auxiliary station." Asalue moved his long neck in a circular fashion.

"I had to leave my stall in the shelter vehicle because the effect was reaching me there. I haven't been able to visit the otterzoid camp for three days. Not that I could do them any good. Murack Five is jealous of her children. K-no-in are her grandchildren, and even we have difficulty fulfilling our nutritional needs. I am surprised your captain didn't rush to aid his species kin first." Flower flexed the claws on her six legs.

"Ryan is in most ways blind to species. Or as much as one can be. If the Great Flyer of the Skies exists, I think she/he spent extra time on him." Asalue flicked his tongue.

"One of those coming is k-no-in," observed Flower.

"Yipya. He is a veterinarian. The taller *Homo sapiens* is Pikeman, a good healer but not one of my favourite beings. The shorter *Homo sapiens* is Ziggy. He served here at the time of the disaster. Pikeman and Ziggy are both males. I mention it because I have trouble telling with *Homo sapiens*."

"I was like that when I started here. There are some I don't think *Homo sapiens* themselves can tell apart. The way they cover themselves in cloth makes it difficult. Smell is the most reliable way." Flower spoke absently as she eyed the approaching group.

BEGINNING OF THE END

Samantha lay on the cot in medical. Pikeman had collected cells to make his stem cell culture. While the procedure hadn't hurt, it had been embarrassing. She unconsciously clutched the hospital robe she wore closed over her buttocks.

"It sounds like they have their claws caught," remarked Mrapp from the other cot.

"I'm glad they made it through. Pikeman may be the biggest prat in the galaxy, but he knows his stuff." Samantha lay back on the cot. The wounds in her skin were sealed and healing, and with each meal, she could feel herself growing stronger.

"I'll stick with the k-no-in. Even if he keeps forgetting I'm not a house pet." Mrapp swung her legs over the edge of her cot and stood. "You served on a hawk, didn't you?"

"The *Moor Hawk*." Samantha hung her head. "I was on leave when the accident happened."

"Sorry."

Samantha swung herself into a sitting position. "It is what it is. I joined the relief effort because, well…"

"I know. My father was on the *Gerrrhissmow*. It makes it hurt less to do something." Mrapp flared her nostrils. "How good is this medical bay? Pikeman was complaining about how primitive it is."

"Pikeman is an ass! This is as good as most hospitals in the U.E.S. The captain kept everything, just less of it. You know, three cots instead of ten. We lucked out."

"You did. It would be nice to have a dedicated felinezoid

unit." Mrapp scratched at the edge of one of her dressings.

"*Homo sapiens* ship. At least Yipya seems able to transpose the readings."

"I caught him looking things up on his handheld."

"Would you want him not to? Divine, he's a vet. What do you think he's going to do? Keep the anatomy and biochemistry of every living thing in his head!" Samantha rolled her eyes.

"Point." Mrapp lashed her tail, leaving a cloud of loose fur in the air. She grew serious. "Do you think they suspect?"

"I don't think they've had time to think about it. It was going to come out sooner or later. We didn't have a choice. If we hadn't, we would have all been dead before the *Star Hawk* reached us." Samantha snagged a crutch that was left by her cot.

"But will the people who weren't here understand?" Mrapp flexed her claws.

"Some will, some won't. It's not like we killed anybody. We used what we had." Samantha slipped from her cot and stood on her remaining leg.

"Where are you going?" Mrapp lay back on her cot and looked at the vital sign readout. The *Homo sapiens* readings ranged from well above normal to well below. Yipya had told her they were normal for her species.

"Washroom. I hate microbot diapers. Then a microbot cleanse. I stink."

"Enjoy. I wish I had a grooming system. It feels like months since I was clean."

"Not likely to be one aboard but ask. They were transporting a mix of species. What have you got to lose?" Samantha leaned on her crutches and hobbled to a door in the back of the medical bay.

She paused to read a brass plaque mounted on the door frame.

'Kadar Al-Qahtani 457 PC to 575 PC. Irradiated Kanga-zoid Relief Effort, Died - Escape from Gaia. We Will Never

Forget.'

"We will never forget," whispered Samantha as she slipped into the washroom.

"Too many thoughts. I need a distraction," remarked Mrapp to the empty room.

"I can assist with that, my comely feline friend. We have books, music, visual images, and the company of a charming AI with many ideas to engage your attention while you recuperate." Henry spoke in felinezoid into the medical bay.

Yipya trotted into the village, pulling an E.S.T.C. He came to a stop before Flower. His mouth dropped open, and his eyes ranged over her.

"When you're done looking, maybe you can close your mouth and do something useful!" snapped the female k-no-in.

"I..." Yipya closed his mouth and swallowed, then spoke slowly and distinctly as if to a child. "I am sorry. I was not expecting to find such a pretty k-no-in on this planet. I'm Yipya. I am an animal doctor. What do you do?"

"If you'll open your ears and stop eyeing my fangs, mister veterinarian, I'll tell you! I am a maintenance tech specializing in environmental systems. I'll also mention that I maintain the k-no-in troop transports that have been remade into radiation-safe shelters for this rehabilitation area. My co-workers and friends need medical attention. While a veterinarian might not be the best choice, you are arguably better than nothing! So, get to work. You couldn't afford me anyway." Flower jerked her head in a dismissive gesture.

Yipya stepped back, looking offended. "Show me to the worst case. I have prepreparing nutrient injections."

"This hut here. She is a healer. When she is recovered, she can help." Flower indicated a shelter to her right with her forearm.

Yipya released the E.S.T.C. he'd been pulling and stepped into the shelter.

Pikeman arrived, and Asalue showed him to a hut.

Ziggy stood in front of Flower. "I'm not a medic, but tell me what else needs doing, and I'm on it."

Flower's ears turned forward. "Do you know how to work a *Homo sapiens'* textile maintenance unit?"

"Laundry. Show me to the machine." Ziggy followed Flower to the side of the waste processing station, where there was a nanobot clothes maintenance unit. A cargo container piled with dirty laundry stood beside it.

"Military surplus. This I know." Ziggy picked up a blanket and scowled at the dried vomit crusting it.

"I fed her a native plant that might have supplied one of her nutritional deficiencies, but the companion chemicals were toxic. Her body expelled it." Flower sounded ashamed.

"When stardust is falling, you try whatever might work. If you get lucky, you live. If you don't, you die a little sooner." Ziggy began feeding the blanket into the cleaning unit.

"Ground forces, I believe. Some things cross all species. I think I am going to like you." Flower flared her nostrils.

Ryan and Kitoy moved about the otterzoid camp, repairing equipment and brushing dust from the solar panels that made up the shelters' outer surface.

Rowan and Coopla did another circle of the shelters. Coopla treated the otterzoids' injuries and the sores on their skin while Rowan would wake them one at a time, feed the patient half a ration pack, then let them collapse back into sleep.

Hours later, the rescuers met by the empty fire pit in the centre of the ring of shelters.

"Asalue called in. The *Homo sapiens* were as badly off

as the otterzoids. Pikeman and Yipya have been giving them nutritional boosters, and they've been fed." Ryan briefed his people.

"Should we head straight for auxiliary station three now that we've dealt with the worst of this?" asked Rowan.

"They're k-no-ins manning station three. I made contact on the radio. They say they can wait. They can eat more local foods and even have imported plants from Srill." Kitoy looked to the sky where the sun was touching the western horizon. "Besides, they'll be starting their night."

Rowan looked up. "It's that late?"

"Busy day," observed Ryan.

Coopla let her eyes range over her companions and spoke querulously. "And now, you can tell me why a *Homo sapiens* has telekinesis as strong as most otterzoids."

"It is a long story," soothed Ryan.

"The nets are set. I will feed the afflicted again after sunset. Until then, I have time." Coopla rose on her hind legs in a show of strength.

Rowan sighed. "Are you familiar with e-entertainments?"

"The *Homo sapiens* experiential dramas. I liked *Cyborg Spy*. The university library had an interface unit. I would book an hour each week. It supplied interesting insights into your species. What about them?"

"Did you ever wonder how they got made?"

Michael sat in a booth at the support town's Garlic Palace. Terry Monk sat opposite him, wearing a smart business outfit. They both had plates of penne arrabbiata in front of them.

"You are seriously looking at a relaunch of *Tales of a Country Vet*." Terry toyed with her pasta with her fork.

"A revisit. A six-month run to update the principal characters. With Sun Valley being decommissioned, I want to cash in on the fans' nostalgia. Let them visit old friends."

Mike sipped his wine.

"And you want me to run it." Terry leaned back in her seat.

"You'd get showrunner status and wages. I'd need you to take controllers fresh out of college. With the Kemetic set region starting up, I'm short of experienced people."

"Would I have to deal with Harvey? He's why I left S.E.T.E. in the first place."

"You didn't hear?" Mike looked surprised.

"Hear what? I've spent the last three years on Silvanus making a documentary about the blight."

"He was visiting New York on Earth and wandered away from his tour group. The story is that a woman lured him into a gang zone. They found his body in the river. All his valuables were taken."

Terry sighed. "I can't say I'm upset or surprised. How's Leila taking it?"

"Last I heard, quite well. She was still listed as the inheritor. She gave up on him five years ago. There is no love lost there." Mike glanced at the face of the antique grandfather clock that was part of the restaurant's decor. "I need to get back to the office. Will you come back for a half-year stint? If this works out, there may be other vintage revisits."

"With Harvey gone, when do I start?" Terry sipped her wine.

⌥⟡⟢

Gunther, Willa, and Angel watched as Valaseau's breathing became easier and her fever dropped. Gunther scanned her mind which, for the first time since he'd met her, seemed rational.

"Thank you all for helping me. I know you were really protecting Toronk, but the effect is still that I'm alive." The felinezoid's tail flicked as her nostrils flared.

"We're glad it worked out." Willa patted the alien's paw.

Angel made a noncommittal snort.

"I'm going to keep you here for a few more hours. Then..." Gunther stared at the alien with a perplexed expression.

Valaseau looked at Gunther. "That is the question. Can you trust me? I know I wouldn't. Even with your telepathy, you have to ask if I have an agenda buried deep in my mind. Killing me like this would cost any of you, but it might come to that. Letting me go? Where could I go but back to the pirates? You tell me there's a break in command. Which side would I choose? Would I become a threat again? You're alone in a canyon, and the herd is stampeding through it."

Gunther stared at the felinezoid. Her tabby stripe markings lent her an innocent quality, and her pupils were dilated. He shifted uncomfortably.

"Gunther, I know what you're thinking. Are you sure?" asked Willa.

Angel stared at Valaseau and sighed. "Maybe with the telepathy booster, you could be sure. I still don't like it."

"Valaseau, if you open your mind to me, there may be a way." Gunther regarded his prisoner.

"I don't have options." Valaseau flared her nostrils. "I trust you to be decent more than my own kind. You fought to defend your world. We came to invade it. Now that my mind is clear, that makes a difference."

"Willa, Angel. Be ready. We're taking Valaseau to the 'telepathy booster.' If she tries anything, snap her neck."

CULTURAL NORMS

Ryan held Rowan in what had become their bed. Passion satiated, he was free to enjoy the closeness.

"How long do we have?" Rowan returned the embrace.

"Never long enough. Privacy off, Henry, time?" Ryan spoke to the air.

"An hour to sunrise." Henry's voice was pitched soft.

"Bring the light up to day levels. Wake the crew. We'll brief over breakfast." Ryan stretched, feeling his spine pop.

"Breakfast is an idea. It's harder to fight a telepathic projection if it ties into something you have in common with it." Rowan rolled to the edge of the bed.

Ryan allowed himself to appreciate the view of her lean, well-proportioned form set against a desert scene bathed in predawn light. "I like how you synced the time on the wall projection with local time."

"Helps to make me feel less jet-lagged." Rowan found the cargo pants and long-sleeved shirt she'd worn the day before, then started to dress.

Ryan followed her example. An hour later, they towed a pair of O.S.C.T.M.s to the otterzoid settlement. Coopla clambered from one of the dwellings. She moved sluggishly, and her limp was more pronounced.

"I don't want that here!" Coopla glowered at Rowan.

A rock hurled itself at Rowan. Rowan's brow wrinkled. The rock stalled in the air, then dropped. Coopla glanced to the side. Another stone sped towards Rowan.

Ryan dropped the O.S.C.T.M. he was pulling and lunged, clutching the otterzoid around the throat. He pulled Coopla back on her hind legs, strangling her. The second rock dropped.

"How dare you?" The red of rage tinted Ryan's face, and his voice held death.

"I do not want that abomination near my people. I had time to review a file about *Angel Black*. She is a killer! To steal my peoples' abilities, then use them to slaughter us." A rock flew towards Ryan. He pulled the otterzoid around and used her body as a shield at the last second.

Coopla grunted as she knocked the wind out of herself.

"They were pirates trying to conquer what I thought was my world," objected Rowan.

"You slaughtered them. Choked them to death with your mind. How could you, pup eater?" Coopla lifted another rock with her mind.

"I have had more than enough of people attacking and disrespecting the woman I love." Ryan tightened his grip on the otterzoid's throat.

"Ryan, it's all right. Let her go." Rowan looked shocked.

"No! I'm done running away. Everything I come across is either trying to blow us up or put us down. It ends here! It ends now! I don't give a pinch of stardust what your issue is, Coopla. So you read a magazine article about *Angel Black* and think you know what it was all about? That isn't even a still image of the situation. Rowan especially, but every member of my crew has taken incredible risks to help the relief workers. If you ever attack any of my people again, I will snap your neck. And if you think you could stop me with telekinesis, you better make your first shot count because you won't get a second. Pup eater!"

Ryan threw the otterzoid to the ground and raised a fist, ready to strike.

Coopla lay in the dirt and looked up to see a savage predator ready to pummel her. The rage was terrifying, the stance deadly. Deep inside, her animal nature saw only one chance of survival. She lay on her back and looked up at Ryan in utter submission. "I... I..." She trembled, then, mastering herself, rolled onto her front and hung her head. "I am sorry."

Rowan looked at the cowed healer. "I accept your apology." Rowan considered, then took a chance. "All is silt in the pond. It will settle and leave the waters clear."

Coopla trembled as she dipped her head to Rowan. "Thank you." She turned to Ryan. "Captain."

"Show Rowan respect, and for my part, it is done."

Coopla made a feeble paw-splashing gesture. "The news of a being such as Rowan swims a stream I am sadly familiar with. Knowing what she did for an entertainment, I was swimming in cloudy waters."

"Remember, I didn't know it was an entertainment until Ryan liberated me. What would you do to protect your world from pirates?" Rowan's voice, if not friendly, held understanding.

"As you say, Rowan. I do need help caring for my people. I have been up all night."

"We'll take over feeding them. Have you located the bodies of the dead? I should move them onto the ship to minimize environmental contamination." Ryan spoke softly.

Coopla groomed her muzzle, nearly dislodging the scab that had formed over her sore. "There is little risk of that."

"Still."

Coopla looked up with pleading eyes.

"Ryan, maybe let it go for now." Rowan touched his arm.

"It needs to be taken care of." Ryan looked confused.

Rowan looked to Coopla, then at the waste treatment facility. "I think it has been."

Coopla groomed her muzzle. "You are perceptive for a female of any species." She looked at Ryan. "It has been largely dealt with. I will let your own species deal with the details."

"Ryan, why don't you give Coopla a lift back to the *Star Hawk*? I can handle the morning feedings." Rowan moved to an O.S.C.T.M. left the day before and extracted the last few otterzoid ration packs. "One each?"

"Yes, they are up to that." Coopla hissed a little through her nose. "Give them a few days, and they will start complaining about the food's quality."

Ryan put the grav lifts under the O.S.C.T.M., helped Coopla climb onto it, then towed them back to the *Star Hawk*.

Yipya awoke to the sounds of movement outside his stall. He stretched his legs, put his feet on the ground, and rose off the sleeping bench that supported his chest and stomach.

"You're awake," remarked a growly rumble in k-no-in.

The voice made Yipya want to go into debt. Turning in the two meters wide by three long sleeping stall, he faced the hatch.

Flower stood in the converted k-no-in troop transport's hallway staring at him. He was again struck by her beauty. Fangs as yellow as her namesake, a light natural stripe pattern going down her sides, large black eyes.

"I've pulled k-no-in ration packs from the supplies. You should eat." Flower eyed him with mild disdain.

"After I have checked on my patients with Pikeman." Yipya moved out of the officer's stall. "I have to say, having a proper sleeping bench is an improvement over the *Star Hawk*. Thank you."

"Benches are there. We may as well use them. I thought Captain Chandler tried to accommodate everyone. Asalue spoke highly of his hospitality." Flower walked beside Yipya down the portable base's three-meter-wide central corridor. Six of the stalls were equipped for k-no-in. The rest had had their sleeping platforms removed and been retrofitted for use by *Homo sapiens* and otterzoids. They came to a three meter by three meter elevator. They stepped in, and she pressed the down button.

"He tried. Our departure was rushed. I had to make do with a *Homo sapiens'* sleeping platform. No real support. They sleep with all their limbs off the ground."

"They are an odd species. I have come to like them for all of that."

"Me as well, though some things confuse me."

The lift opened. They stepped into a hallway identical to the one above, only the stalls lining it were roughly a meter wide and had been set up as animal pens.

"Do the other species stay here often?" Yipya looked into a stall.

"Only during the flood. The river floods for five to eight days every year. When that happens, silt washes down from upstream. The silt is contaminated with radioactive particles. Once it settles, it's too radioactive outside for advanced life forms for several days. Several insect species can cope, and some of the smaller reptiles and mammals that have short lifespans anyway. Anything larger..." Flower let out a puff of breath.

"So, you herd a breeding population of the animals into the troop carriers until the worst of the radiation has passed, and the relief workers take shelter with them. Small surprise that this is my primary posting." Yipya stepped through the troop carrier's hatch and turned to face the rising sun.

"Great Divine, grant me the strength to do thy will."

"Grant us the wisdom to know thy will," added Flower.

Yipya flexed his claws happily as they finished together. "Grant us the courage to live thy will.

"It's nice to have someone to pray with. So few k-no-in on the Switchboard Station practice, and those that do..." Yipya shook his head. "Faith is about inclusiveness. The Divine comes to all and loves all in different guises and ways. Sadly."

"Sadly, there are always those who want to feel superior to others."

Yipya and Flower walked to the human settlement.

Pikeman met them in front of the line of shelters. "All nice and rested," he snipped.

"I believe the game was to draw the long straw. I won. What is the status of our patients?"

"Improving. Watch the one in the third hut down. He is developing a respiratory infection. The body isn't in the disposal station. You should ascertain where it is so we can avoid environmental contamination." Pikeman sneered.

"What is left is in the troop carrier. The otterzoids were very thorough." Flower spoke matter-of-factly.

"What!" gasped Pikeman.

"*Homo sapiens* flesh is closer to otterzoid than any species native to Murack Five. It supplied many trace nutrients, allowing them to survive until you arrived."

"And the otterzoids?" asked Yipya.

"They returned the favour. I didn't understand the concern. It was a life gift. I can see where it would have been a problem with disease transmission if they were the same species, but trading the dead dealt with that. I told the otterzoids and *Homo sapiens* that it would be rude to refuse the gift of life."

Pikeman stepped back. "You told them?"

"Of course. It is no different than using the remains to make the protein nutrient solution to feed the stem cells in Samantha's limb regeneration. Perhaps even safer because they did not eat their own species," explained Yipya.

Pikeman stroked his hand over his scalp. "I cannot argue the pragmatism. I will need to see the remains that are left." He held up his hand. "Later. Now I must sleep."

Pikeman walked away. Yipya and Flower ate M.R.E.s and then started taking meals into the shelters.

The day wore on. The crew from the *Star Hawk* brought E.S.T.C.s of M.R.E.s and medical supplies that soon formed a solid line across from the shelters.

The sun was past its zenith when Flower approached

Yipya with a k-no-in M.R.E.

"It has been a long time since breakfast," she commented.

"It is good work. The *Homo sapiens* are recovering. I do not think I'll ever get used to my patients speaking to me." Yipya flexed his claws.

"I have found you can get used to many things." Flower passed him a ration pack.

"I wish to apologize for when I spoke to you as one mentally deficient. It is simply you are so beautiful, yet you are not on Srill. I could not see how you could have failed the breeding exam except by mental defect." Yipya opened what looked like a bowl of dog kibble.

Flower sighed. "It is a common mistake. I… Rikrana." She spoke the last in a whisper.

Yipya moved close to her and stroked her back with the underside of his chin. "I am sorry. To let you know, I was amongst those who lobbied for the outer zones to be tested before being sterilized. The council was far too harsh for something that wasn't your fault."

"Thank you. I was a month away from my breeder exam when the reactor malfunctioned. My mother and I lived on the other side of the city. We left as soon as the warnings sounded, but that didn't matter. When I reported for testing, they saw my birth city, and I was sterilized and put in service. I got my ratings as a maintenance tech, then specialized in environmental systems."

"And Murack Five." Yipya had left his chin over her shoulders. She leaned into him, coveting the warmth.

"I got tired of everyone thinking I was a dullard because I look nice. When I saw the duty, I thought the other species wouldn't care, and the few k-no-in here would learn. I was half right. Most of the other k-no-in only want me for one thing. That's why I took this assignment."

Yipya pressed down on her back. "They fail the breeding exam by a large margin not to see you in your words."

Flower pulled away and laid her chin over Yipya's back.

"You may be able to afford me. Save up for a while."

Ryan checked his inventory and moved a cargo container out of the *Star Hawk*. He pulled it to the k-no-in troop shelter and pushed it into a stall. Several stalls were full of the station's shipment that wasn't food or medical. Opening his handheld, he spoke. "Kitoy, give me Henry. Over."

"You've got me, hotty boss. Over."

"I'm showing this as everything except for this station's aquatic normal flora tanks. Can you confirm? Over."

"Confirmed. Over."

Retrieving the grav lifts, he carried them back towards the *Star Hawk*.

Outside, the sun was just past noon. "Kitoy, you still have ears on? Over."

"I'm at station. I'd rather be pulling boxes. Over."

"Someone needs to keep Henry company. Over." Ryan looked to the sky. It was close enough in colour to be mistaken for Earth. He tried to convince the knots in his guts that appearances were reality, but he couldn't escape that this was Murack Five.

"Would that it were true. Over," interjected Henry.

"What's the squawk been like? Over." Ryan focused on the work.

"I ran the record for the last forty-eight hours. Not much but normal background. Dichrostigmazoid news piece on the destruction of C-132 and two vessels of suspicious intent. The sycamorezoids are quiet. Over."

"They're probably working out a new way to make life challenging. Can you patch me through to Rowan? Over." Ryan stretched, hearing his back crack.

Rowan's voice issued from his handheld. "It's me. Over."

Ryan smiled. "Rowan, are the otterzoids up to answering some questions? Over."

"They're awake and handling their own bathroom breaks. Beyond that, I think it will be a day or two. Over."

"Find out if they have deployment instructions for the aquatic habitats. I'd like to offload and get out of here. Over."

"On it. You okay? Over."

Ryan wondered how he could tell her nothing was okay for him on Murack Five. "On my way. I can at least bring back an empty. Over.

"Kitoy, I'm done. I'm heading to the otterzoid settlement. When Tim gets back, have him shift the cargo out of the unused quarters. We'll be taking more people back than we brought. He'll need to configure their rooms. Get on with Muperr, find out who and what's term of service is complete. I don't expect much re-enlistment. When we know how many k-no-in are coming back, I'll check with the local k-no-in about any spare sleeping platforms she has. I want to look at one to see if it will integrate with our systems. Over."

"Captain, this is Jacques. Oh yes, over."

"Hello, Jacques. I'm sorry we've left you on your own. Over."

"I understand priorities, Captain, but I now have one. I have been inspecting the local ocean monitoring stations. They are not good. I need the repair parts sent for them delivered to the shore immediately to avoid catastrophic failure. Over."

Ryan stared at the k-no-in transport where he'd stacked the equipment and sighed. "Rowan, I'm going to be a while. Over."

Two hours later, Ryan pulled an O.S.C.T.M. up on a sandy beach by the sea. Jacques's scuttle suit lay on the sand, its legs splayed out. A trough made of ill-fitting repurposed polycarbonate panels thrust out over the ocean. It was full of rotting vegetation. As he watched, a clump of the vegetable matter fell into the sea.

"Over here," called a nanobot-translated voice, followed

by a high-pitched thrum.

Ryan scanned the shoreline, spotting the octozoid, who was waving his tentacles.

It took a minute to push across the sand with its tufts of vegetation, then Ryan lowered the O.S.C.T.M. into the shallow water.

"Thank you, Captain. If these units are not repaired immediately, over a year's data will be lost." Jacques released catches on the side of the case and started sorting through its contents. "Are things as bad as the others say?"

Ryan sighed. "There have been deaths. A day or two later, and there would have been more."

"In this age of wonders that some should die of hunger." Jacques made a whistling sound with his waste orifice. "I am sorry I have not been of more help, but being aquatic…" He waved his tentacles.

"We do what we can. Are you good to maintain the remote sensor stations?" Ryan stepped out of the shallows and sat on the beach.

"Once you drop off my rations, I'll have all I need. An earlier researcher equipped a cave for habitation. The delayed shipments have transformed inconveniences into disasters. I must go. Several of the monitors are in the sunlit zone. It is easier to work with ambient light." Jacques thrust pieces of equipment into a bag that hung from a belt around his bulbous body and vanished into the sea.

"Star Searcher, we are going to have words."

RECRUITMENT

Samantha hobbled forward. The crutch dug into her armpit, and a cut on her leg was irritated by her hospital gown brushing against it, but she couldn't resist the lure of the ship.

Exiting medical, she looked up and down the corridor. Ground forces officer country was to her left. To her right was a hallway with a large door in the side where the rest of medical used to be. A series of smaller doors opened off the other side of the hall that had once granted access to the small arms locker, the morgue and various supply rooms. The elevator was at the end of the meter-wide hall.

Hobbling, she followed the passage. If she squinted, she could believe she was on the *Moor Hawk*. She could imagine Jeff McCaffery walking up and trying to get her to join a poker game or Dyia Ghosh coming on to her.

Tears brimmed in Samantha's eyes as she pressed the call for the elevator.

Henry watched Samantha in silence. He'd retrieved her records from the relief station's mainframe as soon as Pikeman brought her aboard. She was no threat. He had seen enough vets saying goodbye to know the signs. There was no harm in letting her walk the halls with her ghosts.

Samantha rode the elevator to the space flight crew section. She stepped into the hall. Here she could have been on the *Moor Hawk*. Aside from small brass plaques that dotted the hall, this was a Hawk in its glory. The thump-hop of her gait filled the passage as she walked to the officer's mess. The door opened, and she stepped in.

Empty but clean. She sat at the fourth chair down on the door side of the rectangular table.

Conversations and laughter from long ago played in her mind. She half expected the door to open and comrades to step in or a catering officer to appear in a duty uniform and deposit a food tray. "This is a working ship, no fancy dress here. Eat up and get back to station." She mimicked the voice of her old XO.

She debated pulling an M.R.E., but she was still on a schedule as her body adjusted to regular feedings.

She moved back to the corridor. The door to the quarters that corresponded to the ones she had had was locked. She moved on. The laundry was open. The spare uniforms cabinet was empty, but everything else was as she remembered it. She came to the door to the bridge. Her hand trembled as she pressed the button, expecting it to be locked. To her surprise, it slid aside.

A cougar tan felinezoid swivelled in the communication chair and flared her nostrils. A man of partial American First Peoples ancestry smiled at her from the environmental station. Most shocking, a mutilated android turned his chair to regard her.

"Hello, Samantha," said the android.

"I'm sorry. I..."

"Nothing to be sorry for," said the felinezoid. "I'm Kitoy. Take a seat."

Samantha hobbled to the pilot's station, sat, and scanned the board.

"I'm Tim, and our computer officer is Henry." The man spoke in a cultured voice.

"Samantha, but of course, you already know that."

"We know. Welcome to the *Star Hawk*. Ryan, the captain, has been busier than a madam at a hedonist convention, or he would have said hello himself earlier," remarked Henry.

Samantha smiled. She swivelled her chair and scanned the pilot's board out of habit. "You know, you need to clean your grav ports. Half of them have reduced efficiency."

"Told you. It takes explosives to remove the spacer once it's caught hold." The intact side of Henry's face smiled. "I'm on it, baby doll. Just taking a while because my maintenance bots are shuffling cargo. We got time."

"Do you want to run a pre-flight?" asked Kitoy.

Samantha's hands were caressing the controls before she could think. "Aside from the dirty ports, everything is green, and I mean everything. I've seen Hawks fresh out of the yard that didn't have readings this good."

Kitoy flared her nostrils. "I noticed that your term of service for Murack Five is up. What are your plans?"

Samantha swivelled in her chair to regard the felinezoid. "Is this a job interview?"

"First interview, if you like. Ryan has the final say, and Rowan, our navigator, is the procurement officer, but they're both busy, so we decided to do some screening for them." Tim sounded officious. "According to your record, you are qualified to pilot a Hawk in communications and have a General Operating Procedures certification."

"I... I hadn't thought past getting off this miserable rock. I..." A hundred ghosts called out to Samantha. A hundred silent voices said, 'live on. Live on for us, or else what was it for?'

"I would appreciate your recommendations, but I am rusty, and my leg..." Samantha continued the pre-flight.

"Baby doll, you don't need a leg to pilot. If Pikeman does his job, you'll be fixed up and ready to shag in a couple of months anyway." Henry's voice had its usual banter.

"And as to rust. Henry, please lock out the pilot's board and run some simulations." Tim's voice had lost its pompous overtones and could almost be mistaken for his father's.

"Whatever you say, oh desirable captain's son," said Henry.

"Is he always like that?" Samantha started running a simulation.

"You get used to it." Kitoy went back to scanning her board. "That's odd. Henry, have a look at this."

Ryan plodded into the otterzoid settlement. The soaked legs of his coveralls had dried, but they were wrinkled and encrusted with salt. Five otterzoids lounged on blankets in the late afternoon warmth. They all looked malnourished, but as one, they moved their heads to regard Ryan as he approached.

A male otterzoid stood on trembling legs. "Captain Chandler. I am O'lam Fishseeker, administrator of this settlement. You and your crew are sweet fish after a fast."

Ryan hurried to O'lam and sat cross-legged on the ground in front of him. "Please, save your strength."

O'lam partially collapsed onto the filthy blanket he lay on, then made a splashing motion with his paws. "Rowan has told us much about you. She says you wish to know the distribution schedule for the aquatic normal flora modules?"

"They're all that's left to unload, and because of a shipping error, the support units have a limited charge." Ryan let his hand rest on the soil. He imagined he could feel life returning to the nearly-dead world.

"We will not know where to deploy the units until after the next flood. The shelter stations have their own electrical supplies. They may be adequate to maintain the modules. You should talk to Flower about it."

"Flower? Oh yes, the k-no-in technician." Ryan glanced to where Rowan crawled out of one of the shelters, carrying an empty M.R.E. "I will. There is also the matter of the dead and those of your people who have completed their service."

Rowan walked to Ryan's side and kissed him.

He looked at her with shock.

"You're a civilian. Get used to it." Rowan lay her hand on

his shoulder. "I'll tell him, O'lam."

"Thank you, Rowan. It is a strong current in the telling. As to who will be departing, two of my people have completed their sentences. There is no doubt that they will go. You will have to ask Donald about the *Homo sapiens'* camp. We cooperate but have autonomy, and such issues are not my purview. Captain, if you will excuse me."

Ryan could see that the small effort of speaking had exhausted the otterzoid.

"Of course. Enjoy the sun." Ryan stood and walked with Rowan to the edge of the settlement.

"What is the mystery with the dead? We need to take them to prevent contamination," Ryan half-whispered.

Rowan looked grave. "They were desperate for nutrients that Murack Five sources lacked. Meat is meat."

Ryan looked at his boots. "Divine!"

"They did what they had to." Rowan gripped his arm.

"No judgments, Row. I've seen enough to know, 'there, but by the grace of the Divine, go I.' It does pose a problem."

"What?"

"Many species eligible for service on Murack Five have taboos against cannibalism. Recruitment is hard enough." Ryan shook his head.

"People will understand."

"What was your first gut-level reaction when you heard? The first second before you had a chance to think?" Ryan took her hands in his.

Rowan's features clouded. "The first instant? Revulsion."

"Society programmed us that way. Too many people never take the next step and think."

"Henry says that biologics are programmed." Rowan sighed.

"There is nothing like an outsider's perspective to cut through the lies we tell ourselves." Ryan smiled. "Part of why that polymer prat is my friend. He keeps me honest."

"We need to cover the—well, it's not technically

cannibalism, but still—up." Rowan nodded.

"No doubt, but how? The bodies must be accounted for to avoid contaminating the environment or future kangazoid culture. We can't risk some kangazoid archaeologist digging up an otterzoid skeleton in a million years."

"What do we do?" Rowan looked anxious.

"For now, we haul the empty O.S.C.T.M.s back to the ship. Then go to the *Homo sapiens* settlement. Tomorrow, with any luck, we will do auxiliary station three, then it's back to Kangra-la to finish offloading. By then, I should have a plan."

Rowan smiled. "One of your plans. We're in trouble!"

"You are spending too much time with Henry."

Croell and Zandra watched as a pair of emaciated *Homo sapiens* used the settlement's aging grav lifts to walk a transport container out of the *Mary*'s hatch.

Once it was outside, Croell and Zandra took the felinezoid cargo unit and walked towards the village as the *Homo sapiens* moved back into the *Mary*.

"It saddens me that we leave the unloading to these unfortunates. They should be given time to rest," remarked Zandra.

"The *Mary* is a *Homo sapiens* ship. They fit better." Croell focused on the two k-no-in that walked back from the village with the other set of grav lifts. "Star Searcher has much to answer for."

"To think a sentient starves in this age. It is inexcusable," agreed Zandra.

Croell bobbed his head up and down.

Muperr approached along the trail and fell into step beside Croell. "Greetings, Croell and Zandra of Cloud Skipper Sect. May the Great Flyer of the Skies flick tongue upon our meeting."

"Greetings, Director Muperr Trapsetter. You honour us with your formal greeting." Zandra spoke from her end of the cat box.

Muperr's tail flicked happily that the couple honoured him by having the female reply. "I'm sorry I did not greet you immediately. With the supplies, there has been much to do."

"A leader's first duty is to his people. Courtesy may be delayed for a just cause." Croell flicked his tongue.

"Your understanding is appreciated. I have several reasons for our discussion. First, to thank you for braving the dangers of the Murack system."

"The *Star Hawk* cleared the way for us," observed Croell.

"It is about the *Star Hawk* and her crew I wish to speak. I must confirm that you know that all Republic employees in a Republic zone are exempt from honour geasa for the duration of their service."

Croell and Zandra stopped cold. "Do you lie?" hissed Croell.

"I can show you the ruling. I hope this does not change your willingness to help us. Any you seek vengeance against have sanctuary until their service to the Republic is concluded."

"The theocracy would never agree to this," blurted Zandra.

"They had little choice. Your people are not the least advanced in the Republic but against the technologies of the elder species…" Muperr shrugged and lashed his tail.

Croell bobbed his serpentine head and neck. "The Great Flyer of the Skies is merciful."

"Husband?" gasped Zandra.

"Neither of us wishes to see one of our charges dead. With time, a way to fulfill our geis without killing her may become apparent. An opponent too dangerous to have may become an ally invaluable." Croell flicked his tongue and tapped his finger claws on the ground.

"How?" Zandra eyed her husband with fascination.

"Do you recall the exact words spoken to our clients?" Croell flicked his tongue.

"Not the exact words."

"I know with Hunoin, I agreed to deliver Rowan to her for the cell sample. She specifically wanted Rowan alive. Beyond the delivery, the kill was hers to undertake. I have reviewed it in my mind. John led me into a false interpretation of that contract. It is complete in the eyes of the Great Flyer of the Skies."

Zandra bobbed her head.

"Rowan is your target?" Muperr popped his claws and, despite his emaciation, bared his fangs. "She and Ryan have done much for this settlement."

"Calm yourself, Director. Much is happening you do not understand. The laws of the theocracy will be kept by my beloved and myself," soothed Zandra.

"The problem truly starts with John. I was distraught and do not recall my words exactly." Croell flicked his tongue. "It is oddly fortunate that they will have been recorded. If we can experience that record, there may be a way." Croell turned to Muperr. "As to you and your people. We said we would help. That is binding on us. In truth, I welcome the opportunity to meet with Captain Chandler on neutral ground. We have things to discuss."

Ryan walked hand in hand with Rowan down the trail to the *Homo sapiens'* settlement. With her, he could forget the icy fist around his heart. The churning in his gut stilled, and when he looked around, he could see the beauty of the river and the iridescent blues and greens of the swarms of grasshopper-like insects that burst from the reed beds as they walked by.

Rowan pointed to a half dozen creatures that looked vaguely like six-legged hornless buffalo grazing on the other side of the river. "They're impressive."

Ryan squeezed her hand. They were a couple on a walk. With her, he could revel in the moment. He pulled her into a one-armed hug, and they watched the herd. Above, the sun was setting, painting the valley grasses gold.

"When this is over, we should go camping." Rowan's voice was light.

Ryan smiled. "The important things." He sighed. "We need to talk to Flower about hooking the aquatic habitats up to the shelter's system."

Reluctantly, they moved to the edge of the *Homo sapiens* settlement. Yipya and Flower stood side by side, watching the sun kiss the valley's edge. *Homo sapiens* men and women sat outside the shelters.

"Ryan. It is good to see you." Yipya turned to face the approaching humans.

"From what I hear, you've had a busy time," remarked Ryan.

"There have been no new deaths, and the patients are growing stronger. By tomorrow they should be caring for their own basic needs. *Homo sapiens* are a resilient species." The vet dipped his head in a show of respect.

"So, if we depart tomorrow, you'll be able to deal with it all?"

"With the help available. Allow me to introduce Flower. She is the maintenance technician assigned to maintaining the k-no-in troop carriers."

Ryan smiled at the k-no-in female and gave a shallow bow. "It is nice to meet another engineer. This is my trading and navigation officer, Rowan."

Flower dipped her head, returning the bow. "Captain Ryan Chandler, the world saver. It is my honour to meet you."

"I would have been by earlier, except I haven't quite mastered being in two places at once. A skill every captain should acquire."

Flower released the growling sound that served k-no-in as a laugh. "Engineering technicians as well."

Ryan glanced past Yipya, then rushed to aid a man struggling to his feet leaning against one of the shelters. The green coverall the man wore was clean and in good condition, and the blanket about his shoulders was clean and bore the UES ground forces emblem.

"Take it easy," cautioned Ryan.

"Captain, I'm Donald Samuels, director of this station. Where the nova blast have you been? We ran out of food months ago. I'm lodging a formal complaint." Donald lurched and, with Ryan's help, lowered gently to the ground.

Ryan straightened with an angry expression. "I received this duty a little over a month ago. Pirates raided the last two shipments, killing most of the crews. My crew and I were nearly nova blasted getting here. So, you might like to turn your formal complaint sideways and—"

"Captain!" Ziggy appeared at Ryan's elbow, carrying an armload of clean blankets. Ziggy continued in a soft voice. "His wife is the one that didn't make it."

"Thanks for telling me." Ryan let his gaze range over the decrepit settlement.

"It's not as bad as it looks, but it will take days to set the place to rights."

"Do you know who's shipping out? We have quarters available in the *Star Hawk*. It would be fewer for Yipya and Flower to deal with. It should be safe at the otterzoid settlement now, and I want to move on tomorrow."

"Meredith and Wong. Their contracts were up six months ago." Ziggy gestured to a short Caucasian woman with patchy blonde hair that dozed with her back to one of the shelters, and a middle-aged Asian man with short, lank hair. The man looked up with a cadaverous face, smiled, came slowly to his feet, and saluted. "Captain."

"Wong!" Ryan raced to the man's side and helped him to sit.

"You're looking good, Captain. Civilian life must agree with you." Wong smiled at Ryan.

"It has its moments. You joined the relief effort. Is Cai

with you?"

Wong sighed. "Cai and I split six years ago. No one's fault. Maybe if we'd gotten off Earth when her mother died. It was all too much with the crime and poverty. We didn't have the funds to book passage out system, and I didn't want to re-enlist. The stress drove us apart. After the split, I signed up for a five-year relief stint. Figured I could help fix the mess we made and have some credits in the bank when I was done, plus a free ride to the Switchboard Station. How's the *Star Hawk*? I read that you bought her."

"You'll see her soon. I couldn't let those brass hats take her."

Wong nodded. "The *Star Hawk* is too grand a lady to lose over something as stupid as the admiralty."

"You'll be aboard soon. Yipya, is he strong enough to travel?"

"If someone else does the walking," replied the veterinarian.

Ryan pulled out his handheld. "*Star Hawk*, do you read? Over."

"We read, Captain. Over," came Kitoy's voice.

"Tell Tim to ready two quarters in the space crew sector for *Homo sapiens*. Is Pikeman up? Over."

"He's having breakfast. Over."

"Tell him to bring a pair of grav stretchers. An old friend is coming home. Over."

Ziggy cleared his throat.

Ryan looked at his impromptu gunner.

"Wong can have the quarters I was using."

"Ziggy, you're part of the crew," Rowan regarded the recovering addict with a concerned expression.

"You can stay on." Ryan met the fallen soldier's eyes.

"No, I can't! If I have access to memoria, I don't know what I'll do. Here I can live in the now, make a difference. Wash some of the blood from my hands. Yipya and Flower need a *Homo sapiens* to help them interface with our tech, and Donald is willing to give me a five-year contract as a relief worker. Star Searcher can't block that. This is what I came here for. I'm a ground pounder. I'll never be space crew." Ziggy looked pleadingly at Ryan.

Ryan nodded. "You'll always be welcome on the *Star Hawk*. When Pikeman brings the stretchers, you can help us bring Wong and Meredith to the ship if they are good with it?" Ryan turned back to Wong.

"I'll be happy to be aboard, Captain." Wong smiled.

"Anything to get off this rock," Meredith croaked from beside her shelter.

"Ziggy, please help them pack. Use the empty E.S.T.C.s. We'll bring them aboard. They can unpack when they're up to it. Take a few minutes to clear your room and say goodbye to Kitoy. I think she's going to miss you."

"She's not the only one." Rowan squeezed Ziggy's arm.

"Will do, Captain." Ziggy stood at attention, snapped a military salute, then relaxed and shook Ryan's hand. "Thank you." Releasing Ryan, he hugged Rowan, then moved to Wong and slipped into the shelter behind him.

Ryan turned back to Flower. "I need to integrate the aquatic habitats' power systems to an external source. Star Searcher let them run down to critical. Once they're off my power grid, they've got maybe two hours before the support systems flatline."

"That crab fails the breeding exam on all parameters." Flower dug little ditches with her toe claws. "If I supply power for the habitats, that will slow the cleaner runs."

"The what?" asked Ryan.

"A piece of technology you don't know. The galaxy is coming to an end," quipped Rowan.

Flower let out a low growl. "Engineers are universal. I had a false sire who kept up with all the tech dispatches. I felt the same way about him."

Rowan smiled as Ryan sighed and shook his head. "You were saying, Flower."

"I will show you. Come." Flower led the small group about fifty meters upstream from the village to where reeds and grasses dominated the ecology. The fading sun still gave enough light to see clearly.

Ryan spotted it first. A square platform about two meters wide by three meters tall, supported by a host of three decimeter-long, crab-like legs along its edges. The outer surface seemed to be made of solar panels. The device scuttled forward its own length, then stopped. A moment later, there was a sound like a vacuum, then it moved forward again and repeated the process.

"What does it do?" asked Rowan.

"It is a flower picker." Flower bobbed her head.

"A…"

"Flower, I think the *Homo sapiens* need more context," observed Yipya.

"Have you heard of the Gralipa flower?" Flower spun around, snapping at a bug reminiscent of a wasp that was trying to bite her.

Ryan and Rowan shook their heads.

Flower flared her nostrils. "You're fortunate I know *Homo sapiens* nonverbal communication as well as I do. Gralipa is a genetically engineered plant. Their natural progenitor is a common plant on Srill and Murack Five. The plant picks up radioactive materials and sequesters them in its blooms and stem. The cleaner goes over an area and scans it for Gralipa. Mechanical arms on the unit's underside snip the flowers off at the base without disturbing the plants around them. The bloom and stock are then vacuumed into the storage container on the unit's top. When the container is full, the cleaner goes to a preprogrammed site and dumps its load before resuming its pattern. It's how we have managed to clear this area so quickly."

"A plant that likes radiation?" queried Rowan.

"Why not? We use a breed of chrysanthemum that absorbs heavy metals for environmental cleanup." Ryan watched the cleaner move onto another patch of ground. Now that he was looking, he could see a plethora of yellow blooms to one side and in front of the device. To the other and behind it, they were absent. "What do you do with the cut flowers?"

"The goal was to deposit them into a cavern complex left by one of the old gopherzoid cities, but we haven't had the energy for the transport vehicle, so we built a sluice on the beach and dumped them into the sea. Far from perfect, but it is cleaning this section of land, and the currents sweep the radiation into the deep trench off the coast. Auxiliary station three is doing the same thing into a river." Flower dug her claws into the soil.

"Half fix is better than no fix. Nova blasted sycamorezoids! And you can't generate enough power to maintain the habitats and the cleaners." As Ryan watched, the sun dipped below the valley's brim. The cleaner paused, dug the ends of its legs into the soil and stopped.

"The solar panels on them only supplement stored power. They come to the troop carriers for recharge when they run down." Flower watched as, in the distance, another cleaner robot stopped moving. "After the post-flood rush to re-clear the habitation area, I set them to only work in daylight. It's easier on the power storage systems to cycle less frequently."

Ryan nodded. "I don't have a quick solution. The normal flora tanks have to be powered."

"Then we will slow down the cleaning. The land will lose ground so that the river may live. Without the river, the land is dead." Flower sighed dramatically. "And the buffalo-like herbivores were doing so well."

THE SEARCH BEGINS

"**I** am sorry, Angel. I do not understand what has changed, but my mind seems clear for the first time since coming to your world. I am ashamed of the things I have done." Valaseau lay on the cot in the garden shed/prison.

Angel sat beside her, monitoring her IV and suctioning the mucus from the felinezoid's nose at need. "It doesn't make it right. I love Toronk, and he loves me, and you, well, you…"

"I know. I… the odd thing is, Toronk does not suit me. I like males I can dominate."

"And you dated Toronk?" Angel sounded incredulous.

"I know. You are a better match for him. I normally do not approve of mixed-species relationships. There are too many cultural differences and expectations, but I can see it working with the two of you."

The door opened, and Gunther stepped in, closing it behind himself. "The serum is ready."

Valaseau looked at Angel. "I don't know if being sick cleared my head or something else, but before he cures it, please believe me when I say I am sorry. Take care of Toronk. He's a good male."

Gunther pushed the syringe into the IV tubing and depressed its plunger. "We'll know in a few hours."

Troy's hand hovered over the control that would restart the

psychotic feed in Valaseau. He pulled his hand back. "You know, Gene. I think there may be time for a redemption arc. Note that I am discontinuing the psychotic feed in Valaseau. Put it on the board for all controllers. What's the use of having power if you don't use it?"

Samantha sat at the pilot's station on the *Star Hawk*. She was dressed in a green coverall fresh from the clothes maintenance unit with the leg pinned up. Her crutch lay on the floor beside her. Her pre-flight had been done before the rest of the biological crew returned from removing the cargo for station two and loading a k-no-in hygiene station and twenty sleeping benches. Now she had the opportunity to impress Captain Ryan Chandler and maybe secure a posting... job under him, and she had bats in her stomach.

Ryan sat at the engineering console. "Henry, note. The number two scram jet is showing some resistance. Remind me to check on it."

"Aye, hotty boss."

"Request direction coordinates." Samantha reduced the *Star Hawk*'s gravity profile, allowing it to drift into the air.

"North by northeast, make altitude six thousand meters," said Rowan.

Samantha worked her controls, and the *Star Hawk* sped forward.

Rowan focused on her scanners. "Surface rad is climbing."

Ryan finished his checks and moved to the captain's chair. "Outside the cleaned areas, that's expected. Are there signs of life?"

Rowan focused on the big-screen visuals. "Various fauna, and it appears insects. The mutation rate must be through the roof. We're moving into an area of high rad. No apparent life."

"Expected. Keep scanning. Henry, record everything. The

data may be of use to the relief effort. Samantha, how's my lady handling?" said Ryan.

"Like silk, Captain. All piloting systems green." Samantha made a minor adjustment.

"Once we set down, see Pikeman for an update about your leg." Ryan's voice took on a note of regret. "We may have gotten enough material from auxiliary station two for him to prep for the regrowth."

"Aye, sir. Carlotta and I were friends. Oddly, it will be nice to have part of her near."

"Surface rad is dropping. We're starting to get plant life again," announced Rowan. "Two minutes out from auxiliary station three."

Samantha glanced at the main screen where a mountain plateau with the sea well below and beyond was on view. A k-no-in troop carrier sat at one corner of the flat area, looking like a model on a diorama. A peaked kangazoid dwelling covered in tarps occupied the plateau's middle. Bits of forest and cultivated fields surrounded the structure. A stream fed by a nearby glacier on a mountain to the south meandered across the land. A herd of creatures reminiscent of goats but with six legs, no horns, and pushed-in faces grazed at one end of the plateau.

Ryan's eyes fixed on a mound covered in flowers. A bolt of pain went through his heart. "Rowan, shift the view and push down the stream's course."

The image on the big screen shifted. Six flower pickers were moving down the valley surrounding the stream. Forward of the machines, there was a plethora of yellow flowers. Behind them, there were none. A flower picker came up to a tree and did almost a dance as it circled the trunk, removing yellow blooms, then resumed its course.

"Nice clean engineering. K-no-in may be low-tech, but they use what they have. Pilot, bring us to a hover and drop us to a hundred meters. I want to observe this operation," ordered Ryan.

Samantha used the jets to keep them still against a

gusty headwind while dropping their altitude.

Henry swivelled in his chair and winked at Ryan. Ryan nodded as the rusty pilot demonstrated her skills.

"One hundred meters relative to surface," said Rowan.

"Captain, auxiliary base three has made contact," announced Kitoy.

"Put them through. Navigation, split the big screen." Ryan leaned back in his chair and smiled.

The front screen split, half showing the robots clearing the flowers, the other half showing a k-no-in with a ragged coat with old burns marring the left side of his body. He also had a mechanical left foreleg.

"Greetings to the *Star Hawk* and her crew from auxiliary relief station three. I am Director Grann."

"Greetings. We will be landing momentarily. I thought a brief survey from the air might be useful." Ryan watched as one of the robots stopped collecting flowers and scuttled towards the main plateau. He glanced at Kitoy, who was watching him, and casually scratched his ear. She killed the audio transmission.

"Rowan, put the rad levels up on the screen. Kitoy, resume transmission."

"That is courteous, but we have drones for such tasks. Please land in the circle of boulders in the southwestern quadrant of the plateau."

"On our way. Over and out."

The image on screen was filled by the flower picker, which scuttled to a steep slope ending at a cliff. It dumped a tangle of plant matter that tumbled into a deep chasm. The flower picker then started back for its collection zone. The area around the flower picker's course read seven millisieverts annual, while the slope read ten per annum.

"Expand the visual field," ordered Ryan. "Samantha, have you got the quadrant for landing?"

"I have visual on pilot's screen. It's small, but I can make us fit."

"Bring us in, low and slow." Ryan watched the rad

numbers as they came in. Except for the hillside of the flower dump, the plateau didn't top six millisieverts annual.

Minutes later, the ship was locked down, and the loading ramp deployed.

Ryan stepped onto the plateau and inhaled deeply. The smell of life was everywhere.

"Captain." Grann walked up and dipped his head in a bow.

"Director." Ryan returned the bow.

"My people are ready to assist with the unloading." Grann waved with his mechanical arm. A dozen k-no-in walked up.

"Are you strong enough?" Ryan couldn't keep astonishment from his voice.

Grann made a coughing up a furball sound. "K-no-in are better suited to the environment of Murack Five than the other species. While Grandmother does not embrace my kind enthusiastically, she does not deny us. We have been fortunate in our efforts, and this plateau is suitable for habitation. It was our hope to bring a population of our younger siblings here this year, but we have lacked the vehicles and energy to do so."

"The background radiation is low enough year-round to recolonize?" Ryan sounded impressed.

The k-no-in tossed his head happily.

"You have perhaps seen these?" The k-no-in took a yellow flower from behind his ear.

"Brilliant bio-engineering," observed Ryan.

Grann preened. "Sadly, we have been dumping them into the river that runs along the plateau's base, further poisoning it and the sea, but there is little else to be done without power for transport. If we had the power to transport the harvest and more collection robots, we could have this continent clear in fifty years. Kangra-la decommissioned in ten."

Ryan stroked his chin. "Where would you go if the kangazoids occupied this plateau?"

"Our troop transport is still mobile. We would follow the access valley and establish ourselves on the next plateau. It is safe most of the year and once housed a village."

"The separatists have messed everything up." Ryan sighed deeply.

"Fanatics fail the breeding exam by a large margin," agreed Grann. "Shall we begin unloading your ship? While k-no-in can survive on Murack Five, many of our foods will not grow here. Even ration packs would add desirable variety."

Samantha felt guilty as she lay in the infirmary while the rest of the crew unloaded the ship.

Pikeman stood beside the nanobot manufacturing unit checking readings. "Primitive, outdated, antiquated piece of scrap. Why that self-important dictator couldn't set up my unit so I wouldn't have to monitor the process, I don't know."

"Is there a problem?" Samantha was tempted to challenge Pikeman on his vitriol but was held back by the same reasoning that meant you didn't antagonize the mess personnel.

"The otterzoids were most thorough. The... raw materials... will serve for making the inter-tissue structures, but the nutrient solution for the stem cells will have to wait. Even the bone marrow has been... extracted. The unit is disassembling the raw materials into components. When that is done, I will begin."

"We did what we needed to survive." Samantha lay back on the cot.

"Yes, yes." Pikeman moved to her side and ran a handheld over her remaining leg from the knee down. An image of a human leg appeared on a wall screen. Pikeman worked a control. The picture changed from a right leg to a left.

"You have the beginnings of a shin splint. I'll correct it in the regrowth." Pikeman made another adjustment.

The nanobot manufacturing unit hummed as the energy supply field expanded to fill its construction chamber. The device took the calcium and other materials remaining from Carlotta's body and generated the intercellular framework the stem cells would inhabit.

"With this piece of junk, it will take twelve hours. I'm going to check on the other patients. You may dress and go about your business." Pikeman stomped from the room.

Samantha looked at the nanobot manufacturing unit and sighed. "Thanks, Carlotta."

Ryan stood in front of the mechanical nanobot manufacturer in his workshop. Reaching in, he extracted one perfect ceramic heating unit. The unit was generated from the materials of two of the crumbling, used cores. Turning, he input a set of scans into his drafting screen and worked out an adaptation that would bring the mountings on the k-no-in sleeping platforms into keeping with standard UES floor units.

"Henry, can you handle adapting the deck plates? The records show that we will be transporting ten k-no-in back to the Switchboard Station. I'd like them to have a place to strap in if we pull high g manoeuvres."

"You draw them up. I'll build them, hotty boss. A k-no-in and a *Homo sapiens* can fit together, you know." Henry's voice was teasing.

"I don't want to think about it. Only make four units for a start. I'll mount one bench and see how it works. The difference between on-screen and the real world can catch you out."

The door opened, and a maintenance robot came in carrying several hexagonal floor plates with decimeter-long circular devices beneath them.

"Are those..." began Ryan.

"All with fried grav projectors." Henry directed the maintenance robot to leave the floor tiles under the trackway of mechanical arms.

"Good. We'll swap out bad units with good ones we pull to mount the benches." Ryan stepped to the door. "Bring up the scans of the eastern continent. Put them on the ceiling in my quarters. Overlay the position of any equipment larger than a ground suit when the disaster happened. I'll mount the bench when you have the units ready."

"Sure thing, boss. That area's still hot as Rowan in a bikini."

Ryan paused as a mental image brought a smile. "I am a lucky man." He focused on the job at hand. "I skimmed the scans. Most of the surface is down to safe levels with the EVA suits. I'm not going to let history repeat itself. Dying once for this ball of rock was enough."

"Are we going shopping?"

Ryan opened the door to the captain's quarters and stepped in. The maintenance robots were gone, leaving the room barren. Rolling down the couch/bed into its latter function, he lay down and looked at the map on his ceiling. It depicted a land mass with a large half-circle blasted out of its side, infilled with seawater.

"There is everything we need out there if we can find it," observed Ryan.

"And it hasn't been blown up, irradiated, or otherwise smashed." Henry sounded skeptical.

"It's worth a try. Frankly, that ankylosaur is still in orbit. I don't know how to get by it unless we can beef ourselves up. And the relief effort needs everything."

"I put the regions we updated in colour," explained Henry as Ryan settled himself.

"Good idea. Zoom, grid 7F."

The map moved in on one of the coloured sections. A

dot labelled *Osprey* was on the eastern side of the square.

"Bring up the calculated blast force and directionality for this sector." Ryan closed his eyes. "Divine, if you are out there, I hope you know what you're doing. I wouldn't trust me with this."

Ryan looked at the directionality of the blast wave and drew a mental line.

"Henry, grid 6F." The image on the screen shifted. There was an escarpment of rock that caught Ryan's gaze.

"Henry, sub-grid of 6F 3B, enlarge five times."

The image zoomed in on the escarpment. A jagged arch of rock was torn out of it.

"Henry, draw a line between that crevasse and the start position of the *Osprey* during the blast."

A line appeared on the screen.

"Add curvature for planetary gravity."

The line arched around the planet, going off the screen.

"Zoom out and mark where the bodies of the survivors of the *Osprey*'s crash were found."

The screen zoomed out. A red dot appeared on one side of the line marking the projected course. The map section was in black and white.

"Zoom in grid 5E."

The grid zoomed in.

"Add contour lines for the sector elevation."

The line marking the *Osprey*'s course cut across the grid until it slammed into a low range of mountains.

"Mark it. That is our first search area."

"Do you think there will be anything left of the *Osprey*?" asked Henry.

"The *Osprey* was a Hawk, and we know some of her crew managed to get off after the disaster." Ryan's tone spoke with sadness.

"They fought to the end, Captain." Henry's voice was even.

"For all the good it did them. The rad was too high. We will never forget."

"We will never forget," echoed Henry.

"The rad should be lower now. Now start with the coordinates of the *Mrakper*."

"A felinezoid lander. That's ambitious, boss. What about security?"

"Muperr should have authority, and Kitoy's old intelligence clearances might hold up. Nothing on this rock has been updated since the accident. The computers may be shot anyway."

"We don't have that kind of luck."

"Let's get on. Tomorrow we offload the rest of the gear for Kangra-la. We're done running. I won't let some hateful tree sperm kill this world, and I'm done letting the U.E.S. tell me where I can and can't go and who I can and can't love. If someone wants to get in the way of that, someone will bleed!"

"King Arthur has returned. Hope things work out better with Guinevere this time," quipped Henry.

Ryan smiled. "Merlin, my friend, that is one thing I am sure of."

THE END BEGINS

Kitoy watched as the k-no-in aid workers carried equipment from the hangar bay. Her primary task was to scan the boxes and sort the ones to be left behind. The k-no-in seemed to be in good health.

"It shows you, there's no place like home." Rowan moved to Kitoy's side.

"Or grandmother's house. Where's everyone?" Kitoy swished her tail.

"Ryan said he had things to do in engineering. Pikeman and Samantha are in medical. Tim is trying to convince the *Star Hawk*'s ground forces section that fifteen degrees Celsius is a comfortable temperature. K-no-in like it cool. Wong parked himself at the weapons console and has been running simulations. I think we have a gunner." Rowan waved at two k-no-in picking up a two-meter-long by one across crate with grav lifts. "That one is for Kangrala. The one beside it is the one you need."

The k-no-in dipped their heads and put the crate down.

"It will be good to have a trained crew." Kitoy swished her tail. "Where's Asalue?"

"He said something about being a year behind and placing pickups for the living anthropology. He wants to do a quick excavation of this site before the kangazoids get dropped off, then work the next site in detail. Personally, I think he wanted an excuse to fly around and avoid a long goodbye." Rowan smiled.

Director Grann strode up to the two females. "That's the last container. We can deal with the installation of the units and parts."

"Henry, ask Ryan to come down. We are now cargo light for this location." Rowan spoke to the air.

"Listen to the sexy captain's mate spouting the lingo. I've told him, hotty."

"Is the AI a client of yours?" Grann cocked his head to one side.

Rowan blushed.

Kitoy looked at the expression on her friend's face and hissed with felinezoid laughter.

"Henry is a full AI, willing to work on a ship this size. We all put up with him," explained Rowan.

Grann bobbed his head. "My chief maintenance tech consumes histac root. Whenever I think I've found all the plantings, he comes up with another one. When his mind is clear, he can fix almost anything. I watch him and dig up the roots when I find them. You make allowances."

The lift opened, and Ryan stepped out, moving beside Rowan. He paused to briefly kiss her. Rowan looked shocked.

"I'm a civilian now. I'm getting used to it." Turning, he faced director Grann. "That was a quick unload. I haven't got the sleeping benches set up for the departing k-no-in. Have you told them how dangerous this might be?"

"Captain, they don't care. We may not have suffered as the other species, but this…" Grann waved his mechanical arm. "This is like visiting one's grandmother. Having to be on your guard lest you shame the credits your father paid to conceive you."

"Then ask them to come aboard. I want to land at Kangra-la before it's nightfall." Ryan stepped closer to Grann and spoke softly. "Do any of the ones I'm taking know a wrench from a screwdriver?"

Grann bobbed his head. "Rrrikta and Wotra are fair mechanics. I'll ask Shewof to give a discount to any that help. She's going with you. I wanted to warn you about that. Don't let her have any sharp objects." Grann looked at the deck. "She likes to hurt herself."

"Really?" Rowan moved to Ryan's side.

"There are many ways to fail the breeding exam." Grann shrugged.

"We'll deal. Kitoy, put out the call. We're grabbing sky in one hour."

Medwin sat on his mother's battered couch beside Kendra. They were sharing a textbook for the astronomy 101 class. Obert sat in one of the dilapidated loungers, absorbed in a first-year ecology text, while Jessica sat on the stained carpet reviewing a text on the history of psychology. Carol occupied the other lounger, entering data on legal precedence for one of her employer's cases.

Kendra's watch buzzed. "Sorry, guys. It's time for the news."

Medwin looked up from the text. "No sweat. I could stand a change. Stellar formation is a simple concept, but when you get into the math..." He shook his head.

Carol saved her file. "That's most things."

Kendra shuffled forward on the couch, picked up the remote from the pressboard coffee table and turned on the TV mounted on the wall. "Professor Acharya insists that we follow the news on multiple outlets. He calls it a living example of media and persuasion. He wants us to contrast the media and explain how it proves that the medium is the message."

Obert stretched. "I hope they continue the feature on the reduction of funding for tree planting."

A commercial for Skunk Be Gone deodorant played.

"More like smell like one," observed Carol. "My friend Jabir tried it. I had to take him into the shower and hose him down before the party started. He didn't seem to mind."

"Honey, TMI," remarked Jessica.

A sequence of images speeding through the streets of

Sun Valley played with the caption, 'NEWS FOR YOUR LIFE' across the screen. The image shifted to a well-dressed, attractive woman with midnight black hair and stunning blue eyes sitting at an anchor desk.

"Welcome to the news. We start our program today with a piece from our international office."

The image changed. Everyone in the room gasped and glanced amongst themselves. Ulva sat at a news anchor desk. Behind her, a graphic of the Earth turned slowly. She spoke gravely. "Hello, I am Doctor Ulva House, Global Network News Medical Correspondent. The World Health Organization and the Centre for Disease Control have issued a joint statement.

"A species-threatening pandemic has been released by the Wisconsin Separatist Front. This genetically engineered variant of chlamydia, *chlamydia aerosolizes*, while causing only mild irritation of the mucosal membranes, is airborne and highly contagious. Thus far, all cases have resulted in sterility. Agents from the I.I.B. have recovered documentation of the pathogen's structure and life cycle, which are currently under review.

"Efforts are underway to isolate all cases. The community of Sun Valley, where the Wisconsin Separatist Front released the virus, has been quarantined. The authorities ask that people stay in their homes. Follow news on this station for updates and commentary as they become available."

The screen shifted back to the local anchor, who had gone pale. "This just in. Sun Valley has been declared a pandemic disaster area. All save emergency and healthcare workers will be confined to their homes and places of business. The World Health Organization wishes to inform the citizens that they will coordinate with federal and state agencies to establish food drops. Citizens are instructed to leave their current location only as a matter of survival. The authorities are working on this matter. The symptoms to watch for are itching and/or sores on the mouth, genitals, or anus. All but essential businesses are closed. Any employer forcing workers to violate quarantine will be imprisoned for six months and face fines of up to five hundred thousand credits. Police will arrest anyone who violates quarantine."

The news anchor swallowed. "We will interrupt regular programming throughout this crisis as we learn of new developments. Now continuing with our regular programming. A traffic collision occurred on the corner of Boxletter Drive and Tompson Avenue at—"

Kendra turned off the television and looked at Medwin. Medwin vanished into his bedroom, emerging with a large roller suitcase. Unzipping the front pocket, he pulled out a power cord that he plugged into a wall socket, then pressed a button inside the open pocket.

The feeling of static electricity danced over their skins.

"That's a distinction without a difference. Everyone in Sun Valley is either a scheduled red or orange clone. None of us is fertile." Obert shook his head.

"But now everyone will know it," remarked Medwin. "James's wife killed herself because she couldn't handle that."

"Or because the controllers manipulated her to not handle the news. Why though? We know everything, federal or state, is the controllers. Nobody ever tries to leave Sun Valley."

"They're closing us down. This way, they have a perfect reason to isolate us. After a couple of weeks, they open up enough to let the exports out and essential imports in. Schedule orange and red clones have a thirty-year life expectancy. Mike is going to let attrition clean out the city." Medwin went red in the face. "Bastard!"

"You'd rather he kill us?" asked Jessica. "That's what they did last time. Mike and Marcy are the reason that changed."

The phone rang. Medwin shut down the jammer before he picked up the line.

"Hi, Mom."

Pause.

"Yes, I heard."

Pause.

"Not even to come home. All right, I'll keep the gang here. I think there's enough in the cupboard for a few days."

Pause.

"We'll have to wait and see."

Pause.

"I love you too. Stay safe, and remember you need to sleep too."

Medwin put down the phone. "They are taking the quarantine seriously. One of the nursing assistants from Mom's work tried to go home and was arrested. We're all in for a sleepover."

"That sounds like fun." Carol smiled and licked her lips.

"Umm, no!" said Kendra.

"I'm with Kendra on this one, honey. Three is as much company as I want for some things," observed Jessica.

"Probably for the best," added Obert with regret.

Medwin shifted uncomfortably under his friend's scrutiny.

Ryan stood in the large, nearly empty room that had been the ground forces quarters. Ten k-no-in watched his every move. Twenty k-no-in sleeping benches, taken from auxiliary site two, lay on the floor.

The hexagonal floor tiles all glowed green, orange or red.

"Set the benches two meters apart, then pull the grav tiles corresponding to the legs. Like this." Ryan put a U-shaped device over a floor tile, turned it a quarter turn, then lifted out the tile.

"If the tile is red or orange, put it in the E.S.T.C. we're

using for disposal. If it is green, pull a red tile from the floor and put the green in its place." Ryan pressed a button on the U-shaped tool, releasing the tile, then moved to a red tile on the floor and pulled it, slipping the green tile into its place. The tile glowed green. Ryan put the red tile in the waste box. He repeated the process with three more tiles.

"Very elegant," remarked Rrrikta.

"Thank you." Ryan moved to a bench he'd left floating on a pair of grav lifts. "This is the only tricky part." He walked the bench over so its legs hovered above the open holes in the floor. "You take one of these units and attach it to the power feeds in the hole corresponding to the bench's input jack." Ryan held up a cable with a sphere about three centimeters across mounted in its middle. Each end of the wire ended in connection jacks.

"You connect one end to the *Star Hawk*'s feeds, then connect the other to the jack in the bench leg." Ryan demonstrated. "After that, you lower the bench into place."

Ryan dropped the bench, so its legs sank into the holes in the floor. Ryan opened a panel on the bench's leg and pressed a button. There was a clicking sound as the tile's mounting systems secured.

"Try it out." Ryan watched as Wotra lay on the bench and adjusted it to his body.

"Ryan," the breathy, sultry voice Henry had assigned for Kitoy when she used the intercom filled the crew section.

"What is it now?" Ryan sounded resolved.

"Croell and Zandra have called. They want a face-to-face."

"I'll give them a face-to-face with a laser torch. That nova-blasted pirate scum tried to kill me!" Rowan's voice carried over the channel.

Ryan gritted his teeth. "I'll be up shortly. Try and find out what the stardust they want."

"On it." The channel closed.

"I believe we can perform the bench installation. It is nice to deal with tech that is not unnecessarily complicated." Rrrikta measured out the space to the next bench. "We do not require this much room."

Ryan smiled. "If I get the chance, I want to set up walls. It will have to be later. Everyone is busy right now."

"Most kind of you, Captain. We will call if there are problems." Wotra began removing floor tiles.

"Thank you all for your help." Ryan left the room.

Ulva watched the screen dedicated to Gunther's perspective. Valaseau trembled where she sat on the floor of Gunther's basement. The jammer ticked down towards failure. Willa and Angel knelt beside their enemy, stroking her fur in a soothing way.

"And this is true?" Valaseau asked for the tenth time.

"It is true." Gunther's voice was soothing.

"I will kill the controllers. The things I have done. The madness. I..." Valaseau's gaze passed over three of her greatest enemies. Her emotional monitor peaked for shame.

Ulva released an anti-anxiety medication from Valaseau's drug pack. Gradually her emotions stabilized.

"The sickness?" Valaseau wiped her running nose on the back of her forearm.

"Faked. I've gone through the motions for the show. We could still use you to deliver the supposed cure. I have no idea why they've let your mind clear. It might be for that." Gunther pressed the button, releasing CO_2 coolant into the jammer. "We're almost out of time. Will you take the cure to the felinezoids and otterzoids?" said Gunther.

"Do you believe all this?" Valaseau looked at Quinta, who lay on the ambulance gurney wrapped in bandages.

Quinta gingerly took a breath, grimacing as she did so. "Yes."

"Then so shall I. I'll take the supposed cure to my species kin and the otterzoids. Which faction holds the clinic?"

"They have agreed it is neutral ground. Both sides need medics, and there are too few to draw a distinction." Gunther looked at the floor. "Too many dead."

"Too many have died for a silly diversion," agreed Valaseau. "Beings die in war, but this has not been war."

"No, but sadly, more will likely die because the controllers think only of their own benefit and don't value the lives they control," agreed Willa.

"Perhaps it is a war. I will deliver the cure and try to persuade my fellow sentients to join the octozoid cause. Hurast is disliked, so that should not prove difficult." Valaseau lashed her tail.

Ulva noted that the psychotic feed was turned off in Valaseau and checked who was responsible, finding Troy's memo. She smiled. "Maybe coffee isn't such a bad idea."

Croell stood outside the settlement's great hall and watched the *Star Hawk* in the landing zone. The *Mary* was parked back from the edge of the glacial wall. He flicked his tongue, tasting the air.

Zandra stepped out of the hall and moved to his side. "Husband, I have spoken with Ryan. He was less than inclined to meet with us."

"As I suspected he would be." Croell started walking towards the landing area.

Zandra fell in beside him and stroked her chin over his shoulders. "I swore by the Great Flyer of the Skies that we would take no action against him or his crew until they finish their duty to the Republic."

"And?" Croell didn't take his eyes off the *Star Hawk*.

"He understands our ways. He agreed to meet with us."

Croell flicked his tongue. "He knows his prey."

As they approached, the *Star Hawk*'s hangar bay ramp descended. Ryan emerged, carrying a cylindrical object in one hand.

Croell's tread faltered. He fluffed his wings and spoke softly. "My wife, get behind me."

"Be careful, my husband. He is not batzoid. His oath may not hold." Zandra fell back and let Croell precede her.

"He is Ryan. His oath will hold even as he holds ours suspect. That laser torch is the precaution of a faithful man accustomed to dealing with the faithless." Croell spoke soothingly.

"Croell, hatched of Creen, flown by Brock. You come to me under words of truce binding under the Great Flyer of the Skies' laws. For as long as we breathe the winds of Murack Five, we are barred from violence against each other and those each holds under their protection," Ryan shouted.

"I so do come before thee, Captain Ryan Chandler, in peace bond under the Great Flyer of the Skies' laws for as long as we breathe the winds of Murack Five."

"As you are Cloud Skipper sect and Zandra is not bound by your oath, I offer the pledge of peace to her. What says she?" Ryan stepped towards the batzoids, his thumb against a switch on the laser cutter's side.

"I come in peace and will hold you, your crew, and passengers safe from all violence by the Great Flyer of the Skies' laws."

Ryan slipped the laser cutter into a holster on his belt and held his hands where they could be seen.

Croell and Zandra rose on their hind legs and showed open, empty palms.

"You wish to speak." Ryan closed the distance between them.

"We have much to discuss." Croell flicked his tongue. "You have been a cunning opponent. I give you the gift of my respect."

Ryan allowed the ghost of a smile to touch his lips. "You're still breathing. The feeling is mutual. Let's see how we can arrange for all of us to stay alive."

"There may be a way in keeping with my obligations to the Great Flyer of the Skies," began Croell.

The sun was fully down before Ryan called back to the ship, and Rowan joined him and the batzoids in the main hall.

Croell watched Rowan tentatively enter the large room and move to Ryan's side at one of the long mess tables.

"I greet you with open hands." Croell showed his empty palms.

Rowan rubbed her shoulder through the material of the jacket she wore. It hung on her slender frame, front heavy. "Hello."

"It is a pleasure to meet you," Zandra spoke the *Homo sapiens'* nicety while holding her palms open.

"I... You tried to kill me!" blurted Rowan.

Croell shrugged. "It was a contract. Had I known you as I have come to know you, I would not have taken it. Both for your worth as a being and the risk involved. Hunoin is a sentient the galaxy would be better off without. Not a bad Gunlok player."

Rowan went red in the face. Ryan took her hand before she could speak. "Croell may have a way out of one of our predicaments."

"I am bound by my oath to fulfill the geis your John Wilson placed upon me. The geis of Hunoin was fulfilled when she received the stem cells and deactivated the nanobots she supplied you with. I opened the door for her to kill you, and she, through her own actions, failed."

"You poisoned me. I almost died!" Rowan looked flabbergasted.

Croell shrugged. "And would have save that by Hunoin's actions, your death was prevented. Under the laws of the Great Flyer of the Skies, Hunoin lost claim to my services when she supplied the nanobots that prevented your death. That geis is fulfilled."

"So, you only intend to kill me once," snipped Rowan.

"Row, hear them out. Would I have asked you to leave

the ship with them here if I had doubts?" Ryan looked at her imploringly.

"Fine. So that leaves John."

"John Wilson came to us in the set region, commissioned our services, and supplied us with a ship and a Luba bot to act as a piloting interface. We are charged to return to him within the year."

"And this is my concern. Why?" Rowan's gaze darted between the two batzoids. Neither of them looked threatening.

"It is a matter of the wording of our contract. We think we pledged to bring your body before him."

"Not gonna happen." Rowan's hand slipped into her jacket pocket.

"We are hoping we did not state the body's condition." Zandra flicked her tongue.

Rowan looked at the batzoids. Her hand slipped from her pocket.

"But we must be sure. It is possible our exchange with John was recorded." Croell flicked his tongue.

Rowan sat. "We can't go back into Gaia space. I'm not legally a person there, and Ryan is wanted."

"We might be able to lure John to the Switchboard Station. This is a start, Row." Ryan looked at his once enemies. A calculating expression filled his face. "Croell, Zandra, would you be willing to help us all leave this planet?"

"If it is in keeping with the Great Flyer of the Skies' laws." Zandra flicked her tongue.

"I'm going to be unloading all day tomorrow. I need a rad and terrain survey of part of the eastern continent. I'll need one of another few sectors the day after. You could speed things up by doing them for me."

"Of course, Captain. John is paying for the antiproton, so it would be our pleasure." Croell flicked his tongue.

Ryan smiled as a spark of hope kindled.

SHOPPING LIST

Tim yawned and leaned against the corridor's wall. Convincing the *Star Hawk*'s sub-processors to adhere to non-*Homo sapiens* environmental norms was a constant battle. Opening the door to the quarters that had been Jacques's, he found two otterzoids lounging in the water.

"Greetings, Doctor Timothy Chandler," called the mahogany-furred male.

Tim stepped into the room. "Please, Sea-Bird, Tim is sufficient."

Both otterzoids splashed the water with their hands. "We must thank you and your father/captain for providing this pool. We know it is not customary for *Homo sapiens*' vessels to be so well disposed for the comfort of other species."

"Your thanks are appreciated, Skalla. We do what we can. Is the water warm enough?"

The green-furred female swam in a circle, then splashed her paws. "Quite comfortable. And the rations. I never thought field rations could taste so good. I wanted to ask, what are your plans for after we return to the Switchboard Station?"

Tim sighed. "I don't think my father has thought past getting out of the Murack system."

"We would like to speak with him. Murack Five presents unique opportunities for profit if you have the imagination to see them."

Tim eyed the otterzoids. "Wasn't it the pursuit of profit that resulted in you going to Murack Five in the first place?"

The otterzoids cleaned their muzzles. "Yes, we sold rights to land we did not hold the rights to. This, however, is real and can benefit all involved. Your background encompasses elements of environmental engineering, correct?" Skalla spoke enthusiastically.

"Yes." Tim sounded skeptical.

"Will you open your surface thoughts to me so that I may impart information?" Sea-Bird looked up quizzically.

"Only my surface thoughts and only information. I'll draw my own conclusions," said Tim.

Sea-Bird wrinkled his brow. Tim gasped, then smiled. "I'll talk to my father about it. No promises. He hates this planet."

"As do we all, but there is a fortune to be had that will benefit this world. It seems oddly appropriate that Captain Ryan Chandler should be one of those who reap the benefits."

Tim laughed. "And oddly necessary that a craft with the capacities of a Hawk perform cargo runs in the Murack system."

"For a non-telepath, you are most perceptive," remarked Skalla.

"I've known lawyers. Enjoy the pool."

Ryan watched as k-no-in carried the last cases of supplies down the *Star Hawk*'s ramp. Muperr and Kitoy stood to one side of the hangar bay, their tails swishing as they conversed in their species tongue. Muperr's coat was filling in, and he no longer had the exhausted air about him, though you could still count his ribs.

Tim and Rowan were manoeuvring the personal effects of the thirteen *Homo sapiens*, fourteen felinezoids, two otterzoids, and twelve k-no-in from the primary relief settlement, whose terms of service were complete, into their quarters.

Ryan approached Muperr and Kitoy. "Pardon me, Director. Might I have a word?"

Muperr swished his tail. "Of course." He turned to Kitoy. "I still say Mopra Spearmaster was the best defensive player they ever had, but I'll take your point about Mrapp Fisher on offence."

Kitoy flared her nostrils and swished her tail. "Have you seen last year's final?"

"No."

"I have it in my personal files."

"Please, and don't tell me about it."

"When you're done with the captain, come to my quarters. *Homo sapiens* ships have good wall displays." Kitoy swished her tail and walked away.

"She is an amazing female," commented Muperr.

"She is that. Muperr, be careful. She still wears the red sash some days. Let's go to the mess. I haven't had dinner, and I'm sure you could do with a decent meal."

"I could, but a ration pack will have to do."

They started towards the elevator.

"We'll eat in the space crew section. Space navy officer kits only."

Muperr lashed his tail. "You do know how to live, Captain."

In minutes, they sat at the table in the officers' mess with steaming M.R.E.s.

"To cut it short, I need armaments if I'm going to make it off this rock alive, and you need equipment for the restoration effort."

"Yes. Are you staying until the heating units can be revitalized or leaving us a power unit?" Muperr looked optimistic.

"No. Stage four," Ryan said flatly.

"Stage four won't happen for ten thousand years." Muperr lashed his tail.

"So, we accelerate the timetable. The eastern continent

is littered with military hardware. When I did the flyover, we scanned the surface rad. In suits, it's within the safe range. Everything we need is out there."

Muperr nodded. "Security protocols."

"Frozen in time at the moment of the accident, Ground Forces Pack Leader for the southeastern continent."

"And you, Captain Chandler of the UES Space Services. If you have the suits, I have the people. Let us go to the market."

"Then, when we're done, Crach can load a group of kangazoids onto his great sky raft and take them to the land of rivers and fields. Tell station three that they should move their troop carrier. The wallabies are coming home."

"Hop hop kanga, watch a wallaby woo." Muperr lashed his tail as hope kindled in his eyes. "Maybe this hasn't all been for nothing."

⊂══◆⟩

Kitoy tidied her quarters and found the file in her personal database. The entry door chimed.

"That was quick." She opened the door and found herself staring at Tim.

"Hi, I wondered if you wanted to go to mess together. The otterzoids, Sea-bird and Skalla, have an idea I want to bounce off you." Tim smiled in the odd way *Homo sapiens* did. At that moment, that smile was so alien to Kitoy. He was so alien.

"I..." Kitoy lashed her tail. "I'm having Muperr over to watch a Hunters game."

"Oh. They're the Predator team you've told me about, right? Would you like some company?"

"You hate team sports. I think you'd be happier not." Kitoy forced her nostrils to flare, trusting the species barrier to hide her other reactions from the alien. She pushed down on a sense of shame.

"I... Whatever you want." Tim stepped away from the

door, which closed.

Kitoy looked at the charcoal sketch of Kadar and her on the wall. "You don't get a say!" She lashed her tail and tried not to feel ashamed. "Tim will be better off. He has no idea how hard it is being in a mixed couple. Besides, how dare he assume? Muperr is coming to watch a game. Nothing is going to happen. I... Oh, Kitoy, shut up." She went back to tidying her quarters.

Samantha lay on the treatment cot in the *Star Hawk*'s medical bay. A body bag lay open on the floor. With clinical detachment, Pikeman fed tissue and cartilage into the nano-processor.

"The otterzoids didn't let much go to waste." Pikeman finished filling the processor and pressed a button. "This will make enough nutrient slurry to begin the process. I trust that you are competent to refresh the reserve tank as needed. I will prepare a supply of nutrients before you depart."

"I... Don't you feel anything?" Samantha looked at the bones in the bag.

"They are raw materials." Pikeman extracted what looked like a model of a lower leg with the skin left clear and the muscles opaque. "I serve the living."

Samantha imagined a moment of regret crossed Pikeman's face.

Lining the lower leg up, he pushed it onto her stump and secured it with transparent tape. Next, he attached an input valve to its side, extracted nutrient solution and stem cells from the equipment on the wall, and put them into a bottle that he suspended IV-like by the treatment cot.

"You must stay on the cot as the leg fills and the stem cells establish. It will be morning before you can move. That includes bathroom breaks. The nanobot sanitary system is there for a reason. Use it. After that, you'll have to refresh the nutrient solution whenever the reservoir gets low. You cannot put weight on the regrowth unit for a month. I will put it in a cast once I have seen it is established properly. That will support it and remind you. Your leg will be regrown and integrated with your biology in two months."

Ryan sat on the bridge. Rowan occupied the navigator's station. The big screen showed the surface scans Croell and Zandra had spent the day taking.

"Another ankylosaur has moved into orbit. I don't think they're laying mines. They're too stable," observed Rowan.

Ryan smirked. "Mines would be useless. There's a cloud of leftover chaff waiting to chow down on them. I should pass that fact on to Croell and Zandra."

"You can't trust them. They're murderers!" Rowan turned her chair to stare at Ryan.

"They only think they're murderers, doll face. All the hits before Sun Valley were imputed." Henry put a 1920s Chicago accent on his voice.

Ryan and Rowan shared a confused look but let it slide.

"Fine, attempted murderers," Rowan amended.

"My love, if you think about it, we both have body counts far higher than theirs." Ryan took a breath and released it through pursed lips.

"I... I thought I was defending my world." Rowan hung her head.

"And I was serving my species, and Croell was enforcing the laws of his culture. Dealing with other species means stepping into their skins. I don't trust him past his own self-interest. He needs a clear path off this planet. We're his best bet of getting it. Someone needs to do the job, and it got him away from here for the day in case he found some loophole that would let him still act against us. Zoom 5E on the big screen, please."

Rowan adjusted the view.

The screen displayed a mountain slope littered with toppled, blasted trees. A pair of peaks formed a deep valley. There was a gouge in the side of one of the peaks with a jumble of rocks hurled to the west below it.

"Move us forward. Ten meters per second to the west." Ryan watched the screen as if he would bore through it with his eyes.

After twenty seconds, there was a trench of gouged rock and shattered trees.

"Follow that trench." Ryan stood and stepped closer to the screen.

The image tracked forward for ten seconds. The valley widened out and flattened. A large protuberance in the land came into view.

"Centre on that object and enlarge."

"Divine," whispered Rowan.

On the screen, the shattered remains of the *Osprey* lay on its side. The ship's top was sheared off, leaving tangled polycarbonate and metal. Its landing legs stuck out to the side. Several of them were missing. Others were mangled. The hull around the lower decks was largely intact.

"We found her." Ryan's voice was sad.

"I..." Rowan's voice caught. "How bad was it to do that to a Hawk?"

"Bad enough to kill a world. What's the rad level?"

"Twenty-one millisieverts annual."

"Safe with the EVA suits we have. It looks like we're grave robbing." Ryan clapped his hands. "Henry, contact the *Mary* and transmit the next set of map sectors to them. They can look for the *Mrakper* while we deal with the *Osprey*. I want everyone on the EVA team rested and good to go. Rowan, how long until it is first light at the crash site?"

Rowan did the calculation. "It's noon there now, so sixteen hours."

"We're grabbing sky in ten hours. Henry, tell Muperr.

Wake the bridge crew in eight. Mess will be ten minutes after. Wake the EVA team in nine hours, mess and safety checks in transit. I want to take advantage of ambient light. We have work to do."

"Sure thing, hotty boss."

Kitoy and Muperr sat angled on her couch/bed so as not to crush their tails and watched her wall.

"Yes! Go Hunters!" yelled Muperr as an object resembling bolas wrapped itself around a post with a large bird painted on it.

Kitoy swished her tail. "That was a great shot."

"And from a first-year member of the club. Falcon Bowcat is leading the hunt." Muperr looked around Kitoy's quarters as the players set up for the next round. His eyes fell to the charcoal sketch of Kadar and Kitoy on the wall. "That's a nice picture. Not many people work in traditional mediums anymore."

"It was my husband's idea. He tries... tried to support artists." Kitoy looked at the sketch.

"You miss him," Muperr spoke softly.

"Sometimes."

"Was it hard being with a *Homo sapiens*? I have *Homo sapiens* friends. Working on Murack Five, how could I not? But I've never been attracted to one in a physical sense." Muperr looked at Kitoy.

"It took getting used to on both our parts, but no. Being with Kadar was the most natural thing I've ever done. When the spirit is in love, the body will follow." Kitoy's tone dropped as an image of Tim floated to the top of her thoughts.

"That is a lovely sentiment. Kitoy, I—"

"Kitoy, hotty boss says we're grabbing sky in ten hours. All crew up in eight to dress and mess. You might like to sack out. I think Crach, god of mercy, will be working us hard tomorrow. If only." Henry's voice came into the room.

"I should go and see to some things in the village. Ryan has asked that I come along to deal with any active felinezoid systems." Muperr stood.

"We can finish the game later." Kitoy moved to the door. Muperr paused and took Kitoy's hand, massaging its back with his thumb. Kitoy returned the gesture but inside felt hollow. Her door opened, and Muperr stepped out. The door closed. Kitoy looked at her hand. "Kitoy, what do you really want?"

Valaseau and Angel slipped into Gunther's backyard. It was pre-dawn.

"You will take the cure to Chelaa, right? She's the best one to disseminate it." Angel flexed her wings.

"I will. Tell Toronk that I am sorry." Valaseau looked away.

"I will." Angel leapt, drove her wings against the air and cleared the fence around the yard. She caught the updraft rising from the hot street and gained altitude.

Valaseau vaulted the fence and vanished into the shadows. She slipped past the forces maintaining the quarantine and, an hour later, entered the abandoned warehouse the pirates were using as an infirmary. She scanned its grubby institutional walls and took in the background stench of mould and decay.

"I lived like this!" Her lips pulled back from her teeth. "So stupid, so unimaginative. We could have lived like gods by selling advanced technologies to the primitives."

An exhausted-looking k-no-in appeared in the hallway in front of her. "Commander?"

Valaseau took on a defensive stance. "I have a cure. I must get it to Chelaa."

The k-no-in eyed her. "Do you know of the leadership challenge?"

Valaseau lashed her tail. "Yes."

"And that this is neutral territory. All who come here are treated without question." The k-no-in eyed her warily and scratched its claws against the concrete floor.

"I know that now and agree."

"And that by order of the chief medic, Chelaa, there will be no violence permitted here."

"I can agree to that." Valaseau sighed heavily. Given her history, she couldn't blame the k-no-in medic for doubting her.

"Chelaa is in the room to your left. If you harm him, it will be your life. All the k-no-in have agreed to the peace bond, and we will enforce it."

Valaseau sheathed her claws, touched her fingertips together and bowed. "I will heed your words. I swear by my blood and my kin."

The k-no-in dipped its head and stepped aside.

Valaseau entered a room full of cots supporting a dozen felinezoids and eight otterzoids. Chelaa and two k-no-in moved between the stricken, suctioning airways and refreshing bags of IV solution. A chameleonzoid lay on a blanket on the floor, trembling. An IV flowed into its side, and a large bucket was by its head.

"Chelaa." Valaseau moved to the otterzoid nurse's side.

"Valaseau." Chelaa sounded scared.

Valaseau forced her nostrils to flare and tried to look non-aggressive. "Gunther healed me. He sent this." She held up a bottle of clear liquid. "He said two cc's intravenously per patient and to watch for allergic reactions."

Chelaa stared at the felinezoid. "You have made common cause with the defenders?"

Valaseau looked to the floor. Her tail trembled. "Gunther's telepathy booster did for my mind what the serum did for my body. He made many truths plain to me. I no longer see enemies where I could have seen friends."

Chelaa made a splashing motion with his paws. "The

truth is persuasive. Help me distribute this 'cure', then perhaps I can get some rest."

An hour later, Valaseau helped a leopard spot felinezoid move into the washroom. Two k-no-in stood at one end of the infirmary, dishing broth into cups that other k-no-in distributed among the patients.

Chelaa moved to Valaseau's side.

"What about the chameleonzoid?" Valaseau gestured towards the reptilian officer.

"They attempted to put poison in the octozoids' lake. That one got splashed with the poison. I do not think he will last the day."

"How many chameleonzoids does that leave?" Valaseau watched her species' kin and otterzoids recover with a sense of satisfaction.

"I am not sure. The k-no-in are evenly split between sides, but only twenty are left. This insane war against the *Homo sapiens* is ending, no matter who wins our internal conflict. It is just a matter of how much more blood is spilt."

LEVERAGE 26

Ryan hurtled towards a plain of toppled trees. The respirator on his face hissed with each breath. Wind tore at his hair. His service coveralls barely cut the cold. Streaks of light flew towards him, then steered away as the friendly fire protocols took over. He pulled his ripcord. Nothing happened! He yanked it in a panic. Still nothing! The ground came up. There was a flash of light. He jerked awake, screaming.

Rowan wrapped her arms around him, her soft hair pressed tight against his back.

"Divine, I hate this planet," he gasped.

"Kangazoid village?" asked Rowan.

"No." Ryan sighed. "How I took the rad dose."

"That wasn't in the entertainment I experienced." Rowan pulled him down onto the bed and held him.

"Part two. It's also how I became Saggal's breath brother." Ryan let her warmth comfort him.

"What brought it on?"

"What I'm going to do to the *Osprey* is similar to what I did then." He arranged Rowan so that they spooned with her in front. The smell of her, the warmth of her, they drove the demons back.

"The k-no-in troop transports were heavy with plants and animals protected from the radiation wave. The problem was they didn't have flight capacity. We needed them in Kangra-la and the western continent. They were too big to fit in any of the landers."

"So, you came up with a brilliant plan." Rowan kissed his

hand.

"Saggal did. We performed EVAs to wrap ropes around the transports, then made a kind of net that we put over the landers of the more advanced species. Have you ever seen a dirigible?"

"On television. Like a helium balloon on a larger scale," reflected Rowan. She'd learned to navigate the waters of her man's trauma.

"With the grav neutralized, the *Star Hawk* floats on the air. We used that effect and lifted the k-no-in troop transports. We couldn't move very fast because it would overstress the cables. Atmospheric pressure kept us to about five hundred meters above sea level."

"Why not use the grav lasers to lift them?" Rowan couldn't quell her curiosity.

"Can't use a grav laser in atmosphere. The weight of the air molecules you pull in will cave in the ports." Ryan kissed her shoulders. As his stress reduced, other distractions impressed themselves on his consciousness.

Rowan nestled back into him. There was only a brief window of opportunity for learning what was at the base of his fear before his defence strategies would end the discussion. If she pushed, she knew he would shut down. If she went along, the rest of the story would come in time.

"The *Star Hawk* was flying a k-no-in troop transport loaded with plants and animals over the central continent to Kangra-la. Saggal was in a felinezoid grav tank, flanking us and watching the harness and cables. We were almost clear of the land." Ryan kissed her shoulders as his hands began to wander.

"And?" whispered Rowan.

"Later. We don't have much time before the wake-up call. I don't want to waste it."

Angel landed on the third-storey balcony of her apartment,

folded her wings and slipped into her living room.

"Angel!" Toronk set aside a lithium-coated dagger and lashed his tail happily.

The diminutive dark-skinned woman rushed into the tabby stripe felinezoid's arms.

"I've missed you so much." Angel took his hand in hers and rubbed it.

"And I you." Toronk brushed his cheeks against the top of her head.

Angel pulled away and extracted a syringe from her fanny pack. "Gunther says this should inoculate you."

Toronk flared his nostrils. "Good. Inject me, then help me get to bed."

"Best offer I've had in weeks."

Ryan sat in the command chair as the *Star Hawk* coasted to a stop fifty meters over the wreckage of the *Osprey*. "Rowan, bring it up on the big screen, fill the space."

The screen showed the *Osprey*. The top was a tangle of smashed materials. Scuffs ran along the sides.

"Samantha, circle the target. Navigation, keep the image on target. I want a 3D scan. Especially focus on the bottom."

Samantha worked the pilot station. Her left leg from the knee down was encased in a cast.

The *Star Hawk* drifted around the *Osprey*, scanning its condition and position.

"Henry, Kitoy, can you make contact?" Ryan watched the screen.

"We have contact," said Kitoy.

"The auxiliary coordination computer is active. Primary isn't there anymore," added Henry. "It's demanding we identify, or it will fire. Uppity class five."

"Spirit of the hawk. Kitoy, put me through. *Osprey* Coordination Computer, this is Captain Ryan Chandler

Alpha, Alpha, Alpha, command override, permission, Alpha, Beta, Delta, Omega one three two. Cross-reference voice print. Do you acknowledge?"

"Cross-referencing command officer's voiceprint file corrupted. Please submit supplementary verification."

Ryan rubbed his temples as he dredged through his memories. "Bi nilj shi, beekid bi."

"Security phrase accepted. Acknowledging Captain Chandler."

"What was that?" asked Rowan.

"The full extent of my Navajo, and I mangled it. *Osprey* C.C., stand down all weapons systems. Under U.E.S. Space Services regulations, I am assuming command of the *Osprey*. Do you acknowledge?"

"Acknowledged."

"Send all data on ship's condition to the *Star Hawk* and prepare for friendly boarding."

"Acknowledged."

"Rowan, Henry, put it on the big screen." Ryan leaned back and watched as a schematic of a Hawk class filled in with red, orange, and green appeared.

"Nova blast!" commented Wong from the weapons console.

"Nobody sneeze. It might collapse," agreed Ryan. "The cargo transfer system for the lower decks looks intact. Henry, track it out. Is there a way to use it for salvage?"

Seconds passed. "It's a lot of detours, but there's a route from all lower deck ports and systems to the exterior loading port. But boss. The ship is on its side."

"That will be the first thing we fix. Bring up the current antigrav specs on the big screen."

An array of G's covered the image. About a third of them were green, the others red.

"There isn't enough displacement to lift her," said Henry.

"We'll deal. Tell the EVA team to have cables ready." Ryan stood up.

"Wasn't dying once enough for you?" Henry swivelled his

chair to glower at Ryan.

"What choice do we have?" Ryan stared at the android.

"What are you talking about?" demanded Rowan.

"Henry can fill you in while I help with the setup." Ryan looked around the bridge gravely. "Henry, it's not like before. This time I'm not against the clock. There's time to do it safely, and I will be fully suited. I'm the only one with the engineering skills to pull this off, and it needs to be done. I'll be careful."

"If you were careful, you wouldn't go out there in the first place." Henry scowled and swivelled his chair.

"Samantha, drop us down beside the *Osprey*'s top side. Kitoy, tell the EVA team we exit the ship in twenty minutes."

Twenty-five minutes later, Ryan was in the personnel airlock on the *Star Hawk*'s bottom beside the closed hangar bay ramp. The airlock was a twin to the one on top, save that the exterior hatch was its floor. Ryan had draped polycarbonate cable over the shoulder of his suit and held onto a ladder on the airlock's wall. Two of the relief workers with EVA ratings were crowded in with him, also carrying cables. The radio and safety checks were behind them. Now it was time to begin. Cold dread clutched Ryan's heart, but this time Rowan wasn't there.

"Open the hatch. Over," he ordered.

"Opening hatch. Over," replied Henry.

The floor vanished into the hull, leaving the personnel holding onto the ladders on the airlock's walls. Ryan descended a ladder that ran along one of the support legs. He reached the ground. "Afra, come down and stay by the lock. You're safety officer. Cowan, drop your cable and come with me. We need to look for tie-downs on the *Osprey*. *Star Hawk*, do you read me? Over." Ryan took a step.

"We read you, Ryan. Your suit telemetry shows internal rad is green. Over."

"Keep an eye on that for me. Send out team two. Team two, do you copy? Over." Ryan picked his way between shattered, desiccated tree trunks and blasted boulders toward the *Osprey*.

"We copy, Captain. Over," came the reply from Walt, team two's leader.

"As we planned. Attach the cables to the *Star Hawk*'s outer port legs, then feed them out to the *Osprey* in as straight a line as possible. I should have the tie-down points picked by the time you're done. No heroics, no shenanigans. It may not look deadly outside your suit, but it is. Over."

"Understood. Over," replied Walt.

"It would be better with a larger team," observed Cowan's voice.

"Radio protocols. Over," snapped Ryan.

"Sorry, rusty. Over." Cowan's tone was stung.

"I'm sorry. Overreaction. You're right, but I only have six functional suits. When you buy scrap, the government likes to get its money's worth. Over."

Ryan walked to the *Osprey*, which towered over him like a cliff. The floor of the top deck could be seen beyond the ship's torn and twisted upper walls.

"Seeing it up close, I have to ask, can we really lift this? Over," said Cowan.

"Topple, not lift. Over." Ryan began walking along the edge of the stricken ship. After a few strides, he pulled a cylinder off his suit's tool belt and marked a place where two struts formed a triangle with paint. "That's bow one. Over."

Stress sweat dripped down Ryan's sides as he imagined the air in his suit as thin and cold. He walked along the *Osprey*'s side to where another junction of support struts was visible. He marked it and moved on.

⊂═━◇

Rowan watched Ryan on the big screen. "How's he doing?"

Kitoy lashed her tail. "He's not saying much beyond

orders and consults. Pulse and BP are both high for *Homo sapiens* norms."

"If he had any sense, he'd have worn a brown uniform. EVAs are dangerous." Henry sounded concerned.

Rowan swivelled her seat to look at Henry. "What happened before? Ryan got as far as telling me that they were airlifting the k-no-in troop transports like zeppelins."

"I don't want to remember it." Henry turned and faced the redundant human-computer interface on his console.

"Kadar told me. It's how he and Ryan got irradiated." Kitoy's voice was sad.

"Please. He…" Rowan thought of Ryan's reaction if she shared his confidence in her or the vulnerability he revealed only to her. That would be a betrayal to top all others. "I would like to know."

"When the blast hit, it tore through everything. There was damaged equipment everywhere. We were moving a k-no-in troop transport heavy with twenty-five k-no-in, plants and animals. Ryan called them seeds of the future," began Henry.

"There was a *Homo sapiens* portable missile installation on the surface. The crew was dead, but the computer had standing orders to fire on enemy vessels." Kitoy's nose started to run.

"The wind had destroyed its reception dish or the rad and EM pulse its radio input. Either way, it didn't receive the cease-fire order." Tim looked up from the environmental board. "Did you think I wouldn't ask what killed my father's first body?"

"The captain was so driven. He wanted to save anything he could. We all did. We all felt the guilt, but he forged it into purpose. That is what Captain Ryan Chandler does," Wong chimed in.

"When the unit opened fire, Saggal was riding safety and inspection patrols in a felinezoid grav tank. He wasn't expecting an attack because of the ceasefire. When he saw the missile, it was too late to evade it. It slammed into his tank. Somehow Saggal brought the flying brick down in one piece," added Henry.

"Still don't know how he managed that," Wong chimed in.

"The automated system fired on the troop transport next. It took a hit to the side. Kadar had to treat sixteen k-no-in for radiation sickness." Kitoy took deep breaths.

"The captain was stumped. How to stop the missile fire. The unit was targeting the downed felinezoid tank as the perceived greater threat. One clean hit, and it would be over. Someone with command authority had to reach the missile unit to shut it down." Wong's voice took on a hint of awe.

"And hotty boss, madman that he is, came up with the most stardusted scheme in the galaxy." Henry sounded annoyed.

"What?" Rowan eyed her shipmates.

"Friendly fire protocols," Henry and Wong spoke in unison. Henry continued. "*Homo sapiens* weapons under computer control have it encoded into their base programming not to target unarmed *Homo sapiens*. It's a way of preventing civilian casualties."

"Suits count as armour. Ryan broke speed records getting to the hangar bay. He grabbed a respirator and a parachute and was out the airlock," Wong continued.

"With the rest of us screaming for him to stop. The missile system stopped firing on Saggal's tank and the troop transport and focused on Ryan as he went down. The missiles got close enough for their system to confirm an unarmed human, then diverted.

"Here." Henry blinked. The big screen's image split. Half showing the current EVA, the other half showing the image of a man in a space services uniform descending onto a barren of broken trees, mud pits, and boulders on a white parachute with a caduceus on it. He hit the ground, rolled, coming up against a toppled log and released the chute before running towards a dirt-coloured oval on caterpillar treads with long tubes on its top. Something shot out of one of the tubes as the figure ran. The image jostled. "Second hit on the troop transport. The kinetic wave got through."

The figure leapt onto the black oval. Ryan's voice commanded. "Missile platform, you are ordered to stand down and cease bombardment. Captain Ryan Chandler of the *Star Hawk*. Voiceprint confirm."

"Standing down by order of Captain Ryan Chandler. Break in command protocol is noted for review." The voice was mechanical and muffled. The bombardment stopped.

"We set down as quick as we could. Suited personnel went out to help the survivors. Three of the five felinezoids made it. The captain came in as quick as he could, but it wasn't quick enough." Wong looked away from the screen.

"The k-no-in transport's hull was breached, and the door jammed. Kadar threw medical kits through the hole in the hull but couldn't fit through in his suit. He took it off, crawled through and suited up on the inside. He saved a dozen k-no-in, but his exposure was enough to kill him in time." Kitoy's nose was running.

Rowan nodded as she watched the image of Ryan race towards where the *Star Hawk* was setting down. "He gave his life that others might live. Ryan, we are going to have to work on that!"

"I like how you think, hotty," agreed Henry.

The main screen returned fully to the present. The lines had been strung from the *Star Hawk*'s landing legs to the *Osprey*'s shattered hull sections and pulled taut. The EVA-suited figures were walking back to the *Star Hawk*.

"*Star Hawk*, we have finished prep and are coming in. Over." Ryan's voice sounded weary.

"Confirmed. Over."

"Check systems. We'll have enough day left after decontamination to attempt a tilt. Henry, tell the *Osprey* to warm up its grav nullifiers and do the same for ours. Over."

"Just get in the ship. Blasted deranged biologic. Over,"

snapped Henry.

As the sun touched the western horizon, Ryan sat at the engineering station.

"Samantha, make us light and let us drift up."

"Aye." Samantha's hands caressed the pilot's controls. The *Star Hawk* rose into the air, pulling up against the cables attaching it to the *Osprey*.

"Kitoy, Henry, activate all grav nullifiers on the *Osprey*. Samantha, zero-g effect."

On the big screen, the *Osprey* shuddered as the cables pulled taut. The *Star Hawk* tilted to one side. The *Osprey* jerked up and then fell upright. The *Star Hawk*'s deck tipped sharply.

"Level us," ordered Ryan.

The *Star Hawk* levelled, floating above the *Osprey* that now stood on its remaining legs.

"Take us down. We'll untie tomorrow. Henry, how are the support legs on the *Osprey*?"

"She's shaky, boss."

"Will her hangar bay ramp open?"

A moment passed.

"No joy, hotty boss." Henry swivelled to look at Ryan.

Ryan took a deep breath, held it, and then let it out. On the screen, twilight was descending into night. "We're done until morning. Break out the good rations. This is a win."

⊶◇

Tim stood in one of the athletic simulation booths studying for his GOP. His skills weren't needed, and watching the EVA was boring. He needed the distraction from Kitoy… He hung his head. "Pause lecture."

He looked across the *Star Hawk*'s gym.

"It's only natural she'd want to be with Muperr. He's felinezoid. Common background like that crazy sport she's into." He sighed.

The door opened. Samantha clomped in on her

crutches. "Hi, Tim."

"Hi, Samantha. Are you cleared to work out already?" Tim sounded incredulous.

"Refreshing my GOP. It's been a few years."

"I'm taking mine."

"Want to review together? I hate the stock lecture series. I like to touch the systems I'm working on. It's how my brain works."

Tim smiled. "Sure. I've got the text files on my private system in my quarters."

"Then let's go. Beats having them beamed into my brain." Samantha turned and clumped from the room.

TAKING THEM HOME

The sun was full up, and the cables formerly attaching the *Star Hawk* and the *Osprey* were returned to storage. Ryan and Cowan deployed the collapsible loading ramp beside the damaged ship. As Ryan climbed the ramp, he looked at the hull.

"What a mess. Over," remarked Cowan.

"Nothing stealth capable, that's for sure. Over. *Star Hawk*, we're entering through the cargo hatch. Henry, direct us to the hangar bay. Over."

Ryan dropped to his hands and knees as he crawled into the passage. The lights on his helmet came on. Rails for the E.S.T.C. distribution system stretched out before him, occasionally forming junctions.

"Turn right at the first junction, then left at the next. Over." Henry's voice was steady.

"Understood. Over." Ryan and Cowan crawled forward until the tracks split. "We're there. *Osprey* C.C., open the cargo transfer hatch to the hangar bay and increase lighting to day levels."

The hatch slid open, flooding the tunnel with light. Ryan slipped through, came to his feet and froze.

"Divine keep them warm," breathed Cowan.

"And fill them with light," added Ryan.

"What is it? Over." Kitoy's voice entered their helmets.

Ryan scanned the scene. Before him stretched a jumble of damaged equipment and shattered pieces of humanity. Dried blood spattered the walls and floor. Immediately in front of him, a corpse lay on the floor. A troop transport on its side cut the remains in half. The back of the skull was caved in. Bones protruded from the tattered uniform. He turned and saw a head, the skin dried mummy-like against the bones. The jaw broken. Beyond that was a crumpled heap of bones lying against the underside of a U.E.S. field ambulance that was missing a front-drive wheel.

"I think I'm going to be sick," said Cowan.

"Take deep breaths." Ryan stepped forward. Something rolled under his foot. He looked down. It was a human arm, the flesh dried to the consistency of leather.

"We can't disturb them. This is a grave," blurted Cowan.

"We must, or we fill more graves. I promise this to the dead. We will bring you home. *Osprey* C.C., what is the status of the morgue?"

"Stocked within standard U.E.S. space services parameters," the *Osprey*'s auxiliary coordination computer reported in an even voice.

"We process by the numbers. First, the loading ramp, then the suits. Then with more bodies... workers, we begin. You got that, Cowan? Over." Ryan forced himself to see the job. There would be time for the dead when the living were cared for.

Cowan's voice wavered. "Understood, Captain. Over."

Ryan inspected the loading ramp. A grav tank with a hole in its side the size of a large watermelon had slammed against one of the hydraulic struts, warping it. Pulling a laser cutter from his belt, Ryan sliced through a spot where the hydraulic piston was almost snapped. "*Osprey* C. C., lower the hangar bay ramp."

The hangar bay opened with a thud that shook the ship.

"*Star Hawk*, send the rest of the EVA team. I'll check the suit storage, then go up and scrounge parts for a cargo link. Over."

"Understood. Over," Kitoy's voice replied.

Ryan moved to the suit locker. The door had been cut from its hinges. Six suits were missing, leaving fourteen.

"Cowan, survey the room. Try to find grav lifts. Stay clear

of the tank. Over."

"Understood. Getting distance. Over."

Moving to the grav tank, Ryan clambered through its entry hatch. The interior was mercifully empty of personnel.

"*Star Hawk*, when the team is suited, isolate the hangar bay and open its ramp. I'll be bringing in today's load that way. Over."

Ryan smiled at how easy the old patterns re-asserted themselves. Settling in the pilot's seat, he scanned the controls, then tentatively flicked several switches. The display came to life in an array of red, orange, and green.

He hesitantly activated the grav nullifiers. The battered war machine lifted and evened out until it hovered above the exit ramp.

"Ryan, Rowan says, 'I thought you knew how to drive this thing!' Over," came Kitoy's voice.

Ryan snorted. "When did I ever say that? I was a space forces *engineer*! I only learned to drive these things well enough to move them in and out of my repair bay. Over." Ryan pushed a throttle forward a notch. The large ovoid vehicle inched down the *Osprey*'s ramp. The screen showed the *Star Hawk* with its ramp deployed and four EVA-suited figures walking his way.

Flipping switches, Ryan lowered the tank to the ground in front of the ramp. He opened the hatch.

"Cowan, start loading the suits into the tank. We'll check them back home. Over."

"Understood. Over."

"McMillan, you were a vehicle's tech. Anything you can fly, drive, or otherwise get out of our way, get it on its axles, load it with whatever you can find, then get it to the *Star Hawk*. Over."

"Understood. Over," replied a woman's voice.

"*Star Hawk*, have Henry conscript a maintenance robot from the *Osprey* to scrub the grav ports on the *Star Hawk*. Use one of the ones that has become contaminated. We'll be leaving them behind. Over."

"Affirmative. Over," replied Kitoy.

Ryan looked out the hangar bay's opening to the planet beyond. "You haven't got me yet." He turned and picked his way around bodies and debris to the elevator.

"Perry, I'm going to the space crew sector, if I can get the lift to work. Follow me up. Over."

"Affirmative. Over," replied a crisp baritone.

Ryan reached the lifts, which had had the doors cut away and left on the deck. Stepping in, he hit the button for the space crew section and winced as a screeching sound transmitted through his suit to his ears. A minute later, he stepped onto a deck under an open sky.

"*Osprey* C. C., deck plate integrity display."

The plates underfoot glowed in mostly reds, with orange and green scattered throughout. Moving to where the space crew mess had been, Ryan walked up to a ripped-open interior wall. Pieces of track were exposed.

"A couple of meters is all I need." He selected a length of the E.S.T.C. distribution system track and cut off its mangled end with his laser torch. Three more cuts and he had two meter-long lengths of rail.

"This damage is unbelievable. Over," remarked Perry.

"Believe it. Collect the green grav tiles and load them up. Over." Ryan took the two lengths of track and walked back to the elevator.

"Where are you going, Captain? Over," asked Perry.

"To do something you want no part of. Over."

Ryan stepped onto the lift and pressed for the ground forces level. The elevator screeched as the warped tracks grated against the runners. The lift came to a stop a decimeter off level. Ryan stepped out. A body lay smashed against the wall. The shattered bones had torn the flesh, so it didn't look human.

Ryan fought down his sense of dread and checked the radiation levels.

"Seven mSv. Still protecting your crew as best you can,

old bird." Ryan followed the hallway to the small arms locker. "*Osprey* C.C., open small arms locker, Captain Chandler's authority."

The door pulled into the wall with a grating sound. Ryan stepped into a room three meters deep by six long. A device that looked like an EVA suit, only heavier and with tubes mounted on its forearms, was sprawled on the floor. Ryan counted ten kinetic rifles in racks. Twenty portable power packs sat in recharge stations along the wall, and there was a cabinet of pistols and other small arms. Boxes of various types of grenades and RPGs littered the floor.

"*Star Hawk*, do you copy? Over." Ryan began inspecting the suit.

"We read you, Captain. Your signal is barely getting through. Over," replied Kitoy.

"Check the records for someone on board checked out on type seventeen mech armour. Put Henry on the horn. Over."

"I'm here, hotty boss. Over." Henry's voice had a forced quality.

"Are there any empty E.S.T.C.s aboard the *Osprey*? Over."

"Currently thirteen. Over."

"Get them lined up at the ground forces small-arms locker restock port. Over."

"Aye, Captain. Over."

A hatch in the wall opened, and an E.S.T.C. emerged. Minutes later, the boxes of grenades were packed in it. The E.S.T.C. vanished onto the ship's rail system to be replaced by another.

Kitoy's voice came on the channel. "Captain, we have two mech pilots aboard. Over."

"Ask them if they'd like to saddle up. I have a monster to move. Over."

Ryan packed the small arms locker and then turned his attention to removing the power pack recharge stations lining the walls. If he stayed focused, he could forget where he was.

When the room was empty except for the mech, he moved to the next door down the hall.

"Perry, you done up top? Over."

"Unloading the lift. The rest of the team is clearing the last vehicle from the hangar. Over."

"Come up to the ground forces level. Over."

Ryan's eyes darted from the mutilated, desiccated bones and flesh to the door. "*Osprey* C.C., open mortuary."

The door slid into the wall, revealing a room full of large black bags. Ryan stepped in and pulled down a bag before moving to the body in the hall. He enfolded the shattered corpse, sealed the bag and watched as the system activated. Letters formed on a flex screen on the bag as it read the identification chip someplace in the mess of flesh and bone.

> Lieutenant Jane Sanders. Station: *Osprey* ground forces. 3672987. Deceased. Calgary, Alberta, Canada, Earth. Next of Kin Husband Bryan Sanders.

"Divine, I thought I was done with this."

The elevator arrived, and Perry stepped out. "Captain?"

"Load up with the bags we'll need for the casualties in the hangar, but first... Take Jane's other end, and let's get her down. Over."

Hours later, Ryan watched the ambulance with the missing drive wheel hover out of the *Osprey*'s hangar bay carrying a load of salvage. The hangar was now empty save for a line of body bags against one wall. One of the bags sat open. It contained what looked like a handsome Caucasian man with a firm jaw. The body showed no signs of decay or desiccation. The form had been ripped in two at the chest. Ryan knelt beside it and pulled the torn uniform to one side, revealing a spill of wires and circuits.

The bag beside him contained the android's lower body and legs. Reaching into the chest, Ryan felt a shattered half-orb. Moving to the other bag, he found a matching half-orb. He closed the bags.

Master Sergeant Keith. Station: *Osprey* ground forces. AI-25-Copernicus. Deactivated. U.E.S. Space Services. Next of Kin - NA.

Ryan stared at the tag.

"*Star Hawk*. Record for legal purposes. Over." There was a hitch in Ryan's voice.

"Recording bonded statement. Over." Kitoy sounded confused.

"I, Captain Ryan Chandler, formally declare that Henry, Copernicus class AI-16, is my brother under the law. I am heretofore his next of kin. Over."

"Boss." Henry's voice was full of emotion. There was a pause. "Thanks. Over."

Ryan swallowed. "How long until we lose the sun? Over."

"Twenty minutes until sunset. Over," replied Kitoy.

"All personnel. We're done for the day. I'll see you in the *Star Hawk*'s hangar for decontamination. Over.

"Perry, take the other end of this bag. Laura, David, take his legs. We'll carry the Sergeant aboard. Doreen, move the loading ramp away from the *Osprey*'s hull. Tuck it under the ship for the night. Over."

⌖━━▸

Rowan watched the hangar on the bridge screen. A grav tank, a troop transport, and an ambulance were parked in a row. All of them had damage. EVA suits with shoulder crests from the *Osprey* lay on the floor. The suited figures pulled an assortment of equipment from the vehicles and spread it over the floor.

The suit with a captain's insignia on the shoulder set

down a box.

"That's the last of it. What does the scan say? Over."

"You're the hottest thing in there, hotty boss, in all ways. Decontaminate the personnel, then you lot can go to bed. I know that will make our navigator happy. Over."

"Henry!" Rowan blushed.

"Prep for decon. B crew can stow the gear." Ryan sounded tired. Minutes later, he and the rest of the EVA team stripped out of their suits.

Ryan shuffled from the lift to his workshop. He put the two rail sections underneath the mechanical manipulator arms and, yawning, pulled up a schematic he'd made the day before. "Henry, you know what to do."

"On it, hotty boss. You should get some sleep."

Ryan sniffed. "Cleaning first, I reek. Where's Rowan?"

"She says she'll meet you in your quarters."

Ryan's stomach chose that moment to gurgle. Half asleep, he staggered into Rowan's quarters and leaned into the microbot cleanser. He suspected he dozed on his feet because the unit's chime startled him. He turned and was cleaning his back when the door opened. Rowan stepped in, kissed him, then hand-fed him a cake-like emergency ration.

Ryan chewed reverently.

"You can't keep up like this," she remarked.

"It will be easier now with more suits." Ryan accepted another mouthful.

"So, you'll work both shifts. I'll follow you around and nag you if you try."

Ryan let his eyes close. "I must be hungry. The emergency ration is actually edible."

"I spread peanut butter on it."

The cleanser chimed. Ryan followed Rowan to bed. She tossed the ration's empty wrapper in a trash chute, stripped and climbed beside him, pulling up the blanket.

Ryan kissed her once, held her like a child might a teddy bear and plummeted into sleep.

Gunther awoke from a dream than made him blush. *'Jessica, daughter, you're leaking again,'* he mentally projected, then rolled to take Willa in his arms.

"Again?" Willa mumbled, partially awake.

"They're young and, with the quarantine, bored."

"I know, but really?" She nestled back into her husband. "At least we can sleep in tomorrow."

Ryan stood in his workshop with an emergency ration in one hand. His other hand traced the modified rails he'd salvaged the day before.

"Nice work, Henry."

"If Rowan knows you're up, we're both in trouble." Henry's tone was scolding.

"No use lying there awake. How are B crew doing?"

"You could have stayed in bed with the hotty. I would have."

Ryan smiled. "I'll try to get back at the end of her sleep cycle, but Rowan needs sleep. Just because I'm nova blasted doesn't mean I should make her life miserable. About B crew."

"They've swapped out the bad grav tiles for the salvaged good in the ground crew section, got the tools in the cabinets and racks. The extra equipment is catalogued and stowed in E.S.T.C.s. The EVA suits have all been safety checked. Rrrikta and Wotra have taken it upon themselves to repair the troop transport. They said that the ground drive tech wasn't that different from theirs. Per your instructions, they scavenged a drive motor from the ambulance and hull plates from the tank."

Ryan took a deep breath. "I'm getting a new view of k-no-in. Point them in the right direction, show them a little respect, and they'll do you proud."

"They want to do all right. There's a line-up in front of Shewof's bench. Wanna see?"

"No. Henry, no! Their culture, their business. How long until A crew's wake-up call?"

"One hour twenty-five minutes. Samantha is on the bridge running sims. She wants to get it right the first time."

Ryan moved his gaze to the two body bags on the central worktable. "Should I do it now, or do you need time?"

Henry answered slowly. "Do it now, boss. We both know what you're going to find."

Ryan unzipped the first bag, wrestled the android's torso and head onto the workbench, then skinned the abdomen and chest with a laser cutter. Moments later, the chest was open. Black polycarbonate ribs with carbon fibre muscles detached at design breakpoints and lifted to the side. The cracked half-sphere he'd felt the day before became visible. He set it on the counter under the mechanical assembly arms.

"Henry, please scan the unit."

Ryan removed the other half of the sphere from the lower body. Finally, he pulled a square device with a deep v-shaped dent in its housing out of the torso.

"I knew him. Not well. They never let us mechs socialize, but I knew him. We played Divine Creator once. I won, but it wasn't a bad match." Henry rambled as Ryan worked with the hopelessness of a lost cause that demanded you explore every avenue.

He looked up from the broken pieces. "I'm sorry, Henry. The chips along the break are shattered, and the emergency data storage was smashed. There is no way to re-initialize him."

"Another AI slain for the biological masters. I knew he was dead. Has been dead for decades, but..."

"We've seen too much." Ryan patted the wall in front of him. "Henry, you have time to think, but the parts..."

"If a friend can help Samantha walk again, why not me? When you have time, hotty boss."

"When we have time." Ryan returned the shattered android to the body bags.

❮══✦❯

The sun was half over the horizon when the *Star Hawk* lifted a meter into the air and shifted position.

"Ten centimeters starboard, five forward," said Rowan.

Ryan stood outside in his EVA suit as his ship performed a precision manoeuvre it was never designed to do.

"Stall momentum," ordered Rowan.

"Stalling momentum," Samantha stated.

The ship stopped. Ryan moved closer and eyeballed where the loading port of the *Star Hawk* and the derelict now lined up.

"Ease her down," ordered Ryan.

The *Star Hawk* settled onto the dead ground of the eastern continent.

Ryan wedged the loading ramp between the two ships. Climbing the ramp, he placed the adapted rail sections to bridge the distance between the cargo distribution systems.

"*Osprey* C.C., Henry, begin cargo transfer. Over," ordered Ryan.

An E.S.T.C. came to the end of the *Osprey*'s rail system and stalled. Ryan looked it over, then gave it a shove. There was a clicking sound as it slid across the adapted rails onto the *Star Hawk*'s rail system and vanished into the functional ship.

"Send the next one. Over," ordered Ryan.

The E.S.T.C. arrived and jammed. Ryan gave a push. The E.S.T.C. glided into the *Star Hawk*.

"It's workable. When it wears down, it might sort itself out. Kitoy, send the least qualified EVAer we have to this station with a crowbar. Henry, load up our missile tubes, then send the empty E.S.T.C.s back. Have the *Osprey*'s hot maintenance robots unload its racked missiles into E.S.T.C.s. Over."

"Acknowledged. Hotty boss, inventory says there are Rain of Tears aboard. Over." Henry sounded uncomfortable.

"They were made before the ban. Log it as collection for disposal, then stack them in the hangar bay. Over."

Ryan pushed the next box over the hitch in the rails as someone wearing a suit from the *Osprey* climbed the ramp. After watching two boxes transfer, they took the post.

Ryan descended the ramp and walked to the *Osprey*'s hangar bay. He looked at the body bags on the floor. The rest of the EVA team walked up behind him.

"Cowan and Perry, you're with me. Laura, get that mech suit if you can. Use your own discretion and watch the rad. The rest of you are on graves detail. Start with the troop deck, then medical. Move up to officer country. Try to keep the number of trips in the lift to a minimum. It doesn't sound good. Over."

Ryan led the way to the lift and ascended to the ground forces and medical level.

Laura left the group at the door to the small arms locker. She had a pressure cylinder of air under her arm and a portable power pack strapped to her back. The armoury's hatch grated closed once she was inside.

Ryan led the way into the medical facility. It was identical to the *Star Hawk*'s save that there were ten treatment cots. Bodies lay smashed on the floor, some ripped apart. Dried blood sprayed the walls. The remains of a man in surgical scrubs hung semi-upright by his neck. His head had smashed through the front of the nano assembly unit and stuck.

"I'll get body bags. Over," said Cowan.

"Affirmative. I count fifteen. Over." Ryan moved to the corpse projecting out of the nanobot assembler. "Help me with this. Over."

Perry took the other side. They lifted out the corpse. The head fell back, but the soft tissue held it on. By silent accord, they put the body on the treatment table. The device activated, showing zero biological activity. A fast-paced beeping sounded.

"*Osprey* C.C., shut down medical alarms," ordered Ryan.

The beeping stopped. Ryan examined the nano assembler in the wall. "He missed the energy field generator and the nano reserve tanks. With those, it should be easy to fix the assembler at Kangra-la." Ryan began disassembling the unit.

"Sir, permission to speak? Over."

Ryan cringed at the formality. "What is it, Cowan? Over."

"What are we going to do with the bodies? We can't just leave them on the floor for the trip back. Over."

Ryan paused in extracting the nanobot reserve tanks. "Good point. Over."

"We could use the ground forces sleeping racks as shelves. Load them in the hangar bay and walk them and the bodies to the *Star Hawk*. Over," suggested Perry.

"Good idea. Over." Ryan took the components of the nano-assembler and set them in an E.S.T.C. that had appeared in the medical supply port. The box was already half full of medication vials and portable equipment.

Hours passed in emptying the *Osprey* and transferring items to the *Star Hawk*.

Ryan had a wall panel down in medical and was pulling ceramic heat distributors out of their clips and stacking them in an E.S.T.C. when Kitoy's voice intruded. "Ryan, the transfer rails are working without hitching now. Over."

"They wore down? Over."

"The *Osprey* rose up. The hydraulics weren't as bad as we thought. The ship needed to lose some weight. Over."

"Patch me through to Henry. Henry, inventory? Over." Ryan leaned against the wall and rested his eyes.

"The missile tubes are full. Reserve armament is a third

of a standard load. Pikeman is stocking medical. There's plenty of everything. I'll be finished with the E.S.T.C. transfer in two hours. A-team has started hauling over the ground pounder racks. Over."

"What are the rations like? Over."

"Rad free and still on date, barely. Half a standard load for ground forces. Officer and enlisted. Over."

"Anything else? Over."

"There are five hornet drones in the armaments."

Ryan opened his eyes. "Those could be useful. Over."

"If we ever go anywhere with nude beaches, hotty boss. Over."

"Henry, do we have privacy? Over."

"Do now, my sexy captain. Want to talk dirty to me? Over."

Ryan rolled his eyes. "Arrange for the M.R.E.s we keep to be the officer rations. Over."

"Already did. I live with you biologics. I get tired of the complaining. Over."

"Put me on to Rowan. Over."

"Rowan here. Over," came a voice that helped to soothe Ryan's jangled nerves.

"Any sign of the *Mary*? Over."

"They showed on the screens about two hours ago, then went behind the horizon. Ov… Wait, now that is a coincidence. I have them heading this way. Over."

"Kitoy, any communications? Over." Ryan tried to force his shoulders to ease.

"Incoming. Relaying. Over," stated Kitoy.

"*Star Hawk*, this is the *Mary*. We have found our prey. I am transmitting coordinates and a visual survey on a companion frequency."

"He's a polite assassin," snipped Rowan.

"Kitoy, put it on the big screen and tell me, is it the *Mrakper*? Tell Croell thank you and ask him to continue the survey of the eastern continent. Over."

"It's a felinezoid heavy lander. It slammed sideways into

a mountain and split in half. The base portion is on its landing legs, with its aft buried in a hill. The bow is on the other side of the mountain, half-buried in a glacier. Over."

"Call up Muperr. We'll want to cross-reference any schematics. The first thing will be the EVA suits. Tell the rest of the team to bring more ground forces racks than we need for the *Osprey*'s crew. They can serve the same function for the felinezoids. Have them pull green grav tiles from the crew sector as they are exposed. Over."

An hour later, Ryan and Cowan watched two crew in *Osprey* EVA suits load two two-meter-long by one in all other dimensions black boxes that were the ground forces racks into the elevator. Ryan squeezed in beside the cargo.

"These are the last of the bodies. Over," observed a woman's voice.

"How many? Over," asked Ryan.

"Forty-five total. Over."

"Most of the troops were deployed when the disaster hit. Load a hundred of the racks. Over."

Ryan felt a hand grip his shoulder through his suit. "You're taking them home. That's something, sir. Over," comforted the woman.

The lift stopped on the engineering deck. Ryan stepped out with Cowan behind him. Bloodstains covered the walls. Half the lights were out, casting everything into twilight. The pipe-like tubes of the grav laser drive system had smashed through the ceiling, partially blocking the passage. There were scorch marks from a long-dead fire. Ryan squeezed by the grav tubes and moved to the power chamber.

"*Osprey* C.C. Open power chamber," ordered Ryan.

"Cannot comply. Malfunction," the computer's voice replied.

"Do you think we'll be able to get in? Over," asked Cowan.

"All the best stuff is here. See about clearing the hall. Get the mech suit on it. Over," observed Ryan.

Cowan went to inspect the hall. Moments later, Laura, in the mech suit, stepped out of the elevator. Soon there was the sound of crashes and bangs.

Releasing the wall panels, Ryan looked at the door mechanism, then cut the tracks and mounts with his laser torch. Grasping the edge of the door, he pulled it into the hall. The door fell with a crash.

Inside the energy transfer station, it was as if the disaster had never happened. A pair of grav lifts sat in clips against the wall. Ryan checked the three antiproton energy storage units. One hundred per cent, one hundred per cent, fifty-seven per cent.

"It will be nice to be out of debt." He spoke to himself as he pushed the grav lifts under one of the units.

A half-hour later, the second, full, antiproton unit descended on the elevator. The engineering hallway was clear to a hole in the wall opening onto the engineering control room. Ryan stared at a jumble of broken trusses, shattered walls and exploded consoles. Sharp edges abounded. The auxiliary weapons activation and control circuit lay in a jumble of circuits where a strut had smashed through the weapons console. Wires tied the palm-sized chip to the debris.

"There has to be a way to get it without killing yourself," he whispered, then checked his heads-up time display. "Laura, clear the passage down to the auxiliary computer junction if you can. Over."

"On it," replied the mech operator. "I almost forgot how much fun it is to drive one of these things. Over."

"When you're done, log off. We all need rack time. Over."

Ryan moved to the elevator and rode it to the hangar. Switching to the general frequency, he spoke. "That's it for today. Wrap up your current load. Over."

28 NECESSARY RISKS

Ryan crossed to the *Star Hawk* with rain spattering his suit's visor. The grav lifts supporting the full antiproton pack he pulled seemed heavy in his grip.

"Rain might help with decon. Over," remarked Perry's voice.

"Check your externals. Rain's as hot as the rest of this mudball. Over," observed Cowan.

The mech suit walked by carrying the other antiproton pack.

"Captain, how much longer? Over," asked Laura's voice.

"Tomorrow should see us done here. Two or three days at the *Mrakper*, then a day to unload and another to deliver to the auxiliary stations. Then it depends on the moons. Over." Ryan knew he shouldn't let his ire show, but he was too tired to care.

"The moons? Over," said Cowan.

"There are times to start a trip such as ours and times not to. Over." Ryan sighed.

They entered the *Star Hawk*'s hangar bay, counted off, then the bay ramp rose into the ship. Decontamination took an hour, during which most of the suited figures lay on the floor. Some managed to sleep. Ryan checked the work on the troop transport and swapped a pair of grav lifts out of the ambulance to complete the repair.

"Decon is complete. B crew will see to the suits." Kitoy's computer voice spoke into Ryan's helmet.

The A crew stripped and slogged to the elevator while B crew entered the hangar, converging on the salvage.

Rrrikta and Wotra mounted grav lifts on a pair of ground forces racks and moved them to the elevator. Ryan walked the hangar, checking tool racks and cargo. Satisfied, he moved to the elevator.

Rowan met him when he emerged onto the flight crew section. "I've set up a ration pack for you in the mess."

"I'll have an emergency ration. I need to review the…" He looked at an expression as hard as steel.

"You are going to eat and sleep." Rowan took his arm, and her nose wrinkled. "And take a cleanse. Eat first."

Ryan closed his dry eyes as his stomach rumbled. "Fine. Henry, put the images of the *Mrakper* up on the mess wall."

"Henry, don't you dare. Honestly, Ryan! If it takes a day or two more to get away from this planet, it takes a day or two more to get away from this planet."

"The moons don't think so." Ryan's eyes burned.

"What? Never mind. There is no point in rushing if it kills the one captain who might slip by the blockade." Rowan half dragged him to his place at the head of the mess table. Several members of the EVA team stared at him with tired eyes.

Ryan looked at them, assessing people he knew better as EVA suits than face to face. "Half day tomorrow. Spread the word. Tired people make mistakes."

"Thank you, Captain. We were about to say something."

Ryan recognized Cowan's voice. "You should have, but I should have thought of it first."

Rowan deposited an M.R.E. in front of Ryan. The smell reached his nose, and all other considerations left him.

Samantha sat sideways on Tim's couch/bed, her cast supported on the padding. The couch/bed was rolled up into its former position. They both stared at text on the wall.

"I don't get it. The navigator gives the pilot the pull

parameters." Tim looked at the example problem.

Samantha sighed. "A G.O.P. isn't about being a pilot. It's about knowing enough that you can step in and save the ship. In an emergency, you may not have time for a navigator to pick your pull points. You latch the grav laser to what you can see and tug."

"But won't that..."

The door chime sounded. Tim stood. "Door open, please."

"Glad you remembered," remarked Henry's voice.

The door slid into the wall, revealing Kitoy. "Hi. I was wondering if you'd like to take mess together. I... Oh, I'm sorry." Her eyes fell to Samantha.

"Hi, Kitoy. We're working on our G.O.P.s. If you like, you can join us." Tim smiled.

"No. No, I... need to eat. See you on the bridge."

Kitoy walked away. The door closed.

"Awkward," remarked Samantha.

"Kitoy is interested in Muperr. We're just friends."

"Right, and Murack Five will be the next big vacation spot." Samantha shook her head.

"She... We had a start, but, well... I think the species thing got in the way. Which is weird because her husband was *Homo sapiens*."

"People are strange, but I'll tell you this. That cat expected you to be alone. Talk to her." Samantha leaned back on the couch. "I'm not into fur, but she is a sexy piece of cat."

"I'll think about it. I don't want to fight for what should be easy again."

"Some things are worth the fight. I wish I'd realized that when I was still with my ex-wife. Let's get back to the course. Your pull intensity is off."

Ryan lay on the bed in Rowan's quarters. The walls

depicted a starscape. He wearily picked out the constellations. Rowan knelt beside him and held out a pill and a glass of water.

"What's this?" demanded Ryan.

"Pikeman says it will put you out and keep you under for at least eight hours."

"Suppose there's an emergency?" Ryan tried to turn away.

"If we need you, I have an injector of a counteractive in my drawer. Pikeman says you'll be clear-headed in two minutes. Now, get a decent night's sleep before you kill yourself or someone else." Rowan held out the pill.

Ryan popped the pill in his mouth, then accepted the glass of water. "You're bound and determined to save me from myself."

"Comes with being in love." She kissed him, then settled beside him.

"You've saved me so many times. I..." Ryan fell back on the bed, unconscious.

Rowan telekinetically returned the glass to her nightstand and settled beside him.

Ryan sat cross-legged on a metal tray. He looked to his right and saw another tray. He realized he was on an old-time scale. Corpses piled onto the other scale bowl. Kangazoid, felinezoid, k-no-in, *Homo sapiens*. Rowan's shattered body floated to the top of the pile. The scale dropped, catapulting Ryan into orbit.

Huge, armoured dinosaurs flew around him, swinging their club tails. He pulled his sidearm, but the charge meter read zero. Rowan appeared, holding out an energy clip. He slipped it into the pistol. He grew until he matched the ankylosaurs in size and fired at them.

The dinosaurs evaporated, then he fell towards the planet. The wind screamed past, and before hitting the ground, he spasmed and found himself in bed. Cold sweat covered his body. Rowan lay beside him.

"Henry, time," he whispered.

"Three twenty-seven. You should still be asleep, boss," Henry whispered back.

"I…" Ryan felt his head swim. "Make a note. Telekinesis. Divine, I wish we had otterzoid EVA suits. Rowan. Tell her. Don't let me forget or decide against. All our lives. I…" Ryan plummeted back to sleep.

"Note made, hotty boss. Whatever it means."

Ryan stood with a ration bar in one hand, staring at the ground troop area. The k-no-in hygiene unit and benches occupied a small space in front of the door. Then came rows of ground troop racks, each consisting of rectangles two cubic meters square stacked two high, separated by narrow aisles. The floor tiles glowed green as far as the troop racks reached and formed a random pattern of mostly green beyond that.

"Rrrikta and Wotra, you and your crew have done good work here," praised Ryan.

Rrrikta dipped his head in a k-no-in bow. "It is a pleasure to work on a system that is so well designed. The *Hawk* is beyond my understanding, but good structure is good structure."

"Your efforts on the troop carrier were first-rate as well."

"I don't get how people didn't go crazy in transit with only those to live in." Rowan waved toward the troop racks.

"It is rumoured that you are a studio clone. Is that true?" asked Wotra.

"Yes." Rowan sounded defensive.

"Your question makes sense in that case," observed Wotra.

Ryan took Rowan's hand and gestured towards the sleeping racks. "Each rack is set up with an e-rig and programmed to put the body through an isometric fitness program. It's part of why the Hawks have teaching libraries."

Rowan looked at the racks. "They must be worth a fortune."

"Selling off the originals from the *Star Hawk* and my junker went a long way towards paying strip fees and repair costs. Plus, a lot of kids want to sleep in a real soldier's bed." Ryan shook his head. "I can't believe I was ever that young."

Rrrikta stepped forward and laid his chin on Ryan's shoulder. "We all start believing we will be breeders. Regret comes with the years."

Ryan found himself patting the side of the dog-like sentient's face. A moment later, he stepped back. "Log some bench time. The racks should be transferred and mounted by dawn tomorrow. If you can finish the floor, that would be useful."

"As long as the tiles come, it is simple work." Rrrikta dipped his head.

"Rowan." Ryan gestured towards the door.

"Are we going now?" Rowan popped the last piece of her ration bar into her mouth as they entered the hallway.

Ryan sighed. "I don't like this. You aren't EVA-rated, and your telekinesis harms you. I should find another way."

"Stop. Ryan, from what you say, any other way would be even more dangerous to someone. This won't be my first time in an EVA suit, and you'll be with me."

Ryan looked at Rowan. "I love you. I left our suits in the top lock cabinet."

Soon, the suits were donned, and the safety checks performed. Ryan led the way down the *Star Hawk*'s ramp. Rowan scanned the ground, which was littered with dead tree trunks.

"I'm surprised the organics haven't rotted. Over," she remarked.

"Rad kills the decay organisms. In a lot of ways, this is

frozen moments after the disaster. Be careful not to brush against things. There could be sharp edges. Over."

"Are the suits that fragile? Over." Rowan sounded incredulous.

"You don't take unnecessary risks on an EVA. Over."

Stepping into the *Osprey*, Rowan scanned the hangar bay. Rows of salvage covered a third of the floor. Other EVA-suited figures removed sleeping racks from the elevator.

"Captain. Over." Perry's voice came over the radio.

"Go ahead, Perry. Over." Ryan scanned the room, spotting a figure in one of the *Star Hawk*'s suits.

"We've brought down the last racks and tiles from the ground forces section. Cowan has been collecting the personal effects of the dead. Laura has opened the auxiliary computer interface room. The team pulled the textile maintenance unit. It's packed to go. They'll appreciate that in Kangra-la. The old one went belly up. We've been pounding our clothes on rocks in the river. Over."

"Good work. With some luck, we'll move before sunset. Spread the word that we're about to lose the *Osprey*'s C.C. Over."

"There's still a lot to salvage. Over," observed Perry.

"We have what we need today. Over."

Ryan and Rowan took the lift to the engineering floor and stepped into the battered hallway.

"Divine." Rowan looked at the spatters on the walls.

"Cooling fluid. Over," lied Ryan.

"Ryan, I know blood when I see it. Over."

Ryan grimaced. "I..."

"Stop trying to protect me. You can't. Over."

Ryan led her to the engineering room. The sharp edges of broken equipment would endanger anyone in a suit trying to cross the room. Sighing, he pointed out the weapons control circuit.

"It's not too big or far away. I won't need a boost."

Rowan focused her thoughts. The circuit jerked on its retaining clips. Rowan mentally pushed down on the tabs. "These things are a pain. Half the time, you have to pry them up with a screwdriver. You'd think with your tech, you'd have come up with something better. Over," she commented.

Ryan shrugged. The clips depressed, and one by one, the wires pulled free. The circuit drifted over the rubble. Ryan caught it. "Henry, do you have telemetry on Rowan? Over."

Static answered.

"There's a lot of interference here. Over," he remarked.

"I'm fine. Is it really so hard to duplicate these things? Over." Rowan gestured towards the circuit.

"Nearly impossible. There is an AI chip component. Speaking of chips. Over." Ryan led the way down the hall. Sharp metal and polycarbonate surfaces abounded, and they had to pick their way. A door had been torn out of the wall, exposing an intact room a meter square. In front of them was a meter-long object shaped like half a football, with dozens of slender legs around it. The legs clipped into ports in a network of circuit banks. On the side walls were banks of circuits. Most glowed orange. One section was dark.

"Rowan, allow me to introduce the Coordination Computer. Over."

Rowan looked at the football-shaped device. "Why is it so big? Over."

"What do you mean? Over." Ryan sounded confused.

"Henry's CPU fits in his chest with room to spare. Over."

Ryan's smile was lost behind his faceplate. "This unit is ten times the size of Henry's, one-tenth as smart and one one-thousandth the price. With it, the *Star Hawk* can operate with a full crew. It will free Henry from a lot of routine tasks. In biological terms, this is a possum brain to Henry's human. Over."

"Economics. Over." Rowan nodded her head, but the suit hid it.

"Resource management. Over," said Ryan.

"Same thing. What do we do now? Over."

Ryan started undoing the screws that held the dark circuits to the side wall.

"Won't that affect local function? Over." Rowan held open an empty toolbox they brought to receive the circuits.

"This section interfaces the top deck. Nothing left to affect." Ryan stowed the circuits, then stepped up to the C and C module. "*Osprey* C.C., can you read me?"

"Affirmative," replied a mechanical voice.

"This is Captain Ryan Chandler command override, permission, Alpha, Beta, Delta, Omega, one three two. Set all components to local control and prepare for disconnect."

"Preparing. Preparing. Preparing." Lights on the banks of circuits on the side walls flashed. "Prepared."

Ryan grabbed the C.C. by its edges and gave a firm pull towards himself. It slid free. "We're done here. We'll drop this in the hangar bay, then I need to visit officer country."

"I thought Cowan was clearing that area? Over," remarked Rowan as they walked down the hall.

"He's not cleared to access command rank areas or systems. Over."

A half-hour later, Ryan and Rowan carried an E.S.T.C. into the ground forces commander's quarters. The room was pristine.

"Pull the drawers, please. Over." Ryan moved to the private computer terminal on the wall.

Rowan went to work laying folded bedding and uniforms into the E.S.T.C.

Ryan activated the computer and scanned the files. He opened one marked 'mail'.

Dear William.

I hope your studies are going well and you're making some time for fun. I miss you and your mother, but it will be worth it when you graduate debt-free. We made landing though we took several hits and lost some good people. Murack Five is a beautiful planet. We're in a forest region that could be Northern Ontario if you don't look too closely. There are herds of an animal that looks like a cross between a deer and a dalmatian with six legs.

If it wasn't for the war, it would be pleasant.

I don't know when the communications blackout will be lifted, so I have no idea when you'll see this. I'll keep writing until I can send it.

Ryan stopped reading. "Kitoy, can you read me? Over."

"Barely. The interference is getting worse. Over."

"Spread the word. Any personal computers are to be salvaged. Some mail needs to be delivered. Over."

Ryan started disconnecting the private system, loading it into the E.S.T.C. Rowan added a velvet box on top of the pile. Ryan opened the box, seeing three medals arrayed side by side.

Rowan put her arm around Ryan's waist.

"When this is over, I want to go camping. Someplace alive and green where I can forget. Over," said Ryan.

"We will never forget. Maybe if we are lucky, we can forgive ourselves. Camping sounds nice. Over." Rowan's voice was strained.

"No medals for your war. Over," remarked Ryan.

Rowan sighed. "I know my battles on the set region were fake, just a show, but to me, it was real. Real killing, real casualties. The medals don't make up for your wars. Don't make up for anybody's. Over." Rowan closed the E.S.T.C. and they pulled it to the cargo transport access.

The sun was setting when they finished with the *Osprey*. They left its empty hangar bay open. The other EVAers were already carrying the last bits of salvage into the *Star*

Hawk.

Ryan paused to look at the *Osprey*. "Someone will be back for the rest, eventually."

"We have what's important. Over," said Rowan.

Ryan looked at her encased in her EVA suit. "That we do."

They entered the *Star Hawk*. The ramp closed, and decontamination began.

An hour later, Ryan and Rowan stood in front of the auxiliary computer junction.

"This will complete my lady. They lobotomized the ship when they pulled the C.C. units. It will be good to have her back. Henry, you ready for integration?"

"Ready and waiting, hotty boss."

Ryan aligned the coordination computer and pushed it forward. There was a click. All the lights around the auxiliary C.C. turned green.

"C.C. unit, do you acknowledge?" asked Ryan.

"Acknowledged."

"I am Captain Ryan Chandler of the *Star Hawk*. You are now designated *Star Hawk* Auxiliary C.C. Do you acknowledge?"

"Working. Auxiliary *Star Hawk* C.C. unit active. Checking system."

"That will take a few hours. Henry, any issues, let me know."

"Sure thing, hotty boss. I think I'll call it Spot. It seems to like having a ship that works."

"Happy to oblige." Ryan looked at Rowan and grinned. "Now to bed. Tomorrow we loot the *Mrakper*."

HIT ANYTHING HARD ENOUGH

Kitoy sat in her quarters with Muperr. The game finished.

"That was fantastic. The teams were so evenly matched." Muperr swished his tail.

Kitoy found herself nodding, a habit she'd picked up from Kadar. "Muperr, I have something else I need to tell you before we go any further."

"What?" Muperr looked at her. "Kitoy, I know you still wear the red sash some days. I'd be surprised if you didn't. I like you, and I feel this could grow into something. Assuming the relief ships get through, I only have a year left on Murack Five. I'd like to pick up where we leave off when I'm back on the Switchboard Station. That gives you some time."

"I..." Kitoy's nose started to run. "I'd like that. It's easy with you. Easy to be felinezoid. I spend so much time with *Homo sapiens* I feel like I'm losing myself. These quarters, this furniture. It's all so *Homo sapiens*. It's nice to be felinezoid. But I don't want you waiting for me unless you know the truth. I have rutat."

Muperr froze. "Oh." He stood up. "I..."

"It's under control. It doesn't have to make a difference." Kitoy looked at him with pleading eyes.

"Kitoy, I have family on Murrow. I want to be able to visit them. I haven't given up on having cubs of my own. A *Homo sapiens* ex, no issue, but rutat... I'm sorry." He left the room.

Kitoy sat with her nose running for a long time.

Wong scanned the weapons console. He pressed a series of buttons and then made a note on his handheld. "Henry, it isn't practical. With manually selecting the missile types for launch, I'd barely get two shots off a minute. That's assuming I can remember the selection sequence. You'll have to handle the missiles. I can take the particle weapons."

Henry looked across the bridge at the middle-aged man and remembered the green lieutenant of decades past.

The door opened. Ryan and Rowan stepped in. "Morning, Wong, Henry."

"Captain." Wong stood and saluted.

Ryan laughed. "At ease. We're civilians now. 'Morning' is more than enough."

Wong smiled, then sobered. "We have a problem. Without the missile select function, the system is practically unworkable."

"Henry was telling me. Nice work on the mechanical firing chart. Did you finish it?" Ryan slid into the engineering station and started a pre-flight.

"Almost. But it's too cumbersome. In a fight, we'd be pasted."

Rowan moved to the navigator's station and sat.

"Then it's good I come bearing gifts. Let me at the console." Ryan took the weapons activation circuit from the pocket in his coveralls.

"Picked up another dangerous one, I see." Henry winked at Rowan.

"That's illegal." Wong looked at the circuit as Ryan replaced his cobbled-together activation circuit. The console glowed green on all systems.

"I'll put this one in the auxiliary console. We'll take the chart you've made, create a poster for mechanical fire selection, and post it there, just in case. As to the law, only in the U.E.S. and the U.E.S. already want my head." Ryan came to his feet.

"Are you sure you're a civilian, Captain?" Wong smiled. Though Ryan now looked considerably younger than the gunner, Wong could still see the captain, who had become the father he'd never really known.

Ryan smiled. "I'm a civilian. I pay my own crew. Run a diagnostic on the system. After we land, check out the auxiliary. I'm going to enable the auxiliary station now. We grab sky in half an hour."

The door opened. Kitoy stepped in, looking tired. She shuffled to the communications station and started her pre-flight as Ryan left.

"Pilot, bring us to hover. Navigator, focus the big screen on that dark spot on the ground in front of the break." Ryan stared at the big screen where the back end of a ship shaped like an equilateral triangle was visible in the early morning light. The hull was ripped in two, leaving a mass of crumpled plating. Decks and jumbled equipment could be seen through the break. The boxy shape of a felinezoid troop transport bridged the gap between the first deck and the ground a meter below. Its back wheels were tangled in wires which was the only reason it wasn't fully on the ground. The screen closed in on a black cube a little over a meter in all dimensions that had fallen from the broken ship.

"Stardust, it can't be. The power room was the most heavily shielded section of the ship," blurted Muperr, who stood beside Ryan's command chair.

Ryan leaned forward. "Rowan, increase magnification on the antiproton power module."

"Captain, something is moving on the *Mrakper*." Without waiting for orders, Rowan changed the big screen to show a hatch on the derelict that was opening.

"Stardust! Kitoy, open all frequencies. Muperr, abort that launch." Ryan watched a missile streak out of the open port, shooting up, then arcing toward the *Star Hawk*.

Muperr released a series of sounds that put the *Homo sapiens*' teeth on edge.

"Pilot, evasive. Gunnery, chaff. Navigator, track bogey," snapped Ryan.

The missile hurtled towards them as the *Star Hawk* accelerated through the atmosphere. The missile closed on them. A streak of colour shot out of the *Star Hawk*'s stern, exploding like a firework, leaving a cloud of chaff behind them. The missile sped into the chaff. There was a flash of light, and the *Star Hawk* jerked with the shock wave.

"I'm sorry, Captain." Muperr's tail drooped. "The secondary computers are unintegrated. One of the nodes must have recognized a foe. My clearances were no good."

"Not your fault. Samantha, get us over the horizon. Wong, when the *Mrakper* can't see us, activate stealth. We'll try this again."

Minutes passed as the *Star Hawk*, blending with the surroundings, crept up on the *Mrakper*'s aft section. They hovered close to the antiproton power module.

"Rowan, focus on that module. I thought I saw something." Ryan leaned ahead. The big screen filled with the cube. A tracery of fine cracks covered one of the corners.

"Divine!" Muperr's tail lashed.

Kitoy growled as Wong and Henry fell into a dread-filled silence.

"The damage doesn't look that bad," observed Rowan.

"Those things are the best materials tech of the elder races." Ryan stroked his chin.

"If that thing ruptures, it will be the disaster all over again." Muperr took his tail in his hands and started wringing it.

"That is a bad habit," Kitoy remarked automatically.

Muperr released his tail.

Ryan took a deep breath. "I hate this planet! Cowan,

Perry and I will lock down the power cube. I'll fill the cracks with bond strong. Then we bring it aboard for transport. Later we'll plug it into the power converter in Kangra-la."

"What?" gasped Muperr.

"The unit hasn't lost containment. If it had, we'd be in a crater. The best we can do is drain it. You need an antiproton power pack. Muperr, looking at the *Mrakper* as it is, what's the best route to the EVA suits? Rowan, bring the ship up on screen. Samantha, set us down. Be sure we don't disturb the antimatter bomb, please."

Muperr stared at the screen. "The best place would be the lower deck on the right. The vehicle hangar was there, and it was a suit station."

"Rowan, focus on that area, please." Ryan eyed the image as it zoomed in. There was an abundance of ripped hull and scattered debris.

"Kitoy, call Laura. There's mech work to do."

An hour later, Ryan led Cowan and Perry across a field of broken rock and strewn debris to the antiproton power unit.

"Where are the other ones? Over." Perry shifted around as if looking for something.

"One, there were only two. This was a felinezoid bird. It's still powered, so the power module must be in place. We'll leave it there. Over." Ryan inspected the cube. Cracks ran halfway down its side.

"Pass me the bond strong." Ryan held out a suited hand. Cowan put a caulking gun into it. Ryan began filling the cracks with a black gummy substance.

"Give it a few seconds to cure." Ryan turned to watch where the mech suit with a group of EVA suits behind it had reached the edge of the fallen ship. The mech grasped a piece of broken hull and leaned it against the bottom deck, making an impromptu ramp. It then used a wrist-mounted laser to tack weld it before ascending to the hangar deck and bending a broken support strut out of the way.

"That should do it. Let's get the grav lifts under this thing and take it back to the barn. Over." Ryan turned to his work.

The cube lifted out of the dirt, and Ryan's team gingerly levelled it. Ryan knelt to inspect the cube's side and bottom. He checked the unit's power meter. "Fifty-two per cent."

They carefully pulled the power module onto the *Star Hawk* and secured the module by the vehicles.

"Now, let's do some shopping. Over." Ryan led the way back to the *Mrakper*.

Laura felt elation. The power of being in the mech. Here she was safe. The shrinks had diagnosed her with PTSD after the rape. She'd felt so helpless, so weak. She supposed that's why she volunteered for mech duty. The machines looked so powerful. No one could hurt her when she was inside one. She gripped a piece of the hull as thick as her hand and pulled it back, clearing the way for the rest of her team. She took a step forward. Something slammed into her chest plate. Orange lights flashed on her heads-up display.

Without thinking, she lifted her arm and fired. An RPG shot out of her arm tube, slamming into the interior defence installation on the hangar bay's ceiling. It exploded, shaking the ship. A pair of support struts fell, sending a cloud of dirt into the air.

"That left a scratch. Over." Laura looked to her internal rad. It was still safe. "I have suit integrity. I've lost my left arm servos, and my chest armour is history. Over."

"Get back to the ship. Over," ordered Ryan's voice as his unit followed the trail cleared by the rest of the EVA team.

"Sir. Over." Laura started walking back the way she'd come.

"Perry, go with her. Everyone else, don't forget this. As far as this ship is concerned, the war is still on. Get in, get the felinezoid EVA suits and get out. We'll let our friends deal with their own stardust after that. Over." Ryan moved to where Laura had been hit and examined the broken room beyond.

"I count three anti-boarding guns in the ceiling. Over," said Cowan, who stood at Ryan's elbow.

"Muperr, does that sound right? Over." Ryan felt sweat trickling down his sides.

"*Crack, scritt.* Specs say six, but with the *scritt*, some may have been *crack*. Relay my *scrit* clearance through an exterior speaker. The individual audio pickups might still *crackle*. Over."

Ryan rolled his eyes and walked towards the *Star Hawk*. "There's a lot of static in the *Mrakper*. I'll record your audible security code and loop it as we walk. Over.

"Computer, relay incoming message to my suit's outside audio and loop it. Maximum volume," ordered Ryan.

A sound like a large animal in pain filled the air. Ryan returned to the EVA team. A defensive installation tracked him, but it didn't fire.

"Stick to the right. We know that one's blown to stardust. Over."

As the EVAers crept forward, the hangar came into better view. A rectangular, felinezoid troop carrier with a sloped forward section and a top-mounted semi-circular turret lay on its side. A felinezoid field ambulance sat upright. Two felinezoid mech suits were smashed to pieces on the floor amongst at least a dozen felinezoid corpses with varying degrees of dismemberment.

"I think I'm going to be sick," commented a man's voice.

"Try not to look at them. We get in, get out, then it's somebody else's problem. Over." Ryan cringed as the sound of someone being ill came over the channel.

"That's going to be nova blasted to clean. Over," observed Cowan.

"Who was that? Over," asked Ryan.

"Bill Cameron, sir. I'm sorry, it's—"

"You breathing all right? Over," interrupted Ryan.

"It's draining down to my boots. Divine, that stinks. Over," replied Bill.

"Be glad we're not in zero-g, then you'd have real problems. Let's move on. Over."

Coming to the suit locker at the back of the hangar, Ryan pressed the entry button. Nothing happened. He wedged a pry bar from his tool belt against the control plate. The plate pulled away.

"Muperr, do you read? Over."

Ryan waited. His only answer was static.

"All right, people. Form a chain. Three meters apart, back the way we came. Whoever gets the *Star Hawk* with a strong signal is the anchor. You relay exactly the words spoken, and there is no side chatter. Clear? Over," ordered Ryan.

A chorus of, "Clear, over," replied.

The EVAers moved across the hangar bay. Minutes later, the message, "I have contact," was repeated up the line.

"I pulled the door control panel for the suit locker. Which wires do I cross to open it? Over."

Ryan heard the message go down the line three times before it faded into static. Two minutes later, he heard the reply coming back for the first time. "Cross the red and the yellow wires. They're a low-voltage control feed. Over."

The message was repeated twice more, becoming clearer each time.

Ryan pulled the red and yellow wires and wrapped them together.

The door pulled back with a grating sound. When it was three-quarters open, there was a pop, and smoke poured out of the wall.

Ryan shined his light into the locker and saw ten felinezoid EVA suits.

"Call everybody in. We have the mother lode."

Three hours later, in the *Star Hawk*'s hangar bay, Ryan stripped out of his suit, then examined the antiproton storage unit. Muperr and seven other felinezoids inspected the recovered suits.

"I'm calling dibs on the small suits," Ryan shouted.

Muperr looked up, then swished his tail. "I didn't know Kitoy had an EVA rating."

"She doesn't, but it's good for crew safety." Ryan ran a Geiger counter over the antiproton storage unit.

"Speaking of safety." Muperr approached.

"No leakage. Rad is normal. Whoever returns it won't get the deposit back." Ryan moved from the cube and looked at the suits. "How are they?"

"Perfect. I'm tempted to start the salvage today."

"Your choice. If you can drop the EM interference, the control systems may integrate. That would make things go faster."

The sun was setting as Ryan watched Muperr and his team secure the troop transport dangling off the side of the *Mrakper*. The large vehicle hovered up, then backed into the remains of the hangar. With felinezoids doing the work, there had been no more anti-boarding incidents.

Tim stretched at the environmental station. "I should take mess before I run the EVA team through decontamination."

"Permission granted. Check the grav plates again before you go." Ryan looked at his son.

"Everything one hundred per cent except the hangar bay, which is fifty, and the bomb bay, which is max ten per cent. Honestly, Dad. How often do you want to hear it?" Tim smiled and shook his head.

"I like green lights." Ryan returned the smile.

"Kitoy, would you like to join me for mess?" asked Tim.

"I... No, I need to monitor the communications." Kitoy kinked her tail.

"Fine." The smile left Tim's face as he exited the bridge.

"Hotty cat?" asked Henry.

"I'm busy." Kitoy focused on her console.

Ryan moved to the engineering station. Systems he never expected to see out of the orange since the refit were green. "Rowan, what's going on in orbit?"

Rowan checked her console. "Two ankylosaurs and something else. It's a sycamorezoid hull. Henry?"

"It's a scooter, hotty boss," Henry spoke without turning around.

"Put it on screen." A ship shaped like a furry egg appeared on the main screen.

"It's only thirty meters long," observed Rowan.

"It's small, but it's fast, sweetness. It will pull fifty-five g acceleration," explained Henry.

"If we slip past the ankylosaurs, it could hound us to the stargate. That's tomorrow's problem." Ryan returned to the captain's chair. "Rowan, give me a view of the *Mrakper*, top starboard. Then chart the moons' orbits forward in time for the next week. Have Henry confirm your math."

"Aye." Rowan smiled. She knew when her captain was scheming.

The image on the main screen shifted to where a stretch of the derelict's hull was torn away.

⊂══◆>

Muperr deposited a locker of tools into the troop transport. Seeing the *Mrakper* sent pain through his chest. The ship, once so proud, was broken, never to be remade.

"Director, we've cleared the way to the personnel lift. Over," stated a female voice.

"Thank you, Cooper. If I remember correctly, you have an engineering rating, correct? Over."

"I never worked a military ship but have a grade two civilian rating. Over."

"Good enough. You're with me. Over." Muperr strode across the hangar. "When you fill up the vehicles, get them to the *Star Hawk*. Over," he ordered on the open channel.

Coming to the elevator at the back of the hangar, he noticed that its outer doors had been cut away.

"They were jamming the lift. The platform works. Over," explained Cooper.

They stepped onto the platform. Muperr used his tail to press the lift button.

Wisps of smoke rose around the platform's edge, and there was a grinding sound.

He stepped into a hallway. Maybe half the lights glowed, lending the place a macabre air. A felinezoid, so smashed and desiccated that it was hardly recognizable, lay on the floor. Dried blood stains marked the walls. They moved down the hall, stopping at a closed door.

"*Mrakper* operating system, this is Muperr, Ground Forces Pack Leader authorization G R seven two two eight. Voiceprint confirm."

"Matching voice print. Greetings, Pack Leader Muperr."

"Open aft engineering." The door retracted into the wall. The long, narrow room beyond was soot-stained. Muperr could see the *Star Hawk* through the hole at the far end. Shattered and burnt bodies lay on the floor. He and Cooper moved to a console on the far side of the room.

"*Star Hawk*, can you read me? Over." Muperr spoke into his suit. "*Star Hawk*, can you read me? Over." He looked at Cooper, who was examining the singed control board. "Can you deal with the interference? Over."

"There are a lot of exposed wires and short circuits. The EM leakage is acting like a jammer. Over." Cooper lashed her tail.

Muperr kinked his tail tip, and a heads-up display appeared on his visor. He shifted his tail, moving a cursor over the display, triggering a scan of the outside environment. He thought quietly. "Cut power to all useless systems. That might drop the EM interference. Over."

Cooper swished her tail. "I'll start with the ship's drive. Over."

GHOSTS

The sun was fully down when Ryan moved into the *Star Hawk*'s hangar to examine the salvage the felinezoids had brought in. He carried a mug in his hand. Muperr stood by one of the troop transports, looking forlorn.

"Here." Ryan passed the felinezoid the mug.

Muperr sniffed. "Coffee." He downed the cup. "I haven't had coffee in eight years." He looked at the empty mug. "Do you know why I'm on this planet?"

"I felt you'd tell me if it mattered."

"Operating equipment in a less than capable state. I crashed a transport into a lake during an air show. Almost killed a bunch of civilians. I had a three-mug-a-day habit back then. I love coffee, and I hate it!"

"Sorry. I thought you could use a drink." Ryan leaned against the troop carrier.

Muperr leaned beside him. "You were right. You can't even recognize the dead. I could have been stepping around old friends." The felinezoid's nose ran.

Ryan reached up and put his hand on the director's shoulder. "It was long ago."

"I know. I... Did we get the interference down enough for Henry to make contact?"

"He and Kitoy are debating with the *Mrakper*'s computer. It's being stubborn. Henry has suggested that it be subjected to several unsavoury biological practices."

Muperr's nostrils flared. "Your AI is colourful. Perhaps my clearance could carry some weight."

"It might. It keeps saying felinezoid intelligence doesn't

have jurisdiction for cargo distribution."

"None of us in the regs thought much of intelligence. How is Kitoy?"

"Sad."

"If your scheme works, my team will be doing body recovery and not much else. Correct?" Muperr hugged himself.

"If we can get the computer to cooperate, the rest is simple engineering."

"I have an idea that may bring a flare back to Kitoy's nostrils."

"I'd welcome that. She's a good friend. Why…?" Ryan regarded the felinezoid.

"Because, as much as she is extraordinary, I will not give up my family, my world, to be with her. Passion like that is a rare thing. It is a gift only a lucky few ever receive." Muperr flared his nostrils at Ryan. "I envy you. I had a life before I was sentenced here. To be with her would mean giving that up. Her disease comes with consequences I cannot face."

Ryan nodded. "Your species' laws are your enemy. I understand."

"Let us go to your bridge."

"You go. I have work here." Ryan pushed away from the felinezoid troop transport and moved to where the damaged *Homo sapiens* mech suit lay on the floor in pieces.

Muperr sniffed the coffee mug and carried it from the room.

"A Space Services engineer can fix anything with duct tape, beer cans and coat hangers." Ryan smiled as he inspected the chest piece. The outer armour sported a large hole while the inner material was intact. "Step one." Moving to the *Homo sapiens* grav tank, he ran a tool along the edge of a piece of the forward hull. It detached, revealing the under hull. He carried the hull section and set it down on the inner layer of the mech suit. They fit together perfectly.

Two hours later, the tank's turret sat on the deck, and the motor that rotated it was integrated into the suit.

"You fixed it," commented Laura's voice.

"Easy job. If you could run the diagnostics and safety checks, it would help. Rowan has this strange idea that captains need to sleep. A mech will be handy tomorrow." Ryan turned to see a petite, blonde woman in her late middle years dressed in a ground forces uniform with retiree's braids. She smiled, and her blue eyes seemed to sparkle.

"Glad to be of service, Captain. We never met, but I was ground forces for the Batzoid Pirate Suppression."

Ryan nodded. "We did good work there."

"We did. I'll be ready by morning." Laura snapped off a salute.

Ryan returned the salute, then went back to the grav tank. Reaching under a console, he pulled the weapons activation circuit and took it with him.

Rowan watched on the bridge screen as the *Homo sapiens* EVA team clambered over the top of the *Mrakper* in the late morning light. The mech stood guard. A panel started to retract into the derelict's hull. The mech fired an RPG into the widening hole. Flame and debris shot out as hull plates shattered.

"There can't be that many independent control circuits left. Over," observed Ryan's voice.

"Hope not. It's a waste of good RPGs. Over." Laura went back to scanning the hull.

Rowan shifted her view. The work crew had detached two sections of rail, each thirty meters long, and were carrying them towards the open end of the ship.

"The troop transport is coming in heavy," remarked Kitoy from communications.

"I'm sorry. I know this is hard for you," comforted Rowan from navigation.

"You're a good friend, Rowan. No harder than it was with the *Homo sapiens*. It was easier to ignore them since they were in the racks. I see those orange bags laid out in the hangar and... I had an uncle who served here. Suppose he's in one of those bags?"

"War." Rowan adjusted the view to watch the *Homo sapiens* lower the rails to the ground.

"Enough." Henry's voice was firm. "This is not fun. Time for a game."

Half the big screen shifted to a hex pattern, while the other half displayed the EVA team. "Goal is to build the tower. We each lay a piece on our turn and see how tall we can build it. The only enemy is gravity."

"Oh, why not?" said Kitoy.

Rowan watched Ryan on the screen. "As long as I'm stuck on monitor duty. I'm in, but only for a few minutes. I need to finish those lunar projections."

Ryan cut the twisted end off the *Mrakper*'s cargo transfer track and meshed it to the end of one of the salvaged rails. A weld later, the rail stuck out along the ground, almost reaching the *Star Hawk*'s hangar bay ramp. He repeated the process, creating a trackway. He, Laura, Perry, and Cowan moved down the track three meters.

"Get me some clearance, please, Laura. Over." The mech reached down and lifted the rails a handsbreadth off the ground. "Perry, Cowan, that bit of deck plating beside you should do. Over."

The two men pushed a shattered piece of hull under the tracks.

"Set it down, Laura. Over."

The mech lowered the rails. Ryan checked the distance between them, then tack welded the tracks to the hull plate.

"Three more like this, and I'll trust it for our purposes. Over." The group moved further down the track.

An hour later, they stood at the end of the rails near the *Star Hawk*.

"Kitoy, patch me through to Henry. Henry, send the first box down. Over," ordered Ryan.

An F.S.C. hurtled down the rails and shot off the end to slam into a dead tree trunk, filling the air with splinters.

"How'd it go, hotty boss? Over." Henry sounded smug.

Ryan looked at the cat box. "Less than perfect. Tell the *Mrakper* computer it's not throwing the cargo into orbit. Over. Perry, Cowan. Could you get that container into the ship? Over."

The two suited figures moved to push grav lifts under the cat box.

"Looks like you need brakes, Captain. Over," observed Laura.

"Or a slower pitch. Henry. Track the freight as to weight and velocity. We should be able to work out how fast to come off the powered rail to get a nice coast to finish. Over." Ryan inspected the rails and seemed satisfied.

"If I can get Snooty McCatChip to cooperate. For a class five computer, this batch of circuits has an attitude. Over."

"Do your best. Be charming? Over." Ryan watched as Perry and Cowan returned.

"This pound of circuits isn't Fluffy. I liked that coelenteratezoid operating system. It was fun. I'll try. Over."

Another cat box shot down the rails, stalling several meters short of the end of the track.

"Laura, if you would, please. Over." Ryan checked the rails.

Laura walked over and pushed the cat box to the end of the rail, where Perry and Cowan put it on grav lifts and hauled it away.

"Again. And tell the rest of the *Homo sapiens* team to

get grav lifts and rally here."

Several tries later, the cat boxes were consistently stopping at or near the end of the rail. The *Homo sapiens* would take the units and move them into the *Star Hawk*'s hangar bay.

By sunset, the humans were boarding thirty cat boxes an hour.

Ryan moved to Muperr's side on the hangar bay ramp and switched to a private radio channel. "How much longer on your side?"

"We'll be done in an hour. The bodies are all in what's left of the hangar. Once we offload the troop transport, we can fly it back and load them up. I'd like to get it done. Over."

"I understand. The k-no-in can carry the dead to the ground forces barracks while the rest of us get some rest. They'll be respectful."

"I know they will." Muperr looked over the darkening landscape to where both moons were rising. "This used to be an alpine forest." His tail lashed.

"It will be again, because of you." Ryan touched the felinezoid's arm.

"Because of us." Muperr sighed. "The chief engineer's quarters were intact and rad free. Most of it is in F.S.C.s. We brought the sleeping cushion in with the troop carrier. We stripped the room to the lights. Even got some landscape files on the drives."

"Thank you. It's hard for Kitoy being the only felinezoid aboard. I haven't been able to do anything to help."

"Let's finish this and get back to someplace alive. I've had enough of graves."

"As have I." Ryan moved back to the rails where three cat boxes had collided and jammed.

Ryan and Rowan stepped off the *Star Hawk*'s hangar ramp

onto the living soil of the new location for auxiliary station three. She looked to the distance where the old station stood ready to receive its new inhabitants. She regarded Ryan.

"You should have slept more," she admonished.

"I had work to do. Rrrikta and Wotra need some supervision when dealing with tech thousands of years in advance of what they know." Ryan forced a smile.

"You're good at that. I know from experience." She kissed him.

"You're more fun." Ryan pulled her into a one-armed hug and directed her off the loading ramp. The *Homo sapiens* tank exited the *Star Hawk*. The vehicle was stripped of its outer armour, weapons and grav nullifiers. It rolled beside the k-no-in troop transport and stopped. Rrrikta and Wotra strung power cables between the machines.

"Will that be enough?" asked Rowan.

"For now. The antiproton pack in the tank was at fifty-six per cent. Between that and the generating systems on the troop carrier, they should be able to stay charged and expand their clean-up program."

"Why'd you strip the tank?" Rowan walked to a nearby tree and touched its trunk. From the feel, it could have been some exotic earth species.

"The war of death is done here. It's time for the war of life. Stripping the tank makes it lighter. I've suggested to Muperr that it could be converted into an oversized, self-powered Gralipa flower collector. That's why I left the land drives intact."

Grann walked up and dipped his head in a k-no-in bow. "Ryan, Rowan. This is a worthy gift. Thank you."

"You're welcome, Director. Rrrikta and Wotra performed admirably. I believe they've gained from working with the technology of my species. When they return to Srill, I hope they will find it rewarding." Ryan bowed.

Grann made the low growling sound that served k-no-in as a laugh. "I knew it was too much to think we would fool the Space Mink." He sobered. "It pleases me you do not mind."

"I believe measured assistance to your species is in order."

"Thank you." Grann dipped his head.

"Muperr will arrange for *Homo sapiens* engineers and transport techs to consult about retrofitting the tank."

"It will help us heal Grandmother's wounds." Grann bowed his head and walked away.

"What was that?" Rowan looked at Ryan.

"Rrrikta and Wotra have been working with our tech. I'm hoping they picked up some things that will be useful back on Srill. Species charge a fortune for technological advances. The k-no-in entered the Republic barely able to get off their planet with nothing to trade. They seek out places where they can pick up scraps to add to their tech. Rrrikta and Wotra hopefully will advance their people when they get home."

"They're spies?" Rowan made the connection.

Ryan shrugged. "I want the k-no-ins to know that I know."

Rowan rested her head on his shoulder.

The *Star Hawk* settled on the landing for auxiliary station two. Ryan stared at the big screen, watching a herd of bison-like herbivores grazing.

"Exterior readings are green," remarked Tim.

"Ziggy is calling in. He says they can assist with unloading." Kitoy sat at her console.

"Let's do that, then I think we'll spend the night. Time it to arrive at Kangra-la with first light." Ryan nodded.

Rowan turned in her seat to look at him. "That's a change."

Ryan watched the herbivores. "It's alive out there. I think we all need that. Besides, it will be a few days before the moons are where I want them."

An hour later, the *Homo sapiens* ambulance, supported on grav lifts, was walked out of the hangar bay and deposited beside the k-no-in troop transport-cum-radiation shelter. Flower made the power connections between the vehicles.

"The medical cots in this are configured for *Homo sapiens*, and the drugs and equipment we're leaving are *Homo sapiens*. You'll have to adapt." Ryan spoke to Yipya beside the vehicle.

"I am becoming conversant in doing so." Yipya paused as Flower walked up and laid her chin across his back. He bent his head back and brushed her face with his muzzle. "This one will bankrupt me."

"You can afford it." Flower raked her tusks gently down Yipya's back.

Ryan's hand found Rowan's as she moved beside him. "The directors have invited us to join them this evening at their firepit."

"A campfire," observed Rowan.

"Sometimes, you get what you want." Ryan looked at the loading ramp and called out. "Ziggy, hold up."

Ziggy pulled an E.S.T.C. to the side of the trail leading to the village and stopped.

"One second," yelled Ryan, then he and Rowan ran into the *Star Hawk*, emerging with a large case. They trotted to Ziggy and laid the box on the E.S.T.C. he was hauling.

"Captain?" Ziggy looked confused.

"We have something for you. I couldn't spare it before, but things have changed." Ryan opened the box, revealing an EVA suit with *Star Hawk* shoulder patches.

"You'll always be part of the crew," explained Rowan.

"And from the sounds of things, they need someone here to do EVAs when the floods bring down the irradiated silt," added Ryan.

Ziggy looked at Ryan and Rowan as he caressed the suit with one hand. He then snapped off a salute. "Thank you,

Captain, Rowan. With this, I think a short stint may become a future. I'm finding I like it in the present."

Ryan returned the salute.

That evening he and Rowan sat and stared into the fire as old songs from three species were sung, and the moons overhead glowed with a yellowish tint.

At Kangra-la, Ryan and Muperr gingerly walked the damaged antiproton cube to the old U.E.S. ambulance that held the power converter. The door rolled back, revealing Kikkuli, who stood by the old cube. There were a pair of grav lifts under the near-empty cube.

"Now," ordered Muperr.

The old cube rose on the lifts and was rushed out of the vehicle. Heaters throughout Kangra-la blinked off. Muperr and Ryan slid the damaged cube into place, and the heaters came back on. Kangra-la warmed once more.

"That should give you a few years, and with the troop transport and aerial surveys, you can hunt out more if you need them," remarked Ryan.

"As long as it doesn't blow up." Muperr lashed his tail.

"Best way to empty it is to use it. I'm sure only the outer case is cracked."

"Not much for it. Kikkuli, take the empty cube to the *Star Hawk*. I'd rather see you get the deposit than the U.E.S." Muperr held out a Geiger counter and ran it over the damaged cube. The readings didn't change.

"It's under a layer of military-grade shielding. Are you sure we salvaged enough felinezoid M.R.E.s to keep you if the next shipment doesn't get through?" Ryan moved out of the ambulance while Pikeman led a pair of relief workers with an E.S.T.C. of medical supplies and equipment into the ambulance.

"Muperr, I will need additional space for my specialized equipment. There simply isn't room in this vehicle."

Pikeman scowled at the space around him.

"We can set up the felinezoid ambulance across from the door and build a floor, roof and walls between them." Muperr eyed the *Homo sapiens* physician.

"It will do, I suppose. Don't put that there. It goes on the other side. Must I do everything myself?" He harangued one of the workers who had started refilling the shelves.

Muperr lashed his tail as Ryan shook his head. They both left the clinic.

Ryan ascended into the *Star Hawk* to find Kikkuli and Rowan standing by an E.S.T.C.

"Problems?" asked Ryan.

"I was asking Rowan if she knew the ratings for these ceramic heat exchangers. I'm not sure they'll be compatible with our units," remarked Kikkuli.

"They'll work." Ryan smiled.

"You're sure." Kikkuli sounded unconvinced.

"When I designed the heater units, I had to use parts on hand. I was most familiar with U.E.S. tech and had access to it, so I'm sure." Ryan smiled.

"You designed the units?" Kikkuli sounded awed.

"I designed most of the non-standard equipment around here." Ryan shrugged.

Kikkuli grasped his hand. "I've said I wanted to shake the designer's hand for years, and now I get to. If you ever want to stop being an officer, you could be an engineer."

Ryan and Rowan laughed. Kikkuli slid grav lifts under the E.S.T.C. of ceramic heat units and walked it out of the hangar.

"How much longer until we're offloaded?" Ryan looked at the cargo containers spread over the hangar floor. Only the U.E.S. troop transport and parts remained of the vehicles.

"It will take the rest of the day. Are you ready to speak to our next passengers?" Rowan touched his arm.

"No. It's a role too big. I don't want it. But they need me. Muperr has set it up." Ryan stared out of the hangar to where one of the felinezoid troop carriers waited. A large box beside a platform with a microphone attached to it was mounted by the turret.

"Company?" asked Rowan.

"Looking for a promotion." Ryan grinned at her.

"Just don't want some kangazoid wanting to be the mother of a demigod to turn your head." Rowan returned his grin.

Ryan shuddered. "You've never smelled them."

Together they moved to the felinezoid troop carrier. In moments it landed on an open field. Kangazoids bounded up from the surrounding villages. Before the sun was touching the western ice walls, several hundred had gathered.

Ryan climbed to the platform with the microphone. In the box beside him, the holographic image of a kangazoid formed. Ryan spoke into the microphone.

"I am Captain Ryan Chandler."

The image thumped on its chest with its large arms and made the sound "Crach."

"The time has come to begin the return to the land of rivers and fields. The rage of Gramplik is slow to fade, so not all the lands are fit for living. I need two hundred who will travel to a new land. Any who have lived in the high places would be best. I will take you tomorrow, bring all you have. I will carry you in my sky raft to your new home."

The kangazoid hologram pointed to the sun and made an arcing gesture with its large arm, then chopped the hand of the other arm where part of the arc had been indicated. "Wokk." He made an inarticulate roar, said, "Gramplik", then slowly let his arms drift from one side to another. "Wump."

Ryan watched the mix of gestures and sounds, wondering at the translation. A minute later, the kangazoids hopped back to their villages.

"I think that went well," commented Muperr from inside the troop carrier.

"Tomorrow will tell," said Ryan, feeling dirty inside.

When the *Star Hawk* set down amongst the kangazoid settlements, Ryan was shocked to see the crowd that had gathered. Old, young, male, female, they hopped to enter the hangar. It was so different from years before when they had been driven in. They paused, looking in wonder at everything. Ryan stepped out of the elevator before the ramp closed. Several elder kangazoids moved before him, laying carved pieces of wood at his feet.

"Thank you," Ryan spoke into his handheld. "Vrekk," echoed the device.

The elders babbled amongst themselves.

"Kitoy, link in Henry. Henry, I think it best I stay here. Take us up, and let me know when we land." Ryan moved among the kangazoids, touching babies and letting the adults touch him.

The flight ended, and the *Star Hawk*'s ramp descended. The kangazoids hopped onto what had been auxiliary station two. A warm breeze blew. The primitives marvelled at the goat-like herbivores. An elderly kangazoid hopped to the communal dwelling and entered. Others followed. Others raced to the cultivated fields of food plants.

One kangazoid carried a gourd-like container to a fire pit in front of the communal shelter. Several others followed him. They piled kindling and fuel into the firepit and dumped hot coals from the gourd into its base. When the fire burnt, the kangazoids rushed to build a stand over it. Several took spears and bounded towards the herbivores.

Ryan walked towards a mound on one side of the village. He knew what was under that dirt. A people, a way of life. A world almost killed. His thoughts centred on a dying mother pleading with her arms to hold her dying child. Tears welled in his eyes. He could never make up for that. Never atone. A whooping sound caught his attention.

A kangazoid child raced across the field towards him, its mother in pursuit. The child bounded against Ryan's chest. Instinctively he caught it, cradling it with one arm under its feet and one arm around its back. The tiny being gripped Ryan's coverall and pushed its face against his chest. Shock gave way to a warmth that all who have loved a child can understand. The mother bounded up and stopped, watching her child in the arms of her god. Ryan brushed his cheek against the coarse fur of the little one. Somewhere inside Ryan, a piece of ice melted and tight bands around his heart loosened.

Rowan's words echoed in his thoughts. "It was because of you that other kangazoids will get to hold their babies."

"Maybe you're right, my love. Maybe that counts for something too." He kissed the small kangazoid's head, then passed it back to its mother, who took it and regarded him with wide eyes. Ryan stroked her cheek, then started back to the *Star Hawk*. Opening his handheld, he spoke into it. "Kitoy, get everyone started on the pre-flights. One quick stop, then it's back to the stars."

TO THE STARS

Rowan sat at the navigator's station on the *Star Hawk*'s horseshoe-shaped bridge. Samantha sat in the pilot's station. The immaculate blue UES space services coverall with retiree's braids on the shoulder patches seemed to suit her.

The large bridge screen showed the lake that the *Star Hawk* hovered above with four of its landing legs extended below the surface.

"What's the point of taking on all this water?" Tim sat at the environmental station, monitoring the flow in pipes that ran down those particular landing legs.

"Ryan has a plan. You can trust in that," said Rowan.

"Likely insane and/or suicidal, but a plan," added Henry.

On the pilot's screen, images played out as Samantha ran simulations. "Are you sure you got the pull points right?"

Rowan shrugged. "I checked them four times. Is there a problem?"

Samantha sighed. "This is tight. I mean, planetary distance tight, a hundred meters or less clearance."

"Tight's good," remarked Henry.

Everyone ignored the android.

"It's what Ryan wants." Rowan shrugged.

"We'll pull rocks off the surface if we loop the moon like this."

Rowan and Henry shared a look.

"Hotty boss does like getting back to basics." Henry flexed his fingers.

"Throwing rocks. If the ankylosaur is chasing us and the rocks travel vertically relative to the moon…" Rowan stroked her chin in thought.

"The bomb bay is full. I have to ask. Why is the bomb bay set up to be flooded in the first place?" Tim examined the environmental controls.

"The Hawk class was designed to be versatile. You can get a lot of fire in a combat zone. Water bombing could put them out and protect ground-based installations. It can also help deal with natural disasters. After the munitions are depleted, the bomb bay is just empty space. Rigging it to carry water increases a Hawk's versatility," explained Samantha.

"If nothing else, a few tons of water dropped on a platoon can really ruin their day," added Henry. "Ultimate wet T-shirt contest."

The bridge door opened. Ryan stepped in and settled in the captain's chair. All the seats on the bridge were filled except for engineering.

"Kitoy, general quarters. Inform all aboard to brace for high-g manoeuvres. Check with Rrrikta and Wotra that everything is locked down in the old ground pounders' barracks. Rowan, where are our jailers?"

Rowan checked her instruments. "One of the ankylosaur class ships is twenty degrees over the eastern horizon, equatorial orbit. The other ankylosaur and the scooter are behind the planet. The last trajectory placed them in an equatorial orbit."

"We'll worry about the scooter after we break orbit. All it can do is reveal our position. Pilot, grab sky and hold stealth. Accelerate counter-rotation in the troposphere using the scram jets. Tim, Wong. Keep the bomb bay at thirty degrees C."

"Sir? Launching counter-rotation." Samantha sounded confused.

Ryan smiled. "I know it will make us slower to start. Don't worry about it. I'm counting on the stealth to keep them off our back until we enter the thermosphere. Build our speed and increase altitude to compensate for friction. Rowan, how do the numbers look?"

Rowan brought up a navigational plot on her station's screen. "We'll loop the planet by the time we hit the mesosphere and be moving as fast as the scram jets can push us."

"We exit the thermosphere at the equator, longitude 79.879145." Ryan carried himself with pure purpose and determination. Only Rowan and Henry could see the strain that spending weeks on Murack Five had put on him.

"That will have us heading straight for the ankylosaur," reported Rowan.

"Hotty boss, what are you thinking?" demanded Henry.

"Samantha, retract the fill legs and get us moving. I'll fill in the blanks." Ryan leaned back in his command chair.

The *Star Hawk* drifted higher into the air, then the scram jets accelerated them through the atmosphere.

"Rowan, Henry, make scans as we go. It will help update future maps." Ryan felt his stress lessen. Every meter away from Murack Five was a relief.

An hour and a half later, the ship shot out of the thermosphere.

"Activate grav-laser drive. Rotate ports for near-planet acceleration and lock onto the B moon. Twelve gs acceleration."

The inertial dampers kicked in, reducing what the crew felt to 1.2 gs. The main screen at the front of the bridge displayed what looked like a giant, fuzzy egg.

"They've informed the other ships," stated Kitoy.

"They've opened their weapons ports," added Wong.

"Pilot, kill acceleration and show them our belly." Ryan watched the screen as Rowan kept the main view oriented on their foe.

"Wong, open bomb bay doors. Pilot, full 25 g pull to top against the A moon for two seconds."

On the screen, a flight of rockets left the ankylosaur. The

Star Hawk shuddered as water practically exploded from its belly. The water froze in less than a second, leaving a mist of tons of ice particles between the ankylosaur and the *Star Hawk*.

"Bring us straight and rotate us so that top is facing the planet. Coast three seconds, then cycling pull 12.5 g against Moon B. Wong, close her up."

On the main screen, the ankylosaur's rockets impacted the ice particles, detonating well away from their target.

"Gunnery, prep an annihilator salvo top." Ryan stroked his chin as he watched the ice particles drift around the ankylosaur.

"I'm reading a grav-pull against us," reported Rowan.

Ryan smiled. "Samantha, counter grav-pull. Stay on course. Some beings never learn."

The large ship shifted position as the cloud of ice particles was pulled into its gravity laser ports.

"The grav-pull has stopped," reported Rowan.

"They've caved in their forward grav-ports." Henry's voice was pleased.

On the screen, the ankylosaur drew closer, adjusted its position with thrusters, then fired another salvo.

"Countermeasures." Ryan's tone was as cold as death.

"Aye," Wong fired the defensive missiles that moved amongst the incoming and burst, leaving a cloud of nanobot chaff. Several missiles exploded, shrapnel hitting others in the formation. A second rank flew through the cloud of dust. The nanobots adhered to them, tearing the missiles apart and making more nanos to add to the debris field.

"Target will be planet-side of us in three seconds from mark… Mark." Rowan's voice held a note of regret.

"Wong, fire annihilator salvo." Ryan watched as the ankylosaur swept across the screen, and then the angle changed. The view was to the *Star Hawk*'s rear. The missiles impacted the ankylosaur. Jets of gas shot out of the egg-shaped ship's top, driving it into the mesosphere.

The pirate ship glowed red. It jerked up and back for a second. The grav-ports designed for the void collapsed under the pressure of the gases they pulled in. The ankylosaur started to disintegrate as systems never meant to enter an atmosphere were over-stressed. Some of the missiles left from the *Star Hawk*'s salvo slammed home. The huge alien ship's hull opened. Three large boxy sections burst from the ship's core and floated in the atmosphere.

"The power conversion units have ejected and are performing an antigravity drop," observed Henry.

"Kitoy, get word to Muperr. If they can track those nodes, Kangra-la's power shortage days are over," ordered Ryan.

"Are they safe? I mean..." began Rowan.

"The containment and safety measures will hold. The modules will make a soft landing, then it's first come, first serve as to who gets to salvage them." Ryan continued to examine the screen as escape pods burst from the wreck and accelerated into low orbit. "At least some survivors."

"Not necessarily a good thing, hotty boss," remarked Henry.

"The second ankylosaur is coming over the horizon. They've launched a screen of countermeasures," announced Rowan.

Ryan nodded. "Samantha, just like we planned. Loop the moon."

Samantha's hands caressed the controls as the *Star Hawk* careened over the lifeless ball of rock that was Murack Five B. The retired military lander hugged the surface with only a hundred meters margin. The gravity lasers were directed downward, so the ship's momentum pulled around the moon. Dirt and clumps of rock flew up from the lunar surface, making a trail of debris behind the small warship but never hitting it because of its forward velocity.

"I'm reading a grav-pull. The second ankylosaur is line of sight," observed Rowan.

"Expected. Let's test their captain's intelligence." Ryan used the override control in his command chair to shift the main screen to view the ankylosaur. A cloud of dust and rock was accelerating towards it through the void.

"They've cut their pull against us and are pulling out-system," observed Rowan.

"Too bad. Getting hit with a rock would serve them right," remarked Wong.

"Samantha, put all grav laser pull against the A moon, near planet cycling," ordered Ryan.

The *Star Hawk* hurtled forward along the line of the planet's rotation around its sun.

"The ankylosaur has launched an offensive salvo. They're coming up our six," announced Rowan.

"Relative velocity?" asked Ryan.

"They'll reach us just past the A moon," stated Rowan.

"Pilot, loop it! Pop out-system. We'll fix the vector when we have some velocity." Ryan snapped the order as the A moon grew to fill the main screen.

"Aye, sir." Samantha couldn't keep the excitement from her voice. This was flying, and she had missed it.

"Rowan, find points for a twenty-five g pull straight line for as soon as we break orbit with the A moon."

The craters on the A moon's surface could be clearly seen when the *Star Hawk* pulled hard to bottom. Even with initial dampers, everyone's hair flew upwards. The screen displayed the flight of missiles behind them. Some exploded in the cloud of dust and dirt the grav lasers pulled into space. Others shot past, unable to match the turn manoeuvre.

Rowan shifted the main screen to show the ankylosaur closing on the A Moon as the *Star Hawk* shifted its gravity pull points out-system and sped into the void at twenty-five gs of acceleration. The ankylosaur fired another salvo of missiles.

"Rowan?" demanded Ryan.

"Calculating. Our velocity will be too high by the time the

missiles reach us. Wait. Our acceleration is dropping. We're getting a counter pull." Rowan ran another set of numbers. "The missiles will reach us if we don't shake the counter pull."

"Sycamorezoids were never the best at space tactics." Ryan rubbed his chin.

"Their captain can't be that stupid," remarked Henry.

"Maybe they haven't guessed the extent of our armaments. Thank the *Osprey*. Wong, launch four drive busters programmed to disperse when they pass the incoming. Start targeting their incoming missiles with particle beams. Thin the herd."

Four missiles streaked towards the ankylosaur. They passed the incoming missiles and burst into clusters of smaller rockets, each following the line of one of the ankylosaur's grav lasers. The ankylosaur launched countermeasures. Several of the rockets exploded. But others made it through.

Particle beams shot from the *Star Hawk*, picking off the incoming offensive missiles. There were several flashes of light from the ankylosaur.

"We're not getting a counter pull anymore. We will accelerate beyond the offensive fire before it reaches us." Rowan sounded relieved.

On-screen, the ankylosaur rotated. The *Star Hawk* shuddered.

"They've locked on again," announced Rowan.

"Why?" asked Tim from environmental.

"Navigation, expand the screen view." Ryan sat forward in the command chair.

The screen magnification dropped so that the ankylosaur was about the size of a football. Another egg-shaped craft appearing as large as a jelly bean swept past it, following the *Star Hawk*'s trajectory.

"They aren't complete idiots. If that scooter can keep a line of sight with us, it won't matter if we cloak. They'll relay our position, and you can bet there will be sycamorezoid ships prepped to intercept us."

"What are we going to do?" asked Tim.

"A scooter doesn't have the armaments to take us on, and the ankylosaur doesn't have the acceleration to catch us. Rowan, calculate a course to the stargate and send it to piloting. Leave it at a twenty-eight per cent light speed drift, so we have some manoeuvring. Keep the acceleration to two gs until we shake our tail. Samantha, as soon as you get it, execute. Everyone: in-flight safety checks, then we'll go to the civilian watch rotation. We'll take the win and worry about tomorrow after a night's sleep. Be happy, people. We escaped Murack Five."

Pause.

Afterword

Thank you for reading *Arming Freedom*. I hope it brought you pleasure. The story continues in *Freedom's Plan*.

Please review the book and post it on your favourite book review venue. Reviews are life blood for book sales in this day and age.

Remember, the power's in you, please review.

Stephen B. Pearl is a multiple published author whose works range across the speculative fiction field. Whether his characters are wandering the wilds of a post-oil future, braving a storm in a longship, or flying through the interplanetary void in an army surplus assault lander, his writings focus heavily on the logical consequences of the worlds he crafts.

Stephen's inspirations encompass H.G. Wells, J.R.R. Tolkien, Frank Herbert, and Homer, among others. In writing the Freedom Saga, he has, among other factors, drawn on his diverse background and broad general knowledge garnered from preparing for and serving on seminars and panels at numerous shows and events. These panels and seminars range from Intelligent Spacecraft Design to Building Better Aliens. His training as an Emergency Medical Care Assistant, a SCUBA diver, and his long-standing interest in environmental technologies have factored into all his science fiction books, be they on or off the planet Earth.

For more about Stephen and his works visit: www.stephenpearl.com

If you enjoyed *Arming Freedom*, try:

In a universe of gods and gladiators, an extra-galactic intrusion could spell the end of everything.

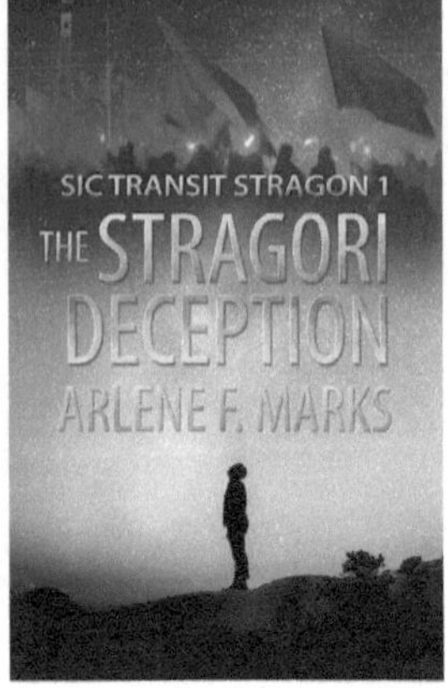

Former Earth Intelligence Service Agents may be the only thing that can stop civil war on Earth's sister world.

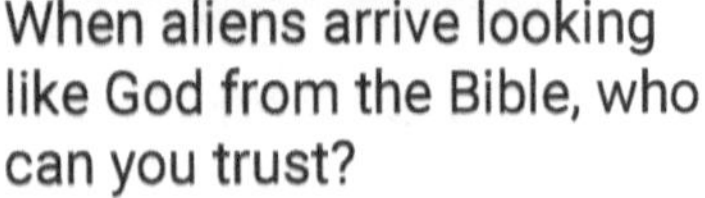

When aliens arrive looking like God from the Bible, who can you trust?

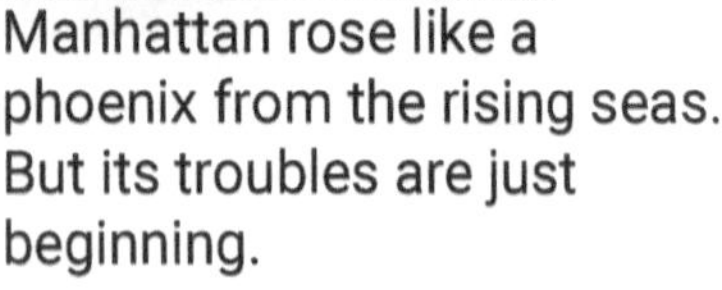

Manhattan rose like a phoenix from the rising seas. But its troubles are just beginning.

See all 50+ titles at

brain-lag.com

www.ingramcontent.com/pod-product-compliance
Lightning Source LLC
Chambersburg PA
CBHW022301310726
48973CB00001B/155